The Princesses and the Dragon

A.I.V. Esguerra

Ukiyoto Publishing

Acknowledgement

There are too many people to acknowledge so I will start with some people.

Like in my first book, The Young Knight and His Metal Steed, I have my family to thank for encouraging me to go on. Like in that book, I also acknowledge "Marq", "Eagle", and "Jegor" for assisting me again with this current book; Marq for examining the Arabic I used and offered corrections where needed, "Eagle" for providing military trivia that was very useful for this story, and Jegor for assisting me in using Russian

For this book, I've gained the help of a few more individuals. While they were kind enough to allow me to use their respective full names, I cannot risk that because of the current political climate. Tragically, I will have to address them with their respective first names. First is "Luis", who assisted me in using Spanish. Next is "Minseok", who assisted me in using Korean. Lastly, there's "Sebail", who assisted me in using Azeri.

Again, I have my professor "J.P." to thank for helping me find that writing is a worthwhile path. I also thank classmates from my college days for their congratulations in becoming an novelist. There will be times where I feel like stopping but with encouragements like these, I won't stop writing.

Contents

Prologue: Beginnings   1

New Orders   4

Rendezvous   20

The Launch   36

The Raid   52

Disguise   68

The Past and the Present   84

Visiting Home   101

Returning to Japan   117

Spying   133

The Truth   148

The Attack   164

Turning Point Part 1   179

Turning Point Part 2   195

Cooperation   211

Shipwreck Assault   228

The New Prisoner   243

The Real Reason   259

Finding a Resolution   275

To Sinpo   292

Heart Attack   308

Epilogue: A New Discovery   325

Author's Notes   329

About the Author   *339*

Prologue: Beginnings

Unknown Location; Enlightenment Point. July 31, 2030; 1400 hours (EP Time Zone)

Reinhard Frühling, the Gatekeeper of Intelligence, approached the throne room of his master, Grand Gatekeeper Sergei Akulov. The former made his salute upon stopping.

"Grand Gatekeeper, I come with news that might burden you yet I must report to you," Frühling told Akulov.

"What is it?" Akulov asked.

"Kravchenko sold Guliyeva."

"What!? To who?"

"Segismundo Alba. He bought Guliyeva from Kravchenko for fifty million UN dollars."

"Get her back. Tell 'SB' to await further orders and give 'LS' files on Kravchenko and Alba to give to the FIS. They need to be punished for this."

"By your will, Grand Gatekeeper."

#

Gatekeepers of Knowledge Safehouse, Bani Al Harith District, Royal Capital of Sanaa; Kingdom of Yemen. 1349 hours (Royal Yemen Time)

In her room at a safehouse used by the Gatekeepers of Knowledge, "SB" practiced Japanese. Sixteen years old, "SB" was a girl with long black hair, light intermediate skin, and dark brown eyes.

She tested herself in Japanese until she heard her smartphone ring. Going to her phone, "SB" found a message sent to her by GOKMail. Opening GOKMail, she found the message was from Reinhard Frühling, calling himself "GIRH". The message read:

To "SB",

The Grand Gatekeeper has given "LS" the task of giving files on both Anton Oleksandrovich Kravchenko and Segismundo Alba for a business transaction not approved by the Grand Gatekeeper. Please await further orders.

Gatekeeper of Intelligence.

Thank Heavens the Grand Gatekeeper has authorized that Kravchenko be eliminated, "SB" thought. While it benefits us, we should have stopped working with a human trafficker like Kravchenko years ago. I wonder if I'll run into Tarou in this mission?

#

OVR Safehouse, Nishinari Ward, Kansai City, Kansai Prefecture; State of Japan. 1600 hours

At the same time, in their safehouse in Kansai City, OVR agents Pyotr Stepanovich Chadov and Karim Olegovich Zhakyanov were summoned to the office of Grand Duchess Tatiana Ioannovna Tsulukidze. "But won't they detect us?" Chadov asked.

"According to what Kapitan Samsonova has said, she claimed that the NUN submarine that spotted the *Studec'* never attempted anything when I last needed it to help me go to Nizhny Novgorod," Tatiana answered.

"But taking in someone again will attract attention from the FIS," Zhakiyanov warned.

"I know, as does the Director. Hopefully, we don't have to accommodate our new guest for long." Tatiana then faced Chadov. "Chadov, prepare the van for tomorrow. I'll start with my belongings."

"Zametano," Chadov replied.

Iron Dutchman, Taisho Ward. August 5, 2030; 0739 hours (Japan Standard Time)

At the dining room of the *Iron Dutchman,* the members of the mercenary group Iron Dutchman Services had their breakfast. Although not a member, Frederick Dirks had breakfast with them. As to why, this was to help act out as their handler because Iron Dutchman Service's current client was the Foreign Intelligence Service of the New United Nations, whom Dirks worked for under the alias "Fred Smith".

Unlike everybody else, Dirks had finished his breakfast. It was then that he felt his smartphone and grabbed it from his right pocket. He found that his IntMail, the communication application used by the FIS, received a message.

Dirks opened IntMail and found that the message came from "Maria Clara" that read:

We have a new mission for you and Iron Dutchman Services. All will be explained later. Please remind Iron Dutchman Services.

Dirks simply stood up and walked to the table where the founders of Iron Dutchman Services, Wouter Vos, Jason Luke Crawley, and Sunan Wattana, ate. Luckily for Dirks, they, too, finished their breakfast. As the former approached, the latter three saw him come to them.

"Something tells me we have a new mission," Crawley guessed as he saw Dirks.

"We do," Dirks answered before he turned to Vos. "Vos?"

"I got it," Vos replied.

New Orders

Iron Dutchman, Taisho Ward, Kansai City, Kansai Prefecture; State of Japan. August 5, 2030; 0819 hours (Japan Standard Time)

All members of Iron Dutchman Services entered their briefing room, which was once the theater room of the mercenary group's namesake ship. Only Wouter Vos and Frederick Dirks did not sit down, as they had to enter the stage of the theater. Tatev Mirzoyan, meanwhile, entered the adjacent room where the projector was located and after laying her laptop computer on the desk where the projector was located, Tatev connected her computer to the projector and the nearby mouse.

After that was done, with the laptop's screen now projected onto the theater screen proper, Tatev opened her computer again. She then turned on the computer's AudComm, an application used only by the New United Nations Defense Forces and the Foreign Intelligence Service. Everyone else in the briefing room now saw the AudComm on Tatev's computer.

"Good, if Miss Mirzoyan contacted me, then that means 'Smith' informed everyone," Alicia Caguiat said over AudComm, with the audio message heard throughout the briefing room through the speakers. "I can assume everyone can hear now?"

Everyone knew Caguiat was the "Maria Clara" assigned to be their Coordinator as it's the FIS that handled mercenaries the New United Nations needed. Iron Dutchman Services knew Caguiat was "Maria Clara" after a contract with the Middle Eastern League ended in failure and that Caguiat personally joined in picking them up, as it was the FIS that allowed Iron Dutchman Services to take up the contract.

"We can," Vos answered.

"Shortly, I'll be sending a file through IntMail. Please wait because that will contain a mission the FIS wishes to avail of your services in addition to your current contract."

"How much will we be paid for this one?" Jason Luke Crawley asked.

"Twice your normal amount. Now please wait as I'm currently uploading the file unto IntMail. When Miss Mirzoyan receives the file and opens it, please refrain from asking until the briefing is over."

Everyone now went silent. Tatev, meanwhile, opened her computer's IntMail and waited until the message from Caguiat arrived. Only after five minutes did the message from "Maria Clara" arrive. Tatev wasted no time in opening the message and found the file attached to the message. She then downloaded the file into the computer and opened it using an application in the computer needed to open the file.

Once the file was opened, the first page was shown to both Tatev's computer and the theater screen. Tatev scrolled down until she found the first proper page of the file as the page between the first and the current page was the table of contents. Upon reaching the file's third page, Tatev, however, froze as if she saw a ghost because the current page contained a picture on the left of a girl who had long brown hair, light skin, and dark brown eyes. Beside the picture was information on the girl from her name until blood type.

"I assume you've opened the file already?" Caguiat asked.

"It's open," Dirks answered. "Mirzoyan scrolled down to page 3."

"Then let's begin. This girl, according to the file, is named Maral Eminovna Guliyeva. Three days ago, the file you're all looking at was left in the Museum of Intelligence Collection. Thankfully, the janitor knew the envelope that contained the file you're looking at now was sensitive so he ran to us and gave us that envelope.

"Miss Mirzoyan, please scroll down."

"R... Right away," Tatev replied before she did as Caguiat requested as the next page now showed a picture of a man in his mid-fifties with no hair on his scalp, dark skin, and dark brown eyes.

"This man is Segismundo Alba, the current leader of the Tijuana Cartel. Publicly, he's a big name within Mexico's corporate world and he managed to separate both by attending to the cartel in its financial matters while having subordinates he can trust handle the more... 'unsavory' matters within the cartel. The file stated that he bought Miss Guliyeva. We don't know who sold Miss Guliyeva. Regardless, we have a way to get her."

Caguiat then asked Tatev to scroll down again. As the latter scrolled further down into the file, the next page shown on the screen now showed a younger man on the left. Unlike Alba, he had short black hair in a crew cut.

"This man is our informant in the Tijuana Cartel, Sergio Ortiz," Caguiat said as she resumed her explanation. "Formerly in the Special Warfare Flotilla, he joined the cartel as a mercenary, but we recruited him into the FIS to infiltrate the cartel. He will assist in this mission by providing us with the location where Guliyeva is kept, how to enter, and the weapons needed. You may ask your questions now."

"So we're going to help you take down the cartel?" Vos asked.

"Not yet. We need Mr. 'Smith' to go to Tijuana and meet up with Mr. Ortiz."

"So why does 'Smith' have to see him?" Sunan Wattana asked.

"He must save Miss Guliyeva by himself. Mr. Ortiz will provide him information where Miss Guliyeva is kept at because Alba is a big name in Mexico's corporate world, yet he manages to keep it separate from his duties as cartel leader. In addition, he can secure weapons Mr. 'Smith' will need for the rescue."

"And where do we come in?" Jason Luke Crawley asked.

"You won't be accompanying Mr. 'Smith' to Mexico," Caguiat answered. "Once he secures both Mr. Ortiz and Miss Guliyeva, they'll escape through a plane whose pilot Mr. 'Smith' will contact after he meets with Mr. Ortiz. For those who'll volunteer, we need you at the safehouse in Yao and to wait there until Mr. 'Smith' returns to Japan.

"Before I end this transmission, there's one last thing I must tell you: we've received a report that the 'Phantom sub' is currently in Japanese waters. That could mean the OVR agents involved in the abduction of Maria Hoshikawa must be doing something. We need one of you to monitor the OVR's safehouse in Kansai City. "

Once silence filled the briefing room, Tatev exited AudComm. "You heard her. Who wishes to volunteer for this?" Vos asked his subordinates. "I'll do so."

"Count me in," Wattana answered while she raised her right hand.

"Same here," Crawley added as he raised his hand.

"Not you, Crawley," Dirks replied as he faced Crawley. "We will need your van, but I need you to stay here and keep an eye on Ganji."

"Why me?"

"Other than Ganji, we still have to monitor those OVR infiltrators. Who knows what they may be up to, especially with that warning 'Clara' gave about the Phantom sub." Dirks then turned to a burly man in his early twenties with light intermediate skin, light brown eyes, and no hair on his scalp. "Qazvini, we'll be needing you for this."

"... Roger that," the man named Qazvini replied.

He better improve his English while I'm in Mexico, Dirks thought before he turned to Vos. "We're done here. Have everyone make their preparations to go to the safehouse."

Vos simply nodded and turned to his subordinates. "Dismissed."

All stood up and left the briefing room. Dirks, however, stayed. He then saw Tatev Mirzoyan leave the projector room with her laptop computer and the mouse she used. Dirks seemingly left the stage, but continued walking toward Tatev. The latter saw the former walking up to her and stopped.

"You needed something, Mr. 'Smith'?" Tatev asked.

"Yes," Dirks answered sternly. "Please stay. I have a few questions for you."

Those near the door of the briefing room proper were Vos and Crawley. "This looks bad," Crawley said to Vos as they saw Dirks about to be alone with Tatev.

"Get out of here!" Dirks shouted as he turned to Vos and Crawley.

"Alright, alright," Crawley replied while he was forced out by Vos. Dirks then resumed looking at Tatev.

"Now then, I heard you hesitate when 'Clara' told you to scroll down," Dirks said as a preface to his first question. "Why?"

Tatev gulped upon hearing Dirks' question. She feared what would happen if she refused his question, yet she also feared the picture of Maral Eminovna Guliyeva. She lowered her head and kept silent while closing her eyes.

"Should have known this would happen. I imagine you know Guliyeva?"

As she heard Dirks' second question, Tatev gulped again, briefly opening her mouth. *He… he could tell?* Tatev pondered in her mind.

"I will not rush you for answers. Just answer yes or no."

"I do know her," Tatev defiantly answered, making Dirks open his mouth. "If… I may, mind if I please accompany you on this mission?"

"W… Why you?" Dirks asked.

"It's… related… to what I told you when we first met… "

Should have known Mirzoyan would act this way once human trafficking became the agenda in this mission, Dirks thought. *I can understand, but why would she ask to join us for this mission?*

"Why don't I take it up with Vos?" Dirks asked as a stopgap answer to Tatev's request. "Just go back to your room for now. I apologize for keeping you here."

"Thank you," Tatev replied before she left the briefing room.

Unbeknownst to Tatev, Wouter Vos stood to the right of the door yet as the former left the briefing room, she didn't notice the latter. Dirks, however, caught a glance of Vos upon exiting the room and turned to his right side.

"Couldn't resist listening, could you?" Dirks asked.

"Why don't we talk about it in the library?" Vos asked.

#

0905 hours

Both Dirks and Vos reached the *Iron Dutchman*'s library. They chose the table where the former tested Tarou Ganji in his Japanese months before to see if he can infiltrate Nishi High School.

"What was that about?" Vos asked Dirks.

"Mirzoyan asked if she can join us for this mission," Dirks bluntly answered.

"Should have known it would come down to this."

"What do you mean?"

"Did Mirzoyan ever tell you the full story when we rescued her in Somalia?"

"What 'full story'? She simply told me that you rescued her from the John that bought her in Somalia last year."

"There's more to that. You ready to hear about the rest of it?"

"I didn't think mercenaries like you would be the type to keep that a secret. Should I have bribed you into spilling your guts?"

"I may be a mercenary, but I wouldn't do that. Thankfully, Jair Rodrigues kept his mouth shut about Mirzoyan and Ganji when he first met them. Now then, as to why Mirzoyan omitted most of what happened, there was one detail she refused to bring up ever since we saved her that day."

"And what's that?"

"She used a gun on someone just to save Ganji. And it's the same gun someone put on her head."

"Sounds like that contract of yours got you into deep trouble?"

"It did. I'll spare you the details as to who hired us and what our objective was, but as soon as the shooting started, vital documents and equipment needed to access the information in those documents were being destroyed. Ganji, although the fastest in eliminating that last of the armed opposition we encountered, found a room with a supercomputer. The last 'scientist', as I can put it now, had Mirzoyan at gunpoint to prevent Ganji from going any futher. One henchman Ganji seemingly killed, had enough strength left to take Ganji with him and during that struggle, Mirzoyan managed to fight back by pushing down the man aiming the gun at her and took it. From what Ganji told me, between the two of us, mind you, was that Mirzoyan used the gun to kill the man attempting to kill Ganji. As for that scientist, he had cyanide on him and used it to avoid talking. I saw that part at least."

"I can see why Mirzoyan omitted that part of her past. I also imagine she never brought up how she was sold into slavery? All she told me was that she came from Armenia."

"Same."

"Now, what do we do about her asking to join us in this operation?"

"We can't let anyone know that I told you about what happened that day. We promised Mirzoyan we wouldn't do that."

"Seems to me you care an awful lot about her."

"I'm still human. With Ganji, I can understand why he opted to fight with us, but Mirzoyan clearly doesn't want to be reminded of her past."

"I can understand myself. I have twin daughters."

"That's a first. An FIS agent blurting out that he has a family."

"I may do some unsavory things, but I'm still a human being. It's why I joined the FIS in the first place: to give my daughters a world far different from where I came from before I joined the FIS."

"Either way, we need to be careful with Mirzoyan."

"Does she even have a schedule of what she does every day?"

"Not really. After eating with us, it's either going to the Internet or helping out when needed. Only in the day. If it's nighttime, she just resumes going to the Internet until she's too sleepy to stay awake."

"If Mirzoyan wishes to join us, we need to notify Hamilton."

"Doc? You're right about that, but we'll need Ganji to drop her off here tonight. Problem is, he's focusing on his summer homework."

"Get him to practice his Muay Thai with Wattana."

"That could work. We can tell Doc about this here tonight."

"Then it's settled. Text Hamilton and Ganji tonight. As for me, I need to get to buying a ticket for a flight to San Diego."

"That's the US. I thought you're going to Mexico?"

"I need to meet up with someone in San Diego before going to Tijuana. From there, I'll get a bus to travel to Tijuana."

Nishi High School, Higashiosaka Ward. 1629 hours

At Nishi High School's Judo club, Both Tarou Ganji and Maria Hoshikawa wore their respective *judogi* as the latter charged at the former. Tarou, however, kept evading yet after his third evasion, he stopped.

How foolish of you, Maria thought as she charged at Tarou again. However, as she was half a meter toward Tarou, she was unable to move and that it wasn't of her own volition. She briefly moved her head toward her arms and found Tarou touching her *judogi's* sleeves at the portion near her elbows.

Oh n- Maria thought before Tarou quickly laid on the floor with his back, pressed his left foot against Maria's stomach, and flipped her with his hands. Maria then fell on her back.

Tarou then got up and offered his right hand to Maria. Maria reluctantly accepted and got up with Tarou's help. An older man then approached them with the former two bowing.

"Nicely done, Ganji-kun," the man said.

"Arigatou, Nishizawa-sensei," Tarou replied.

"We're dismissed for today," the man named Nishizawa announced.

Everyone else in the Judo club began to leave the room. Tarou and Maria then faced each other.

"That was a nice Tomoe nage," Maria said in English.

"Thanks," Tarou replied before he faced the door like everyone else was. "I best get going."

"I'll see you tomorrow."

#

Hamilton-Ganji Condominium, Hoshikawa Condominiums. 1758 hours

Tarou was now at the condominium he and Anita Hamilton resided at. Due to the mission in Iran, he spent his summer finishing make-up assignments due to his frequent absences.

However, his smartphone, given to him by Frederick Dirks, rang. Despite his homework, Tarou answered and found that the message came from IntMail. The message came from Hamilton and it read:

I've closed the clinic for today, please pick me up.

Tarou then grabbed his phone and began to leave the condominium.

#

Iron Dutchman/Hoshikawa Shipyards. 1901 hours

Tarou and Hamilton then arrived at Hoshikawa Shipyards, where the *Iron Dutchman* was docked. After parking the PCX scooter Tarou used to travel across Kansai City, he and Hamilton proceeded to the *Iron Dutchman*, yet they found Sunan Wattana waiting alongside Dirks and Wouter Vos.

"Miss Wattana, why are you here?" Tarou asked.

"I know you've been busy, but you need to brush up on your Muay Thai," Wattana explained. "Shall we?"

"Sure. I'm almost done."

"After practice, why don't you two stay for dinner," Vos added. "It's been a while."

"Sure," Hamilton answered.

"Wait, there's something I need to whisper to you, Hamilton," Dirks warned. "Can I go over to your left ear?"

"Sure," Hamilton replied. Dirks then walked up to the left ear of the former and whispered. Everyone else watched with curiosity until Vos used body language to remind Wattana to take Tarou away. Reluctantly, the latter two left.

"We don't leave until we don't see Wattana and Ganji," Dirks instructed as he stopped whispering.

Vos and Hamilton made sounds while keeping their respective mouths closed as a sign of agreement. The three watched until Wattana and Tarou vanished. The former three began to follow but slowly.

1926 hours

Vos, Dirks, and Hamilton reached the library. They reached the table the former two used earlier that morning.

"Let me guess: we waited for Tarou and Sunan to go elsewhere so that they didn't know we had to talk in private here?" Hamilton surmised upon realizing why she had to talk to Vos and Dirks in the library.

"That's right," Dirks answered. "I apologize for having done so, but there's something Vos and I need to discuss with you."

"I can imagine it's a mission, since we're not allowed to have Tarou with us."

"You guessed right," Vos replied. "Sunan knows too. Hence why we had Tarou brush up on his Muay Thai while we're here."

"Am I needed for this mission?" Hamilton asked.

"Hopefully no," Dirks answered. "We need you to make sure Ganji continues his summer homework."

"Why?" Hamilton's tone when she asked now showed suspicion.

"I... told 'Smith' here about Mirzoyan's past," Vos answered with guilt, also coming out of his tone.

"Why did you do that? You know how scary it is for Tatev to be reminded about it."

"She volunteered to be a part of the upcoming mission," Dirks answered to assuage Hamilton's fears.

"How come?" Hamilton asked.

Vos and Dirks began to explain to Hamilton the mission the former two were given. By the time they stopped, the latter closed her eyes, moved her head downward, and slightly opened her mouth while gritting her teeth.

"I'm surprised someone from Tatev's past is alive," Hamilton said. "She never did tell us about how she was sold off into sexual slavery in the first place."

"We may end up knowing how once this is all over," Dirks cynically added.

"So, what do we do now?" Vos asked. "Ganji's here and should he know about this mission, he'll want to join us and we can't risk it because we need to have him continue keeping an eye on Hoshikawa."

"Tell everyone that Mirzoyan will be joining us after dinner," Dirks ordered before he faced Hamilton. "After dinner, tell him that you'll be leaving for him to resume his studies."

"Understood," Hamilton replied.

"Come on, we best go to the dining hall," Vos commanded. "Barto's probably done, and it's best to start as soon as Ganji and Sunan join us."

#

2107 hours

All members of Iron Dutchman Services, save for Tarou and Hamilton, appeared at the briefing room. At the stage were Vos and Dirks, with the latter walking up to address the other members.

"Before the mission launches, we have one update as to who'll be joining us," Dirks announced before he faced Tatev Mirzoyan. "Mirzoyan, please come on up here."

So it's time? Tatev pondered in her mind before standing up and walking to the stage, surprising everyone else.

After climbing onto the stage, Tatev joined Dirks and faced the other mercenaries. "Mirzoyan here will be joining this mission. Like Vos, Wattana, and Qazvini, she'll remain at the safehouse in Yao."

"And why is she joining us?" Jake Crawley asked.

"Allow me to explain," Tatev announced. "Maral Eminovna Guliyeva is a girl I knew in my past, which all of you know. I intend on seeing her again by participating in this mission. That is all."

"That will be the only update I will make," Dirks continued. "As soon as possible, I will be leaving for JGSDF Camp Yao tomorrow to secure it as my landing zone once I return with Guliyeva. That is all."

Both Dirks and Tatev stepped aside once Vos began to face his subordinates. "Dismissed," he commanded.

2150 hours

Alone, Jake Crawley wandered into the firing range that was once the disco room of the cruise ship the *Iron Dutchman* used to be. *Is Tatev even ready to use a gun should there a need to?* he pondered.

"There you are." Crawley reared his head to find that Sunan Wattana followed him. He then turned his entire body to face her properly.

"What are you doing here?" Crawley asked.

"I could ask you the same thing," Wattana answered.

"I'll be frank: I'm feeling disturbed about Tatev joining you on this mission."

"We all are. We felt this way too when Mirzoyan opted to learn how to use a gun again."

"It all goes back to that day, doesn't it?"

#

Abandoned Mosque, West Mogadishu District, Mogadishu Capital Region; Republic of Somalia. January 10, 2029; 0100 hours (East Africa Time)

At an abandoned mosque facing the Indian Ocean, the National Police (NP) of Somalia surrounded the mosque. As a result of the Third World War, Somalia fell apart in a civil war. Only the south, where the capital of Mogadishu was situated in, was able to rebuild itself as the Republic of Somalia and acquired membership into the African Federation (AF) for assistance in reconstruction. This mosque, however, had yet to bear the fruits of reconstruction and as a result, armed men occupied it, with the NP surrounding them as a result.

The National Police were the result of South Somalia, as it's commonly called, joining the AF. Despite being police, the NP were given equipment needed for small armies from assault rifles to armored personnel carriers (APCs). The entrance to the mosque, the only one as it was surrounded by the ocean on three sides, was barricaded by APCs.

Among those with the National Police were the mercenaries Wouter Vos and Sunan Wattana, clad in armor provided to them by the NP. The former carried an R10 assault rifle while the latter aimed its sniper rifle variant, the SR10, at the mosque. While Vos used his right hand to carry the R10, he used his left index finger to press an earpiece connected to the ear above the finger.

"Ganji, Crawley, Where are you now?" Vos asked.

"Ganji here," Tarou Ganji replied on his end. "Near the mosque. The guards have not spotted us."

"Have Odawaa's men completely surrounded those hostage-takers?" Jason Luke Crawley interjected over the earpiece.

"They have," Vos answered. "How are the Boarders?"

"Two of them already infiltrated the mosque while stealing disguises and weapons from those inside," Crawley answered. "Ganji and I are ready to rush in there should things get nasty. Abdalla and Hussein will cover us when Ganji and I charge in there."

However, gunshots were heard. Everyone's eyes widened as a result and when gunshots were heard, everyone knew what that meant.

"Maya!" an NP officer screamed as he joined Vos and Wattana. "Those gunshots must have come from the mosque! The infiltrators must have been discovered!"

"Ganji, Jake, you heard that?" Vos asked immediately as he used his earpiece again.

"We did," Tarou answered over the earpiece. "Something must have happened to Hassan and Kamas."

"Stay where you are."

"Got it," Crawley interjected.

"I see the door opening," Wattana added while she began to look through her SR10's scope with her right.

She now saw a man leaving the mosque. However, he didn't face the NP as he put aside his AKM assault rifle and grabbed something from inside with both of his arms.

"What's he doing?" the NP officer standing beside Vos asked.

"Who knows?" Vos asked in response. "It could be-"

"I'm seeing a dead body being dragged out of the mosque," Wattana warned.

Both Vos and the NP officer now looked at the entrance of the mosque. Wattana, however, was able to see what was actually happening as the man with the AKM dragged a dead man out of the mosque. He then went back inside and dragged another corpse out of the mosque.

"What do you see?" Vos asked as he and the NP officer turned to Wattana.

"One gunman dragging two dead men out of that mosque," Wattana answered.

"Then it must be the two infiltrators," the NP officer deduced.

"The gunmen inside must have found out," Vos added to the suspicion.

"That's it! I'm ordering the assault now!"

"Odawaa, Wait-" Vos attempted to say until another gunshot was heard.

#

Iron Dutchman, Taisho Ward, Kansai City, Kansai Prefecture; State of Japan. August 5, 2030; 2216 hours (Japan Standard Time)

"It all went to hell due to that gunshot," Wattana claimed in the present. "Some woman made a desperate dash for freedom because of those Boarders, thinking she would be saved. Due to that, we didn't get much money after that mission."

"Yet we met Mirzoyan due to that mission." Both Wattana and Crawley turned to where the voice came from. Wouter Vos now joined them at their shooting range.

"Why are you here?" Crawley asked.

"I could ask you the same thing," Vos answered.

"We were thinking about that mission in Somalia," Wattana explained.

"I was going to think about that too." Vos then stopped as he was barely one meter apart from the man and woman who helped him create Iron Dutchman Services. "Concerned about having Mirzoyan join us?"

"Yep," Crawley answered with his tone showing a lack of resistance.

"I can understand. I didn't think Mirzoyan would want to do this. Sure, money became an issue after we took her in, but having her help with chores and finding contracts was good enough for her to be with us."

"Exactly why I don't feel good about her joining in this mission," Wattana added. "It's clear she's forcing herself to join us because of that Guliyeva girl."

"Still, depending on what happens next, it will become clear once 'Smith' does get that girl and takes her to that safehouse in Yao."

"That does remind me: why is 'Smith' going to Mexico by himself?" Crawley asked.

"Good question," Vos said. "Fighting the Tijuana Cartel? I mean, it's the FIS we're talking about. I doubt saving a girl will help destroy it."

"We can't ask 'Smith' either," Wattana warned.

"Either way, we best get to sleep already," Vos ordered. "We have a lot to do tomorrow."

"Got it," both Wattana and Crawley replied in unison.

#

Kajaran, Kajaran Volost, Syunik Uyezd, Armenia Governorate; Eurasian Tsardom. August 1, 2020; 0659 hours (Caucasia Time)

"PLEASE!" a woman shouted, waking up a girl with light skin, a short and thin body, dark brown eyes, and black hair. "PLE-"

That… that… was Mother… the girl thought, motivating her to get out of her bed. After putting on her slippers, the girl exited her room but found not only where the source of the screaming came from but what happened.

The girl was frozen as she saw an older woman who looked like her laying on the floor with a knife between her breasts and a man standing on a chair tying up one end of a rope with the other end already tied to a nail that was half-stuck on the ceiling.

"F… Father, what are you doing?" the girl asked. "W… What happened to Mother?"

"Is that you, Tatev? the man standing on the chair asked before he wrapped his neck with the rope. "Think you could please help with the chair?"

#

Iron Dutchman, Taisho Ward, Kansai City, Kansai Prefecture; State of Japan. August 6, 2030; 0657 hours (Japan Standard Time)

The same girl, Tatev Mirzoyan, woke up in the present. Upon rapidly waking up, she breathed as if she was struggling to do so.

Figures I would remember that moment, Tatev thought. *I can't believe that coward is my father! Because of him, I was sold into sexual slavery and who knows what would have happened had Iron Dutchman Services not rescued me that day. Now that Maral is alive, I can help her like how Mr. Vos, Tarou, and everyone else helped me.*

Tatev then got out of her bed. This time, she knew what was outside.

Rendezvous

Ishiguro's Firing Range, Outskirts of Kansai City, Kansai Prefecture; State of Japan. July 14, 2030; 1137 hours (Japan Standard Time)

Outside Kansai City was a portion of land owned by one Akira Ishiguro. Ishiguro, a man in his fifties, had short black hair in a crew cut, very light skin that darkened because of constant exposure to the sun, and dark brown eyes and gave what appeared to be a never-ending frown. He was once in the New United Nations Ground Force until he opted to retire. Until his time came, he opted to run a shooting range where he can teach people wishing to use a gun for the first time.

His recent student was Tatev Mirzoyan. Both Ishiguro and Tatev wore goggles that covered their eyes, and a headset that blocked their ears. The former had to because he needed to watch the latter use her P9 semi-automatic pistol as she fired it at a target.

She managed to improve after a month's worth of classes, Ishiguro thought. *If she does wish to be of more help, she'll need to learn more than pistols.*

Far from Ishiguro and Tatev were two men: Jason Luke Crawley and Tarou Ganji. Although far enough, the two men were still able to hear the shots from Tatev's P9.

"Is this even a good idea?" Tarou asked.

"She wants this," Crawley answered.

The firing stopped. Both Tarou and Crawley now saw Ishiguro and Tatev looking at the target, now filled with shells, and joined them. Unlike the latter two, the former two were stunned that most of the bullet holes neared the center of the target, with one having hit the center.

She's definitely improving! Crawley thought with his eyes widened.

Tarou's face, however, remained the same. *It may have been a month, but she needs to constantly practice,* Tarou thought. *Everyone's celebrating too soon.*

"Lunch is ready!" a woman shouted as she appeared, making all turn to her.

The woman was Ishiguro's wife, Sayuri. Only fifty years old, Sayuri's face didn't show signs of her actual age. Unlike her husband, her black hair was shortened and her skin was paler because she hadn't been exposed to the sun.

"Tatev, we're stopping for now," Ishiguro ordered to Tatev. "Take everything to the table."

"Roger," Tatev replied.

#

Iron Dutchman, Taisho Ward, Kansai City. August 6, 2030; 0450 hours

Thanks to his smartphone acting as his alarm clock, Jake Crawley woke up. He yawned after rising from his sleep.

He then got out of the bed and, once he put on slippers, he left his room, presumably to wash his face by using the Iron Dutchman's washroom. However, he realized that someone was outside his room and turned to his right, finding Frederick Dirks.

"Glad you're up," Dirks said. "I'll help you go to the washroom because I need you to take me to Camp Yao."

"Ryoukai," Crawley replied with one word of Japanese he managed to remember; his tone still showing that he wasn't entirely awake. Despite that, he and Dirks continued toward the *Iron Dutchman's* washroom.

I really hope Tatev doesn't get to use that gun of hers, Crawley thought.

#

JGSDF Camp Yao, Yao. 0521 hours

Both Dirks and Crawley, the latter now wearing proper attire for going outside, were now at the office of JGSDF Camp Yao's commanding officer, Juzo Izubuchi. "And when will you be returning with this private jet?" Izubuchi asked after listening to what Dirks explained about his mission and why he needed the airstrip used by both Camp Yao and Yao Airport.

"I have an asset that I intend to take to my safehouse," Dirks answered. "That is all you need to know."

"Very well."

"Thank you, Colonel."

Both Dirks and Crawley then left Izubuchi's office. "Can we get breakfast?" Crawley asked. "I don't think my stomach can wait any longer."

"Sadly, that stomach of yours will have to wait," Dirks replied. "Since I forced you to take me here this early, I'll pay for it."

#

Iron Dutchman, Taisho Ward. 0815 hours

All members of Iron Dutchman Services in their namesake ship were now gathered at their briefing room. This time, Tatev Mirzoyan was seated beside everyone else as opposed to the projector room while Dirks and Wouter Vos were on the stage.

"Now that I got Izubuchi's permission to use Camp Yao as my landing spot once I return from Mexico with Guliyeva, now I must get the plane ticket I need to go to San Diego, in which I am to meet up with someone from the FIS that will help acquire what I'll need then I'll go to Tijuana. After that, I'll get to packing up as soon as I get my ticket."

"So when do we go to Yao?" Sunan Wattana asked while she raised her hand.

"I'll give you a text that will authorize that," Dirks answered. "I still need to meet with Ortiz to discuss how we'll rescue Guliyeva."

"Any questions before we dismiss?" Vos asked to his subordinates.

"I have one," Tatev Mirzoyan said upon raising her hand.

"Yes?" Dirks asked.

"Might I be allowed to take my pistol with me?"

Damn it! Crawley cursed in his mind. *Please say no, "Smith". Please so no!*

"I'll allow it," Dirks answered, shocking everyone other member of Iron Dutchman Services. The former then turned to Vos, who hardly attempted to hide his shock that Tatev would have a gun with her for the mission. "Vos?"

"… I'll allow it as well," Vos hesitantly answered before he turned to Tatev. "Mirzoyan, I suggest you start practicing until we're told to go to Yao."

"Roger," Tatev replied.

"Anything else?" Vos asked to his subordinates. Wattana raised her hand again.

"Yes, Sunan?" Vos asked.

"Does Mirzoyan have a vest?" Wattana asked.

"Get her one BEFORE I tell you to go to Yao!" Dirks ordered. "A vest isn't that hard to find."

He then turned to Vos. "Vos, while Crawley keeps an eye on Ganji and those infiltrators, you'll take the Townace and when I tell you to pick me up, use it."

"Roger," Vos replied. Dirks then turned to Crawley.

"Crawley, when I hear from 'Smith', give Vos the Townace keys," Dirks ordered to Crawley.

"Got it," Crawley replied.

"Anything else?" Vos repeated his question to his subordinates. This time, they replied no. "Then we're dismissed."

#

International Travel House/Outside International Travel House, Minato Ward. 1100 hours

Later, Dirks alone traveled to International Travel House, a travel agency located in the portion of Minato Ward that wasn't destroyed during the Third World War. He had been to International House the day before to acquire a plane ticket for San Diego International Airport and while managing to pay for it, he was told to claim it the following day. Today was that day.

Dirks then entered International Travel House. He then informed the female clerk about his purchase from the previous day.

"Please wait," the clerk instructed.

Dirks found chairs behind him that he could sit on. Luckily for Dirks, the wait wasn't long as the clerk called him out with the ticket he ordered. The former then stood up, claimed the ticket, said thanks, and left.

Returning outside, Dirks now heard his stomach demanding food. Miraculously, there were restaurants nearby, but Dirks couldn't afford to be picky. After going past an office building to the left of International Travel House, Dirks found one restaurant and proceeded to have his lunch there.

#

Iron Dutchman, Taisho Ward. 1307 hours

Tatev arrived at the *Iron Dutchman's* shooting range. This wasn't her first time in the shooting range for this day because she came earlier to clean up her P9 semi-automatic pistol before using it. Since that was hours ago, it was now time for Tatev to practice using her gun.

Before starting, she grabbed a chair painted with a red target. After laying the chair, Tatev then returned to the table where she left her pistol and moved it near a portion of the floor marked for those who practice, shown with two strips of masking tape laid on the floor and crossing each other to make an X. Before grabbing her pistol, she put on her goggles and headset needed to protect her eyes and ears while shooting.

She then got her P9. After that, she loaded it with the magazine filled with 9x19mm rounds and began to face the target.

Now facing the target, Tatev turned off her pistol's safety and took aim. Once she adjusted her position to aim at the center of the target, Tatev began firing her P9.

Upon emptying her magazine, Tatev briefly took off her goggles. She found that she had yet to hit the very center of the target, opting for her to reload. She then grabbed one of the additional magazines also on the table and after loading the pistol, she put on the goggles again and aimed. After a brief inhale and exhale, Tatev squeezed the trigger again and continued until she exhausted the magazine.

Tatev again removed her goggles. She now found a hole at the center of the target. *I did it*, Tatev thought. *Maybe one more before I stop for the time being.*

She then grabbed the last magazine on the table and loaded it onto the P9. After putting on the goggles again and aiming, Tatev fired again.

#

1419 hours

Later, Tatev appeared in a different room carrying the chair she used for target practice. The room was where past targets were disposed of after being riddled with bullets. Tatev found Vikas Mistry outside.

"Done practicing, I presume?" Mistry asked.

"That's right, Mr. Mistry," Tatev answered.

"Just leave the chair there. Please wait while I open the door"

"Thank you," Tatev replied as Mistry opened the door.

Tatev proceeded to the open room. Inside were chairs that have been filled with bullet holes. Once Tatev brought the chair, she used to a vacant spot. She left the chair there and left the room herself. Mistry then closed the door.

#

2014 hours

All passengers of the *Iron Dutchman* gathered again in their briefing room. Like it was earlier that morning, Tatev was seated with everyone else. Vos and Dirks stood again on the stage and faced the subordinates of the former.

"Now that I have my ticket, I must tell you that my flight tomorrow will be at 1000 hours," Dirks announced. "Again, for those assigned to my safehouse in Yao, wait for my signal, then you're to transfer there."

Dirks then turned to Jake Crawley. "Crawley, I'll need you to drive me to KIX tomorrow and I'd rather be extremely early, so I'll go to sleep first and wake you at 0500 hours tomorrow morning."

"Again?" Crawley asked.

"You can rest up for two hours because I need you to spy on the warehouse that we now know to be used by OVR or Soviet agents."

"Why haven't we moved against them?" Wattana asked.

"We don't have proof of who they are," Dirks answered. "Japan has taken in refugees from the Eurasian Tsardom and the Soviet Remnant. Easy for infiltrators to do that and outright questioning them is bad. We need proof to move against them."

Dirks then resumed facing Crawley. "I need you to start connoitering that safehouse," Dirks ordered. "While I'm in Mexico, keep updating me on their movements."

"Yes, sir," Crawley replied; his tone now showing enthusiasm.

"Now, as for tomorrow, I suggest everyone go to sleep now so that I wouldn't have any trouble sleeping myself." Dirks turned to Crawley again. "Crawley, that goes for you as well. I need you to wake up when I say so."

"Yes, sir."

"Then we're dismissed," Vos declared. "Everyone wash up and go to sleep."

#

Hoshikawa Shipyards. August 7, 2030; 0655 hours

Crawley had the Townace prepared in front of the *Iron Dutchman*. He kept himself desperately awake, as it was clear he still needed sleep. By contrast, Dirks began to exit the *Iron Dutchman* with two bags: a messenger bag and a rolling suitcase. Seeing Crawley about to sleep, Dirks walked up to the Townace and knocked on the right front seat.

Finally, Crawley thought while managing to hear Dirks' knocking. He then turned to find the latter and unlocked all the Townace's doors.

From the outside, Dirks now saw and heard that all doors of the Townace were unlocked. He opened the right rear door and, after opening it, he loaded his rolling suitcase inside first. After that, he boarded while carrying his messenger bag.

Once he closed the door, Crawley locked all doors. He then began to move the Townace out of Hoshikawa Shipyards.

Near the OVR Safehouse, Nishinari Ward. 1014 hours

Later, Crawley arrived near a building near the Sembonmatsu Bridge. On the surface, it was used by a delivery service, but while the Foreign Intelligence Service and Iron Dutchman Services now know it's a safehouse, they didn't the warehouse was used by a cell of the Eurasian Tsardom's foreign intelligence agency, the *Otdeleniye Vneshney Razvedi* (OVR).

Once he stepped out of the Townace, Crawley rushed to where he could hide. He then brought out his smartphone and aimed it at the building's entrance. He continued aiming until he saw the door open, forcing him to hide.

However, Crawley continued to aim his smartphone at the building while making sure he wasn't seen. The risk, however, came when he had to take the photograph, as he needed to figure out the face of the man who joined the OVR cell. He immediately pressed the button to take the picture.

Once he heard the sound that indicated the picture was taken, Crawley pushed his smartphone further to him so that it wasn't detected. He then accessed the application on his smartphone named "Pictures". Going to photographs taken on August 7, or rather, the only picture taken during that day, Crawley opened the picture. Miraculously of good quality, Crawley found four individuals in the photograph. While Crawley knew who the other three were, the third man was new to him.

How did they sneak a new guy here? Crawley pondered. *I best leave and tell "Smith" later.*

Crawley looked again at the building and found that the man had vanished. With the door of the building closed, Crawley rushed back to his Townace.

San Diego International Airport, San Diego, San Diego County, State of California; United States of America. August 6, 2030; 0649 hours (Pacific Standard Time)

Dirks ultimately arrived in the United States of America. He looked around outside San Diego International Airport as he was instructed to meet up with someone who will provide him with what he needs for the mission.

He went over all signs raised by those expecting arrivals. He then found a sign that said "Fred Smith", prompting him to go to who raised that sign. Dirks stopped because he was shocked as to who was expecting him: John Vue.

"Vue?" Dirks interjected. "What are you doing here?"

"I was assigned to assist you," Vue answered. "Glad to see you again, 'Smith'."

"Same here… I guess."

"Come on. I got us a hotel where you'll be staying for tonight. We have plenty to discuss and we can do that over breakfast."

#

Rest Inn Express San Diego International Airport. 0717 hours

Both Dirks and Vue arrived at the Rest Inn near San Diego International Airport. After checking in with the latter assisting in making sure the former got his room, they made a quick trip to the room for Dirks to drop off his luggage before they helped themselves to free breakfast.

Once in the hotel's restaurant, Dirks and Vue immediately occupied the first vacant table they found. Seeing the free breakfast was a buffet, and that there was a line, Dirks was the first to stand up and leave to get his food.

As a Green Beret at heart, Dirks mostly counted on fruit but added some meat. However, there was one temptation he couldn't resist: a cinnamon roll. Once he got his coffee, which he kept black and sugarless, he returned to the table he shared with Vue. Now, it was Vue's turn to stand up and get his breakfast.

Since he was an analyst, Vue was a civilian. While he still remembered physical fitness was a necessity for a long enough life to see his daughter Mary finish her education and help her find someone to settle down with, Vue still remembered that no breakfast would be complete with pancakes. He grabbed three pieces and filled each with butter and syrup. After that, he helped himself to two strips of bacon and one cinnamon roll. Unlike Dirks, Vue's coffee was an iced mocha. He then re-joined Dirks at their table and, by contrast to Vue, the former already started his meal.

"I must ask: why did they send you?" Dirks asked after swallowing the strip of bacon he was chewing earlier.

"I wasn't busy at the time, save for my teaching job," Vue answered just as he cut up the respective lower left edges of his three pancakes before impaling them with his fork.

"You teach when you're not being an analyst?"

"I always wanted to be a teacher. High school to be specific. I work in the Company because Deputy Director Saetang heard about me through my prof and offered the job as additional money to help me become a high school teacher."

"And the Company is to make sure you get a scholarship?"

"A little cheat-ish but I do have a wife and daughter. Old Man Boettger isn't going to help as I told you when we first met in Hawaii, so I have to do stuff like this."

"Which school do you wish to teach at?"

"In my hometown of Merced. I hope to move there with Rose and Mary after I get my scholarship."

"Did you always want to be a history teacher?"

"That I can confirm. My grandfather was a history teacher and listening to his stories about Laos before he and his family had to flee as they opposed the Pathet Lao. I argued with my father about it as he's an officer in the NUN Air Force, but he relented on the condition I join either the NUN Defense Forces or the US military. I joined the United States Army and when my service was up, I entered college.

"Anyway, enough of me. Do you have a list of things I can provide for you?"

"Hold on." Dirks summoned his smartphone and accessed an application called "Notes". He accessed a file named "List to show to FIS Operative in San Diego" and gave the phone to Vue.

"Let's see... " Vue said as he looked at the list on Dirks' phone. "You need 90,000 UN dollars for your stay in Mexico and a plane to use for your escape once you retrieve Miss Guliyeva."

"That's right," Dirks replied. "Think you could provide."

"I've already been assigned these tasks." Now it was Vue's turn to bring out his smartphone. After opening his Notes application, he accessed a file named "Places to go to" and gave the phone to Dirks to look at the list.

"Checks out," Dirks said before he and Vue returned their respective phones to each other.

"What will you do now?"

"Find a bus to take me to Tijuana."

"I can take you to the station so that you can get a ticket for tomorrow."

"Thanks. Now, before we discuss further, we best finish our breakfast. We can resume in my room because the rest of it must remain between us."

"Got it."

#

0853 hours

Both Dirks and Vue returned to the room of the former. Once the door was locked and the drapes closed. The latter sat down on the only bed in the room.

"Now, what is it you needed to tell me and me only?" Vue asked.

"Before I go to Tijuana, think you could contact the PF?" Dirks requested. "Ortiz's handler in the PF needs to know I'm coming and that I need to see *her* to meet Ortiz."

"*Her?*"

"Detective Rosarita Sanchez."

"Consider it done."

"Thanks."

"What will you do now?"

"Get that bus ticket, walk a bit, get lunch, walk some more, then I return to the hotel for dinner and after an hour, an early sleep, depending on how early I need to be awake for my bus trip."

"Kirk will keep an eye on you until you leave for Tijuana."

"Got it. I best get going now."

#

FIS Headquarters, McLean, Fairfax County, Commonwealth of Virginia. 1205 hours (Eastern Standard Time)

At his office in the headquarters of the Foreign Intelligence Service, Alberto Pérez received a message in his IntMail. As he opened it, the message came from Yanin Saetang, his Deputy Director of Intelligence, whose name in IntMail is "Y Saet". The message read:

Vue got back to me about "Smith". He's currently buying his bus ticket for Tijuana and wishes to contact Rosarita Sanchez in order to meet with Sergio Ortiz. Please warn the DI before contacting Villanueva.

Pérez began to type a message addressed to one "CP DI".

#

IC Headquarters, Lambeth, Greater London, England; United Kingdom of Great Britain and Northern Ireland. 1811 hours (British Summer Time)

In the Vauxhall District of the London borough of Lambeth was the headquarters of the Intelligence Collective (IC), where all intelligence gathered throughout the New United Nations was delivered to. This building was meant to be the headquarters of the United Kingdom's foreign intelligence agency, the Secret Intelligence Service (SIS) prior to its dissolution upon the creation of NUN.

Despite that, and the Third World War that brought upon the creation of NUN, construction continued. Rather than let the efforts of the construction crew go to waste, the building that was meant to host the SIS was made into the headquarters of NUN's Intelligence Collective.

At her office, Cecilia Parnell, the Director of Intelligence, received the message Alberto Pérez wrote to her about Frederick Dirks' mission in Mexico through her desktop computer's IntMail application. The message read:

Received an update from the Directorate of Intelligence. "Fred Smith" from the Covert Action Center will be traveling to Tijuana to meet up with Rosarita Sanchez from the Policía Federal, Sergio Ortiz's handler. Permission to contact Villanueva.

Parnell immediately wrote "Permission granted" and pressed "Send". She then stood up and left her office.

#

FIS Headquarters, McLean, Fairfax County, Commonwealth of Virginia; United States of America. 1213 hours (Eastern Standard Time)

Pérez received Parnell's reply. After reading it, he began contacting someone with the name "OV PF-DI". However, his message was quick because he began to hear his stomach.

It only took a minute for Pérez to finish his message. Once he finished, he pressed "Send".

#

PF-DI Headquarters, Miguel Hidalgo, Mexico City; United Mexican States. 1115 hours (Central Standard Time)

At his office in the headquarters of the *División de Inteligencia* (DI), Omar Villanueva received Pérez's message. The message was written in Spanish. He had light intermediate skin and no hair on his scalp, with his eyebrows being the remnant of his black hair.

When the United Mexican States joined the New United Nations, it dissolved its only intelligence agency, the *Centro Nacional de Inteligencia* (CNI). To gather intelligence against criminal activity, the duties, personnel, and resources that belonged to the CNI were given to the DI of the *Policía Federal* (PF), also created when Mexico joined NUN to replace the Mexican Army's 1st Military Police Brigade, the Federal

Attorney Police, the Federal Highway Patrol, and the counter-intelligence unit of CNI's predecessor the *Centro de Investigación y Seguridad Nacional* (CISEN).

The current Director of DI was Omar Villanueva. A descendant of Lebanese immigrants, Villanueva was the third Director of DI after his two predecessors. Once he finished reading the message, Villanueva downloaded a copy into a USB device. After disconnecting the USB, he stood up and walked to his office's printer. Once he plugged the USB into the printer, Villanueva made a physical copy of the message he received from Pérez and began to leave his office.

#

PF Headquarters. Álvaro Obregón. 1216 hours

"So, what does this 'Fred Smith' want?" Angela Éliane, the Commissioner-General of the *Policía Federal*, asked after reading the physical copy of Pérez's message after Villanueva gave it to her. Both Éliane and Villanueva were in their fifties; the former having very light skin, graying blonde hair, and blue eyes as a contrast to the dark brown eyes of the latter.

"He's asking for permission to meet with Officer Sanchez in order to meet with 'Fantasma'," Villanueva answered.

"I'll contact Asensio. I'd like to dismiss you, but because neither of us has eaten lunch yet, why don't you join me before you return to your office?"

"Gracias, Comisionado-General," Villanueva replied.

#

PF Tijuana Field Office, Tijuana, Tijuana Municipality, Free and Sovereign State of Baja California. 1115 hours (Pacific Standard Time)

Patterned after the United States of America's Federal Bureau of Investigation (FBI), the *Policía Federal* built various field offices throughout Mexico. Tijuana hosted one such field office.

A woman in her late thirties with long black hair tied into a bun, dark brown eyes, and dark skin approached the office of Chief Inspector Rodrigo Asensio, the commander of the PF Tijuana field office. In his early fifties, Asensio had his black hair in a crew cut, an angular build, and the same eyes and skin color as the woman who entered his office.

"You called for me, Inspector Jefe?" the woman asked.

"Glad you made it, Officer Sanchez," Asensio said. "Now, as for your question, yes. I've been given an order by the Comisionado General."

"And what might that be?"

"A man named 'Fred Smith' will be coming here to Tijuana from San Diego in the United States tomorrow. He intends to meet 'Fantasma'."

"Did you say 'Fantasma'?"

"Sí."

"Has he stated how he'll be coming to Mexico?"

"He's in the middle of acquiring a bus ticket."

"I need to know when because if he's coming to see 'Fantasma', we need to meet somewhere where *they* cannot see us suspiciously."

"I'm sure he'll announce it soon. Of course, it will take a while until we hear of it because he's FIS."

"I understand."

"Now please get lunch. I'll let you know when Señor 'Smith' will be coming to Tijuana tomorrow."

#

Rest Inn Express San Diego International Airport, San Diego, San Diego County, State of California; United States of America. 1200 hours

Frederick Dirks ultimately returned to his hotel room. He found John Vue still inside.

"You should have gotten yourself a room if you wanted to use mine," Dirks said to the analyst, startling the latter.

"Y… You're back?" Vue asked.

"I am. Got the ticket."

Dirks brought out the bus ticket. Sensing that Vue wants to look at it up close, the former gave it to the latter.

"It says you have to reach the terminal tomorrow at 7PM," Vue read out of the ticket.

"Then I'm going to make the most of this trip before tomorrow morning," Dirks declared. "Know anywhere good for lunch?"

"You can join me in visiting my older sister, Kim. She invited me over for lunch. Luckily, she hasn't started cooking yet, but if you say yes, I can contact her now and she can prepare more for you."

"You don't have to do that. You already got me this room, which came with free breakfast."

"I insist."

"... Fine." Dirks, however, made a facial expression that made him realize he had something else to tell Vue. "Wait, there's one thing I need to warn you."

"What is it?"

"Jason Luke Crawley warned me that the cell in Kansai City has a new member."

"A new member? That Phantom sub must have brought him or her to Japan."

"It's a guy. Here's the photo."

Accessing his smartphone's Photos, Dirks found the photograph Crawley took. He then showed the photograph to Vue. After looking at the photograph, Vue nodded and faced Dirks again.

"Order Crawley to keep an eye on that man," Vue requested.

"Will do," Dirks replied.

The Launch

PF Tijuana Field Office, Tijuana, Tijuana Municipality, Free and Sovereign State of Baja California; United Mexican States. August 6, 2030; 1755 hours (Pacific Standard Time)

"Will he arrive at that time?" Rosarita Sanchez asked her superior Rodrigo Asensio.

"He may be FIS, but if he's coming here for a mission, he won't lie," Asensio answered. "You haven't eaten, right?"

"No."

"I suggest you eat now, then wait an hour or two because you need to wake up early to meet with Señor 'Smith' tomorrow."

"Sí, Inspector Jefe."

\#

Tijuana Central Bus Station. August 7, 2030; 0755 hours

Frederick Dirks was now in the United Mexican States. Upon exiting the Tijuana Central Bus Station, he found a woman raising a sign that said "Fred Smith". The FIS agent walked up to the woman, who then lowered the sign as she saw Dirks approach her.

"¿Es usted el Señor 'Smith'?" the woman asked.

"¿Sí?" Dirks asked in response.

"I'm Rosarita Sanchez," the woman said in English. "I've been told you came here to see me?"

"Indeed," Dirks replied in English. "Is 'Fantasma' ready to meet me?"

"Not yet. I've already contacted him last night but right now, he's looking for free time to see you. I've already arranged the meeting place. I've also arranged where you'll be staying for today."

"Good. Please take me there if I'm to wait for 'Fantasma' if *he*'s ready to see me."

"Then get in." Sanchez gestured to a Crown automobile.

#

Rio Tijuana Motel. 0843 hours

Both Dirks and Sanchez arrived at a room in the Rio Tijuana Motel, named after the river it faced. Once they closed the door behind them, Dirks unpacked his belongings while the latter sat on the room's only bed.

"So tell me, why are you here to see 'Fantasma'?" Sanchez asked.

"Whatever comes out of my mouth must not leave this room," Dirks replied sternly. "Is that understood?"

"Sí."

Dirks stopped packing and joined Sanchez in his bed. The former explained why he came to Mexico and throughout his explanation, the latter widened her eyes the longer the conversation went. Sanchez lowered her eyelids once Dirks finished.

"I can see why your Director of Foreign Intelligence had to contact the Director of Intelligence," Sanchez said once Dirks finished his story. "I guess it was too much to ask if this would put an end to the Tijuana Cartel forever."

"You do know another cartel would simply take its place, right?" Dirks warned. "Based on that, it sounds like you joined the Federal Police for a more personal reason."

"I had an older brother who died in a shootout with some cartel gunmen. The survivors were pardoned. You can guess why."

"Too many friends in high places."

"One day, those cartels must be told that this can't go on."

"That's enough. How long do I have to wait until I hear from 'Fantasma'?"

"He's normally free at lunchtime. Please give me my cellphone number. I need to contact you when I hear from 'Fantasma'."

"Hold on." Dirks stood up to make it easier for himself to drag his smartphone out of his pocket. After going through the password he installed to make sure no one would use the phone easily, Dirks found his phone's "Contacts" application and opened it. After that, he found his own number and showed it to Sanchez.

Sanchez also got out of the bed and brought out her phone. Like Dirks, she locked her phone with a password and after opening the phone, she went to her Contacts and pressed the "New Contact" function.

After typing in "Fred Smith", Sanchez looked at the number Dirks showed her. She had to keep looking in-between numbers. This didn't last long, as Sanchez was able to finish typing the entire contact number and pressed a check.

"And now, I'll rest up," Dirks announced as he laid his phone on his bed before following the phone.

"How early did you get up?" Sanchez asked.

"5 in the morning."

"This work makes you busy?"

"Like you wouldn't believe."

"I have to go back to my office. If you have to eat, let me know first."

"Will do."

#

1130 hours

Dirks woke up after getting the sleep he wanted. However, it was the sound of his smartphone that woke him up and, while unable to see clearly, he was able to pick it up and found that it was Sanchez calling him.

"You awake?" Sanchez asked on the other end of the phone.

"I am… " Dirks answered.

"Wash your face. I got a call from 'Fantasma'. You'll be meeting him at Pollos Tijuana. You can get your meal there."

"Gracias."

Pollos Tijuana. 1242 hours

Sanchez and Dirks then arrived at a restaurant named Pollos Tijuana. After parking, the two went inside and after Sanchez told the waiter that they'll be sharing a table with a man she gestured at, the waiter let them inside.

Dirks and Sanchez sat on the same table as Sergio Ortiz, codenamed "Fantasma". He was drinking a glass filled with ice and C-Taste Orange soft drink as he saw his PF handler and the FIS agent joining him.

"You're 'Smith', right?" Ortiz asked.

"I am," Dirks answered. "I take it you heard everything from Sanchez?"

"I'm surprised you're here for the girl only. I thought you came to help put an end to the cartel."

"Let's not get ahead of ourselves."

"But if I'm going to help you, you must help me escape the cartel. For good."

"Consider it done. I need to know where the girl is kept, a schedule of what Alba does in order for me to plan the raid, and weapons."

"I can get all of those. Now, how will you get me out?"

"I plan on getting a plane for our escape. However, I need money because I intend to relocate to a different hotel."

"Then get your money and plane first."

"Will do."

Ortiz then turned as he heard footsteps, with Sanchez and Dirks following. They found a waitress appearing with food and drinks on the tray she carried.

"I got us lunch," Ortiz said to Dirks and Sanchez when they resumed facing each other.

"Gracias," Sanchez replied.

Racedog East Village Terminal, San Diego, San Diego County, State of California; United States of America. August 8, 2030; 0857 hours

Dirks returned to the United States of America. Once his bus arrived at the Racedog bus terminal located in San Diego's East Village area, he got his belongings and, after exiting his bus and the station, he found John Vue and Kirk waiting for him.

"Back so soon?" Vue asked when Dirks approached him.

"I need that money and the plane now," Dirks demanded as he answered.

"Easy there. Why don't we talk this over in my sister's house?"

"I could use a hideout until my business here is done. Very well."

"Then take your belongings to the trunk."

#

Mallory Residence. 1022 hours

The car Kirk drove with Vue and Dirks riding on it arrived at a house in the San Carlos neighborhood in the east of San Diego. Once the car stopped in front of the house, the latter two exited the vehicle. Dirks then got his belongings in the trunk and after that, he joined Vue on the sidewalk. Kirk then left the two.

Both Vue and Dirks proceeded inside the house. This wasn't the first time the latter went to the house as this house belonged to the sister of the former, yet the surname plate on the mailbox contained the name "Mallory".

After Vue unlocked the door, he and Dirks went inside. The former locked the door again.

"I'm surprised you're allowed to even stay here, even though your sister is a married man," Dirks commented. "It's as if you live here because you have keys."

"I take this key with me," Vue answered. "I take it with me every time I have to visit Kim and Mick. In any case, let's sit down."

Both walked to the dinner table. Dirks left his luggage by the door they came from.

"I told Sanchez and Ortiz why I came to Tijuana," Dirks explained to Vue. "I asked Ortiz to get me weapons, Alba's schedule, and the location as to where Guliyeva will be held."

"He hasn't been outed as a traitor yet, but do you trust him to get you the weapons and information?" Vue asked.

"He's a Swiff. As a former Green Beret, a former operator must always help another former operator."

"What do you want to do now?"

"Get the money and the plane."

"I can secure you the money but the plane… "

"What is it?" Dirks sternly asked.

"… You'll have to wait a day or two until that plane is secured. I apologize."

"Should have expected this. I just need to inform Sanchez. She, in turn, will tell Ortiz."

"Do you need somewhere to stay after we get you your additional money?"

"That I can manage on my own."

"Let me know after we get your money. Until then, you can stay in the guest room."

I best hurry up with my search for the cheapest motel before things get bad between Vue and his sister, Dirks thought.

#

Cheney Bank Grantville. 1200 hours

"Now that we have your money, what will you be spending on it first?" Vue asked after he and Dirks came out of a Cheney Bank in the Grantville neighborhood.

"My new hotel," Dirks announced before he brought out his smartphone and showed a hotel he spotted using his D-Maps application. "Awfully cheap too. Still plenty for the pilots and for my new hotel once I return to Tijuana."

"Careful now. You still need money to feed yourself."

"Sure, sure. The motel for here may not have free breakfast so I can still save for when I need food in Tijuana. Speaking of which, let's get lunch."

#

Alvarado Motel. 1351 hours

Dirks was now settled at his new "residence", a motel named after the Alvarado Road. He brought out his smartphone and located the number that belonged to Rosarita Sanchez when she called him the previous day.

After that, Dirks then typed in the number while using his "Text" function. Once he finished typing in the number, he began to compose his message.

#

Alvarado Diner. 1806 hours

Hours later, Dirks was at a restaurant, also named after Alvarado Road, but it was located behind the Alvarado Motel. Unbeknownst to him, Vue entered the restaurant, and he approached Vue's table.

"There you are," Vue said, making Dirks turn to him.

"How did you know I was here?" Dirks asked. "I didn't contact you."

"We're both with the Company. In any case, mind if I sit?" Vue gestured to the empty chair.

"Sure," Dirks answered with Vue helping himself. "I imagine you have something to tell me?"

"I got through with the plane."

"You did?"

"It'll be here tomorrow. However, you'll have to go to Miramar."

"Why Miramar?"

"The plane's privately owned. We're leasing it from a rich fat cat Deputy Director Saetang knows."

"Good to know. What time tomorrow?"

Marine Corps Air Station Miramar. August 9, 2030; 1405 hours

Dirks and Vue were brought to Marine Corps Air Station Miramar (MCAS Miramar), located in the neighborhood of San Diego that became the base's namesake. Prior to the Third World War, this military installation hosted the United States Navy's Strike Fighter Tactics Instructor Program (SFTI Program), famously called "TOPGUN". That ended after the war and with the creation of the New United Nations, the SFTI Program was merged with two other programs from the dissolved US Navy into the New United Nations Maritime Force's Naval Aviation Warfighting Development Center (NAWDC). MCAS Miramar, by contrast, was simply given to the New United Nations Marine Corps (NUNMC), who inherited all resources of the former United States Marine Corps.

Once let inside, Kirk drove until he, Vue, and Dirks reached the airstrip of MCAS Miramar. Upon reaching the airstrip, Vue and Dirks proceeded on foot until they found a Citation Longitude business jet. As they got close to the Citation, Vue and Dirks met the captain of the plane.

"I take it you're the passengers?" the captain asked.

"He is," Vue gestured to Dirks.

"Call me 'Fred Smith'," Dirks said.

"Jacob Wong. Mind telling me why my employer leased me to you?"

"In the plane."

"Fair enough."

#

Iron Dutchman, Taisho Ward, Kansai City, Kansai Prefecture; State of Japan. August 10, 2030; 0859 hours (Japan Standard Time)

"Alright, everyone, I got a text from 'Smith'," Wouter Vos announced to his subordinates in the briefing room of the *Iron Dutchman*. "He's secured the plane and is currently on his way back to Mexico.

"Sunan, Mirzoyan, Qazvini, it's time to move out. We are on standby at the FIS safehouse in Yao until we hear from 'Smith' that he's made it to Japan."

Vos then turned to Crawley. "Jake, I'm taking the Townace with me. I'll need it to pick up 'Smith' once he returns to Japan."

"But what about me?" Jake Crawley asked. "How will I move around?"

"Just walk. You could use an exercise."

"Fine."

#

Crater Shore North Testing Range. 1530 hours

Due to how large Crater Shore was, the New United Nations Ground Force acquired a section of the north as a testing range. This portion of Crater Shore was used and guarded by the 1st Mechanized Light Assault Regiment.

As it was when the regiment acquired the first batch of the New United Nations Defense Force's first bipedal Walgear, the MWG3 Minuteman, the regiment was now in the middle of an Operational Force (OPFOR) exercise yet their Walgear units have lost to their OPFOR, the mysterious Walgear Solbein. Therefore, all but one Minutemen were being washed of the paint rounds that hit them during the exercise, yet it was targets planted on the Minutemen that were hit.

Early in their assignment by the Foreign Intelligence Service, the mercenary group Iron Dutchman Services discovered a mysterious Walgear while rescuing their dependent Maria Hoshikawa. Although it functioned normally that anyone who's already experienced in using a bipedal Walgear wouldn't have any problem with it, this Walgear was still a mystery for those who discovered and used it.

Only one Minuteman had yet to be hit by paint rounds fired by the carbine used by Solbein, which the Minuteman was equipped with. The carbine in question was the T91, the latest iteration of the T65 rifle series, built to be used by Walgears.

Inside Solbein's cockpit was none other than Tarou Ganji, who used Solbein when he, Frederick Dirks, Wouter Vos, Jason Luke Crawley, and Sunan Wattana escaped with Maria.

The Minuteman's pilot was able to evade every shot Tarou fired as he used Solbein's rifle. As this was a practice fight, the rifles were built only for practice which necessitated the invention of paint rounds chambered at 30x173mm. When it was the Minuteman pilot's turn to fire, Tarou evaded as well.

Out of all the 1st Mechanized Light Assault I've dealt with today, Private Bernstein's giving me a hard time, Tarou thought. *I'll circle around him to coax what she's thinking.*

Tarou then moved his left leg that was wearing the panel needed to control Solbein's left leg further to the left and did the same with his right leg, making Solbein do the same with its right leg. In his Minuteman's cockpit, Louise Bernstein witnessed this. Twenty-three years old, Bernstein had very light skin, black hair in a crew cut, and blue eyes.

What could Mr. Ganji be thinking now? Bernstein pondered. *That could be it. He's trying to force me to do something, hoping he will take advantage of it.*

Bernstein switched to using his Minuteman's wheels. She then moved her gearshift lever to reverse, represented by an "R" and then pressed the left foot pedal, making the Walgear move backward with its wheels. After that, she pressed the right foot pedal, making the Walgear stop as the right foot pedal was the Walgear's breaks when it used its wheels. While keeping her right foot on its corresponding pedal, Bernstein pressed the pedal corresponding with her left foot again, making the Minuteman briefly spin. She then took aim against Solbein and pressed the second button of the control stick on the right side of her Walgear's cockpit as that control stick allows the pilot to use the Walgear's right arm.

Once that button was pressed, the Minuteman fired its rifle. Tarou managed to dodge the shot. *Should have known you would trick me into getting shot,* Tarou thought. *Since I'm out of ammo, how about I do this!?*

Tarou then threw away his Walgear's rifle and readied its Strike Knuckles. *Like with getting shot by paint rounds, if any of the targets are hit by a punch from the strike knuckles, it's game over for me,* Bernstein thought. *I just thought of an idea but I best time my shots wisely for it to work.*

Bernstein continued moving backward and firing at Solbein. However, Tarou kept dodging all shots fired by the former, yet he continued to fire. *What are you even trying to do?* Tarou pondered. *Doesn't matter.*

This continued until Bernstein saw that she was running out of ammunition. *Now!* Bernstein thought before she threw away her rifle and stopped moving his Walgear. Tarou then charged at Bernstein's Minuteman as a result.

Fool, Tarou thought as he got close and prepared to punch the Minuteman with the Strike Knuckle of Solbein's right arm.

However, as Solbein's right fist neared the target found on the Minuteman's chest, the latter evaded the punch. Immediately after that, it was the Strike Knuckle of the Minuteman's right fist that hit the target found on Solbein's left arm.

"I win!" Bernstein boasted as she used the communicator in her Minuteman's cockpit to tell Tarou.

Tarou, upon hearing Bernstein's declaration of victory, closed his eyes, smiled, and quietly made a sound before opening his eyes. "That you did," Tarou replied. "Excellent work."

#

Hamilton-Ganji Condominium, Hoshikawa Condominiums, Higashiosaka Ward. 1716 hours

Tarou now returned to his condominium. He then felt his smartphone ring, but only picked it up after he removed his shoes and entered. Once he got his phone, he found that it was a call from Anita Hamilton and answered.

"Doc, what is it?" Tarou asked. "Sorry I responded late. Just got back from Walgear practice"

"It's alright," Hamilton answered. "I'll be coming home late. Someone in the main factory is suffering from a badly injured leg. Mr. Hoshikawa and I are considering taking him to the hospital. I'll allow you to get enough money for your own dinner tonight. Remember, don't eat unless you're hungry. Do your homework until then."

"Got it."

"I'll see you tonight."

The call ended. Tarou then returned to his bedroom and began doing his homework.

1813 hours

While finishing his homework, Tarou now heard his stomach. *It's time,* Tarou thought. However, there was another sound: a knock on the door.

What now? Tarou stood up regardless. He then exited his room and found that the knock came from outside the condominium and proceeded to the door he came from almost an hour before.

He opened the door and found Maria Hoshikawa outside. "M… I mean, Hoshikawa-senpai, what are you doing here?" Tarou asked.

"Came to check up on you," Maria answered. "Also, we're alone so you can call me 'Maria'."

"Wakarimashita". Tarou stepped aside to let Maria inside. He proceeded further into the condominium to give Maria space for her to remove her shoes. She then followed Tarou once she finished.

"How are things?" Maria asked as she joined Tarou in one of the sofas of the condominium's living room.

"The usual for me on weekends after school," Tarou answered. "Walgear practice, then homework. I was going to get money for dinner because Hamilton-sensei won't be home until later."

"Father told me to join you until Hamilton-sensei is free. Where did you have in mind for dinner?"

"I was considering a Korean restaurant near Hakodonocho Junior High School, but it would upset Doc if I went there by myself. She told me about it from one of your father's employees and told me once that we should eat there together."

"The owner of that restaurant is a brother of the employee who told Hamilton-sensei about that restaurant. In any case, we best find somewhere nearby because Father's trying to save up enough money for gas."

"Isn't there a yakiniku place near Nishi High?"

"Which one?"

"The one near the Higashi Gymnasium."

"Father sees it as 'near enough'. He sees anything beyond the school as far."

"Then I just need to get my money."

"I can pay for it."

"You don't have to."

"You've been doing your job ever since you saved me in Sakhalin Island.

"I'll be using the money that came from that operation."

"… Right. I apologize for that."

"It's alright. You already know who I really am, so I can't burden you any longer for my sake."

Tarou then stood up and walked to the other bedroom in the condominium that belonged to Hamilton. Maria then joined him there and found him grabbing yen bills.

"How much did you get?' Maria asked.

"Enough for the both of us," Tarou answered. "Consider that an apology for refusing your offer earlier."

"I see… "

"Before we go, I just need to find an envelope to hide this money. After that, we go to my scooter."

"I can have Ugaki-san drive us there. Please allow me to provide that."

"Very well."

#

Pollos Tijuana, Tijuana, Tijuana Municipality, Free and Sovereign State of Baja California; United Mexican States. August 9, 2030; 1559 hours (Pacific Standard Time)

"Here's the list," Sergio Ortiz said as he gave a piece of paper to Rosarita Sanchez while they shared a table again in Pollos Tijuana.

"Gracias," Sanchez replied. "But what about the weapons?"

"I'm keeping them with me until I see Señor 'Smith'. Location of where the girl is kept is also in the paper."

"Thank you again. I must hurry. No doubt one of your men is coming to see where you vanished to."

"Agreed."

Sanchez stood up, grabbed her bag after hiding the paper she received inside, and left. However, she bumped into a man who had just entered the restaurant. After the apologies, Sanchez reached her car.

\#

Alvarado Motel, San Diego, San Diego County, State of California; United States of America. 1610 hours

Good, Frederick Dirks thought as he looked at the e-mail sent to him by Sanchez. In the e-mail was the pictures of the paper she received from Ortiz. *Once I return to Mexico, I'll need to contact Sanchez as soon as I get my new hotel room. As for that, I need to start reserving and then I need to tell Wong when we're to leave.*

Dirks began to use his phone for the tasks he thought of. For him, this would be the last time he would have to travel between California and Mexico.

\#

Hotel Aeropuerto, Tijuana, Tijuana Municipality, Free and Sovereign State of Baja California; United Mexican States. August 10, 2030; 1141 hours

Now settled into his room in Hotel Aeropuerto, named as such as it's near Tijuana International Airport, Dirks began to call Rosarita Sanchez. The wait was mercifully short.

"Señor 'Smith', is that you?" Sanchez asked on the other end.

"Sí," Dirks answered. "Just got back from San Diego. The plane's on standby at the airport. Have plans for lunch because I could use a meal and an escort, but *not* in that sense."

"Don't worry. I can go to Hotel Aeropuerto. Just be patient."

"Gracias."

1239 hours

Dirks exited the hotel and found Sanchez and her Crown outside. Once the former boarded the Crown, the latter left the hotel.

"Do you have the schedule?" Dirks asked.

"I never kept it elsewhere," Sanchez answered. "I want tacos. What about you?"

"Fine with me."

Unbeknownst to the two as they neared the left turn needed to find the taco restaurant Sanchez mentioned, a car was following them, yet it was far from the Crown, driven by two men hiding their faces with black ski masks. One man then brought out a T4 assault rifle and switched to semi-automatic. Although he was in a moving vehicle, the man was able to aim the rifle at the Crown.

He then closed his left eye while aiming at the right rear wheel of the Crown and pressed the trigger with his right index finger. The 5.56x45mm round was launched out of the muzzle and just as the Crown began to turn, the bullet hit the rear left wheel instead. Whether this was intended or not didn't matter as the car began to spin until it hit the building it would have passed.

Both Dirks and Sanchez were now unconscious. The two men parked their car and exited. The driver, as a contrast to the man who disabled the

Crown, carried an SAF submachine gun. They aimed their guns upon reaching the crashed Crown but found Dirks and Sanchez unconscious.

"No need to kill them," the man with the T4 said. "We need them alive."

"Then we better hurry," the man with the SAF warned. "The police we'll be here soon."

The Raid

Unknown Location. August 10, 2030; 1330 hours (Unknown Time Zone)

Fredrick Dirks began to come about. Once he finished blinking his eyes, how now saw that he was in a room whose only light was a ceiling bulb that was thankfully turned on.

W… Where am I? Dirks pondered. *Last I remember, Sanchez and I- Sanchez!*

He wisely turned to his left. Miraculously, he found Rosarita Sanchez, but she had yet to come to. She was tied to a wooden chair by all four of her limbs.

I remember now. Our car spun out of control and we were just near the taco restaurant Sanchez was going to take me to. If Sanchez is tied to her chair…

Dirks began to stretch his neck down as much as he could while turning to his left shoulder. He was not able to bring its adjacent arm forward. Next, he turned to his right leg and attempted to make it move forward, but it was no avail.

It's official: me and Sanchez were attacked and captured. But by who? The Tijuana Cartel only lasted as long as it did because they wouldn't do something like this. Alba would sell out the soldados responsible for such an attack. Who could have done this?

Before Dirks could hypothesize who abducted him and Sanchez, the only door opened. As it was far from where the two were located in the room, only the opening of the door confirmed where the door was and that it was the only one in the room. Two men began to enter the room just as Sanchez came to.

"W… Where are we?" Sanchez asked.

"Hopefully we'll find out soon," Dirks optimistically answered despite the situation not offering the opportunity to be optimistic.

The two men who entered the room were the same men who attacked and abducted them. They not only remained in the same masks they used but had their respective weapons, a T4 assault rifle and an SAF submachine gun, slung across their backs. Naturally, Dirks and Sanchez turned to their captives.

"¿Quién eres tú?" Sanchez asked.

"Nosotros hacemos las preguntas aquí!" the man with the SAF replied as he brought out the submachine gun and aimed it at her.

"¡Dejala en paz!" Dirks replied.

"¡Juan, detente!" the man with the T4 ordered to his partner-in-crime. The man with the SAF named Juan complied.

The man with the T4 then turned to Juan. "Ahora protege la entrada."

"… Ententido."

Juan then exited the room. Once he was gone, the man with the T4 removed his mask. Dirks widened his eyes upon seeing the man, which perplexed Sanchez.

"I know you," Dirk said. "You're 'Ben'!"

"Glad you recognize me, 'Fred Smith'," the man named "Ben" said. "I apologize for everything. We've been monitoring Tijuana for a month, especially the three of you."

"Three?" Sanchez asked. "You mean-"

"Sergio Ortiz. We've bribed the owner of Pollos Tijuana to be our eyes and ears whenever Ortiz went there for lunch. I'd like to know why you've been seeing him."

"Does it matter? You'll probably use this to wage a war against the Tijuana Cartel."

"You're right about that. Though I get the feeling you think a policewoman like you can make a difference by making sure Tijuana is free from the drug trade. Let me be blunt: that will never happen."

Sanchez screamed like a dog while gritting her teeth and moving, despite being tied to her chair. "Stop! Stop!" Dirks screamed. "We have no time for this! Look, we'll tell you everything you want to know. Just let us go."

"You better hurry. You and Sanchez here haven't had your meal yet."

Dirks quickly summed up why he came to Mexico and why he had been working with Sanchez and Ortiz. He also explained the plan he and

Sanchez devised on how to rescue Maral Eminovna Guliyeva. "Ben" nodded after every sentence.

"I see," "Ben" said when Dirks finished his story. "Very well. I'll have you released. Please wait."

"Ben" left the room. For Dirks and Sanchez, the wait was long but worth it, as "Ben" and Juan returned, carrying black bags and putting them on the former two. Neither Dirks nor Sanchzez questioned what will happen next, as they hoped they would be returned to civilization.

#

Hospital Otay, Tijuana, Tijuana Municipality, Free and Sovereign State of Baja California; United Mexican States. 1623 hours (Pacific Standard Time)

Dirks now woke to find himself in a hospital. As his vision became clear, he saw a man approach him.

"Heard from Sanchez what happened," the man said. "I can imagine who abducted you."

"And you are?" Dirks asked.

"Chief Inspector Rodrigo Asensio. As you could tell, I'm Sanchez's superior."

"How did you find us?"

"Tijuana Municipal Police received a report of two hooded individuals left in the sun to be burned. From what the doctors told me, neither of you has eaten for hours. Food will be sent up to you soon. Until then, rest."

"What about those who abducted us?"

"As Sanchez warned me, we might be dealing with *them*, so I've told the rest of my men to be prepared. Again, rest for now. I'll have someone take you back to the hotel and Sanchez back to her house."

"No. We need to meet up with O- I mean, 'Fantasma'. We need to formulate a plan on how to find Guliyeva."

"I know, but you need your rest first. I'll see what I can do about a new car for you to use because Sanchez's Crown isn't so useful anymore.

Again, rest and eat up. When the doctor says you can leave, you can leave. Now, if you excuse me." Asensio then exited the room.

Café Tijuana Plaza Aeropuerto. August 11, 2030; 1314 hours

Sergio Ortiz traveled to a Café Tijuana located in the Plaza Aeropuerto, the mall closest to Tijuana International Airport where travelers staying at the Hotel Aeropuerto can go to. Once he arrived at the café, he found Dirks and Sanchez at one table, with Ortiz joining them.

"So, why do we have to meet here?" Ortiz asked. "You do know I'm always followed, right?"

"We know that," Sanchez answered. "However, Señor 'Smith' and I were ambushed yesterday and abducted. They learned about us because of the staff of Pollos Tijuana."

"Should have known *they* would be making a move. Didn't think it would be this soon."

Sanchez then brought out the piece of paper that she received from Ortiz two days before. She then flipped the paper, showing maps of the same rectangular building.

"We need to enact the raid tomorrow," Dirks warned. "There's a high chance *they* will move depending on what I told 'Ben' yesterday."

"You talked to *those from Sinaloa*?" Cold anger filled Ortiz's tone.

"I told them so that they can let us go. That's all they wanted to know, which is why Sanchez and I are still alive."

"Is my escape still guaranteed?"

"I can have the plane prepared tomorrow morning, but I need to find a way to enter the hotel without being spotted."

"I can take you there but remember, I'm being watched. *They* always keep an eye on all of their members. Including me."

"I have an idea about that, but I need those weapons today."

"Deal."

#

1430 hours

Ortiz began to leave Plaza Aeropuerto once he reached his car, a Beetle. Another man who stood beside his car, a Yaris, saw the Beetle and immediately boarded. He kept observing Ortiz and his Beetle while they left and once they reached the street, the other man also left, intent on following Ortiz.

Unbeknownst to the other man, Dirks, Sanchez, and another man watched. Once the car following Ortiz began to leave, the former three rushed to another Yaris.

#

Alcoholería Independencia. 1519 hours

Ortiz now arrived in front of an alcoholic beverages store named after the street it faced. This perplexed the man with the Yaris that, after Ortiz parked his Beetle in front of the store, he parked his Yaris behind.

Just as when the man with the Yaris entered the store, Dirks, Sanchez, and the man driving the other Yaris arrived and found the two cars in front.

"Deténgase aquí," Sanchez ordered the driver. The man stopped his Yaris without a reply. Dirks began to exit the vehicle.

"Estévez, espera aquí," Sanchez added.

"Entendido," the man named Estévez replied a second as Sanchez also rushed out of the vehicle.

Sanchez then joined Dirks as he hid on the left side opposite of the store's door. "What's going on?" Sanchez asked.

"Ortiz's cornered," Dirks replied while managing to stretch his neck backward to face Sanchez. "I just need to wait until he least expects someone else to enter because that may be Ortiz's 'guardian angel'."

Inside the store, Ortiz bought three cans of beer. The man who followed him began to exit the store, but as he opened the door, Dirks immediately rushed inside and covered the man's mouth. This horrified Sanchez, yet she couldn't do anything, as she was still shocked by what Dirks did.

Ortiz then walked backward, but once he was far enough, he used his right leg and propelled it upward, hitting the man at his groin. Ortiz kept the leg there until the man lost consciousness and fell into the store's floor.

Dirks then entered the store. Now that it was over, Sanchez overcame the shock and joined him inside. "Why did you do that?!" Sanchez screamed.

"He would have told his superiors about Ortiz," Dirks argued as he faced Sanchez. "We need him out of the way until tomorrow."

"Yo... puedo ayudar... " the owner of the store said.

"¿Tienes cuerda?" Ortiz asked.

"Sí."

"Entonces úsala para atarlo," Dirks requested before he crouched, flipped the man, and found an Ultrastar semi-automatic pistol and gave it to Sanchez. He then turned to Ortiz. "Now take us to where Guliyeva is."

"What about Hernández's car?" Ortiz asked, referring to the unconscious Yaris owner."

"I'll use it," Dirks answered before he turned to Sanchez. "Sanchez, please wait here with Estévez. Ortiz and I need to see where Guliyeva is kept."

#

Hotel Independencia. 1544 hours

Dirks and Ortiz then arrived at a hotel also named after the street it faced. They parked their respective vehicles, Ortiz's Beetle and Hernández's Yaris, in front of a house beside the hotel.

Dirks only joined Ortiz once the latter faced the hotel. "This is where she's kept," Ortiz said as he pointed to his left toward the hotel.

"And I know a way to enter without being spotted," Dirks replied as he pointed to the house to his and Ortiz's left.

"But how will you enter that house?" Ortiz asked.

"We need a ladder, but it will require Sanchez's cooperation. Let's rejoin her at that beer store and discuss how to get one."

#

Alcoholería Independencia. 1604 hours

"First, we're turning this store into our private cell and now we need a ladder to enter someone's house illegally!?" Sanchez exclaimed after listening to Dirks's plan. "And you need me to assist you with this!?"

"Sadly, yes," Dirks admitted.

Sanchez sighed, as it was clear everything was becoming less legal with how to fight the Tijuana Cartel. "But where can we get a ladder on such short notice?"

"Tengo una," the proprietor of Alcoholería Independencia said, making Dirks, Ortiz, and Sanchez face him.

"¿Por qué nos ayudas?" Ortiz asked.

"Porque no es algo que sucede diariamente."

"¿Cuál es su nombre?"

"Sandro."

"¿Dónde está su escalera?"

"En mi espalda. ¿Lo necesitas ahora?"

"Sí, por favor."

Sandro left to get the ladder. Dirks resumed facing Ortiz and Sanchez.

"Now, about the weapons," Dirks continued.

"I've kept them in the trunk of my car," Ortiz answered. "Please wait."

Ortiz then rushed out of the store. Dirks and Sanchez saw him open his Beetle's trunk and getting a metal box. Once he placed the box on the pavement in front of the store, he dragged it inside. He opened it next, showing an SAF submachine gun.

"Where did you get this?" Dirks asked.

"You don't want to know," Ortiz answered. "Now, as to where the girl is kept, she's kept in the basement. I... must caution that you will not like what you will when you do find her."

"Why?"

"I underestimated how much of a monster Alba is."

"I can't promise that this will destroy him. Right now, we need to plan out how to launch the operation tomorrow."

"I'll enter the hotel tomorrow," Ortiz replied. "Carry on as if it were normal. You and Rosa enter the house beside the hotel and use the ladder to get in. You'll also need it to climb to the right side of the house, because that will be how you're going to enter the hotel without being spotted."

"What about the car we just stole?" Sanchez asked.

"We'll use it as our escape vehicle," Dirks answered. "We'll race to the airport and rush to the Citation. As I said before, I'll have it prepared for launch tomorrow morning so that by the time we reach it, it's ready to take off."

"Good," Ortiz replied. "We end this tomorrow."

"Aquí está la escalera," Sandro announced as he returned with it. Everyone faced him, collectively said "Gracias" and resumed facing each other.

"Until tomorrow morning, I'll have Estévez keep it," Sanchez said.

"I'll sleep early to check out," Dirks added. "Where do we meet before we launch the operation?"

"Here," Ortiz answered.

"It's cutting it close, so all of us have to be here tomorrow at 0700 hours."

"Right," Ortiz and Sanchez replied.

#

Hotel Independencia. August 12, 2030; 0801 hours

Ortiz then arrived at the Hotel Independencia acting as if it were a normal day. After a "Buenos dias" from a guard carrying an MP5 submachine gun, Ortiz parked his Beetle. He then entered his office.

Once inside, Ortiz brought out a logbook and turned to a particular page. The page contained the words "El Sr. Alba vendrá de visita hoy, él no debe ser molestado por el momento" with the date 07/12/2030 and the time 6:00 PM written beside the sentences.

And now I must wait for "Smith", Ortiz thought.

Near Hotel Independencia. 0839 hours

The two Yarises appeared in front of the house beside Hotel Independencia. Dirks' Yaris, which he took from the Tijuana Cartel hitman Hernández, was parked directly in front of the house. After he got out, Dirks waited at the gate as Sanchez and Estévez got out of their Yaris.

The latter two rushed to the Yaris' trunk as the ladder needed was kept there. Once they got the ladder, they placed it on the gate. Dirks then climbed onto the gate using the ladder and once he was on the very top of the ladder, he jumped. Despite his weight, Dirks was able to make a quiet landing without getting impaled by the spikes on the gate.

The owner of the house exited to see what was happening, but Dirks used his right index finger and emulated a kiss to make the owner keep quiet. After that, Sanchez and Estévez pushed the ladder upward with Dirks rushing to get it. He managed to get it before the ladder hit the ground.

"Get out of here now!" Dirks quietly ordered to the PF agents.

"Vaya con Dios," Sanchez replied before she and Estévez rushed back to their Yaris.

Now inside the house, Dirks rushed to the house's right wall that faced Hotel Independencia. Finding the nearest position to the left roof of the hotel, Dirks planted the ladder there. Once it was planted, he began to climb, but stopped because the guard who greeted Ortiz earlier watched the direction where Dirks was coming from. Only when the guard wasn't looking was Dirks able to resume. It was then that Dirks reached the roof, making him jump to it.

However, Dirks had to jump to reach the roof. His landing created a loud noise.

Me and my luck! Dirks cursed in his mind.

#

Hotel Independencia. 0928 hours

"¡Mátalo!" a voice shouted that Ortiz heard in his office.

It's time, Ortiz thought as he grabbed his Ultrastar and left his office for the last time.

He now saw the hotel guards firing at Dirks. Ortiz immediately turned off his pistol's safety and began firing. Once the guards turned on him, Ortiz had just killed his second target.

Dirks now jumped off the left roof. By this time, he saw cartel guards rushing to intercept Ortiz from his left and right, making him fire again. He fired in one direction at a time, allowing Ortiz to finish off the rest who were encircling him.

Both Dirks and Ortiz resumed killing those in the courtyard, but one guard hid in a room. Ortiz then jumped into the courtyard, as did Dirks. They immediately rushed to each other.

"Find the girl!" Ortiz requested. "I'll deal with Vargas."

Dirks opted not to reply before separating from Ortiz. The latter then rushed to the room where the guard he called Vargas ran to. He then found Vargas using a phone, prompting Ortiz to shoot him.

Ortiz then ran to the phone Vargas used. Upon picking it up, he found that he used a certain number that made his eyes widen. He then threw the phone against the bed and shot it, grabbed Vargas' AKS-2000U, and left the room.

#

0935 hours

Dirks now entered the basement of the hotel. However, he found that the lights were kept off and yet he was able to see someone sitting down, yet he could only see the legs.

Those thin legs, it must be her! Dirks thought. *Now, where could the lights be?*

He looked at his left, but the light switch wasn't there. Only when he turned to his right did he find the switch. Pressing it, the lights were on, but Dirks now regretted having turned them on.

This is- Dirks found tables with various items, some that looked like normal tools. He then remembered the legs he found before he turned on the light and now he found Maral Eminovna Guliyeva. Guliyeva was wearing a white latex leotard and heeled shoes of the same color. She wasn't able to see, much less know, what was happening as she was blindfolded and she keep moaning because she wore a red-colored mouth gag. Her legs were bent as they hanged as she was made to sit on a wooden triangle hanging from the ceiling and that the object was between her legs, pinning her groin. Her arms were tied together by rope with the left arm above the right arm.

It's official, Alba's a monster! Dirks thought.

"We have a-" Ortiz said until he saw Guliyeva. Dirks then turned to Ortiz.

"… Did you know about this?" Dirks asked.

"I… I do… " Ortiz answered with guilt evident in his tone.

"Then help me get this girl out."

"More of Alba's men are coming here!" Ortiz warned as a knee-jerk reaction.

"What!?"

"Vargas managed to call for reinforcements before I killed him."

"Then get this girl out of here! And get her some clothes. How much time do I have before those reinforcements arrive?"

"Ten minutes."

"Then get started. I'll secure as much weapons and ammo as I can before they arrive."

#

1011 hours

As Ortiz warned, a black RAV4 compact crossover utility vehicle (CUV) appeared. Dirks saw it approach while aiming at its right front wheel with an AKS-2000U. As soon as he closed his left eye, Dirks pulled the trigger. The 5.45x39mm round then flew out of the muzzle and toward the wheel.

When the bullet hit the wheel, the RAV4 tumbled until the sunroof hit the street, destroying the compact CUV and killing everyone inside.

"Nicely done." Dirks turned to find Ortiz carrying Guliyeva with his shoulders. Guliyeva now wore a plain white shirt, pants, and normal shoes.

"Get her to the Yaris," Dirks ordered. "I'll cover."

Ortiz then raced to the Yaris with Guliyeva while Dirks walked backward to cover them. Once the latter reached the former two, he rushed to the front left seat and unlocked the Yaris.

Now inside the Yaris, Dirks unlocked the other doors. However, he and Ortiz heard the engines coming from their rear. Once they reared their heads, they found another RAV4.

"Shit!" Dirks screamed before he turned to Ortiz. "Get the girl inside and start up the car. I'll cover us."

While quick enough to kill two of the gunmen who came out of the RAV4, Dirks had to evade when the surviving gunmen fired back. Luckily, Ortiz finished starting up the Yaris.

"Get in!" Ortiz shouted.

Dirks then rushed to the left rear seats of the Yaris and closed the door. He then shot the rear glass window to continue firing. However, Ortiz then got the Yaris to move. Even with the wrecked RAV4 in his way, Ortiz continued to push forward, saving Dirks from being shot by the surviving gunmen.

#

Near FAR-MEX Avenida Canon Jhonson. 1051 hours

"Are we still being followed?" Ortiz asked while driving.

"For now, no," Dirks answered.

"Good. Where in Tijuana International Airport is that plane of yours located at?"

"I told the pilot to wait for us by the cargo terminal. It's directly facing the wall dividing this city and San Diego."

"Good."

However, as soon as Ortiz turned left, Dirks now saw another RAV4 appearing. "Now we have company!"

"I'm flooring it!"

PF Tijuana Field Office. 1157 hours

Both Sanchez and Estévez were now summoned to Rodrigo Asensio's office. All knew why the latter two had to see the former, but they met regardless. Asensio had a radio on his table.

"No time to reprimand us!" Sanchez said in a hurry. "Where are they now?"

"According to the Municipal Police, they should be in front of SIMNSA. Go to the airport now! I'll keep you updated."

#

Near Baja Fuel/Baja Fuel. 1300 hours

"And now we're out of fuel," Ortiz said in defeat as he found the fuel gauge blinking yellow.

"Just great!" Dirks screamed while he fired the last rounds of his AKS-2000U's penultimate magazine.

Suddenly, Dirk's phone rang. While Ortiz moved to dodge fire from one cartel hitman, the phone flew out of Dirks' pocket. The call came from Rosarita Sanchez.

While managing to keep one hand on the wheel, Ortiz used his right hand to reach for the phone. As a result, he slipped, causing the car to move, yet Ortiz was able to press the green indicator to accept the call. He then returned to using both hands for the wheel.

"This better be good!" Ortiz screamed.

"We know where you are," Sanchez responded on the other end of the smartphone. "We're on our way."

"Then help Dirks and Guliyeva. I'll be dropping them off at a Baja Fuel."

"What!?" Ortiz paid no attention as he turned to Dirks.

"It's as I said. I'm dropping you off!"

"What!?" Dirks screamed.

"Get your phone and the girl, and go! I have an idea."

Ortiz then stopped at a Baja Fuel. Dirks reluctantly acquired his phone and, after doing so, kicked the left rear door. He then grabbed his SAF before rushing out of the Yaris.

However, the pursuing gunmen neared them. Dirks fired what remained of the SAF's ammunition against them.

"Go!" Ortiz screamed.

Dirks then slung the the SAF across the body and grabbed Guliyeva. He flew her out of the Yaris and began to run. As a result, the gunmen stopped and began to exit the Yaris. As soon as Dirks and Guliyeva ran close to the gas station, Ortiz turned back and rushed toward the gunmen.

"Ortiz, no!" Dirks screamed, yet it was useless as Ortiz charged toward the gunmen.

The gunmen fired their weapons, as they now knew why Ortiz was charging at them. Despite getting shot, Ortiz continued charging until he used what little strength he had left to spin the driving wheel left and hitting the brake.

As a result, the Yaris faced its left, but it was its right that hit the two RAV4s. With how fast Ortiz moved and turned, the RAV4s flew until their sunroofs hit the road. Reluctantly, Dirks dragged Guliyeva with him while the gunmen were distracted by surrounding Ortiz.

Unbeknownst to the gunmen, Ortiz hid a grenade. When one gunman opened the left front door, Ortiz released the pin.

"¡Granada!" the gunman shouted before the grenade exploded, killing the remaining gunmen.

It was then that Sanchez and Estévez appeared on the Yaris of the latter. They not only heard the explosion, but saw it. They raced to the station regardless and found Dirks and Guliyeva watching.

"Are you alright?" Sanchez asked Dirks.

"I…" Dirks said, or attempted to say, because it was clear he couldn't respond immediately after what happened.

"Why did he do that!?"

"He wanted me to get the girl out no matter what… " Dirk's answer made Sanchez focus on what Ortiz died for.

"And we will." However, growls from the stomach were heard.

"And Ortiz would have wanted us to get food first," Dirks reminded as a joke at the expense of a dead man.

"It's a little far, but Estévez and I just passed a soul restaurant. I'm not sure if you're into that."

"Doesn't matter. Oh, I forgot, this is Maral Eminovna Guliyeva." Dirks then gestured to the girl beside him.

Sanchez attempted to offer her hand, but Guliyeva walked back. "It's alright," Dirks said. "She's a friend."

"Üzr istəyirəm amma başa düşmürəm," the girl replied.

Figures she wouldn't understand English, Dirks thought. "¿Entiendes Español?"

"… Si," Guliyeva answered.

"I find that hard to believe an Azeri girl would easily pick up Spanish," Sanchez said.

It's like with Maria Hoshikawa, Dirks thought before responding to Sanchez. "Either way, we need food now."

#

Alma Tijuana. 1439 hours

Everyone was now at the restaurant called Alma Tijuana, which served soul food. Guliyeva's order was simply *Moros y Cristianos* and a glass of water. Only Sanchez and Estévez prayed before the meal as Dirks started. Guliyeva, however, moved her chair backward and moved half of her body toward the food, then her neck downward. She then pushed her mouth toward the food as if she were a dog, shocking everyone in the restaurant and forcing Sanchez to stop before she ended her prayer with the Sign of the Cross and pulled Guliyeva from her meal.

"¡Para!" Sanchez shouted while pulled Guliyeva from her plate. Guliyeva's face was now filled with black beans and rice. "¿Acaso no te dijeron cómo comer bien?"

Dirks then used his right index finger to touch Sanchez at her left shoulder. He then got closer to her, intent on whispering something to her. Sanchez simply allowed it, but once she listened to what Dirks had to whisper to her, her eyes widened and she faced Guliyeva as she attempted to eat like a dog again.

Sanchez stopped Guliyeva, but this time, she raised her spoon and made Guliyeva watch. Everyone now watched Sanchez acting like a mother teaching a child how to eat for the first time, despite Guliyeva being sixteen years old.

There's a special place in hell for an animal like Alba! Dirks thought. *And a separate one for who turned Guliyeva into that!*

#

Tijuana International Airport. 1634 hours

Dirks, Sanchez, Estévez, and Guliyeva now arrived at a terminal in Tijuana International Airport, dedicated to receiving cargo deliveries from planes. Once Dirks and Guliyeva exited the Yaris, they walked to the Citation Longitude whose pilot Dirks hired to fly him and Guliyeva out of Mexico and back to Japan. Jacob Wong then ran up to the two.

"Where's the one you call 'Fantasma'?" Wong asked.

"He's dead," Dirks answered.

"Then let's go!"

"Wait one second." Dirks reared his head to the PF agents. "Thanks for everything!"

"Now go!" Sanchez replied. "Make sure Ortiz's death isn't in vain."

#

Alba Group Headquarters, Hermosillo, Free and Sovereign State of Sonora. 1737 hours (Mountain Standard Time)

PF agents in helmets and protective gear used an enforcer battering ram to destroy the door of Segismundo Alba's office. Three men armed with SAFs and a man with only a vest found Segismundo Alba, a man in his mid-fifties with no hair on his scalp, very light skin, and light brown eyes, having destroyed his own window.

"¡Ríndete ahora, Segismundo Alba!" the PF offcer demanded.

"¡Nunca!" Alba screamed before jumping.

Disguise

FIS Headquarters, McLean, Fairfax County, Commonwealth of Virginia; United States of America. August 1, 2030; 0459 hours (Eastern Standard Time)

A janitor unlocked the front entrance of the Museum of Intelligence Collection, a part of the Foreign Intelligence Service's headquarters. This museum was built not only to accommodate the contents of the original museum that was a part of the headquarters of the United States of America's Central Intelligence Agency but to allow those interested in the world prior to the Third World War to read up about the CIA after its dissolution. When the New United Nations was created and the US joined, it dissolved the CIA as a part of the move to avoid repeating the mistakes of the past that led to the Third World War. The museum was only open on weekends and the janitor was to clean it up before it was open.

However, the janitor found a manila envelope laying on the floor. "What's this?" the janitor asked as he kneeled to claim the envelope.

A document left here, the janitor thought after standing up and looked at the envelope. *I think I should give this to someone—anyone in the FIS. It seems too dangerous to read.*

0718 hours

Stanley McAllister and Yanin Saetang arrived at Alberto Pérez's office. The latter looked at the documents that came from the manila envelope the janitor found hours before in the Museum of Intelligence Collection.

"I assume those documents are the reason why you summoned us?" Saetang asked.

"Indeed," Pérez answered. "Rodney was wise to make sure these documents go to us."

"And what are they about?" McAllister asked.

"Anton Kravchenko," Pérez answered.

"He's alive?! Blavatsky claimed he was killed!"

"Says here that he was successfully rescued and had been hiding in Sinpo ever since and that he resumed having women kidnapped and sold off to rich perverts. Among these documents is that of a girl named Maral Eminovna Guliyeva who was just sold recently by one Segismundo Alba."

"Rare for the boss of the Tijuana Cartel to make such a risky purchase."

"We can do what the Eurasians failed to do by getting Kravchenko. However, we need to get Guliyeva out of Alba's clutches."

"I'll have Caguiat contact 'Smith' immediately."

"Wait!" Saetang interjected. "I think it's too early to plan anything."

"What makes you say that?" Pérez asked.

"We might be walking into a trap if we act on this information. We could at least prepare for contingencies."

"Fair enough. You have two days to figure out how to avoid any pitfalls based on the information."

"Thank you, Alberto. As soon as I return to my office, I'll summon Vue and giver the order."

#

McAllister Residence, McLean. 0339 hours

Now at his house, McAllister began to use his secret laptop. Once he opened his GOKMail, he typed:

The Director of Foreign Intelligence has received the documents. Gave the Deputy Director of Foreign Intelligence time to analyze those documents. Will update you when the latter finishes and presents her findings to the former.

Devotee-Infiltrator Stanley McAllister.

McAllister pressed "Send" and hastily quit GOKMail. He then turned off his computer and hid it from his wife Cynthia.

Unknown Location; Enlightenment Point. 1429 hours (EP Time Zone)

Reinhard Frühling, the Gatekeeper of Intelligence, approached the throne room of his master, Grand Gatekeeper Sergei Akulov. The former made his salute upon stopping.

"I've received a report from our Devotee-Infiltrator in the FIS," Frühling told Akulov.

"What is it?" Akulov asked.

"The file 'LS' left at FIS Headquarters is currently being analyzed by Deputy-Director Saetang. Director Pérez will not act until after he has to hear what Saetang has to say."

"Simply wait for our Devotee-Infiltrator to tell us if Saetang is finished."

"By your will, Grand Gatekeeper."

#

FIS Headquarters, McLean, Fairfax County, Commonwealth of Virginia; United States of America. August 2, 2030; 0930 hours (Eastern Standard Time)

"I assume you've finished analyzing the information?" Pérez asked as Saetang was in his office with John Vue beside her. McAllister stood beside Pérez.

"We have," Saetang answered. Pérez then turned to Vue.

"Vue," Pérez said as he turned to Saetang's subordinate.

"It's as Deputy-Director Saetang warned, it's a trap," Vue explained. "It's suspicious that we're told that Anton Kravchenko is alive and that the boss of the Tijuana Cartel bought a girl from Kravchenko with the girl as the bait. If we're to launch an operation to rescue Guliyeva, we need to do it in a way Kravchenko will know and that it will make him careless."

"You said this will be a trap. You're suggesting that we make our own trap."

"According to those documents, Kravchenko has a small army of Korean mercenaries. It's not specified as to how he has them but he will use them to try to get Guliyeva back. We must be wary of that after we rescue Guliyeva from Alba."

"We can have 'Smith' hide Guliyeva at our safehouse in Yao," McAllister added. "That way, we can force Kravchenko's hand. We don't know how but he'll find some way to get his Koreans into Japan. We can ambush them, get one alive, and use him to get to Kravchenko."

"Should we get Iron Dutchman Services involved with this?" Pérez asked.

"We could," McAllister answered. "We can just pay them separately from what we pay them for guarding Maria Hoshikawa."

"We need to let Parnell know of this first. She'll then have to talk to the Secretary-General. No one is to do anything until we hear from Parnell. Also, this conversation must not leave this room."

"Understood," McAllister, Saetang, and Vue replied in unison.

#

August 3, 2030; 1000 hours

"Parnell just got back to me," Pérez announced to his subordinates. "The Secretary-General will be holding a meeting with the Security Council over this matter. The meeting will be held tomorrow."

He then turned to Vue. "Vue, I need you to accompany me to this meeting."

"W… Why me?" Vue asked.

"You analyzed those documents. The Secretary-General and the Security Council would like to hear it from you. I suggest that you make a presentation today and finish it before you go home because you'll need to sleep early. Tomorrow, meet me at the helipad because an Osprey will take us to Andrews, where a plane will take us to Newfoundland. The troops there will provide a ride to St. Anthony."

"Y… Yes, sir."

"Now get to it."

New United Nations Headquarters/St. Anthony Crater, Newfoundland and Labrador Province; Canada. August 4, 2030; 1100 hours (Newfoundland Time)

Vue and Pérez arrived at the headquarters of the New United Nations situated near the crater where the Canadian town of St. Anthony once stood before the Third World War. Getting off the JLTV that drove them from St. John's International Airport, the two men from the FIS proceeded inside NUN Headquarters. They stopped upon seeing Cecilia Parnell, the Director of Intelligence.

"Glad you made it, Al," Parnell said.

"Thank you, Ceci," Pérez replied. Parnell then turned to Vue.

"So you're John Vue," Parnell said. "I assume you have everything we need?"

"Here," Vue replied while raising the laptop bag he carried.

"Then follow me."

#

1130 hours

Pérez, Vue, and Parnell now arrived at the Situation Room found in the underground portion of NUN Headquarters. Here, the Secretary-General of the New United Nations met with the Security Council over matters of security and defense throughout the supernational union.

The room was built to accommodate a circle of tables and their respective chairs, reminiscent of the old United Nations Security Council. The difference between the two was who occupied the tables. The three topmost tables were respectively occupied by the Under-Secretary-General of Defense, the Secretary-General, and the Director of Intelligence. The rest of the seats were occupied by the Chairman of the Joint Chiefs of Staff, the President of the Security Council, and the five members that are elected every ten years from various NUN member-states respectively assigned to bring up matters within their areas of responsibility. Pérez and Vue sat on two vacant seats beside Parnell's with Vue's seat normally going to the Under-Secretary of Inter-State Affairs;

absent due to a murder in the Bolivarian Republic of Venezuela where the victim hailed from the Republic of Colombia, a NUN member-state.

Once the Director of Intelligence and the two FIS men sat down, Vue stood up again and removed a laptop computer from the bag he was carrying. He then rushed to a table nestled to one of the four monitors surrounded by the council seats. Placing the computer on the table and turning it on, Vue connected it to a cable. He then pressed a button on the upper-left portion of the table that turned on the monitors and opened the presentation he made the previous day.

Then, the two doors of the entrance opened with two men each standing in front of the doors, prompting Vue to rush back to his table. The Secretary-General, Yusuf Charaf, entered the room. Everyone already in the room stood until Charaf sat down on his seat.

Seventy years old, Charaf was a man who had no hair on his scalp, dark skin, and brown eyes. In his youth, he was naturally drawn to join the Sahrawi Liberation People's Army. For him and many Sahrawis, the end of the Third World War was an opportunity to achieve real independence for Western Sahara and when the New United Nations was created, it joined and thus, the Sahrawi Arab Democratic Republic was born as a NUN member-state. After the war, Charaf opted for politics and joined the New United Nations government. His decades of experience allowed him to become Secretary-General.

"Ladies and gentlemen, thank you for coming here on such short notice," Charaf said to start the meeting before he turned to Pérez. "Director Pérez, I'll allow you to start this meeting properly."

"Thank you, Mr. Secretary," Perez replied. "Now, I'll have Mr. Vue explain to us all how we must tackle this situation."

"Mind if I get water first?" Vue asked.

"You may," Charaf answered. Vue then stood up and rushed to the nearest table with a jug and paper cups. After helping himself, he then returned to the table and monitors surrounded by the council seats. He then returned to the presentation he opened earlier and moved to the next slide, showing the file on Maral Eminovna Guliyeva. However, Vue then faced Charaf.

"Thank you, Mr. Secretary," Vue said before he stopped looking at Charaf. "My name is John Vue. While I'll be happy to entertain questions, please refrain from asking until I finish explaining each slide. Two days ago, I was assigned to analyze the documents we received three days ago as someone left them in the Museum of Intelligence Collection for us to find. Here is Maral Eminovna Guliyeva, and she is the subject of our presentation because she had been purchased by one Segismundo Alba."

"Did you say Segismundo Alba?" Kristen Parton, the elected council member from the United States of America, asked.

"Yes, Segismundo Alba." Vue switched to the slide containing the document on Alba. "He bought Guliyeva on July 21 and is using her as his personal concubine."

Vue now switched to the slide that showed a document with a picture of a man in his early sixties with no hair on his scalp, very light skin, a blond moustache that was graying, and blue eyes.

"This is Anton Oleksandrovich Kravchenko," Vue said. "Sixty-three years old, he operates the human trafficking ring that sold Guliyeva to Alba. His father Oleksandr Konstantinovich Kravchenko was formerly a KGB official who was involved with the Sparrow School. Like his father, Anton joined the KGB but when the Soviet Union collapsed after the Third World War, both father and son started a prostitution business as Oleksandr used his experince from the Sparrow School, since it's an institution where women who joined the KGB were trained to seduce men in foreign governments and/or militaries. As a result, it was easy for him to acquire women and sell them. Oleksandr died in 2019 with Anton inheriting the business. However, he opted to acquire underage girls. The Eurasian government cracked down on this but Anton miraculously escaped and restarted the business in the South Korean city of Sinpo."

"So why do we need this meeting to go after a pimp?" Preston Godfrey, the Chairman of the Joint Chiefs of Staff, asked.

"Because the Eurasian Tsardom doesn't know he's alive," Vue answered. "Director Pérez and I came to propose an operation to capture Kravchenko, but by using Guliyeva as bait."

"And how do you propose this will lead us to Kravchenko?" Charaf asked. "If we agree to it, of course."

"It was discussed prior to this meeting." Vue then switched to a slide that contained a document full of redacted information with a picture meant for its subject replaced with a giant question mark. The only piece of information that wasn't redacted was the name "Fred Smith". "We will use one of our agents named 'Fred Smith' to infiltrate the United Mexican States to rescue Guliyeva. Before we inform 'Smith' of this mission, we will consider hiring the mercenary group Iron Dutchman Services to assist in hiding Guliyeva. After we acquire their assistance, we will have 'Smith' prepare our safehouse in Yao where we will keep Guliyeva until Kravchenko makes his move."

"And what do you suppose he will do?" Jeanne Soglo, the Under-Secretary-General of Defense, asked.

Vue then switched to the next slide as his answer. "He will use his personal cadre of Korean mercenaries. We don't know how he will get them inside Japan but if he can avoid being spotted by the Eurasians despite reports of their hyper-competence and how we didn't know he's hiding in Sinpo until we were given those documents, anything's possible."

"Do we even have a way of ascertaining how to find Guliyeva?" Touji Minagawa, the elected council member from the State of Japan, asked.

"We have our operative in the Tijuana Cartel," Parnell answered. "We call him 'Fantasma'. We can get him to assist 'Smith' with Officer Rosarita Sanchez of the Mexican Federal Police as our intermediary."

"I don't mean to sound cynical, but what will we do with Guliyeva after we capture Kravchenko?" Cynthia Romero, the High Commissioner for Human Rights, asked.

"Sadly, not much we can do," Vue answered with disappointment evident in his tone. "The document on Guliyeva only mentioned she came from the Azerbaijan Governorate. Chances are, she doesn't have a family. We could put her in an orphanage, but considering what she has been made to do, I doubt she can survive a month, if she's lucky, because she wouldn't know any other language other than Azeri."

"I, for one, accept the plan," Charaf declared. "Shall we put a vote on this?"

"Majority wins," Parnell added. "Who votes yes?"

She immediately raised her hand. Charaf, Pérez, and Vue followed Parnell with their raised hands.

Unknown Location; Enlightenment Point. August 5, 2030; 1439 hours (EP Time Zone)

Both Reinhard Frühling and a woman in black with her mouth wearing a surgical mask entered and saluted Sergei Akulov. "As you can see, 'SB' has joined us," Frühling declared, referring to the woman beside him.

"Any report from our Devotee-Infiltrator in the FIS?" Akulov asked.

"The Secretary-General approved of the operation."

"Order our Devotee-Infiltrator to continue as usual." Akulov then turned to "SB". "As for you, I need you to go to Japan. Tell our Gatekeeper there of this operation because we need him to secure transport routes and accommodation for the equipment and personnel needed."

"By your will, Grand Gatekeeper," "SB" replied.

"After that, go to South Korea and inform Kravchenko of this operation."

"Grand Gatekeeper, forgive me for making such a request but before I go to Japan, permission to go to my safehouse in North Yemen? I wish to acquire what I need to go to Japan."

"I will allow it."

#

Isfahan Refugee Camp, Isfahan County, Isfahan Province, Region 2; Islamic Republic of Iran. February 1, 2023; 2200 hours (Iran Standard Time)

"There you are, Tarou," a girl said as she approached a boy looking at the night sky. The girl had her black hair hidden by a veil, light intermediate skin, and dark brown eyes. "We should go to sleep already."

"Just one more minute," the boy named Tarou pleaded. He had black hair, very light skin, and the same eye color as the girl, who decided to join him.

"You like looking at the stars, don't you?"

"They're free, unlike us." Both Tarou and the girl moved their respective heads downward to a large metal wall in front of them.

"I told you. We live like this for our own safety."

"Why is that?"

"I heard the older children learn this. The giant ship that came from the sky caused lots of bad things to happen. Balochs like me were forced to leave and settle here."

"I see."

"Was it because I said 'Balochs like me'? I'm sorry about that."

"I'm not really a Baloch, am I?"

The girl was unable to answer. Or rather, she had an answer in her mind, but feared the consequences of answering. But the longer she looked at Tarou. She resigned with a sigh.

"T... There is something I heard from Mother and Father," the girl ultimately answered. "But please don't tell anyone that I told you."

"What is it?"

"You were found beside a woman. She wasn't able to respond to any of Father's or Mother's questions when they found the two of you together."

"Would that woman be... my mother?"

"Shireen, Tarou, what are you doing out here!? It's time to go to sleep!"

#

Wings of the Defenders C-141/Sanaa International Airport, Royal Capital of Sanaa; Kingdom of Yemen. August 5, 2030; 1513 hours (Royal Yemen Time)

"Please wake up," a woman with a visor, one of the stewardesses on the Gatekeepes of Knowledge's C-141 Starlifter transport plane, requested as he stood too close to "SB". The latter screamed as a result.

"W... Where am I?" "SB" asked.

"We're in the Kingdom of Yemen. It's natural this would happen because you fell asleep upon my announcement."

"My apologies. Thank you for this."

"By the Grand Gatekeeper's will." "SB" repeated it.

"SB" then stood up and acquired her belongings. She then exited the C-141 through its rear ramp. Once she left the plane, her feet were now on the soil of the Kingdom of Yemen. She then found a man hiding his scalp with a turban and his eyes with sunglasses.

"Glad to see a familiar face," "SB" said as she got closer to the man. "You know where I'm needed."

#

Gatekeepers of Knowledge Safehouse, Bani Al Harith District. 1545 hours

"SB" now entered a safehouse used by the Gatekeepers of Knowledge to shelter agents such as herself. The safehouse, located beside a water treatment plant, was what one agent needed. It simply consisted of a bedroom with two beds that each accommodated four people, a kitchen, and a bathroom.

"SB" traveled to the bedroom. There, she opened a cabinet where she acquired actual clothes she needed to blend in. After getting the clothes, she began to leave the safehouse.

#

Wings of the Defenders C-141; Above the State of Oman. 2120 hours (Gulf Standard Time)

"SB" now looked at the clothes she acquired. *If it weren't for all of this, I wouldn't have traveled the world,* "SB" thought. *I may have lost everything that day seven years ago, but I'm able to travel across the world like I wished to do since childhood.*

Now, I wonder what you're doing right now, Tarou?

"SB" then closed her eyes as the flight wouldn't end for another seventeen hours. Her mind began to drift into childhood memories, yet these were memories no one should have experienced in the first place.

Isfahan Refugee Camp Elementary School, Isfahan Refugee Camp, Isfahan County, Isfahan Province, Region 2; Islamic Republic of Iran. February 12, 2023; 0920 hours (Iran Standard Time)

A large explosion was heard throughout the Isfahan Refugee Camp. The elementary school built in the refugee camp was no exception, that classes were stopped without a word.

What was that? the girl named Shireen pondered.

Suddenly, an engine was heard. "Everybody, please calm down," an older woman instructed, the teacher to the children, instructed. "Whoever came to our school might enter this room so please be patient."

The wait wasn't going to be long as everyone now heard loud footsteps. They knew that meant someone was coming and that he was in a hurry. Their guesses were right as a soldier of the Islamic Republic of Iran Army Ground Forces appeared. He wore a green-colored uniform that consisted of a cap, tunic, and trousers. The trousers were held up by a black-colored belt. His feet wore black-colored boots. Slung on his back was a Type 56 assault rifle.

"Everyone, we must evacuate the school," the soldier urged.

"Is this related to what we heard just now?" the older woman asked.

"Baleh. It's an explosion, therefore we must go to the shelter now."

"Why?"

"The Eurasians have declared war on us. The explosion earlier was most likely their doing, and many others occurred throughout the country. We need to hide in the shelter until we don't hear any more explosions."

#

Isfahan Refugee Camp Bomb Shelter. 1000 hours

Every man, woman, and child began to converge in front of a gray-colored structure that simply had a metal door colored red. This was the refugee camp's bomb shelter, needed when there was an explosion like what was heard almost an hour before. More soldiers of the Iranian Ground Forces guarded the structure. Two also carried Type 56s while two carried G3 battle rifles.

Among those appearing outside was the class Shireen was a part of. However, she saw the boy named Tarou and was able to join him as no one was looking. Despite being surrounded by others, which invited noise, Tarou heard the footsteps and reared his head to find Shireen approaching him. He turned his entire body just as Shireen stopped.

"Tarou, you made it," Shireen said.

"Same goes to you," Tarou replied.

"Do you know what will happen next?"

"I doubt all of us will be able to enter that shelter."

"Why?"

"Because we wouldn't be out here."

"What do you mean you can't let all of us in!?" a male voice shouted.

"That's Father's voice," Shireen guessed before she moved to where the voice came from, with Tarou following.

Both pushed their way across others in front of the shelter. They found an older man and a woman beside him arguing with one of the soldiers.

"It is Father," Shireen repeated. "And Mother is with him."

"I'm sorry, the shelter is full," the soldier explained.

"Then how will everyone else be protected if there's another explosion?!" the man added.

"Please be patient."

"Pedar!" Shireen shouted as she rushed to the man and woman she recognized as her parents, with Tarou following her. Both parents turned to the approaching children.

"Shireen, you're here," Shireen's father said as his daughter stopped. He then grabbed Shireen and resumed facing the soldiers.

"As you can see, I have a daughter," the man said to the soldier, resuming their argument. "What will happen to her if-"

Suddenly, sirens were heard. This was followed by the sound of jet engines and because it was loud, everyone outside the shelter turned to where the sound came from. They looked above the shelter and found an Su-25

Grach close air support aircraft flying above them. It flew fast enough that it vanished, which should have been a relief for those below.

However, that relief would make way for more suffering as a bombshell was dropped. It was too high for anyone to see, but as it got lower, it split into two. Balls of metal came as a result of the bomb splitting in two and began to fall into the ground. No one noticed as the balls fell slowly.

Below, one soldier received a call from his portable radio and answered it. Everyone watched as they knew the possibilities that came from the call. Unbeknownst to all, the metal balls were low enough they should have been seen. In a split second, they began to explode.

#

Wings of the Defenders C-141; Above the Indian Combine. August 5, 2030; 0439 hours (India Time)

"SB", the grown-up Shireen, now woke up. She breathed as if she survived after holding her breath while underwater.

That dream again, The Gatekeepers of Knowledge agent thought. *I guess it's natural for me to have that dream. It's why I joined the Gatekeepers.*

"Breakfast!" the stewardess who woke Shireen up in the Kingdom of Yeman announced as she appeared with a wheeled tray. The latter raised her hand for the former to see.

#

Nagoya International Airport, Toyoyama/Nishikugai District, Aichi Prefecture; State of Japan. 1539 hours (Japan Standard Time)

After going through customs with the documents she also got from Sanaa, Shireen had stepped out of Nagoya International Airport. She now wore the clothes she also got from her safehouse in Sanaa.

Now dressed normally, Shireen looked like her mother, who died in that bombing that struck the Isfahan Refugee Camp seven years before. She then found a man in a suit approaching him.

"Are you 'SB'?" the man asked.

"I am," Shireen answered.

"Please follow me. We're to see Gatekeeper Japan."

Japan Tachyon Particle Receiver, Seto. 1600 hours

Shireen was then brought to the Japan Tachyon Particle Receiver complex in the city of Seto, also in the Aichi Prefecture. After being allowed entry, Shireen and the man who picked her up parked their car and proceeded inside. They reached the office of Gatekeeper Japan. Once it was explained to the Gatekeeper's secretary, Shireen alone approached the office of Gatekeeper Japan. Both clenched their fists and saluted.

"So you're 'SB'?" Gatekeeper Japan asked with Shireen nodding. "Please sit."

Shireen then sat down. "I've been instructed to assist with a mission. Think you could please explain to me what that mission is?"

"I am to retrieve a girl named Maral Eminovna Guliyeva. However, it will require that Guliyeva be brought here to Japan by the FIS's 'Fred Smith'. Guliyeva was sold to one Segisumundo Alba by mistake and that the FIS have been informed about it. They'll order 'Smith' to retrieve Guliyeva and bring her here to Japan."

"And how am I to help?"

"I plan on going to South Korea and inform Anton Oleksandrovich Kravchenko of this. I am to use his Korean mercenaries but they will need weapons, vests, clothes, food, a ship to deliver all the weapons they need to them, a safehouse for them to hide until we hear that 'Smith' returned to Japan with Guliyeva, routes that will lead to the safehouse, vans to use for travel, and a Walgear for me to use should the situation call for it."

"Before I am to help, how many of Kravchenko's men will you bring with you?"

"Two nine-man squads."

"Then I'll arrange for AK-05s, Type 69 RPGs, ammunition for the aforementioned weapons, vests, a radio, earpieces, and rations to be brought over here to Jpan while I can get shirts, pants, belts, and shoes to the safehouse. I can also start arranging for Minagawa to provide the trucks needed to deliver everything and everyone to the safehouse and the vans. As for the safehouse, it's in Kansai City; northwest Crater Shore."

"Perfect. We can launch from there to attack the FIS safehouse in Yao as soon as we hear from our Devotee-Infiltrator in the FIS that 'Smith' returns to Japan with Guliyeva."

"I assume that's all?"

"One more thing: that Walgear has to be an SH-6."

"There's already an SH-6 for you in the *Pacific*. We'll have it delivered as soon as you return to Japan."

The Past and the Present

Japan Tachyon Particle Receiver, Seto, Aichi Prefecture; State of Japan. August 5, 2030; 1700 hours (Japan Standard Time)

At the room in the Japan Tachyon Particle Receiver, Gatekeeper Japan appeared. All Gatekeepers of Knowledge personnel working in the room turned to him. Like their Gatekeeper, they were hooded and covered their entire bodies with cloaks. The cloaks had armbands on the right sleeves yet there were different colors for those in the room.

Within the Gatekeepers of Knowledge, a rank system was used within the organization and the color of the armband determined the rank. Those with the green armbands bore the lowest rank within the Gatekeepers, named "Initiate". Above them were "Devotees", who wore red armbands. Above Devotee was the Gatekeeper assigned to manage all affairs within a nation-state with his or her armband colored white.

Gatekeeper Japan was then approached by a female Devotee. Both saluted each other.

"Glad you're here, Devotee Matsutani," Gatekeeper Japan said. "Please get me to Gatekeeper Russia."

#

RSFSR Tachyon Particle Receiver, Federal Capital of Vladivostok; Russian Soviet Federative Socialist Republic. 1803 hours (Vladivostok Time)

At the same room in the TPR that serviced the entire Russian Soviet Federative Socialist Republic, Gatekeeper Japan appeared on a large monitor. "Attention, Gatekeepers RSFSR, I am Gatekeeper Japan," the Gatekeeper addressed. "I am calling for Gatekeeper RSFSR. Please notify him."

A male Devotee saluted Gatekeeper Japan. "By the Grand Gatekeeper's will," the Devotee replied.

1833 hours

Later, the Devotee returned to the room with Gatekeeper RSFSR. Gatekeeper Japan saw and once his RSFSR counterpart faced him, they saluted each other.

"What can I do for you, Gatekeeper Japan?" Gatekeeper RSFSR asked.

"I need enough AK-05 rifles and Type 69 RPGs for nineteen men," Gatekeeper Japan answered.

"Why?"

Gatekeeper Japan explained to Gatekeeper RSFSR why. Everyone listened with surprise except for the latter as he remained stoic.

"Consider it done," Gatekeeper RSFSR replied after listening to Gatekeeper Japan. "What about the delivery of the weapons?"

"I'll have a ship travel to Vladivostok to get the weapons," Gatekeeper Japan answered. "I assume you can get Kovalchuk to help?"

"He has no choice."

#

Novaya Lubyanka Building. 1852 hours

Despite the creation of the Eurasian Tsardom, a portion of the former Union of Soviet Socialist Republics remained in the southeast, near the People's Republic of China and the Democratic People's Republic of Korea. This portion was commonly called the "Soviet Remnant" as a result and with assistance from its neighbors, rebuilt the city of Vladivostok as its capital since it was bombed during the Third World War.

As a result, new structures were built that the city appeared to be a different one from the one destroyed in the war, despite using the same name. One example of this was the Novaya Lubyanka building. Built as a homage to the building that housed the *Komitet Gosudarstvenoy Bezopasnosti* (KGB) in the Lubyanka Square located in Moscow prior to its destruction, the Novaya Lubyanka building was to fulfill the same purpose as the original Lubyanka Building did in hosting the resurrected KGB.

Leaving his office was Oleh Bohdanovich Kovalchuk, the current Chairman of the KGB. However, he felt that his reason for leaving would be different from having dinner. He sighed as he knew what he felt in his bottom-rear. Despite that, he left the office and raced to the nearest bathroom.

#

1930 hours

Now in a bathroom, Kovalchuk not only washed his hands but also the object that made him go to the bathroom in the first place. Once both were washed, Kovalchuk raced to the air dryer and when his business there was finished, he returned to the sink.

There, he opened the tip of the object as it was shaped like an egg. The object was none other than a pager, a communication device no longer used. Kovalchuk, however, used it as it was something he could use when he was in KGB headquarters. Upon turning on the pager, Kovalchuk found a message that read:

Devotee-Infiltrator Kovalchuk, we request that you provide us a map of Vladivostok's sewers and of the headquarters of the 1st Brigade of Border Guard Ships because we intend on stealing the weapons stored there for an operation that will involve acquiring the assistance of Anton Oleksandrovich Kravchenko.

Gatekeeper RSFSR.

Thank goodness it's just the maps, Kovalchuk thought. *That I can quickly provide.*

#

Isfahan Refugee Camp Bomb Shelter, Isfahan Refugee Camp, Isfahan County, Isfahan Province, Region 2; Islamic Republic of Iran. February 11, 2023; 1020 hours (Iran Standard Time)

Shireen Baloch began to come about. Upon doing so, she heard ambulance sirens and shouting. As she opened her eyes, she saw the morning sky, yet there was smoke.

"Shireen!?" a voice shouted.

Shireen now saw Tarou. Unbeknownst to her, she was almost buried by a corpse that Tarou was attempting to push away. The former turned her head to her left, but she found a corpse. She widened her eyes upon seeing a dead man, but it was then Tarou succeeded in pushing the corpse off Shireen. She got up, but her legs remained on the ground and immediately turned to her right as the corpse Tarou pushed out of Shireen was her mother.

"M… Mâdar… " Shireen said as she identified the corpse beside her.

Shireen rushed to her mother's corpse. "Please, wake up!" Shireen screamed.

Shireen repeated her pleas and added pushing, thinking her mother was still alive. Tarou simply watched. After three tries, Shireen found that it was hopeless and simply laid on the floor and cried. Two paramedics spotted Tarou and Shireen and rushed to them.

\#

Wings of the Defenders C-141; Above the Republic of Korea. August 5, 2030; 1830 hours (Korea Standard Time)

"Are you okay?" the female attendant asked as she appeared before Shireen's face, causing the latter to startle. Shireen promptly looked at her left and right before facing the attendant.

"… How long was I not responding to you?" Shireen asked.

"For almost an hour," the attendant answered. "I gave you your dinner ten minutes ago. I suggest you eat now because we'll be approaching Wonsan International Airport in less than fifty-three minutes."

"I apologize for this. I've been reminiscing as of recent."

"I understand. Please eat, because you'll need some time to brush your teeth afterward."

\#

Wonsan International Airport, Wonsan, Gangwon Province; Republic of Korea. 1859 hours

With her belongings with her, Shireen stepped out of the Starlifter and into the Republic of Korea (ROK). Specifically, she was now in Wonsan; formerly a part of the Democratic People's Republic of Korea (DPRK).

During the Third World War, the ROK ultimately moved to reunify the Korean Peninsula due to the chaos of the war with assistance from the United States of America due to the DPRK increasing relations with the Union of Soviet Socialist Republics after the destruction of the Moscow Kremlin that started the war. The unification wasn't complete by the time the war ended, but among the spoils of this campaign was Wonsan.

Shireen then saw two men waiting by a Starex van. "Nal delileo on geot gat-eunde?" Shireen asked in Korean.

"Ye," one of the two men answered. "Please get in."

#

Sinpo Box Factory, Sinpo, Hamgyong Province. 2039 hours

The Starex now arrived at the Sinpo Box Factory. This factory was a recent addition to the city of Sinpo, a noteworthy target during the Third World War as it hosted the South Sinpo Shipyard, a valued possession of the DPRK's military industry. The city was notoriously bombed as a result.

The bombings only stopped after the war ended. Reconstruction only started once the 21st century began, and that it was to only cater to civilian matters though the naval base that was also a target in the world war was rebuilt to be used by both the Republic of Korea Navy and the New United Nations Maritime Force.

Once the Starex was allowed inside, the driver stopped before the entrance of the factory's main building, with Shireen exiting the van. Many of those who only saw it as a factory that made boxes weren't aware of the secret it hosted. While it was built from a bombed-out fish factory, that wasn't the secret.

As Shireen proceeded further inside, she found the factory's actual secret: the continuation of Anton Oleksandrovich Kravchenko's human trafficking ring. Shireen pressed on to find Kravchenko's office, despite being surrounded by crates being carried by trolleys. These crates contained tubes for the girls to breathe in until they arrive at the respective residences of the individuals who purchased them. Also filling the air was the sound of girls who have yet to be sold, reacting to the *training* forced upon them before they were to be sold.

Shireen then arrived at Kravchenko's office. She knocked on the door.

"Who's there?" Anton Oleksandrovich Kravchenko asked from inside his office.

"It's 'SB'," Shireen answered.

"You may come in."

As a result, Shireen allowed herself inside the office. She found Kravchenko simply focused on a *particular* video. Shireen knocked on the door as she entered to make sure he had her attention.

"Sorry about that," Kravchenko replied, making him exit the video in a hurry before facing Shireen again. "Please close the door and proceed further."

Shireen did as Kravchenko requested. After that, she sat on the sofa to the left of Kravchenko's desk.

"So, what brings you out here?" Kravchenko asked."

"Maral Eminovna Guliyeva," Shireen simply answered.

"Please don't kill me! Business wasn't good and Alba offered me enough. I assure you-"

"I'm here to assure you that the Grand Gatekeeper won't have you killed."

Kravchenko gulped upon hearing what Shireen said. Not long after, he sighed, then faced Shireen.

"So… how can I help?"

"I need your men. We've arranged a scenario where the FIS will get Guliyeva from Alba and that they'll take her to their safehouse in Yao. We can get Guliyeva back from them."

"Will you provide my men with weapons?"

"That will be Gatekeeper Japan's responsibility."

"Anything else I can help with?"

"The Grand Gatekeeper intends on finishing where Henderson left off with Guliyeva. We'll send him here in due time. Please continue hosting the experiment and only that."

"… Right."

"Now, if you excuse me, I need to find somewhere to stay until the ship arrives."

#

Hotel Federal, Venustiano Carranza, Mexico City; United Mexican States. 0819 hours (Mountain Standard Time)

Located southwest of the Mexico City International Airport was the Hotel Federal, near the *Poliforum Central de la Colonia Federal* cultural center. In one room of the Hotel Federal, a man used his laptop computer. Twenty-five years old, the man had short but voluminous black hair, light skin, and dark brown eyes.

The man had a GOKMail application on his computer. His GOKMail received a message that read:

To "LS",

"SB" is currently preparing the troops needed for the assault on the FIS safehouse in Japan once she hears from our Devotee-Infiltrator in the FIS about "Fred Smith's" movements. The Grand Gatekeeper demands that information proving that Segismundo Alba leads the Tijuana Cartel and evidence of his deeds being covered up by his allies within the Mexican government must be delivered as soon as possible.

Gatekeeper of Intelligence.

I have the list of people I need to see to accomplish this task, the man thought before bringing out his smartphone and opening its "Notes" application. Finding a note titled "List of People to Find", the man began reading a list that consisted of three pairs of people. Three were grouped under CEO (Chief Executive Officer) and three were grouped under "President". Two people were under one number and the number pertained to one company.

Since I'm in Mexico City, I'll start with the CEO and President of TV Azteca.

#

Outside 1st Brigade of Border Guard Ships Headquarters, Federal Capital of Vladivostok; Russian Soviet Federative Socialist Republic. August 6, 2030; 0900 hours (Vladivostok Time)

A van appeared outside the headquarters of the 1st Brigade of Border Guard Ships, one of the four brigades of the naval branch of the Soviet Border Guards. Although under the KGB, the Border Guards functioned as a separate military solely dedicated to guarding the borders of what remained of the Union of Soviet Socialist Republics, hence the need for a naval branch.

Men in black hiding their faces with gas masks came out of the van. No one, however, was able to see the men nor the van. These men brought out a ladder and one of them carried a detonator.

"Headquarters in sight," one man said. "Detonating gas bombs."

The man wasted no time in pressing the detonator. As a result, a large purple gas cloud erupted from every building of the headquarters complex. The gas cloud affected the guards near the gates of the headquarters complex and, as a result, they lose consciousness.

The men began to charge at the south end of the headquarters complex with their ladder. They planted the ladder onto the south gate with one man climbing onto the ladder.

#

1st Brigade of Border Guard Ships Headquarters. 0950 hours

The men in black began exiting every building in the headquarters complex with four wooden crates and two other crates made of metal. The latter two bore "5,45 mm". In addition, the men wore vests filled with magazines, also loaded with 5.45x39mm rounds.

"Chen, Thomas, open the gate," one man ordered to the two men lowering the metal crates to the ground.

"Roger," the men named Chen and Thomas replied before rushing to the south gate where they all came from with the ladder no longer there.

Finding the gate's controls, Chen and Thomas open the gate. Seeing the gate open, one man who stayed with the van rushed toward the headquarters complex. Once the truck stopped, the crates were immediately loaded. Everyone then rushed inside the van with the driver returning to the gate where he had entered. He briefly stopped to pick up Chen and Thomas, who immediately rushed to get inside. As soon as they boarded the van, the driver rushed out of the complex.

Vladivostok Border Entry Seaport. 1041 hours

The van now arrived at another Border Guards installation, the Vladivostok Border Entry Seaport, a portion of the city's harbor needed to inspect supplies and visitors coming to the RSFSR. Like with the headquarters of the 1st Brigade of Border Guards Ships, the installation was also struck by the same gas cloud, but it had yet to go away. Just as the men in black began exiting the van carrying the crates they stole, another van arrived.

This van was also filled with men in black wearing gas masks. Unlike the earlier van, these men brought with them cardboard boxes. The men who brought the wooden and metal crates then saw those who brought the cardboard boxes.

"Now we need to find a ship to take all of these boxes and meet up with the *Pacific*," one man said.

#

Eastern Bosphorus. 1130 hours

A Border Guards ship taken by the men in black now appeared in the middle of the Eastern Bosphorus. The men then stopped the ship.

Suddenly, a submarine rose from the depths of the Eastern Bosphorus and moved slightly toward the ship. It resembled the *Perun*-class ballistic missile submarine of the Imperial Eurasian Navy. However, it didn't carry nuclear missiles, but as soon as it stopped beside the ship, it lowered a large ramp to connect to the ship.

As a result, the men in the ship began bringing the crates to the ramp. Once all the crates were loaded onto the ramp, men from the submarine rushed to get the crates. The ship moved away from the ramp and began to return to Vladivostok. By the time the ship turned its back on the submarine, the latter closed its ramp as the crates were taken inside the submarine.

Sinpo Box Factory, Sinpo, Hamgyong Province; Republic of Korea. 1700 hours (Korea Standard Time)

"How did you get these men?" Shireen asked while she stood beside Anton Oleksandrovich Kravchenko as they looked at the eighteen men gathered at the factory complex. These men were within the age range of eighteen to twenty-nine. Despite physical differences with their bodies, these men had black hair and light skin.

"I can command favors from the Supreme Leader," Kravchenko answered. "These men are actually from the Korean People's Army and they've infiltrated this country before, thus you will be using them for your mission into Japan."

"Do they know where they're going and why?"

"I simply told the Supreme Leader they're to assist in extracting an RGB cell." Kravchenko then turned to Shireen, intent on bringing up another subject. "What of the weapons and other supplies?"

"Gatekeeper Japan is still working on it," Shireen answered. "I'm going to need your help with getting these men to come with me to Japan, but you might have to hide them here."

"How may I help?"

#

Hotel Sinpo. 2009 hours

At her room in one of the few hotels in Sinpo, Shireen began using her smartphone's GOKMail. Addressing her message to one "GJYS", the message read:

Kravchenko gathered the men I need. I request that you ask Minagawa to prepare his trucks to accommodate the men because I intend to take them with me to Japan by making them hide in the boxes made in Kravchenko's front. I assume you've acquired the supplies from the Soviet Remnant at this point, but I can also imagine it will take a while for Minagawa to get them, so Kravchenko's men come first.

"SB".

Shireen then pressed "Send".

Fortress of Knowledge; Enlightenment Point. 1610 hours (EP Time Zone)

Reinhard Frühling appeared at the office of one Robert Willard. Willard served as the Gatekeeper of Defense, Frühling's equivalent in the Defenders of Knowledge. Both men saluted each other before Frühling sat down on the couch in the office.

"How can I help you, Gatekeeper Int?" Willard asked.

"Please ask Sub-Gatekeeper Mansur to have our plane in the Republic of Korea to wait for my agent 'SB'," Frühling requested.

"Isn't she supposed to leave tomorrow with Anton Kravchenko's men?"

"That hasn't changed. However, she intends on having them hide in boxes until they reach the safehouse Gatekeeper Japan prepared for them."

"Why boxes?"

"No one would suspect that men are inside the boxes. In addition to that, Gatekeeper Japan will arrange for trucks to hide the boxes."

"I'll talk to Mansur about it."

#

TV Azetca Headquarters, Tlalpan, Mexico City; United Mexican States. 0545 hours (Mountain Standard Time)

A guard at the headquarters of TV Azteca, one of the three media companies in the United Mexican States that owned a news channel, appeared for his shift. As he made his last step before starting work, he felt something touching his left foot.

The guard lowered himself upon seeing what his foot felt, a package. Picking up the package, the man found that the package contained a message in Spanish that read:

Para el Señor Yan y el Señor Herrera.

Tu Ángel Guardián.

Hotel Sinpo, Sinpo, Hamgyong Province; Republic of Korea. 2239 hours (Korea Standard Time)

Simply wearing lingerie, Shireen heard that she received a message. As soon as she got her phone, she opened her GOKMail. The message came from Frühling and it read:

Mansur ordered the plane to remain at Wonsan International Airport. Crew have been alerted of the additional cargo. I suggest you wake up early and tell Kravchenko of this because he will need to prepare his trucks as soon as possible.

Gatekeeper Int.

Finally, Shireen thought before writing "Order acknowledged. Thank you" and pressing "Send".

She then put down the phone and wrapped herself in her bed's blanket.

#

Sinpo Box Factory. August 7, 2030; 0611 hours

Anton Oleksandrovich Kravchenko arrived at his factory. However, after he parked his car, he found Shireen waiting by the entrance, making him pause as if he stepped on a minefield.

"W… What are doing here?" Kravchenko asked.

"We need to start packing everyone up into boxes," Shireen commanded. "Now."

"Y… You mean now?"

"Now!"

#

Wonsan International Airport. Gangwon Province. 1810 hours

Trucks began to appear at Wonsan International Airport. They parked near the Gatekeepers of Knowledge's C-141 Starlifter, still parked at the airport. Shireen got off one truck and found the loadmaster rushing to the trucks as boxes containing tubes at the very top were being laid on the tarmac.

"I take it this is the 'additional cargo' Sub-Gatekeeper Mansur spoke of?" the loadmaster asked.

"Yes," Shireen answered. "Any news about the supplies from the Soviet Remnant?"

"The *Pacific* has left Soviet waters. The ship owned by Minagawa's waiting at the rendezvous point."

"Good. Please make sure all boxes are loaded inside. I need to get into normal clothes because I need to ride on the Minagawa trucks once this plane lands in Japan."

"By the Grand Gatekeeper's will."

#

Wings of the Defenders C-141/Nagoya International Airport, Toyoyama/Nishikugai District, Aichi Prefecture; State of Japan. 2000 hours

Once the C-141's rear ramp was lowered, Shireen was the first to step on Japanese soil. She was now in civilian clothing. She then found a man approaching her.

"Ganji Mahsa desu ka?" the man asked.

"Hai," Shireen replied in Japanese. "Minagawa gurūpu de hataraite imasu ka?"

"Sou desu. Kansai-shi e o-dzure shimasu."

"Wakatta."

#

Sea of Japan. 2059 hours

The submarine that left Vladivostok, called the *Pacific* by the Gatekeepers of Knowledge, rose from the depths of the Sea of Japan. Spotting the submarine was a container ship that contained a crane. Once the submarine stopped rising, it lowered its left ramp, connecting the submarine to the container ship.

The crates stolen from the Soviets were delivered onto the container ship. Once the last crate was taken to the container ship, one crate was dragged to the ramp. This crate, however, was taller than those that were stolen from the Russian Soviet Federative Socialist Republic.

The crate was two meters tall. Despite that, it was delivered to the container ship by its crane. Once the crate landed, the submarine closed its ramp. It began to submerge with the container ship staying put.

#

Maizuru, Kyoto Prefecture. August 9, 2030; 1700 hours

The container ship now arrived at Maizuru. The seamen working on the ship disembarked with a trolley containing the boxes from the RSFSR. They found men rushing to them as soon as they set foot on Japanese soil.

"Are you with Minagawa Group?" one of the men from the container ship asked.

"Hai," the man opposite to the seamen replied. "We'll take these supplies to Kansai City."

"Arigatou."

#

Abandoned Shipwreck, Crater Shore North, Kansai Prefecture. August 10, 2030; 1500 hours

Inside a shipwreck located in the northwest portion of Crater Shore, the Koreans began opening the boxes delivered to them by Minagawa Group. The open boxes contained rations needed for survival. Shireen and a man beside her watched.

The boxes being opened were made of wood and metal. The wooden crates contained AK-05 assault rifles and Type 69 rocket-propelled grenade launchers. One wooden box contained additional RPG rounds. The metal crates were next to be opened and as the "5,45" showed, the crates were filled with 5.45x39mm rounds as the AK-05 was chambered for that caliber.

The last to be opened were the additional cardboard boxes. These contained vests for body protection and magazine storage, a radio, and earpieces.

"Now that we have everything, we wait until we know when the target is coming and where she will be kept at," Shireen said.

"And how will we know?" the man asked.

"We wait until I've been contacted by my superiors, Song."

#

Minagawa Group Headquarters, Nakamura Ward, Nagoya City, Nagoya Prefecture. 1429 hours

While Hoshikawa Group was based in Kansai City, the Minagawa Group dominated the capital of Nagoya. Like Hoshikawa Group, Minagawa group rose by acquiring companies that struggled in the wake of the Third World War.

Office space was one business Minagawa Group dominated in all of Japan, allowing it to have an edge against Hoshikawa Group. Minagawa Group Headquarters, located in the Nakamura Ward and the tallest building in all of Nagoya, showed how much the *keiretsu* dominated Nagoya.

Alone in a bathroom for men was Minagawa Group's President, the bald Chiaki Minagawa, fifty-five years old, was now in a bathroom. Other than his hands, he was also washing the same egg-shaped object Oleh Bohdanovich Kovalchuk kept injected into his body.

Unlike his corporate rival Daisuke Hoshikawa, Minagawa's life was more privileged. He avoided the dangers of the Third World War, which many assumed to be the luck of the Devil while he was in the United States of America studying. He never served in the military as a contrast to Daisuke, who joined the Special Operations Brigade of the New United Nations Ground Force. Another contrast he had with Daisuke was that he remarried but in less than acceptable circumstances due to the timing in between his first wife's death and his second marriage and that it was rumored his second wife was his mistress.

Once he opened the object, he began to use the built-in pager. He began typing in a message despite the small screen and the lack of buttons with letters and numbers. Despite that, he typed in his message and pressed the "Send" option that was on the screen.

Minagawa then moved to a toilet stall. After closing the stall door, Chiaki began to return the pager with the egg-shaped cover to where he kept it in his body.

#

McAllister Residence, McLean, Fairfax County, Commonwealth of Virginia; United States of America. August 12, 2030; 0311 hours (Eastern Standard Time)

Stanley McAllister rushed to his bedroom with the door already open. As he turned on the light, he found his wife Cynthia asleep and her bathrobe.

"She's fine," a male voice said. "I simply gave her a sleeping pill and naturally, I had to bathe her."

Knowing where the voice came from, McAllister turned to see the man who was in Mexico. "Who are you!?" McAllister screamed.

"Call me 'LS'," the man said. McAllister stopped being angry; his face showing that he's familiar with the initials "LS".

"W… What are you doing here?" McAllister asked with fear evident in his tone.

"To give you orders from the Grand Gatekeeper himself," the man called "LS" answered.

#

Abandoned Shipwreck, Crater Shore North, Kansai Prefecture; State of Japan. August 12, 2030; 1530 hours (Japan Standard Time)

Shireen approached the "living quarters" of the shipwreck she and her Korean "mercenaries" were using. Seeing them eat and sleep, she knocked on the nearest metal wall she could find.

"Listen, everyone!" Shireen shouted. "I've heard that our target has left Mexico. She will arrive at Yao Airport tonight. I need someone to accompany me to Yao Airport."

"I'll go," the man she talked with the previous day said as he raised his right hand."

"Daleun salam?"

Another man raised his hand. Shireen turned to him. "Neo-neun?"

"Hong Ji-seok."

"Then we move out at 2000 hours. No weapons because this is simply for reconnaissance."

Visiting Home

OVR Safehouse, Nishinari Ward, Kansai City, Kansai Prefecture; State of Japan. August 2, 2030; 0630 hours (Japan Standard Time)

N ow awake, Tatiana Ioannovna Tsulukidze began to use her smartphone's SatCom application. She found the message came from her superior, Vyacheslav Leonidovich Puzanov, the Director of the OVR. The message read:

Dobroye utro, "Elizaveta",

You have a mission and this will require that you be picked up by the Studec' tomorrow underneath Osaka Bay like before. It will take you to Nabil'. From there, you'll be taken to an Imperial Air Force plane at Nogliky Airport that will take you to Nizhny Novgorod. I will tell you the details when you appear at my office.

"Nizhny".

I best make my preparations for tomorrow, Tatiana thought.

#

Osaka Bay Park. August 3, 2030; 0400 hours

Tatiana, along with her subordinates Pyotr Stepanovich Chadov and Karim Olegovich Zhakiyanov, arrived at the Osaka Bay Park. As it was still dark, it was frequent for the OVR agents to come here.

Only Tatiana and Zhakiyanov got out of the van, a fourth-generation Stepwgn. Tatiana carried with her a sports bag and wore some of the equipment needed for diving, including an air tank. Zhakiyanov was to accompany her due to his bulk so when they came across the fence, Tatiana put down her bag and briefly jumped to hang on to the fence. Zhakiyanov then rushed to push her into the other side by placing both of his hands on her right foot. He pushed with enough force that Tatiana leaped into the park. After that, Zhakiyanov threw the sports bag to Tatiana. Tatiana then opened the sports bag, finding the other equipment needed for diving. Once she extracted what she needed, she threw the sports bag back at Zhakiyanov.

"Spasibo, Karim," Tatiana said.

"Pozhaluysta," Zhakiyanov replied.

Tatiana rushed toward the water. Zhakiyanov then returned to the Stepwgn with Chadov and they left Tatiana as this was routine for them. Once she reached the shore, Tatiana installed the rest of the diving equipment. After putting on the hood, mask, snorkel, mask, and fins, Tatiana turned her back, sat on her buttocks, and fell into the water.

#

Studec'; Underneath Osaka Bay. 0520 hours

"Kapitan!" Andrey Egorov shouted as he rushed to his captain, Yelena Abramovna Samsonova. "I've just heard from Stárshiy Serzhánt Danylo. He said someone is knocking on the glass bottom door."

"That must be the Grand Duchess," Samsonova deduced. "Order Stárshiy Serzhánt Danylo to open the door and let her in."

"Zametano, Kapitan."

#

0549 hours

Tatiana was now in the control room of the *Studec'*. Both Samsonova and Egorov faced.

"Glad to be working with you again, 'Elizaveta'," Samsonova said.

"You too, Kapitan," Tatiana replied. "How are the NUN submarines?"

"Same as always: watching us but not making a move."

"Do you think today will be different?"

"I hope not."

"Then we need to move fast."

"Zametano."

Underneath the Pacific Ocean. 1059 hours

The *Studec'* exited the gap between the western prefectures of the Kansai region and Shikoku Island. Samsonova, meanwhile, arrived at her intercom and pressed a particular button.

"Attention all hands, this is your captain speaking," Samsonova announced. "After we exit the gap between Kansai and Shikoku, we will turn one hundred degrees to port before using the *Chernyy Marlin*."

#

NUNS *Busan*; Off Uruppu Island, Nemuro Subprefecture, Hokkaido Prefecture. 1315 hours

Casimir Kowalski, the Captain of the *Cheyenne*-class submarine NUNS *Busan*, picked up his intercom. He then pressed the button for the sonar room.

"Conn sonar," Kowalski said.

"Conn aye!" a female voice said rapidly on her end. "Captain, we're picking up a large sonar reading. I might be coming this way."

It must be that "Phantom sub" again, Kowalski thought. *But I have my orders.*

"Acknowledged," Kowalski replied. He then turned to his officers.

"We carry on as usual," Kowalski ordered.

"Aye, skipper," one officer replied.

#

Nabil' Naval Base, Nabil', Nogliki Volost, Nogliksky Uyezd, Sakhalin Governorate; Eurasian Tsardom. August 4, 2030; 1518 hours (Sakhalin Time)

The *Studec'* arrived at Nabil'. This was one of the three naval bases for the Imperial Eurasian Navy's Pacific Fleet; the other two being Petropavlovsk-Kamchatsky and Vilyuchinsk in the Kamchatka Peninsula. By contrast, the naval base in Nabil' was new. This naval base was built because the Imperial Eurasian Navy was in need of a forward base if in the event of a campaign to take the southern half of Sakhalin Island dominated by the Russian Soviet Federative Socialist Republic. A notable reason why this naval base was built was to accommodate facilities for maintenance of the Pacific Fleet's submarines due to the destruction of the Bechevinka facility in the Kamchatka Peninsula during the Third World War. As a result, Nabil''s economy thrived from local tourists and those from countries that have diplomatic relations with the Eurasian Tsardom. Once the *Studec'* docked, Tatiana got off while carrying her buoyancy compensator as if it were a backpack. Upon stepping onto Eurasian soil, she saw two men approach her.

"Glad you made it, 'Elizaveta'," one man said. "Please follow us. Your plane's waiting at Nogliki Airport."

"Spasibo," Tatiana replied.

#

Nogliki Airport, Nogliki. 1733 hours

Tatiana and the two men that picked her up at Nabil' arrived at Nogliki Airport. Unlike Nabil', Nogliki was a target of an air strike by United States Navy aircraft during the Third World War. Mercifully, the target was only the oil facilities in Nogliki and that conventional weapons were used. When northern Sakhalin Island was annexed by the Eurasian Tsardom during the Reunification War, the Gatekeepers of Knowledge not only assisted with the reconstruction of the oil facilities but also helped turn the urban locality into a small city. The airport was a part of this process.

The plane that was to take Tatiana to Nizhny Novgorod was an Imperial Eurasian Aerospace Force An-74 transport aircraft that was built for VIP (Very Important Person) transportation. A variant of the An-72 that was originally built to be used in harsh weather conditions. The Third World War changed that when many who were able to flee the Soviet Union during the war made off with most of the An-72s and some An-74s. The survival of this line of transport aircraft was only possible when Ivan Vladimirovich Tsulukidze's forces captured all facilities that belonged to the Antonov Design Bureau during the Reunification War. While the line was resurrected, all future iterations were designated "An-74".

Once Tatiana neared the An-74, a woman wearing a VKK-6 flight suit rushed to her. Tatiana stopped as soon as the woman saluted her.

"Are you 'Elizaveta'?" the woman asked.

"Da," Tatiana answered.

"Stárshiy Leytenánt Gulnaz Nurbekovna Boldjurova. Please follow me inside."

"Spasibo."

#

OVR Headquarters, Nizhegorodsky District, Imperial Capital of Nizhny Novgorod. 1106 hours (Novgorod Time)

Tatiana now arrived at the office of the OVR's Director, Vyacheslav Leonidovich Puzanov. "Glad you made it, Gospazitza Tsulukidze," Puzanov said with sarcasm evident in his tone.

"I apologize, Director," Tatiana replied. "I needed to rest after my flight. I left the hotel at 1300 hours but I needed a meal first before coming here."

"I understand. As I promised, I will tell you the full details of the mission. Please sit."

Puzanov immediately gestured to the seat in front of his desk. Tatiana sat down in response.

"Now then, your mission this time is to take Vladimir Nikolayevich Mirov with you back to Japan," Puzanov resumed.

"Why him?" Tatiana asked.

"After Iron Dutchman Services' appearance in the Iran Governorate, we realized that if we wish to defeat them the next time we have to fight them, we must know how they operate. Leytenánt Mirov will be staying with you, of course. You're to pick him up at the Sevastopol Base and after that, you're to help him infiltrate Kansai City."

"Does he know how to dive?"

"He's with the Naval Infantry. He's trained to do so."

"Very well. Should I go to Sevastopol now?"

"Net. I must inform Contre-Admiral Khachikian first. At most, you can go to Sevastopol tomorrow."

"Zametano."

"Before I dismiss you, why don't you visit the Kremlin?"

"Excuse me?"

"Your parents just got back from their annual trip to their *dacha* in the Tajik Governorate. Will you at least find time to visit?"

"I'll think about."

"I'll start calling Contre-Admiral Khachikian as soon as you leave. He'll assist with getting you somewhere to stay while you're in Sevastopol." Tatiana then stood and while Puzanov looked, his left eye caught a glance of a certain file. He gulped as he saw Tatiana no longer facing him.

"Wait!" Puzanov shouted. "There's one thing I should give to you before you go."

Tatiana then faced Puzanov again. "What is it?" she asked.

#

Nizhny Novgorod Kremlin. 1340 hours

Tatiana was now inside the Nizhny Novgorod Kremlin, specifically the Kremlin Palace found in the Kremlin's southwest. For Tatiana, she wasn't to treat it as home as she was born before it was built and only lived there until she was sent to a boarding school for girls. The palace was built from 1992 until 1999 as it was built on the grounds of the former Transfiguration Cathedral that once stood in that portion of the Kremlin until it was turned into the House of Soviets in 1931. When Tsar Ivan Vladimirovich Tsulukidze opted to make the entire Kremlin his seat of power, he began to eliminate all traces of Soviet influence save for the military equipment that served as exhibits. The House of Soviets was the primary target, and Ivan opted to build a palace in its place. Prior to her adolescence, Tatiana grew up watching the palace being built and despite her reluctance, she took what little free time she was given, especially now, to explore the palace.

She then passed a woman who worked as a maid. While Tatiana paid little thought other than getting out of her way, the other woman briefly stopped just as Tatiana resumed moving.

"Tatiana, is that you?" the woman asked; her voice making Tatiana pause.

"Mat'?" Tatiana asked upon turning to see the woman remove her hood. This woman was Tatiana's mother, Tsarina Consort Yekaterina Borisovna Tsulukidze (née Afonina). Seventy years old, Yekaterina had gray hair, very light skin, and gray eyes. Despite the differing hair color, Tatiana was a spitting image of her mother in her youth.

"Da," Yekaterina replied. "What are you doing here?"

"Work. Director Puzanov recommended that I visit before I leave tomorrow."

"Where are you going after this?"

"Sevastopol. That's all I can tell you."

"I understand. Will you join us for dinner tonight?"

"Tonight?"

"Please. Your father would desperately want to see you since you're here."

"Very well. But dinner only."

#

1920 hours

Tsar Ivan Vladimirovich Tsulukidze arrived at the dinner table. Upon seeing Tatiana home, he stopped and widened his eyes.

"Tatiana, what are you doing here?" Ivan asked.

"Mother asked me the same thing hours ago," Tatiana answered. "I came here because Director Puzanov gave me an assignment. I'm only here at Mother's urging, so after this, I must leave tomorrow as a part of that assignment."

"Of course. I must not get in the way of your duty after all."

"Enough of that," Yekaterina complained. "Ivan, please sit down."

"Zametano," Ivan replied before sitting down, unaware of the silent giggle her daughter made. Once she heard Ivan move his chair, she stopped.

Both Yekaterina and Tatiana did the Sign of the Cross, yet Ivan watched as this was his wife and daughter saying Grace before the meal. Once they finished, Yekaterina and Tatiana did the Sign of the Cross again. All ate afterward.

#

Sevastopol Air Base, Belbek, Sevastopol Volost, Crimea Uyezd, Ukraine Governorate. August 5, 2030; 1000 hours (Kiev Time)

Tatiana was now in Sevastopol. Despite its name, Sevastopol Air Base was located in the village of Belbek as it was close to Sevastopol. The runaway used by this base was also used by the civilian Sevastopol International Airport. This was the result of Tsar Ivan opting to have a civilian airport built. That allowed the air base to be used while civilian airliners appeared.

Once Tatiana exited the An-74, she found two infantrymen from the Imperial Eurasian Navy approaching her. "I assume you'll take me to Contre-Admiral Khachikian?" Tatiana asked.

"Da," the Naval Infantryman replied. "Please follow us."

#

Sevastopol Naval Base. 1150 hours

Tatiana now sat alone on a chair in the office of Levon Samvelovich Khachikian, the commander of the Black Sea Flotilla of the Imperial Eurasian Navy's South Seas Squadron. However, Tatiana was only aware of the Sevastopol mentioned in history, as the current-day city was a casualty of the Third World War. Sevastopol Base, the destination of the *Loshad'* Tatiana rode on, was the cause and the result of the city being a target.

During the Third World War, the city was a target because of the naval base it hosted. As a result, the city was struck by a nuclear weapon with the focus on the naval base. As a result, Sevastopol Bay, which hosted the naval base along with the city's civilian port, was geographically changed because of the damage wrought by the nuclear warhead that fell into the base. Both were only rebuilt with assistance from the Gatekeepers of Knowledge, with the new naval base serving as the headquarters of the Black Sea Flotilla.

Khachikian himself just entered his office with Tatiana standing up as he began to face her. "Glad you made," Khachikian said. "Please sit." Tatiana immediately complied.

"I assume you know why I'm here?" Tatiana asked.

"Da," Khachikian answered. "Unfortunately, Leytenánt Mirov is busy training the cadets and after that, he'll need to eat. I can imagine you came here without having lunch. Neither did I. How about we eat lunch together until we can summon Leytenánt Mirov to this office?"

"Good idea."

#

1347 hours

As it was hours before, Khachikian was at his desk with Tatiana seated in front of him. It was then that Vladimir Nikolayevich Mirov appeared. Once he closed the door, Khachikian stood up with Mirov saluting him. Khachikian saluted in return.

"You called for me, Admiral?" Mirov asked.

"Da," Khachikian answered. "I have a mission for you, but our guest will be the one to explain it to you.

"Guest?" Tatiana reared her head to face Mirov, shocking the latter in the process.

"Y- You're-"

"She came as an OVR operative. You're to call her 'Elizaveta' for the duration of this mission."

"Zametano."

"Now please get a chair and sit on it."

Mirov found another chair and began to get it, allowing Tatiana to stand up and move her chair to her left, but she positioned it facing her right. Once she moved and sat down again, Mirov positioned his chair where

Tatiana's chair was positioned earlier. Seeing Tatiana facing him, Mirov understood why without speaking and positioned his chair facing Tatiana. He then sat down.

"Before I explain my mission, you must make sure this information must not leave this room," Tatiana ordered. "Is that understood?"

"Zametano," Mirov replied.

"Then let's begin. I came here today in relation to your failure in eliminating the mercenary group Iron Dutchman Services when they assisted the Brotherhood of Freedom in the Iran Governorate."

"Y… You came here because of that?"

"Da. You're to accompany me back to Japan, where I lead an OVR cell. There, you are to secretly spy on one particular member. I have a file here you must read. However, this is eyes only."

"Zametano."

Tatiana then brought out the file Puzanov gave to her the previous day. As he grabbed and opened it, Mirov saw that the paper in the file had a picture of Tarou Ganji. He read it twice with Tatiana and Khachikian watching. Once Mirov finished, he slovenly lowered his arms with the right arm still carrying the file, but with how he moved them, it was only a matter of time before the file fell.

"This boy, he's-" Mirov said incompletely.

"Surprising, isn't it?" Tatiana asked. "Now give me the file."

"… Right." Mirov gathered enough strength to move his arms. He then pushed his right arm toward Tatiana with the file in hand. Tatiana then took the file from Mirov's right hand.

"I… I can't believe the man who killed my students in Sakhalin and who defeated me in Iran was none other than a teenage boy… " Mirov said with horror evident in his tone.

"I was surprised too when I read that file," Tatiana replied. "The boy was assigned to keep an eye on Maria Hoshikawa because of his age. We don't know why, but that could mean NUN's FIS is aware of my cell in Japan."

"Either way," Khachikian interrupted, making Mirov and Tatiana face him. "this mission is simply reconnaissance." Khachikian then focused his attention on Mirov. "Leytenánt Mirov, you're to accompany 'Elizaveta' back to Japan and you'll be instructed to spy on this Tarou Ganji. This is to be of great help the next time we fight these mercenaries."

"But how long must I do this?" Mirov asked. "Won't we be detected if we approach Japan?"

"I've taken that risk many times," Tatiana answered. "The only thing that's changed recently is that they now know about the *Vyšen'* submarines. Luckily, they're just watching us. Now, as to how long we need you in Japan, three days at least."

"If this mission is to be kept amongst ourselves, what should I tell my subordinates?"

"I have an idea about that," Khachikian answered. "Before that, we need to discuss where you'll be staying for tonight."

#

1410 hours

Both Mirov and Tatiana, in their respective seats, were now located on the left side of Khachikian's office. The door then opened, with Mirov standing up and rushing to stand beside Khachikian. Two men and a woman also wearing Imperial Eurasian Naval Infantry uniforms, Giorgi Paatovich Kipiani, Talgat Aibekovich Yusupov, and Nadezhda Anatolyevna Aslanov, entered the office. Once the door was closed, they saluted Khachikian with the admiral saluting in kind.

Both Kipiani and Yusupov had light skin, light brown eyes, and buzz cuts, but had other differing features. The former had an average build and brown hair, and the latter had a stout physique and black hair. Aslanova had very light skin, auburn hair, and blue eyes.

"Glad you made it," Khacikian said. "Leytenánt Mirov summoned you here to tell you that he has been given an assignment only he can accomplish alone."

"Alone?" Aslanova asked.

"Da," Mirov answered. "Our guest here will explain."

Mirov then gestured at Tatiana, who began to stand up. Kipiani, Yusupov, and Aslanova turned to see their guest approach the admiral's desk.

Grand Duchess Tatiana is the guest? Aslanova pondered. *What's she doing here?*

Tatiana stopped at Khachikian's left. "I can imagine one of you knows who I am, but for the sake of this mission, you must call me 'Elizaveta'. Is that understood?"

"Zametano," Kipiani, Yusupov, and Aslanova replied in unison.

"Also, this discussion must not leave this room."

"Zametano."

"Good. I'll be taking Leytenánt Mirov with me on a mission that will require him to infiltrate Japan by himself. As you can guess with the name 'Elizaveta', I'm with the OVR and that I'm in command of the OVR cell Leytenánt Mirov will be assigned to. As to why Leytenánt Mirov is to come with me, he is to conduct reconnaissance on Iron Dutchman Services."

"Wait, did you say 'Iron Dutchman Services'?" Kipiani asked.

"Da," Tatiana answered. "Everything Leytenánt Mirov will learn while he's with me in Japan will help the next time all four of you will have to fight the mercenary group the next time you encounter them."

"And how will that help?" Yusupov asked. "With all due respect, the pilot of that silver Shagokhod damaged our Shagokhods that they're still being repaired."

"That's exactly why Director Puzanov explicitly asked for Leytenánt Mirov," Tatiana answered. "He's the commander, so it falls upon him to learn from the mercenaries. I assure you that we will only keep him with us for three days at the least."

"Why Japan?" Aslanova asked.

"I'm prepared to tell you, but you must not keep this to yourselves. Is that understood?"

"Zametano."

"Then allow me to explain," Mirov said. He began by summarizing everything he read from the file Tatiana showed to him earlier. This widened the eyes of his three subordinates.

"So all of this started because the Wolves of Turkmenia were hired to kidnap this Maria Hoshikawa and that the brief war we had with the Asian Pact was a result of this?" Aslanova incredulously asked.

"I didn't believe it either," Mirov answered. "However, no one actually knows why all of that happened in Sakhalin Island. The FIS have only kept those mercenaries around Gospazitza Hoshikawa to figure out who hired the Wolves of Turkmenia to kidnap her and why."

"Adding to the mystery is that silver Shagokhod," Kipiani added. "How could a teenage boy use a Shagokhod like that?"

"That's why I'm undertaking this mission," Mirov answered. "I wish to know myself."

"I understand," Aslanova replied.

"Do what you have to do, Leytenánt," Kipiani added. "We can use what you learn to make that Tarou Ganji pay a hundredfold for humiliating us back in Iran."

"When will you leave?" Yusupov asked.

"Tomorrow," Tatiana sternly answered.

"Why don't we go out together for a night in the city before Leytenánt Mirov leaves?" Kipiani cheerfully answered.

"But we don't have enough money," Aslanova argued. "Even if we pool in all our money, we wouldn't have enough for a taxi in the event most, if not all of us, get drunk."

"I'll contribute," Tatiana replied.

"You will?" Mirov asked.

"Let her, Leytenánt," Kipiani answered. "It's not every day a child of the Tsar will treat us commoners to a night out."

Khachikian forced a cough; everyone knew what that entailed. "I assume that is all?" he asked.

"Da," everyone replied in unison.

"Wait, I'll need to ask for your numbers," Tatiana requested as she brought out her smartphone. "I need to find a place to stay for tonight, then I'll inform you as to where and when to meet up for dinner. However, this is only for tonight, because I will delete your numbers tomorrow."

Everyone complied with Tatiana's request. Mirov was the first to use Tatiana's phone to give his number. He then gave it to Kipiani and after he gave his number, Kipiani gave it to Yusupov. After him was Aslanova, who then gave the phone back to Tatiana after she provided her number. "Leytenánt Mirov, Mládshiy Leytenánt Kipiani, Mládshiy Leytenánt Aslanova, Mládshiy Leytenánt Yusupov, you're dismissed," Khachikian added.

Mirov rushed to join his subordinates. Once he stood beside Kipiani, they, along with Yusupov and Aslanova, saluted.

"Zametano," all four said in unison.

#

Privdenna Hostel. 1500 hours

Tatiana now arrived at a hotel that bore the name of the bay that helped make up the civilian port of the city. Once she got off the *Loshad'* used by the two Imperial Eurasian Naval Infantrymen assigned to guard her while she's in Sevastopol, Tatiana proceeded inside the hostel. She then stopped at the concierge.

"Welcome to the Privdenna Hostel," the female concierge announced to Tatiana. "How may I help you?"

"I was given a reservation at this establishment," Tatiana explained. "It's under the name 'Alžbieta Uladzimirovna Kostyukova'."

#

1533 hours

Once Tatiana entered her room, she found the room she was given already occupied. Three women in their late twenties had settled into the room while there was a fourth bed that had yet to be claimed. It was now an awkward situation for both parties as Tatiana was warned beforehand, yet neither she nor Khachikian, who handled the reservation prior to her arrival, knew how old were the girls whom Tatiana had to share the dormitory room with.

"So you're Gospazitza Kostyukova?" a woman with short blonde hair asked.

"Da," Tatiana answered. "And you are?"

"Hania Markovna Smetanina."

A woman wearing glasses over her blue eyes with short brown hair tied in a braid raised her hand, signaling her intent to introduce herself. "Aleksandra Petrovna Sedova."

"Are you from the House of Sedov?"

"I… I am… "

"What's with that question?" a woman with medium-length black hair asked. "We came here to cheer Sasha before her arranged marriage. Also, my name is Arpi Gareginovna Galstyana."

"My apologies. My business does involve dealing with the nobility," Tatiana replied.

"Why are you here?" Savarynova asked.

"Visiting relatives. I'm staying here for the night because tomorrow, I'll be returning to Nizhny Novgorod tomorrow."

"What is it that do you do?" Sedova asked.

"I'm a paralegal for Golitsyn Luxury Goods."

"That's interesting," Galstyana commented. "Please, make yourself at home."

"Spasibo." Tatiana began to settle on her bed. Once she finished, she brought out her smartphone but seeing that its screensaver was a picture of her surrounded by two men and another woman, Tatiana looked around. She turned to her left and after going through her phone's password, she went to the phone's clock application. She then set a timer that would go off at two hours. By the time she finished and laid her phone to her left so that no one would see it, she found Galstyana approaching her. Once Tatiana turned to Galstyana, the latter froze once the former spotted her.

"I… Sorry about this," Galstyana replied.

"You have something to ask, don't you?" Tatiana asked.

"How long will you be here in Sevastopol?"

"Until tomorrow morning. I apologize if my presence is causing you some problems."

"Not really… " Galstyana briefly glanced at Aleksandra. Unbeknownst to the former, Tatiana also glanced at Aleksandra until Galstyana stopped and resumed looking at Tatiana. "We had a friend who had to change rooms because you were hastily given this room."

"What's her name?" Tatiana asked, hiding her suspicion about Galstyana glancing at Aleksandra.

"Alla Arkhipovna Utkina. Be thankful her boyfriend joined us because she can stay with him."

"Again, I apologize."

"It's alright. Speaking of which, what were you doing earlier?"

"I plan on taking a nap for two hours, so I set an alarm. I intend to treat the relatives I talked about to dinner tonight."

#

Punjab Foods. 1800 hours

"Why are we eating at a Punjab Foods?" Kipiani asked as he, Mirov, Aslanova, Yusupov, and Tatiana appeared at an Indian restaurant named Punjab Foods. "I just ate here yesterday."

"I said I would help pay, so consider my choice as to where we're eating to be payment," Tatiana said. "Besides, I wanted to go here yesterday."

"Zametano."

"Though why are we eating now?" Aslanova asked.

"I'm to leave early tomorrow," Tatiana answered. "So quit wasting time and let's go."

Returning to Japan

Sevastopol Air Base, Belbek, Sevastopol Volost, Crimea Uyezd, Ukraine Governorate; Eurasian Tsardom. August 5, 2030; 0830 hours (Kiev Time)

Tatiana Ioannovna Tsulukidze, Vladimir Nikolayevich Mirov, Giorgi Paatovich Kipiani, Talgat Aibekovich Yusupov, and Nadezhda Anatolyevna Aslanova were brought to Sevastopol Air Base. The An-74 transport plane that brought Tatiana to Sevastopol Volost was prepared to fly with its captain Gulnaz Nurbekovna Boldjurova waiting by the left side ramp already laid for Tatiana and Mirov to use.

"Mládshiy Leytenánt Aslanova, I leave the training to you," Mirov said to Aslanova.

"Zametano, Leytenánt," Aslanova replied.

"I must get going now. Do svidaniya." Mirov saluted with his subordinates saluting in kind.

He and Tatiana immediately boarded the An-74. Boldjurova followed and once she was inside, she closed the ramp.

#

Imperial Eurasian Aerospace Force An-74; Above Voronezh Governorate. 1149 hours (Novgorod Time)

"Have you decided on what you'll be ordering?" Tatiana asked while holding a large piece of paper wrapped in plastic while looking at Mirov, who also held the same piece.

"Da," Mirov answered. "More importantly, it doesn't appear to be that we're going east." Mirov turned to his left to the window beside the table where he and Tatiana were seated at.

"That's why I asked about your order. We're going to Nizhny Novgorod for supplies. Our respective orders will be among those supplies needed for the rest of the flight, which required a stopover at Nizhny Novgorod because if we fly straight from Sevastopol to Nogliki, that will require flying above the People's Republic of China longer than needed."

"I apologize. Please give me one more minute."

As a soldier at heart, he seems more accustomed to rations, Tatiana thought.

#

Above the Bashkotorstan Governorate. 1728 hours (Yekaterinburg Time)

Both Tatiana and Mirov had finished their respective lunches. Mirov simply watched in silence as Tatiana said Grace after the meal. After doing the Sign of the Cross, she faced Mirov.

"Leytenánt, what could you tell me about your fight with Tarou Ganji?" Tatiana asked.

"Why is an OVR agent asking me this?" Mirov asked in response.

"This is off the record. I just want to know how you were able to survive that fight because that silver Walgear used by Ganji is capable of destroying an entire team by itself."

"Might I please know what will you do with what will come out of my mouth?"

"Nothing. I simply wish to know how you survived."

"Very well. Listen properly."

#

Studec'; Nabil' Naval Base, Nabil', Nogliki Volost, Nogliksky Uyezd, Sakhalin Governorate. August 6, 2030; 0748 hours (Sakhalin Time)

"An honor to meet the 'Lighning Baron'," Yelena Abramova Samsonova said after Tatiana and Mirov arrived at the bridge of the *Studec'*; her words focused on Mirov while looking at him. She then gestured to Andrey Egorov. "This is my executive officer Andrey Yevgenyevich Egorov."

"An honor to meet you," Egorov replied.

"He is to accompany me back to Japan," Tatiana declared.

"And how long will that be?" Samsonova asked as she turned to Tatiana.

"Three days at the least."

"Good enough with me. Shall we leave already?"

"Of course," Mirov replied.

"Before I do, I must tell you this important fact about this submarine and those in the same class. Before I even do so, you must swear that you will keep this to yourself when you return to the Tsardom."

"Zametano."

"Then listen carefully about the *Chernyy Marlin*."

#

Underneath the Pacific Ocean. 1059 hours (Japan Standard Time)

"Attention all hands, this is your Captain speaking," Samsonova announced throughout the *Studec*'s PA system. "We will be using the *Chernyy Marlin*. Please find something to hold on to because you will need it. I say again, find something to cling to. This is my last warning."

So it's time, Mirov thought. *Best do as she says.*

Mirov began to lay on his stomach while laying his head on his bed's pillow. After that, he began to cling to the legs below the pillow. He then closed his eyes for what was to come next.

"Activating *Chernyy Marlin* in 3… 2… 1!"

The vibrations began. Mirov desperately held onto the legs below his pillow to avoid falling off his bed. *Does the Grand Duchess always back and forth between Japan and the Tsardom in this manner!?* Mirov thought while he struggled to remain on his bed.

#

1309 hours

After two hours, the vibrations stopped. Although his eyes remained closed, Mirov now felt the lack of vibrations. *It's over?* Mirov pondered before opening his eyes.

As he opened his eyes, the first thing he saw was his pillow. He slowly let go of the legs below and rose his head from the pillow, looking in both directions. After that, he rotate his body so that he can lay on his bed with his back as it should be.

"Thank you for enduring our usage of the *Chernyy Marlin*," Samsonova announced over the PA system. "As soon as it's safe, we will resume our course to Japan. Remain as you are until your bodies are safe to be moved."

I haven't endured this much since my third fight with Tarou Ganji months ago, Mirov thought while he placed his palms on his pillow and pressed his head against them.

#

Near Bushehr Airport, Bushehr, Bushehr Uyezd, Iran Governorate. July 17, 2030; 1724 hours (Tehran Time)

Four Imperial Eurasian Navy SH-6s charged toward Solbein. Vladimir Nikolayevich Mirov led this team. As Mirov and his team got closer, Solbein faced them and charged against them in kind.

"There you are!" Vladimir Mirov shouted as he saw Solbein charging at his SH-6 through the screen of his Walgear's control panel. "Aslanova, move back, stop and fire. Kipiani, divert to the right, Yusupov, divert to the left."

"Zametano," Nadezhda Anatolyevna Aslanova, Giorgi Paatovich Kipiani, and Talgat Aibekovich Yusupov replied in unison.

Having did as ordered, Aslanova, Kipiani, and Yusupov moved to the directions Mirov assigned to them. While Mirov continued moving forward, he fired his SH-6's AKS-74U carbine. Aslanova, Kipiani, and Yusupov followed with their respective Walgears' carbines. Just as when the rounds fired were about to hit Solbein, it jumped to the horror of the four Eurasian Walgear pilots.

Mirov, Kipiani, and Yusupov stopped. However, Aslanova didn't in time as Solbein managed to catch up to her and fired the SH-6's carbine, depriving her Walgear of its primary weapon.

"Nadia!" Kipiani shouted before going back with his SH-6 to help Aslanova.

Upon reaching Solbein, Kipiani fired his Walgear's carbine at Solbein. The attention of the latter was now focused on Kipiani, with its two eyes glowing red.

As Kipiani got close, Solbein jumped again. The former stopped his SH-6 and fired but the silver Walgear was able to evade his shots.

"Nevozmozhno!" Kipiani shouted before Solbein landed in front of his SH-6's right arm.

Before Kipiani could even aim his Walgear's weapon at Solbein, the latter used its right leg for a roundhouse kick, damaging the SH-6's right arm. "That won't stop me!"

Kipiani attempted to use the Strike Knuckle of his SH-6's left arm but Solbein was shot in response. Responsible was Mirov and Talgat Aibekovich Yusupov.

"Help Mládshiy Leytenánt Aslanova!" Mirov ordered in the communicator of Kipiani's cockpit.

"… Da," Kipiani replied.

While Kipiani resumed rushing to Aslanova's SH-6, Solbein charged toward Yusupov's SH-6 yet Mirov followed and fired. Yusupov continued to move back and fire, even if meant wasting ammunition.

Through his cockpit's monitor, Mirov saw how Solbein continuously evaded Yusupov's shots. *Whoever's inside cannot be human!* Mirov thought until he saw 30x210mmB rounds through his monitor, forcing him to evade.

However, Mirov now saw that Solbein neared Yusupov's SH-6 and fired his Walgear's carbine in response. This caused Solbein to charge toward Mirov instead. While Mirov reversed and fired, Solbein jumped to evade.

NOW! Mirov shouted in his mind before turning and while turning, he aimed his Walgear's AKS-74U again. Mirov then pressed the trigger that allowed the Walgear to do the same but upon doing so, Solbein jumped again in the middle of the air to evade the 30x210mmB rounds.

That can't be possible! Mirov thought as he saw what happened before his very eyes through his cockpit's monitor. Once Solbein landed, an SH-6 rushed toward it but Solbein threw it aside. Through his monitor, Mirov saw that the SH-6 was missing its left arm yet it was empty.

But who- Mirov thought until he heard someone shout Yusupov's name.

Mirov now saw two fully intact SH-6s charge toward Solbein. "Kipiani, Yusupov, what are you doing!?" Mirov shouted.

"Got Aslanova to get out while I took her SH-6," Kipiani answered over the communicator in response. "Leytenánt, get to a safe distance and aim! Yusupov and I will keep this demon busy!"

Rather than pull rank, Mirov rushed to find somewhere to aim his AKS-74U against Solbein. However, as he got the carbine for his Walgear, he saw that neither Yusupov nor Kipiani were able to hold off Solbein for long as he saw the latter grab the right arm of Yusupov's SH-6 and the left arm of Aslanova's SH-6. It didn't take long for Solbein to rip both arms off, forcing Yusupov and Kipiani to eject.

Mirov then saw a discarded AKS-74U and rushed to it. Meanwhile, Kipiani and Yusupov continued to fight despite their respective SH-6s missing an arm. Despite their efforts, Solbein always evaded their respective blows until it hit, forcing everyone to stop and see that Mirov fired the shot with his SH-6's left arm using the other AKS-74U it picked up.

"Yusupov, Kipiani, eject at once!" Mirov ordered. "I'll finish this!"

"But Leytená-" Kipiani pleaded.

"Eto poryadok!"

Both Yusupov and Kipiani ejected from their respective SH-6s. Immediately afterward, Mirov tossed the carbine he picked up in front of Solbein.

"Pick it up!" Mirov demanded toward Solbein while using his SH-6's speakers. "Now we'll finish this fair and square."

Although he expected it, Mirov heard nothing from Solbein's pilot, Tarou Ganji, while watching Solbein pick up the carbine. *He's still picking up the AKS-74U despite how he fought earlier,* Mirov thought. *Who are you and how could you fight like this?*

As soon as Solbein now carried the AKS-74U, Mirov was the first move and aim but to his horror, Solbein moved faster than he did and as Mirov found out too late, Solbein appeared behind Mirov's SH-6 and fired first, hitting the left arm of Mirov's left forearm just as the latter attempted to block the shots. While the rest of the Walgear survived, the SH-6 was unable to use its left arm, yet it didn't matter to Mirov. He continued firing but Solbein evaded and after that, Solbein fired. This time, Mirov evaded.

I don't have an advantage if we keep fighting like this, Mirov thought.

"Y... You're pretty good... " Mirov said while looking at the screen of his Walgear's control panel as it showed the damaged Solbein. "How about we toss aside our rifles and resort to our Strike Knuckles?"

Without saying a word, Tarou managed to remove Solbein's carbine. Mirov followed with his SH-6's AKS-74U.

Mirov then made his first move by using the Strike Knuckle of his Walgear's right hand, but as he made his strike, Solbein evaded. The latter used his Walgear's right Strike Knuckle in response but the former evaded it.

Impressive, Mirov thought. *Ganji can still fight despite the damages his Walgear sustained.*

Solbein struck again but Mirov not only evaded, but used the Strike Knuckle of his Walgear's left hand. Solbein turned and used his Walgear's left Strike Knuckle to intercept the Strike Knuckle of Mirov's SH-6.

It now became a battle of willpower. Both Solbein and Mirov's SH-6 pushed their respective Strike Knuckles against each other, but they knew that their respective Walgears were at their limit, especially with the damage the left arm of Mirov's Walgear sustained. Solbein, however, continued to push its left fist further, increasing the damage of the SH-6's left arm.

Solbein again punched Mirov's Walgear, but this time, he used Solbein's right Strike Knuckle. The electric discharged disabled the electronics of Mirov's SH-6 and just as when Tarou attempted another punch with Solbein's left Strike Knuckle, the Walgear stopped.

So it's come to this, Mirov thought while he closed his eyes. *Maybe I can meet my maker.*

However, he heard many sounds but none were of explosions. He still saw the darkness of his cockpit.

#

Studec'; Underneath the Pacific Ocean. August 6, 2030; 1334 hours (Japan Standard Time)

A knock on the left rear leg of Mirov's bed in the present forced him to wake up. After being startled, Mirov saw that it was Tatiana Ioannovna Tsulukidze waking him up.

"Now that you awake, the Captain is calling for the both of us to see her at the wardroom," Tatiana said. "Now get up."

"Z… Zametano," Mirov replied.

#

1343 hours

Both Mirov and Tatiana arrived at the wardroom of the *Studec'*. All officers of the submarine were now gathered. The former two saluted, with the latter standing up and saluting in return.

"At ease," Yelena Abramovna Samsonova ordered with Mirov and Tatiana complying. "Now please sit."

"Zametano," Mirov and Tatiana replied in unison before finding two empty chairs near Andrey Yevgenyevich Egorov and sitting on those chairs.

"Please be patient with the food," Samsonova added. "The cooking only started as soon as I gave the order to resume going to Japan."

Everyone replied with a "Zametano". "Now then," Samsonova continued before turning to Mirov. "Leytenánt Mirov, I must ask: do you know how to dive?"

"Da," Mirov answered.

"Good. I'll order Stárshiy Serzhánt Danylo to let you borrow his diving suit when we reach Osaka Bay."

"What are we having for today?" Tatiana asked.

"Rassolnik," Samsonova answered. "It'll take thirty minutes for it to be prepared."

"Eto khorosho."

Samsonova then resumed looking at Mirov. "Leytenánt, I know 'Elizaveta' told you not to tell anything about why she's taking you with her to Japan, but I must ask: what will you do after your mission?" she asked.

"Go back to training cadets in Wa- I mean, Shagokhod fighting," Mirov answered.

"That's good. We could use more people like you."

"Leytenánt Mirov, I have a question," Egorov interjected.

"Da?" Mirov asked as he faced Egorov.

"Why did you become a Shagokhod pilot? Did your father try to-"

Mirov, however, looked down at his portion of the table. Everyone else stared at Egorov, with the latter realizing what was happening. He widened his eyes as to why and turned back to Mirov.

"Mne zhal'," Egorov said. This made Mirov face him.

"It's alright," Mirov replied. "It's just… I didn't want to talk about my father."

"Again, I apologize. Though why did you become a Shagokhod pilot?"

"I liked the machine. Therefore, as soon as I heard about the SH-6, I applied to be one of its test pilots. Then we invaded Iran."

This is the second time I encountered someone dealing with a past too difficult to be open with, Tatiana thought as she attempted to listen to Mirov's tale. *Reminds me of what Galstyana and I talked about in Sevastopol.*

#

Privdenna Hostel, Sevastopol, Sevastopol Volost, Crimea Uyezd, Ukraine Governorate; Eurasian Tsardom. August 5, 2030; 1733 hours (Kiev Time)

With her smartphone ringing, Tatiana got up. Upon grabbing it, she turned off the smartphone's timer. She then began to text Vladimir Nikolayevich Mirov and his subordinates. Her message read:

"Meet me at the Punjab Foods near the naval base."

She then pressed "Otpravlyat'". After that, she began to exit the room with Arpi Gareginovna Galstyana, sleeping beside Aleksandra Petrovna Sedova, noticing.

"Seeing your relatives?" Galstyana asked.

"Da," Tatiana answered as she stopped. Unbeknownst to Galstyana, the former glanced at the latter at the bed of Aleksandra. "My suspicions are correct."

Tatiana's words made Galstyana gulp. *What suspicions?* Galstyana desperately pondered. "I… What are you talking ab-"

"We can talk about this outside the hostel. If you wish."

#

1741 hours

Both Tatiana and Galstyana were now outside the hostel. "You're in love with Sedova, aren't you?" Tatiana asked.

"W… What are you talking about?" Galstyana asked.

"I can tell by the way you talked to me before you introduced yourself. Then you were sleeping at Sedova's bed."

"I… " Galstyana then sighed, realizing there was nothing else she could say to hide her real feelings. "I'm not sure if I could call it 'love'. I do, however, find it uncomfortable that Aleks had to marry a man."

"When did you and Sedova first meet?"

"When my parents used to work for the House of Sedova. She was a lonely girl and therefore, I became her friend. That didn't last as my family had to move out to find work after her parents died and that her uncle became the Baron of Sedov. When we met again in tertiary school, her uncle had Aleks engaged because the man he chose for her is from the House of Volkonsky."

And such an arrangement is because Baron Advey is in debt and became the Baron of Sedov because he's the younger brother of the previous Baron, the previous Baron not having any sons, and neither does Baron Advey, Tatiana thought before resuming her discussion with Galstyana. "I have an idea, but it's incredibly risky."

"What is it?" Galstyana asked.

"I need to whisper it to you first. The Okhrana could be listening. Even watching."

"Go to my right ear." Tatiana raced to Galstyana's right ear and whispered. The latter stood in surprise the longer the former whispered, yet the two Imperial Eurasian Naval Infantrymen who are to take Tatiana wherever she wishes to go were unable to figure out what Tatiana and Galstyana were talking about as this was why Tatiana resorted to whispering. She remained that way even after Tatiana stopped.

"But won't the Ohkrana stop us if we attempted that?" Galstyana argued.

"I know some people who've done it," Tatiana retorted. "You just need to plan it well. In fact, allow me to help. But promise me you will keep this to yourself and Sedova."

"And how can you help?"

Tatiana then returned to Galstyana's right ear whispered again. Everything that came out of the former's mouth was more shocking for the latter to hear, even after Tatiana finished whispering.

"Y… You're joking, right?" Galstyana desperately asked.

"Net," Tatiana answered bluntly. "In fact, I came here to Sevastopol, and that is all I am going to tell you. Hold on."

Tatiana then brought out a memo pad and a ball pen. She wrote quickly, much to Tatiana's curiosity. Once Tatiana finished, she gave the note to Galstyana.

"Use that number if you are interested," Tatiana said. "Now, if you excuse me, I have 'relatives' to go to."

#

Studec'; Underneath the Pacific Ocean. August 6, 2030; 1405 hours (Japan Standard Time)

"Gotovo!" a cook shouted in the wardroom of the *Studec'* as he appeared with a tray filled with food and water. This ended Tatiana's reminiscing of the previous two days.

The cook began to distribute the *Rassolnik* stew he prepared and glasses of water. Yelena Abramova Samsonova and Andrey Yevgenyevich Egorov were the first to receive their respective bowls filled with *Rassolnik* stew and glasses of water. While the cook continued to distribute, everyone who received their stew and water waited until everyone else at the table has a bowl and a glass. Even when the cook had yet to leave, the officers waited. Only when he left did they begin with a prayer. After that, they began eating their stew.

#

Underneath Osaka Bay. 1755 hours

"Good, you made it," Samsonova said in her chair as she noticed Tatiana and Mirov arriving in the *Studec*'s bridge. "I called you up here because we're near Kansai City."

"When do we make preparations?" Tatiana asked.

"Soon. I need Stárshiy Serzhánt Danylo to prepare his diving suit for Leytenánt Mirov to use. Also, you'll have to wait a little while longer because it's too early to appear in Osaka Bay Park at this time, is it not?"

"Agreed," Tatiana and Mirov replied in unison.

"Just go back to your respective beds for the time being. I'll have Stárshiy Serzhánt Danylo himself notify you when you two can launch."

"When it is time, might I please be allowed to contact my men?" Tatiana requested.

"But that will require surfacing," Samsonova argued until she sighed, understanding why Tatiana made her request. "Very well, I'll surface to allow you to use SatCom. But only when I say it's time to launch."

"Spasibo."

"Now return to the officers' cabins."

#

OVR Safehouse, Nishinari Ward, Kansai City, Kansai Prefecture; State of Japan. August 7, 2030; 0100 hours

"Zhakiyanov, vstavat'!" Pyotr Stepanovich Chadov shouted as he knocked on a door. This didn't last long as he heard the doorknob move, making him stop. As he moved backward, he saw Karim Olegovich Zhakiyanov open the door.

"Chto eto?" a drowsy Zhakiyanov asked.

"I received a call from the Grand Duchess," Zhakiyanov warned. "She'll be at Osaka Bay Park. We have to pick her up now!"

"Hold on. I need to wash my face first, then dress up."

"I need to dress, too. I'll take you to the bathroom."

#

Studec'; Underneath Osaka Bay. 0256 hours

"Ready?" Artem Viktorovich Danylo asked as he and his Imperial Eurasian Naval Infantry *Spetsnaz* unit looked at Tatiana and Mirov, both wearing diving gear. Out of Danylo's unit, only Dahlia Vadzimirovna Kaminskaya was also dressed in diving gear.

"Da," Tatiana and Mirov replied in unison.

"Popov, open the door," Danylo ordered to his subordinate Popov.

"Zametano, Serzhánt," Popov replied.

#

Osaka Bay Park, Taisho Ward, Kansai City, Kansai Prefecture; State of Japan. 0400 hours

Using night vision binoculars, Pyotr Stepanovich Chadov saw an arm rising in the middle of Osaka Bay. He then lowered a ladder behind him and placed in front of him while holding it. The hand he saw then reached the ladder. Another hand then grabbed it, allowing the owner of the hands to start climbing and getting near enough, used the left hand to cling to Japanese soil and immediately used the other hand to cling further. The diver then moved the arms further into Japan and once far into Osaka Bay Park, the diver jumped and was able to land despite being wet. The diver began to remove the mask and snorkel, making Chadov see that it was Tatiana Ioannovna Tsulukidze, whom he helped.

"Glad you're back," Chadov replied.

"Spasibo," Tatiana replied. "What about the man I said that will be joining us?"

"He should be- He's touched the ladder," Chadov said upon seeing another diver, whom he now knew as Vladimir Nikolayevich Mirov, grabbing the ladder.

"I'll get out of the diving gear. Also, someone from the Naval Infantry Spetsnaz is with us. She'll get Leytenánt Mirov's gear after he climbs into Japan."

"Zametano."

#

OVR Safehouse, Nishinari Ward. 0455 hours

"So this is where you operate?" Mirov, now in a plain white shirt, black pants, and black boots, asked as he, Tatiana, Chadov, and Zhakiyanov asked as they entered the safehouse used by the latter three.

"Da," Tatiana answered. "And for the next two days, you will be living here. Do as we say and no one will get into trouble."

"And how long have you been here?"

"Three years," Chadov answered. "We pretended to be defectors from the Soviet Remnant. We work as couriers that deliver anything, no matter who the client is. The money we earn from these jobs gets us food and clothing."

"And I imagine you three were able to learn Japanese?" Mirov asked.

"Da," Tatiana answered. "Later, you'll have to spend the rest of the day doing so. For now, get some sleep."

"Zametano," Mirov replied.

#

0913 hours

"Vstavat'!" Zhakiyanov said to Mirov while standing close to him. As a result, Mirov woke up.

As he opened his eyes, he saw Zhakiyanov. Because the latter was close like an animal, Mirov screamed and moved away from Zhakiyanov. "As you can see, I'm awake now," Mirov replied. "Why did you have to be so close!?"

"Because 'Elizaveta' prepared breakfast," Chadov said as he looked at both Zhakiyanov and Mirov.

"The Grand Duchess prepared breakfast?" Mirov asked as he turned to Chadov.

"Da. Now come on, you two."

With Chadov proceeding ahead to the only dining table in the safehouse, Zhakiyanov and Mirov followed. The latter two found glasses filled with milk beside each chair on the table and Tatiana placing a plate filled with circular bread on the table.

"Glad you're awake, Leytenánt," Tatiana said as she saw Mirov.

"Is that... oladyi?" Mirov asked.

"Da. Please sit, but wait, I just need to prepare the jam."

"Spasibo." Mirov, Chadov, and Zhakiyanov sat down and began looking at the *oladyi* that Tatiana prepared. The wait wasn't long as Tatiana brought out a jar of blueberry jam and laid it on the table.

"You made this oladyi?" Mirov asked.

"Da," Tatiana answered upon sitting down and lowering utensils on the table.

"We worked hard to get the recipe for this," Chadov said to Mirov. "Luckily, we made enough for you."

"You know how to make oladyi?" Mirov asked to Tatiana.

"Da," Tatiana answered as she gave Chadov, seated beside Mirov, his utensils. "My mother taught me."

Tatiana then gave Mirov his utensils. After that, the former sat on her chair beside Zhakiyanov. "Before we begin, we'll pray," Tatiana announced. She then started the prayer, but Mirov didn't partake, yet he kept silent and persevered until the prayer ended. Tatiana, as soon as she ended the prayer, noticed but avoided talking about it.

"As they say here in Japan: 'Itadakimasu'!" Chadov announced. Everyone began eating. Mirov, however, was quick to swallow after an adequate amount of time needed for thorough chewing.

"Didn't you say you work as couriers?" Mirov asked after his swallowing. "Shouldn't we be preparing for work?"

Mirov's questions made Tatiana and her subordinates briefly stop. Everyone else then resumed their chewing, but they were faster than Mirov was and they swallowed not long after.

"We should get a call soon," Tatiana answered. "Now please resume your meal."

"Mne zhal'," Mirov said before he used his utensils to cut a piece of the *oladyi* and putting it in his mouth. He resumed chewing, but this time, it was slower.

This oladyi, I feel as if I'm a child again… Mirov thought while he chewed. Unbeknownst to him, Tatiana looked at him while she was also chewing her food. *Should have known he would act like he's in another warzone,* Tatiana thought.

#

1017 hours

Both Zhakiyanov and Chadov rushed to the Stepwagn they owned. Once inside, they started up its engines. After that, they immediately left the safehouse.

Unbeknownst to Chadov and Zhakiyanov, a man watched without being obvious about it. While he saw the Setpwagn leave, he brought out his smartphone and took a picture of the Stepwagn.

How did they sneak a new guy here? Jason Luke Crawley pondered. *I best leave and tell "Smith" later.*

Spying

Minagawa Electronics Service Center, Suminoe Ward, Kansai City, Kansai Prefecture; State of Japan. April 7, 2030; 1115 hours (Japan Standard Time)

A man brought Pyotr Stepanovich Chadov and Karim Olegovich Zhakiyanov to a section of the service center owned by Minagawa Electronics, a subsidiary of Minagawa Group, filled with nineteen cardboard boxes. The latter two froze as if they saw ghosts upon seeing the boxes.

"W… We have to deliver these?" Chadov asked.

"Hai," the Minagawa employee answered. "However, because of the number of boxes, you are to take four trips at most from here to the destination of these boxes."

"And where are we to deliver these boxes?" Zhakiyanov asked.

"I have a map and directions for your two trips from here to that destination," the Minagawa employee answered as he brought out a map of Kansai City marked with red lines that start from the location of the service center. Marked in a red circle was a portion of Crater Shore's northwest section, with both red lines leading to the encircled portion of the map. Both Zhakiyanov and Chadov looked at the map with caution.

"Do we know who lives in that portion of Kansai City?" Chadov asked while he and Zhakiyanov held the map with the latter continuing to look at it.

"No," the Minagawa employee answered. "You and Sadykov-san are to simply leave the boxes at least one meter near the location. No further questions about who ordered these boxes, the exact location as to where they're to be taken, what are inside the boxes, and why."

"Wakarimasu."

Crater Shore North. 1300 hours

Chadov and Zhakiyanov arrived near a shipwreck located in the northern portion of Crater Shore, near the Crater Shore North Testing Range used by the 1st Light Mechanized Assault Regiment of the New United Nations Groud Force. Once they found that they were one kilometer near the shipwreck, the two OVR agents parked their Stepwagn.

After parking, Chadov and Zhakiyanov began to remove the first four crates that were loaded inside the Stepwagn. Both had to unload one crate at a time due to how long they were.

"It's disappointing we can't know what is inside these boxes!" Chadov screamed while he and Zhakiyanov unloaded their first box and lowered it into the ground. "Whatever's inside these boxes is heavy."

With the first box lowered, Chadov and Zhakiyanov continued to unload the boxes. Unbeknownst to the two OVR agents, the box they unloaded contained Shireen Baloch. She waited inside with a knife.

#

1330 hours

The first four boxes that Chadov and Zhakiyanov delivered were now alone near the shipwreck. Shireen then used her knife to free herself from the box. Once she escaped her box, she desperately breathed upon finding that she's in Japan.

Thank heavens I'm alive, Shireen thought while she breathed. *After five breaths... I... must hurry and... free... the... others. The deliverymen will return with more boxes.*

#

OVR Safehouse, Nishinari Ward, Kansai City. 1936 hours

Both Chadov and Zhakiyanov returned to their safehouse. They found that Tatiana Ioannovna Tsulukidze and Vladimir Nikolayevich Mirov waited for them at their dinner table with a Dutch oven filled with *borscht*, smaller bowls, utensils, and glasses filled with water.

"Is… that borscht?" Chadov asked.

"Da," Tatiana answered sternly. "And you're late."

"Prosti za eto," Zhakiyanov replied. "Today's delivery was taxing and strange."

"How strange?"

"Can we please talk after eating?" Chadov pleaded. "Ya goloden!"

"Otlichno!" Tatiana screamed in response. "Teper' my mozhem nachat'!"

"Spasibo!" both Chadov and Zhakiyanov replied before to their seats at the table.

#

2029 hours

"Nineteen heavy and long boxes?" Tatiana asked after everyone finished dinner and that Chadov and Zhakiyanov told her about the delivery.

"Da," Chadov answered. "We were told simply to leave the boxes one kilometer near a shipwreck in Crater Shore. We weren't allowed to know what were in the boxes, who was asking for them, and why they were to be delivered one kilometer away from the shipwreck."

"Thank you for warning me of this. Did you at least get paid?"

"Da," Zhakiyanov happily answered.

"Though we were told of another shipment that will be delivered to Kansai City in three days," Chadov added. "We don't know yet if it's going to the same location."

"Either way, be prepared," Tatiana replied. "Now then, we're to begin cleaning up the table."

"Zametano," Chadov and Zhakiyanov replied. Tatiana then noticed Mirov's silence.

"You too, Leytenánt," Tatiana warned, making Mirov gulp. "Remember, you're to answer to me for three days at the least. Until then, you're to help us maintain this safehouse. Consider that an order."

"Z… Zametano," Mirov replied.

Near Nishi High School/Tadakono Drug Store, Higashiosaka Ward. April 8, 2030; 1638 hours

"What are we doing here?" Mirov asked as he and Tatiana neared Nishi High School.

"This is where Tarou Ganji studies at," Tatiana answered.

"How old is he?"

"Not sure about his age. He does study at this school. Even now, that surprises me. In any case, we're here so that you can see who it is that defeated you twice. However, he's in the middle of Judo practice, so we need to wait."

He takes up Judo? Mirov thought before opening his mouth. "How will we wait?"

"We buy from there." Tatiana pointed at the nearby pharmacy, Tadakono Drug Store. Both Mirov and Tatiana proceeded to the pharmacy. Once inside, they found sandwiches and *onigiri*, but they split up after getting baskets, with Tatiana eyeing the liquid products. Thankfully for Mirov, he found signs in English, allowing him to get what he can. Once he bought the sandwiches and *onigiri*, he placed them in his basket. As he arrived at the cashier, so did Tatiana with the water she bought.

After the payments were made, Tatiana and Mirov exited the pharmacy with the former using her and finding that it was 16:55. "It's time," Tatiana announced. "We best return to the school, but before that, hold my bag."

Mirov simply grabbed the plastic bag containing the liquid bottles Tatiana paid for. The latter then brought out a picture of Maria Hoshikawa with Tarou Ganji and gave it to Mirov.

"I assume the boy is Tarou Ganji?" Mirov asked.

"Da," Tatiana answered. "Please give me back my bag. Remember, you're to see Ganji only. After that, we leave."

"Zametano."

Both Tatiana and Mirov returned to the school. They now found that the students started to leave. The former two said nothing yet waited. The wait wasn't long as they saw Tarou Ganji leave while dragging his PCX motor scooter until he turned to where they were. Both Mirov and Tatiana stepped away to make sure Tarou didn't notice them and it worked as they weren't spotted by him. Once he was unwittingly in front of Mirov and Tatiana, Tarou started up his motor scooter. The former two watched Tarou use the PCX to return to his condominium.

Not only is he still in school, but he manages to use a motor scooter, Mirov thought. *He must earn a lot of money to even have a motor scooter.*

"Done looking?" Tatiana asked. "It's time to go."

"Zametano," Mirov replied.

However, a limousine caught the respective glances of Mirov and Tatiana. Despite her order, Tatiana opted to stay with Mirov, assuming that she changed her mind. They now saw Maria Hoshikawa moving to the limousine, carrying her school bag on one hand and her *judogi* on another. Ugaki, her driver, rushed out of the driver's seat and opened the rear right door for Maria. Once Maria was inside, Ugaki returned to the driver's seat and began to leave; neither he nor Maria were aware they were being watched. Mirov then turned to Tatiana.

"That's the girl from the picture," Mirov said.

"Da," Tatiana answered. "Her name is Maria Hoshikawa."

"That's Maria Hoshikawa?"

"We'll continue this discussion later. We best leave."

"Zametano."

Both Tatiana and Mirov began to leave but as soon as they began to be lost within the horde of Nishi High School's students, Tatiana glanced at a black Townace van with its blond male driver looking at her and Mirov. Tatiana then brought out her smartphone as she was able to see the license plate on the Townace, but waited until she was no longer within sight of the owner. Once she and Mirov were behind the Townace, they stopped with Tatiana putting down her bag. While this confused Mirov, Tatiana reared her head at the Townace's rear and found the rear license plate. She then moved her phone to her left hand, discreetly allowing her to aim the lens of her phone's camera against the rear license plate. Unknowingly, she was able to aim the lens at the license plate by the time she pressed the button needed to take the picture. She then saw her picture and nodded in agreement that the photograph she took was flawless, allowing her to hide the phone and pick up the bag.

"What was that for?" Mirov asked.

"Just wanted to take a picture," Tatiana answered. "We best resume moving."

#

OVR Safehouse, Nishinari Ward. 1820 hours

At the dining room in their safehouse, Mirov sat alone as he looked at the picture he looked at hours before while Tatiana began heating up the sandwiches they bought at the pharmacy beside Nishi High School. Once Tatiana had every sandwich inside the conventional oven, she then joined Mirov.

"Still looking?" Tatiana asked.

"Prosti za eto!" Mirov sputtered while putting down the photograph. "I now have more questions than answers and I don't think staying here for another two days will help me the next time I encounter Tarou Ganji in battle."

"Why do you think that?"

"What I do understand is that he's undercover as a student to keep an eye on Maria Hoshikawa, who is important. However, I find it difficult to reconcile that the man, or boy as I learned today, I fought twice is simply a teenager."

"I was surprised too when I found out about Tarou Ganji. What little I found about Hoshikawa, by contrast, surprised me more."

"Kat tak?"

"Before I answer that question, how much do you know about the death of Tsesarevich Viktor?"

"He died of an illness." Mirov stopped after giving his answer, widening his eyes for one second until he realized the implication of Tatiana's question. "You don't suppose-"

"Da. I find it hard to believe a perfectly healthy man like Tsesarevich Viktor, my brother, would die of a mere illness. Then there's the story of how my future sister-in-law Svetlana Eduardovna Sonina committed suicide in the Far East and that her body wasn't found. Not only that, a mysterious plane was spotted at around the same time her death was ruled as suicide. You can imagine what came next."

"And how is Maria Hoshikawa involved in this?"

"Almost a year ago, my subordinates and I assisted with acquiring the garbage from Nishi High School. Hoshikawa must have volunteered to give us the garbage and somehow, a piece of her hair was stuck in the trash. Zhakiyanov got the hair out of the trash and naturally, we got a strand." Tatiana, however, stopped. This puzzled Mirov, yet he remained silent. "Before I continue the rest of this story, you promise to keep this to yourself?"

"Zametano," Mirov replied.

"During that ordeal, I noticed a faint resemblance between Maria and Tserarevich Viktor. Once I got a hold of the hair strand, I traveled back to the Tsardom and told my father, the Tsar, about this and asked him if he can have his DNA compared with the DNA found in the strand."

"Any results yet?"

"So far, none. Again, no one else must know that we had this conversation."

"Zametano."

"My doma!" Pyotr Stepanovich Chadov announced as he and Karim Olegovich Zhakiyanov arrived in the safehouse. "What are we having for dinner tonight?"

"Sandwiches and *onigiri*," Tatiana answered as she and Mirov saw Chadov and Zhakiyanov return. "How was today's delivery?"

"It went well." Chadov and Zhakiyanov then joined Tatiana and Mirov at their dinner table. "Today, we got an unexpected client."

"Who?"

"Most likely an Iron Dutchman Services member. We could tell because we got to see the *Iron Dutchman* itself and, as we suspected, Iron Dutchman Services is being sheltered by Hoshikawa Group."

"What did the client want?"

"A... I.... don't know how to tell this to you." Tatiana then realized what the woman ordered as she guessed from how Chadov hesitated to be concrete with her answer because Tatiana realized the "package", in *both* senses of the word, was something a woman like herself would use and that Chadov hesitation in answering was to avoid an accusation of sexism.

"A sex toy, isn't it?"

"But it was... *long*."

"Never mind. That reminds me, those sandwiches must be finished heating up by now. I'll get them." Tatiana stood up and returned to the kitchen. Behind her back, Chadov resumed the discussion about the delivery she and Zhakiyanov fulfilled, getting Mirov into the conversation.

#

1909 hours

"Gochi sou sama deshita," Tatiana, her subordinates, and Mirov said in unison once they finished their dinner. Tatiana then turned to Mirov.

"You got that one right," Tatiana said, referring to how said "Gochi sou same deshita".

"Arigatou," Mirov replied.

"Speaking of which, I just remembered something about today's delivery," Chadov interjected.

"What is it?" Tatiana answered with suspicion in her tone while not looking at Chadov. Both Mirov and Zhakiyanov assumed that Chadov wanted to resume discussing what he delivered.

"They own a Townace and just as when we left, it returned to that portion of Hoshikawa Shipyards."

"Did you say a Townace?" Tatiana's tone as she asked indicated extreme interest.

"Da," Chadov answered, but was still shaken by how Tatiana asked her question.

"Was it black?"

"Da," Zhakiyanov answered.

"Mirov and I encountered a black Townace when we spied on Tarou Ganji today. Hold on, let me get my phone." Tatiana then stood up and rushed out of the dinner table. Luckily for Chadov, Zhakiyanov, and Mirov, the wait was short and Tatiana returned with her smartphone and showed the photograph she took hours before.

So that's why she took the photo, Mirov thought.

"Did the Townace have this license plate?" Tatiana asked.

"Da," Chadov answered as he and Zhakiyanov leaned toward Tatiana's phone to look at the license plate in the photograph.

"Spasibo." Both Chadov and Zhakiyanov stopped leaning. "The owner of the Townace was most likely keeping an eye on Ganji. We might need to know why."

"Zametano," Chadov, Zhakiyanov, and Mirov replied in unison.

"Now please assist with the trash."

#

August 9, 2030. 0900 hours

Mirov, Chadov, and Zhakiyanov gathered at their dinner table again that morning. They found that Tatiana prepared bread with jam and butter on their separate containers; all laid out on the table.

"Glad you're all here," Tatiana announced. "Before we eat, I received a call from Minagawa."

"Is it about the other cargo they wish for us to deliver?" Chadov asked as he, Mirov, and Zhakiyanov sat down.

"Da. In fact, this is a good opportunity for us. The shipment will arrive at the service center tomorrow morning. We must be there at 0900 hours at the earliest to begin delivering the shipment to the same shipwreck. Since it won't be here until tomorrow morning, we can use today as an opportunity to place a tracking device on the Townace used by Iron Dutchman Services."

"Why do we need to track them?" Mirov asked.

"Because we can't afford to take our eyes away from those mercenaries while we have to deal with tomorrow's delivery," Tatiana answered after she turned to Mirov. "Like yesterday, you and I will go to that pharmacy, buy sandwiches, *onigiri*, and bottled water again."

"Zametano," Mirov replied. Tatiana then turned to Chadov and Zhakiyanov. "Chadov, Zhakiyanov, I need the two of you to follow us with the tracking device. Once you see the Townace, deliver it to the Townace."

"Zametano," Chadov and Zhakiyanov replied in unison.

"Now let us pray before we begin eating," Tatiana ordered.

#

Near Nishi High School, Highashiosaka Ward. 1654 hours

Like it was in the previous day, Mirov and Tatiana stood near Nishi High School with bags filled with food and water from Tadakono Drug Store. Tatiana brought out her phone and typed "Near the school. Where are you?", followed by pressing "Otpravlyat".

She kept her phone with her right hand while looking in both directions. She then felt her phone and found Chadov's reply, which read:

"We spotted the Townace. Do something to distract the driver because he will detect me and Zhakiyanov if we start placing the tracking device."

Tatiana then typed "U menya yest' mysl'", followed by pressing "Otpravlyat".

"Ya vizhu Gandzhi," Mirov said as he saw Tarou Ganji dragging his PCX scooter out of the school. Tatiana then also saw the boy leaving the school.

"Sledi za mnoy," Tatiana ordered before she moved toward Tarou. Mirov didn't respond as he immediately kept an eye on Tatiana as she walked up to Tarou.

Once Tatiana began talking to Tarou, Jason Luke Crawley saw what was happening and began to use his binoculars to see Tarou and Tatiana. As a result, he was unable to see Chadov and Zhakiyanov appearing on the rear-view mirror. The two OVR agents wasted no time in inserting the tracking device, which resembled a poststamp but with a tiny red glass circle in the middle, below the license plate. As soon as they were able to stick the tracking device, Chadov and Zhakiyanov wasted no time with their escape.

At this point, Tatiana's distraction worked as Crawley continued to keep an eye on Tarou leaving with his PCX scooter, unaware of the tracking device. Tatiana then signaled Mirov that they're finished and that they must leave. As she and Mirov began to leave, the former brought out her phone and texted Chadov, writing "Byli sdelany. Vremya ukhodit'", then pressed "Otpravlyat".

#

OVR Safehouse, Nishinari Ward. 1822 hours

While Mirov, Chadov, and Zhakiyanov were seated by their dinner table, Tatiana, however, connected her phone to the dish she used for SatCom. However, she was using a different application in phone but it still required the dish.

The application, called "Treker", showed a map of Kansai City and a blinking red circle. The red circle was now in Hoshikawa Shipyards. She then joined her subordinates and Mirov at the dinner table.

"We can now track that Townace," Tatiana announced. "Tomorrow, I will partake in the shipment."

"Why you?" Chadov asked.

"Someone has to follow that Townace."

"Might I make a request?" Mirov asked as he raised his hand.

"What is it?" Tatiana asked as she turned to Mirov.

"I wish to follow Tarou Ganji tomorrow when he leaves the school. I wish to know where he lives."

"I can lend you a tracking device. Just don't get caught."

"Zametano."

The sound of a timer went off. Everyone at the table knew that the sandwiches Mirov and Tatiana bought were now heated.

"And now, we can begin dinner," Tatiana declared. "But after this, we wait two hours, then we sleep because all of us need to wake up early tomorrow." She turned to Chadov. "Chadov, I need you to go to

Hoshikawa Shipyards and keep an eye on that Townace. Text me if it's leaving."

"Zametano," Chadov replied.

#

Near Hoshikawa Shipyards, Taisho Ward. April 10, 2030; 0910 hours

Chadov now stood outside Hoshikawa Shipyards. He looked at the front gate of the shipyards with binoculars. However, he opted to continue using his right hand with the binoculars while he brought out his smartphone with his left hand.

He then switched which item was to be held with his right hand, with the binoculars now on his left hand. Now using his right hand to control his phone, Chadov texted "Ya snaruzhi verfi" and pressed "Otpravlyat".

The Grand Duchess will take her time with her reply, so I can go back to observing the gate, Chadov thought as he began to put aside his phone. However, he felt his phone vibrate, which meant that a reply came.

He then found that Tatiana wrote a reply that read:

Zhakiyanov and I are almost at the service center. Continue to observe what the mercenaries are doing.

Chadov, however, then heard engines. He hurriedly hid his phone and resumed using his binoculars with both hands. He now saw the black Townace owned by Iron Dutchman Services leaving the shipyards. Wrapping the strap attached on the binoculars around his neck, Chaodv brought out his phone again and immediately replied to Tatiana, writing "The Townace is leaving the shipyards" and pressed "Otpravlyat".

Tatiana's reply this time was faster. It read:

Now return to the safehouse and attach the phone to the satellite receiver and use Treker. Found out what the mercenaries are up to.

#

OVR Safehouse, Nishinari Ward. 1001 hours

Filled with sweat, Chadov returned to the safehouse. Despite the sweat, he rushed to Tatiana's office, where the dish she used, the satellite receiver, was kept. Chadov then connected it to his phone and accessing his Treker application, he saw the map of Kansai City and the red circle that was the tracking device he and Zhakiyanov planted on the Townace the previous day. However, he found that the Townace was taking a different route, far from Nishi High School.

Chadov immediately began to write another text message to Tatiana and after pressing "Otpravlyat", Chadov returned to Treker to see where in Kansai City was the Townace at. He now saw that the van was approaching the neighboring city of Yao. It was then that Tatiana's reply came, with Chadov opting to respond to it. The reply read:

Gde seychas furgon?

Chadov wrote "Furgon nakhoditsya v Yao" and sent his reply. After that, he rushed back to Treker and found that the Townace stopped at a certain location. Chadov then zoomed in to see where in Yao the Townace was. He found that the Townace was near JGSDF Camp Yao, at one Horikawa Bathhouse. He immediately returned to the "Messages" application and added another message for Tatiana that read:

Found where that Townace is at. It's at a bathhouse that has the surname "Horikawa" with it. Presumably family-owned. What should I do?

Chadov then pressed "Otpravlyat". Only after one minute did Tatiana reply and it read:

Zhakiyanov and I have the delivery to finish. Unlike the large boxes you dealt with two days ago, Zhakiyanov and I are dealing with smaller boxes. Although there are larger ones, we'll deal with those after our first trip to that shipwreck. We'll discuss our findings tonight. For now, I need you to help the Leytenánt with his plan to plant another tracking device onto Tarou Ganji's scooter. Don't disturb him because he's practicing his Japanese right now. Wait until lunch to tell him you'll help him.

Chadov then wrote "Mind if I take the Leytenánt with me to that yakiniku restaurant near the hardware store? I have enough money for the both of us" and sent it afterward. Curiously to Chadov, Tatiana immediately replied. The reply read:

Fine. In fact, I just realized that with how early we started, Zhakiyanov and I can be finished at roughly 1300 hours. When you and the Leytenánt finish eating at that yakiniku restaurant, return to the safehouse immediately.

Chadov then wrote "Zametano" and pressed "Otpravlyat".

Crater Shore North. 1139 hours

Elsewhere in the Kansai Prefecture, Tatiana and Zhakiyanov arrived a kilometer near the shipwreck; the same destination where Chadov and Zhakiyanov had to drop off packages two days ago. Once Zhakiyanov parked their Stepwagn, he and Tatiana immediately got to work on unloading their cargo.

Upon opening the side doors, Tatiana and Zhakiyanov began to unload the first box they can grab. However, the boxes were long, and that Tatiana didn't have the bulk Chadov's body had to offer whenever he helped Zhakiyanov so Tatiana positioned herself on side of the Stepwagn while Zhakiyanov stood on the other end, intent on doing most of the lifting to help Tatiana.

There must be a weapon inside this box, Tatiana thought as she pushed. *Could this be like what happened when we had to accommodate Serdar Muhadow months ago?*

Despite that, Tatiana continued to push. As she continued to do so, Tatiana bended her body's upper half to continue pushing the box out of the van. Once the box was halfway outside the Stepwagn, Zhakiyanov moved backward to continue holding to his end until Tatiana moved further inside the van. As a result, the box now stood vertically and when Tatiana gave the final push, Zhakiyanov desperately placed the box on the ground just as Tatiana returned outside.

I must tell Slava about this, Tatiana thought.

#

OVR Safehouse, Nishinari Ward, Kansai City. 1316 hours

Tatiana and Zhakiyanov returned to the safehouse. They found Mirov and Chadov at the dinner table.

"Good, you two are here," Tatiana said just as she and Zhakiyanov sat down. "Now that we just got paid, we need to plan what to do next after Mirov plants that tracking device on Tarou Ganji's scooter."

"Do we even know where Ganji lives?" Chadov asked.

"That's what I wish to determine," Mirov answered. "That way, you three can plan for future operations once I leave."

"That's a good idea," Tatiana added. She then brought out her smartphone and pressed a tab for an application named "Karty". Tatiana used her fingers to point at Japan, narrowing it to Kansai City. She continued narrowing until she reached Nishi High School, as it was near the Hanazono Central Park; both venues occupying large amounts of land throughout the Higashiosaka Ward. Tatiana continued looking at the map fervishly with her subordinates and Mirov leaning toward her until she was finished. Tatiana examined the map twice, then stopped, making the latter stop looking at her.

"Considering who Hoshikawa's father is and that we're dealing with a mercenary group, Daisuke Hoshikawa himself must have provided a degree of help. He owns a condominium complex near the school. Since Ganji uses a scooter, he could be living there."

Tatiana then turned to Zhakiyanov. "Zhakiyanov, I need you to stand by the gas station near the school."

"Zametano," Zhakiyanov replied. Tatiana then turned to Mirov and Chadov; seated beside each other. "Mirov, Leytenánt, go to the pharmacy and buy anything until Ganji leaves. However, if you're to follow him, Mirov must do so by himself for the time being.

"Chadov, you're to follow Mirov, but make sure you're at least five meters apart from him because if you're too close, it'll arouse suspicion."

"And if Ganji does reach Hoshikawa Condominiums, I'm to infiltrate the condominium complex by myself in order to plant the tracking device?" Mirov asked.

"Da," Tatiana answered. "Any more questions?"

"What about the Townace being in Yao?" Chadov asked.

"After we get that tracking device into Ganji's scooter, I'll inform the Director about everything we discovered. Any more questions?"

"Net," Chadov, Zhakiyanov, and Mirov answered in unison.

"Khoroshiy. Before we launch this operation, we must have our cheque turned into yen bills."

The Truth

Near Nishi High School, Higashiosaka Ward, Kansai City, Kansai Prefecture; State of Japan. August 11, 2030; 1653 hours (Japan Standard Time)

Outside the same pharmacy near Nishi High School, Vladimir Nikolayevich Mirov stood and watched Nishi High's students exit. He observed as if he was an animal waiting for prey. That prey was none other than Tarou Ganji.

Mirov then stopped looking at Tarou as to avoid arousing suspicion. Unaware that he was being spied on, Tarou got on his PCX motor scooter and started up its engine. Facing the direction leading to his condominium, Tarou left, unaware that Mirov intended to follow him to his condominium.

As soon as Tarou got the scooter to move, Mirov observed carefully. However, he avoided moving until he was far enough for Tarou to not notice him if he followed. Once Tarou moved past the pharmacy, Mirov followed while keeping an eye on him and the scooter. Pyotr Stepanovich Chadov, standing near a *Nihon Kirisuto* church beside Tadakono Drug Store, then followed Mirov. Unbeknownst to the OVR agent and the Imperial Eurasian Naval Infantry Walgear pilot, Jason Luke Crawley also watched from outside the pharmacy. As soon as he could only see Chadov, Crawley began to follow the OVR agent.

#

Outside Hoshikawa Condominiums. 1739 hours

Chadov now arrived at Hoshikawa Condominiums. However, he found Mirov waiting by the metal fence that separated the parking space for bicycles owned by the condominium complex's residents from the street. Mirov himself was directly in front of Tarou Ganji's PCX scooter.

"What are you doing?" Chadov asked Mirov.

"You made it," Mirov said after he turned to Chadov. "My apologies. I'm trying to figure out how to get inside the condominium complex without getting spotted by the guard."

Mirov politely directed Chadov to the guard assigned to the front gate of the condominium. "Ya ponimayu," Chadov replied. "I have an idea. You can be quick, right?"

"Da."

"Don't move until I've distracted the guard."

"Zametano."

Chadov then directly moved to the front gate. Mirov watched until Chadov began talking to the guard. Although he couldn't hear them, Mirov saw that as the signal to infiltrate the bicycle parking lot. He then jumped through the fence. Thankfully for Mirov, his landing was silent, allowing Chadov to continue distracting the guard. Now inside, Mirov rushed to the PCX and planted the same tracking device Chadov planted onto the Townace used by Iron Dutchman Services. He placed the device close to the rear wheel where no can see it. Once that was finished, Mirov immediately jumped back outside. Chadov then saw Mirov exiting the bicycle parking lot and thanked the guard. However, he left slowly to avoid attracting the guard's suspicion. Chadov then joined Mirov where he found him.

"Posadili apparat?" Chadov asked.

"Da," Mirov answered.

"Pora idti."

"Zametano."

#

OVR Safehouse, Nishinari Ward. 1900 hours

Both Chadov and Mirov returned to the OVR Safehouse. However, they found Tatiana Ioannovna Tsulukidze and Karim Olegovich Zhakiyanov waiting for them; Tatiana's face was evident of her anxiety in waiting for the former two. Food was prepared and that the entire table was filled with it, glasses of water, plates, and utensils.

"Ty opozdal," Tatiana said to her subordinate and the Imperial Eurasian Naval Infantry Walgear pilot.

"Prosti za eto," Mirov replied. "I had difficulty infiltrating the condominium complex, so I had to get Gospodin Chadov to help me"

"Never mind that. Just join us because the food isn't going to remain warm for long. You can bathe after this. Consider this your punishment for arriving late."

"Zametano," Chadov and Mirov replied before sitting down.

#

2030 hours

Tatiana plugged her smartphone with the satellite receiver. She then began to use the SatCom application on her phone. However, she found that she received a call from "Nizhny".

"Finally, you responded!" Vyacheslav Leonidovich Puzanov, the Director of the OVR, said, with desperation evident in his tone.

"Da," Tatiana answered with her tone showing suspicion.

"I'm making this call to warn you that I've heard something urgent from our spy within the Soviet Remnant and that I must warn you about it."

"What might that be?"

"The Soviet Border Guards suffered a series of thefts. Other than the usage of a sleeping gas, no one was hurt. However, weapons and ammunition were stolen."

That must be it, Tatiana thought as she had in mind her recent deliveries. "I was just about to tell you something, but before that, I must ask: when did this happen?"

"Five days ago."

"My men and I have been making strange deliveries. Boxes to go to a shipwreck northwest of Kansai City. However, we weren't allowed to know what was inside the boxes, among other denials. It could be weapons."

"Then it must be the weapons that were stolen from the Soviets."

"Also, I've been placing tracking devices on vehicles owned by Iron Dutchman Services. Their van is in Yao right now, particularly at a bathhouse. Perhaps the theft of these weapons and their presumed arrival here in Japan, along with why Iron Dutchman Services brought their van to Yao, are connected."

"If they are, investigate further. You might have to keep Leytenánt Mirov with you."

"Zametano. I'll have Chadov find this bathhouse early in the morning."

#

Nishigori Parking/Near Horikawa Bathhouse, Yao. August 12, 2030; 0900 hours

Using the Stepwagn, Pyotr Stepanovich Chadov arrived in Yao's Takasagocho neighborhood. Finding a parking lot, he brought out his smartphone and by accessing Treker, he found that the parking lot was where the Townace used by Iron Dutchman Services was there because the blinking red circle in Treker that represented it was at that very parking in Treker's map.

Those mercenaries must have placed their van there because there isn't parking close to that bathhouse, Chadov thought. *I best park as well and continue on foot.*

Chadov then entered the parking lot but parked elsewhere to avoid attracting unnecessary attention if he parked beside the Townace. After parking, Chadov began to walk across Takasagocho. After passing through a cemetery and crossing the street, Chadov turned to his right and continued. As he did, he began to use his phone's Karty application. He was then able to find where in Yao he was located at and saw how long he had to walk until he reached Horikawa Bathhouse. Despite that, Chadov carried out his order. Just as he neared Horikawa Bathhouse, he stopped as he saw a woman with dark skin appeared in front of him. He waited until the woman turned in front of him.

Chadov then continued and as he turned to his left, he saw that he found Horikawa Bathhouse. He then used his phone's camera and took a picture of the entrance. After that, he bought from the nearby vending machine and once he got his drink, he proceeded to return to the Stepwagn.

OVR Safehouse, Nishinari Ward, Kansai City. August 12, 2030; 0800 hours

All OVR agents and Mirov gathered at their dinner table. Tatiana Ioannovna Tsulukidze now used her phone's Treker application. On the application's map of Kansai City, there were now two blinking circles. One was the red circle that represented the tracking device planted on Iron Dutchman Service's Townace; still in Yao. Another was a green circle, and it was moving toward Nishi High School; this represented the tracking device that Vladimir Nikolayevich Mirov planted on Tarou Ganji's PCX motor scooter.

"Ono rabotayet!" Tatiana boasted as she looked at the map. "Now that we can keep track of what Tarou Ganji does, we can figure out what the last thing Leytenánt Mirov needs to learn before we have him return to the Tsardom."

"But how will we contact Kapitan Samsonova?" Vladimir Nikolayevich Mirov asked.

"Prior to arriving at Nogliki, I told the Kapitan to always raise the sail for one hour. It has a satellite dish as well, so we can contact her. We just need to do it tonight where there's less attention toward Osaka Bay."

#

Unknown Location; Enlightenment Point. 0950 hours (EP Time Zone)

"Good," Sergei Akulov said after listening to a daily report by Reinhard Frühling. "Anything else?"

"Yes, Grand Gatekeeper," Frühling replied. "Our Devotee-Infiltrator in the OVR has told us that the Director warned Grand Duchess Tatiana about the theft of the weapons from the Russian Soviet Federative Socialist Republic. Also, the OVR are tracking activity about Iron Dutchman Services."

"What have they found?"

"The Townace van used by the mercenaries was taken to Yao. Most likely, the mercenaries are using the FIS safehouse that uses Miyako Horikawa's bathhouse as a front."

"They're most likely preparing to receive Frederick Dirks once he returns to Japan with Maral Eminovna Guliyeva. Inform 'SB' of this update at once and tell her to await further orders."

"By your will, Grand Gatekeeper."

#

OVR Safehouse, Nishinari Ward, Kansai City, Kansai Prefecture; State of Japan. 2050 hours (Japan Standard Time)

"Has Leytenánt Mirov learned a lot?" Yelena Abramovna Samsonova asked on the other end of Tatiana's smartphone, which was connected to the satellite receiver needed for the latter to use SatCom.

"Da," Tatiana answered. "He intends to stay for another two more days to analyze Tarou Ganji, then he'll prepare to return to the Tsardom."

#

Horikawa Bathhouse, Yao. 2100 hours

At the bathhouse in Yao owned by Miyako Horikawa, Wouter Vos received a text message through IntMail from one "FS" that read:

Vos, I'll be returning to Japan tonight. Be prepared to pick me up along with the girl I saved.

Vos then told Qazvini. Both then traveled to the room where Tatev Mirzoyan and Sunan Wattana stayed at but knocked. "What is it?" Wattana asked from the other side of the door.

"'Smith's' on his way back here," Vos warned. "We need to gather now."

"Tatev and I are about to put on shirts. Please wait."

#

2110 hours

Vos and his subordinates were now gathered at a table on the first floor of the bathhouse. "For now, it's just a simple pickup," Vos explained to his subordinates. "I'll drive the Townace tonight. I only need one of you to accompany me. Whoever's willing to, please raise your hand."

"I'll go," Wattana said as she raised her right hand. "Anything's better than lying around."

"Then we best put on proper clothes. After that, we rush to the Townace."

\#

OVR Safehouse, Nishinari Ward, Kansai City. 2130 hours

At the OVR safehouse, the occupants all gathered at their dinner table. "I imagine those mercenaries are up to something since you dragged us here?" Pyotr Stepanovich Chadov asked.

"Da," Tatiana answered before showing the map of her phone's Treker application. The green dot that represented Iron Dutchman Service's Townace now moved toward JGSDF Camp Yao. Chadov, Karim Olegovich Zhakiyanov, and Vladimir Nikolayevich Mirov showed their surprise upon seeing the green dot move.

"I need someone to accompany me to Camp Yao," Tatiana requested. She then glanced at Mirov. "Someone other than Leytenánt Mirov."

Mirov remained silent as he knew why Tatiana didn't want him to come with her. "Ya poydu," Zhakiyanov said as he raised his hand.

"Then we best get into proper clothing."

\#

Near Japan Ground Self-Defense Force Camp Yao, Yao. 2215 hours

"My sdelali eto," Tatiana muttered as she and Zhakiyanov, using their Stepwagn, reached Yao, particularly JGSDF Camp Yao.

Tatiana then brought out her phone and opened her Treker application. The map now showed the red circle representing Iron Dutchman Services' Townace almost reaching the entrance to the base. "Zhakiyanov, please find us somewhere to hide," Tatiana ordered. "Those mercenaries are nearby, and it will be a problem if they detect us."

"Zametano," Zhakiyanov replied before moving the Stepwagn backward. He then realized that he moved past somewhere to hide, opting to switch gears. After that, he moved the Stepwagn forward, then switched to the reverse gear, then moved backward again and turned. Now, they were at a position where the incoming Townace wouldn't spot them.

"And they're just parking," Tatiana said as she continued looking at Treker. "What are they here for?"

Suddenly, the sound of a jet plane's engines was heard. *A plane at this hour?* Tatiana pondered cautiously. *Could that mean-*

The plane's engines became louder. Both Tatiana and Zhakiyanov then realized that was what the mercenaries came to JGSDF Camp Yao for.

"Zhakyanov, stay here," Tatiana ordered as she turned to her subordinate. "I'll go down and position myself as near to the base as I can. Hopefully, I can figure if this plane and the mercenaries are connected. Just wait here."

"Zametano." After Zhakiyanov's reply, Tatiana got off the Stepwagn. She then ran as fast as she could until stopping at the nearby fire station. Upon stopping, she panted. Despite that, Tatiana gathered enough strength and willpower to bring out her phone and use its camera. She then switched to its night-vision function. She was then able to see past the gate leading to Camp Yao, particularly Iron Dutchman Services' Townace.

If those mercenaries parked their van nearby, that could mean the plane that landed just about now must have something or someone they need to leave with in a hurry, Tatiana thought as she looked with her phone's camera.

Wait, I'm seeing three people leaving, Tatiana thought as she saw Wouter Vos, Sunan Wattana, and a girl with had long brown hair, light skin, and dark brown eyes wearing a plain white shirt, pants, and shoes.

Another teenager? Tatiana pondered. *I'll take a photo of this, then rush back to Zhakiyanov. It's time to get out of here.*

Unbeknownst to both the mercenaries and Tatiana, Shireen Baloch watched from afar but with better equipment. She then moved somewhere else and seemingly touched the air with a clenched fist. Another Stepwagn van then appeared as a result. She then got inside the van with the van vanishing after that. A metal object with four legs followed Shireen inside the seemingly invisible van.

Unknown Location, Mariupol, Mariupol Volost, Donetsk Uyezd, Ukraine Governorate; Eurasian Tsardom. January 2, 2020; 2302 hours (Kiev Time)

In an isolated room, girls populated it. The youngest of these girls was seven, while the oldest was fourteen. Two girls of the same age sat beside each in one corner. The door then opened. Every girl knew what that meant and continued looking as they stood up.

A man in his early sixties with no hair on his scalp, very light skin, a blond moustache that was graying, and blue eyes appeared in the room. He focused on the two women who were sitting beside each other and grabbed one of them. The already-unfortunate girl had light skin, a short and thin body, dark brown eyes, and black hair. The girl, however, showed no fear when the man began to drag her away. The other girl, who had the same physical features as the girl with black hair, albeit with her hair being brown, clung to her.

"Tatev, yox!" the girl with brown hair shouted before the man kicked her.

#

Outside Horikawa Bathhouse, Yao, Kansai Prefecture; State of Japan. August 12, 2030; 2208 hours (Japan Standard Time)

In the present, the girl with brown hair, Maral Eminovna Guliyeva, woke up. It was then that Wouter Vos and Sunan Wattana, who had picked up Frederick Dirks and Guliyeva, had arrived at Horikawa Bathhouse.

Once Dirks, seated beside Guliyeva, opened the rear right door, Guliyeva began to scream and struggle out of the seatbelt. Both Dirks and Wattana covered their respective ears, but since Guliyeva was seated close to them, their efforts to protect their eardrums appeared to be futile. It was then that Tatev Mirzoyan, the girl Guliyeva clung to in her horrible memory, appeared with Miyako Horikawa.

"Nani ga kotodesu ka?" Horikawa asked.

While Dirks gave his answer in Japanese, Tatev examined the screaming girl. She wasn't able to say anything, but she seemingly recognized Guliyeva. *It can't be,* Tatev thought. *If that is Maral, I can see why she's screaming. There's only one thing that could help. I just hope I get the lyrics right.*

Tatev then began to sing, making the chaos go away. Neither Dirks, Horikawa, Vos, nor Wattana questioned why was Tatev singing, nor were they urging her to stop. Although Tatev sang in Azeri, a language the latter didn't understand, everyone felt at peace listening to Tatev's song, Guliyeva most especially. Not only did it allow her to calm down, but she was able to remove her seatbelt and exit the Townace without any further incident, but walked slowly toward Tatev. "T... Tatev?" Guliyeva asked once she looked at Tatev. "Siz... siz... Tatev Mirzoyan?"

"Bəli," Tatev replied with tears appearing on her bottom eyelids.

Guliyeva simply rushed to Tatev and cried as the latter hugged her. The former, still crying, kept silent but smiled.

#

Horikawa Bathhouse. 2224 hours

Dirks, Vos, Wattana, Tatev, Guliyeva, and Horikawa were now in the dining room of the bathhouse. They were joined by Jawed Qazvini. Guliyeva was then given a glass of water and she drank slowly. Everyone else watched with varying feelings about what happened.

What on Earth is that spook thinking? Wattana anxiously pondered. *He got the girl out from the Tijuana Cartel. What now?*

Guliyeva, however, felt as if she can understand the thoughts of those surrounding her. She then rushed to finish her water, but Tatev grabbed her left forearm.

"Etmə!" Tatev warned. "Yavaş-yavaş için. Biz sizi tələsdirmirik."

Guliyeva simply nodded and just as soon as Tatev let go of her left forearm, the former continued to drink slowly. *Should I have taken Tatev with me to Mexico?* Dirks pondered.

Tatev also looked at Guliyeva with fear as the latter drank her water slowly. Not the fear of her tantrums, but of others that no human should experience nor tolerate if it's done to others. *I hate to admit this, even to myself, but I didn't think Maral would even be alive,* Tatev thought.

Thankfully for everyone looking at Guliyeva, she was almost done with her water. However, it was the same: Guliyeva took a pause longer than needed after each gulp. This was the last because after this was her last gulp, ending with an empty glass.

"Çox sağ ol," Guliyeva said.

"That means 'Thank you' in Azeri," Tatev said to her fellow mercenaries, Dirks, and Horikawa.

"I don't mean to be rude but, does she know any other language beside Azeri?" Wattana asked.

"Other than Spanish, just that and Azeri," Dirks answered.

"Actually, she also knows Armenian," Tatev added. Maral then added to what Tatev said but she spoke in Azeri. "Oh, if anyone's wondering that meant, Maral said that she also understands Russian and Ukrainian."

Guliyeva then felt a certain uneasiness from her groin. "Burada hamam var?" she asked. "She's asking if there's a bathroom in this bathhouse," Tatev explained.

"I'll take her there," Dirks said before he stood up and faced Guliyeva. "Por favor sígame." Guliyeva then stood up. As Dirks began to leave the dining room, Guliyeva followed.

"I'll return to my room for now," Horikawa said before she also stood up. "I might be asleep, so if there's anything else you need, just knock within one hour."

"Hai," the Iron Dutchman Services members replied in unison as they faced Horikawa.

After a smile, Horikawa then left the room. The mercenaries then faced each other.

"She seems to know how to ask to go to a bathroom and can follow 'Smith' around," Wattana commented about Guliyeva's request to go to the bathroom.

"We… were at least told to clean ourselves up daily," Tatev answered with reluctance, as evident by her tone. "Those who were willing to pay didn't want to do it with dirty women. And when I mean dirty-"

"I get it!" Vos replied with his avoidance to hear more shown by both his words and body actions. "Awfully pragmatic, though."

Everyone then heard that Dirks returned with Guliyeva, prompting the former to turn to the latter two. "Where did Miss Horikawa go?"

"She's in her room," Vos answered. "Why?"

"I was hoping to get Guliyeva here to sleep with her."

"She can sleep with us," Wattana replied. "I'm sure one more girl can fit with me and Tatev."

"Please direct me to your room."

Both Tatev and Wattana stood up and were the first to leave the room. Dirks and Guliyeva followed soon after.

"And while we're at it," Vos said before he stood up. "I'll return the van to the parking lot. We have at least sixty plus minutes before midnight."

#

2320 hours

Both Dirks and Tatev then returned to the dining room. They found Vos, Wattana, and Qazvini looking at them; their eyes showed that it was clear they couldn't afford to hide their suspicions about the real motive behind the mission any longer.

"I assume you have questions?" Dirks asked.

"You guessed right," Vos answered. "You're the one getting us paid but, please, for the love of God, tell us why we have to keep Guliyeva here?"

"Tatev and I need to sit down first," Dirks replied. "Then I'll explain."

The other mercenaries didn't continue. Dirks and Tatev took that as permission and sat down again. "Alright, I've withheld this because you didn't need to know. Now, you do."

"Something tells us there's more to this than a possible war with a Mexican drug cartel," Wattana replied.

"Indeed. We need Guliyeva as bait to draw out the man who sold her into sexual slavery."

"All this just to get to her pimp?" Vos incredulously asked.

"He's no mere pimp," Dirks retorted. "His name is-"

"Anton Oleksandrovich Kravchenko," Tatev answered defiantly, causing everyone but Qazvini to gasp.

"H… How do you know that?" Dirks asked.

"Because he had me abducted, trained me to be a sex slave, and sold me."

"You?" Wattana asked. "Why?"

"I didn't know it, because I was only seven, but as I got older, I realized I was collateral. My parents suffered financial problems. They met with a man for more money and when they couldn't pay it off, which I was able to hear because my parents argued about it, they opted to die. Well, my father, at least. He murdered my mother, then he asked me to assist in his suicide. The man they met, Kravchenko, came that day and took me away and imprisoned me in an apartment in Mariupol. It was there that I met Maral."

"What's her story? Or rather, did she tell you?"

"Unlike me, her parents just sold her. Somehow, she knew Armenian, hence why were able to talk. I even learned some Azeri from her and the both of us were able to pick up Russian and Ukrainian. Everything Kravchenko and his partners-in-crime did, we endured by thinking of each other, even when we were separated. We hoped that one day, we would escape. However, on January 2, 2021, I was sold off."

"Who… purchased you?" Dirks asked.

"I didn't know their names. They hid their faces in masks when they… 'inspected' me. When I was brought there, I was blindfolded. I wasn't blindfolded when I kept at my room and to make sure I didn't ask too many questions, they spoiled me. Books, computer with internet access, food, decent clothing… "

"And this was all in Somalia," Vos interjected. *No wonder she was reluctant to say more about herself when we first met,* he thought. *It would be rude of me to ask why didn't she say she knew Russian.*

"Why were you purchased?" Dirks asked to make Tatev resume her tale.

"I… I don't know," Tatev replied. "However, I was injected with something. After that, they made me hear mysterious sounds. This went on for years until Mr. Vos, Mr. Crawley, Miss Wattana, and Tarou saved me."

"Now then," Vos interjected as he faced Dirks; his intention made clear to his subordinates. "why did you bring Guliyeva here?"

"We, as in the FIS, intend to use Guliyeva as bait to draw out Kravchenko," Dirks answered.

"And how will you do that?" Tatev asked.

"We simply keep her here. No doubt Kravchenko would bring his private army of Korean mercenaries and have them scouring the city. All that needs to be done is to wait for one of henchmen to appear, then we grab him, and use him to get to Kravchenko."

"And why is the FIS trying to get him?" Vos asked. "I apologize for being rude about this in light of everything Mirzoyan has told us, but why do you want to get Kravchenko?"

"Because the Eurasian Tsardom failed to do so. We intend to use Kravchenko as a bargaining chip for potential deals with the Tsardom."

"Didn't you say he has a private army of Korean mercenaries?" Wattana asked.

"That's why you don't dismiss him as a mere pimp," Dirks answered. "Kravchenko was only able to operate his business because he learned it from his father, Oleksandr Konstantinovich Kravchenko, a former KGB officer who was a part of the Sparrow School that trained women to seduce foreign government and military officials. Kravchenko only inherited the business after his father died, but then he made the boneheaded decision to kidnap, train, and sell girls like Tatev and Guliyeva. The Okhrana launched one nasty campaign to end Kravchenko's flesh business, but he somehow escaped. The Eurasians even assumed him dead."

"So you intend to rub it into the Eurasian's faces that you could do what they couldn't?"

"That's right."

"What now?" Vos asked. "We have the girl. So, we simply wait?"

"Yes," Dirks answered.

"I have another question: how do you know about the Eurasian attempt to arrest Kravchenko?" Tatev asked.

"It happened a year after you were sold off to those scientists. The FIS assisted the External Intelligence Directorate of the Commonwealth of Euro-African States in helping an Okhrana officer named Volodymyr Vsevolodovych Blavatsky flee from the Tsardom. The EID agent I worked with for this case personally rescued Blavatsky with the aid of the Ukrainian Unification Force while I had to get his wife and daughter out through Turkey. When we were able to get him out of the Tsardom, he told us about Kravchenko and his sex trafficking ring. As payment, he ratted out a client of Kravchenko's from Free Ukraine, who used Turkey-based couriers to purchase a girl Kravchenko turned into a sex slave. The next thing you know, the Ukrainian National Police arrest one Lev Rustemovich Bohantenko, the owner of Free Ukraine's largest shipping company, at his office in Odesa."

"Now the real question is, how did Kravchenko even escape and acquire his own private army?" Wattana asked.

"We can ask Kravchenko that once we get him," Dirks answered. "For now, we go to sleep."

#

August 13, 2030; 0001 hours

Both Wattana and Tatev returned to their room in the bathhouse. They found Guliyeva, no longer wearing the shirt, pants, and shoes given to her by Sergio Ortiz but in her white latex leotard and still not asleep yet. "Maral, yatmaq vaxtıdır," Tatev warned.

"Mən... mən... yata bilmirəm... " Guliyeva replied with despair evident in her tone.

Both Tatev and Wattana turned away from Guliyeva and sighed. "Didn't think this would happen... " Wattana regretfully said before she turned to Tatev. "Mirzoyan, you'll have to sleep with her."

"W... Why me?" Tatev asked.

"This is between you and her. I'll just be a stranger butting in where she shouldn't at best. I'll do all I can to ask Horikawa if I can sleep with her."

"... Got it." Both Tatev and Wattana returned to the room. Tatev reluctantly but miraculously got Guliyeva to stand up, allowing Wattana to grab her futon and pillow. Once Wattana left and closed the door, Tatev took Guliyeva to her futon and as the former kneeled, so did the latter.

"Do you at least remember how to cross your legs?" Tatev asked.

"Bəli," Guliyeva replied.

Tatev stopped kneeling and turned. As she sat down, she crossed her legs. Guliyeva managed to copy Tatev's movements.

"I'm surprised... you're alive," Guliyeva said.

"So am I," Tatev replied, then looked at Guliyeva. She looked away in an instant. *What can I ask her after all these years?* Tatev pondered desperately. *Those scientists didn't hurt me in any particular manner, but with Maral... Wait, I think this might help.*

"How did Mr. 'Smith' and Sergio Ortiz treat you?" Tatev asked once she looked at Guliyeva again.

"They... took care of me... " Guliyeva answered; her hesitation evident with her tone. "Mr. Ortiz, he... "

"He gave his life to save you and Mr. 'Smith', didn't he?"

Guliyeva nodded. Tatev then stopped looking at the former and closed her eyes. *I can't tell for certain if she's appreciative of Ortiz's sacrifice or not, but it is a fact to Maral that he nor Mr. 'Smith' are the same as Kravchenko or Segismundo Alba since they risked their lives to save her.*

Guliyeva then looked at Tatev. "Your Azeri is better than when I first taught you," Guliyeva said, making Tatev open her eyes. Tatev then turned to Guliyeva.

"Y... You think so?" Tatev asked.

"How did you improve on it?"

"The one who bought me didn't intend on making me a sex slave. However, I was injected with something and made to hear certain sounds. Despite that, they spoiled me by allowing me to learn many languages, allowing me to improve on my Azeri... I apologize for even saying this. You must think I had it easy... "

"You seem to know who Cənab Smit is."

"That's a far longer story to tell... but I guess we have time."

The Attack

Unknown Location; Enlightenment Point. August 12, 2030; 2220 hours (EP Time Zone)

Reinhard Frühling appeared at the throne room occupied by Sergei Akulov. The former saluted the latter after he stopped walking.

"I assume you have news from 'SB'?" Akulov asked.

"I do, Grand Gatekeeper," Frühling answered. "Maral Eminovna Guliyeva has now arrived in Japan. She's under the protective custody of Frederick Dirks and Iron Dutchman Services."

"Allow 'SB' to launch the attack against the safehouse."

"By your will, Grand Gatekeeper."

#

Horikawa Bathhouse, Yao, Kansai Prefecture; State of Japan. August 13, 2030; 0819 hours (Japan Standard Time)

Sunan Wattana approached the room she moved out of the previous night. Before she could knock, she heard Tatev Mirzoyan's voice. She knocked regardless. Tatev then opened door, allowing Wattana to see her and Maral Eminovna Guliyeva.

"What were you up to?" Wattana asked.

"Teaching Maral English."

"Breakfast is ready. You can teach her later."

#

0822 hours

Wattana appeared the bathhouse's dining room with Tatev and Maral Eminovna Guliyeva following. Miyako Horikawa, Wouter Vos, Frederick Dirks, and Jawed Qazvini saw who'll be joining them.

"Glad you could join us," Dirks said. "Please sit."

"Thank you," Guliyeva replied, shocking everyone but Wattana and Tatev as the three women sat down.

"H… How did you pick up English?" Vos asked.

"Maral learned a little from Mr. 'Smith' before arriving here last night," Tatev answered. "She and I got up earlier than everyone else so that I can teach her some more."

"Can we please resume this discussion later?" Horikawa asked politely in English despite her Japanese accent evident in her tone.

"Right," Dirks declared. "Itadakimasu."

"Itadakimasu," everyone else but Guliyeva replied. It was then that everyone else realized that she doesn't know Japanese yet. Tatev, seated beside Guliyeva, immediately turned to her with embarrassment evident with her facial language.

"I apologize for not telling you about this," Tatev said. "In Japanese, they say 'itadakimasu' to begin eating."

"Never mind that," Horikawa said. "We can start eating already." Tatev then briefly stopped looking at Guliyeva.

"Wait, one last thing I need to say to Maral," Tatev warned before she turned to Guliyeva again. "After finishing a meal, say 'Gochi sou sama deshita, then, do this." Tatev then clasped her hands together. Guliyeva did the same and repeated what Tatev said.

"I assume it's in Japanese?" Guliyeva asked.

"It means 'Thank you for the meal'."

"Can we eat already?" Wattana asked. "You can teach her later."

"Sorry," Tatev and Guliyeva replied in unison.

Unlike in Mexico, Guliyeva was able to use her metal utensils well. Tatev glanced while chewing her food.

I'm surprised Maral can use utensils, Tatev thought. *Perhaps Mr. 'Smith' taught her how to use them. At least those scientists taught me how. I must have learned a lot before I was saved by Mr. Vos, Miss Wattana, Miss Crawley, and Tarou…*

Abandoned Mosque, West Mogadishu District, Mogadishu Capital Region; Republic of Somalia. January 10, 2029; 0104 hours (East Africa Time)

In her room, fifteen-year-old Tatev Mirzoyan heard gunshots. She dropped a book she was reading in response.

What was that? Tatev pondered.

Suddenly, a male scientist with dark skin barged into the room. "Doctor, what's the matter?" Tatev asked.

"Armed men are here," the scientist answered. "We have to get you out of here."

"But-"

"Just come with me. I promise to protect you."

Tatev then stood up and left the room with the man. However, they found Somali National Police fighting armed men in plain clothes. The former used R10 carbines while the latter used MP5 submachine guns. The scientist grabbed Tatev by her right wrist and dragged her with him as he ran. Unbeknownst to both, Tarou Ganji spotted them.

The scientist and Tatev then saw two more gunmen in plain clothes; unlike the armed men with MP5s, these gunmen used KAAN carbines. "Naga fogee iyaga!" the scientist ordered.

"Haa mudane," one gunman replied.

The scientist hurriedly moved, forcing the gunmen to move away. The former and Tatev arrived at a room whose door contained a sign with "Information". Once inside, the scientist locked the door.

"W… Why are we here?" Tatev asked as she saw the supercomputer. Gunshots followed.

"I just need to do something," the scientist replied before rushing to a desktop computer located to the left of the door.

As he reached the computer, he turned on the computer and, after typing in his password, began to access the computer's hard drive. He pressed commands that led to all data within the supercomputer to be deleted.

Suddenly, the door was kicked. The scientist then rushed to Tatev and grabbed her, using his left arm to prevent her from moving by constricting her neck and using his right hand to bring out a Zigana semi-automatic pistol and aim it at Tatev's right temple. The one who kicked the door was Tarou Ganji, and he aimed his R10 rifle at the scientist.

"Put the gun down and let the girl go!" Tarou demanded.

However, everyone heard a gunshot, with Tarou managing to avoid the bullet. This caused the bullet to hit the left knee of the scientist, allowing Tatev to free herself and grab the Zigana. Seeing the one responsible, one of the two gunmen that tried to prevent Tarou from reaching the information room, Tatev shot him.

Both Tatev and Tarou turned to the wounded scientist. Despite losing blood, the scientist had enough willpower to laugh.

"F... Fools, I may be dying, but you'll never get the information now," the scientist weakly boasted.

Tarou turned to the computer the scientist used. He saw that the data in the supercomputer was almost deleted. Just as he faced the scientist again, the former found the latter biting a cyanide pill. This hastened the scientist's death.

#

Horikawa Bathhouse, Yao, Kansai Prefecture; State of Japan. August 13, 2030; 0900 hours (Japan Standard Time)

"Gochi sou sama deshita," everyone said at the table once they finished breakfast. This included Guliyeva, who perfected the words and action needed.

You got that one right, Tatev thought with a smile while she looked at Guliyeva while making sure no one else noticed.

"Now I'll clean up the plates," Horikawa announced.

"I'll help," Wattana announced while raising her right hand.

"Arigatou," Horikawa replied as she looked at Wattana.

"That means 'Thank you' in Japanese," Tatev whispered to Guliyeva's left ear.

Both Horikawa and Wattana gathered all plates, dishes and bottles. Once that was done, they left the table.

"Before we discuss our next move, we wait until Wattana and Miss Horikawa are done washing the dishes," Dirks instructed. "We need Wattana with us on this discussion."

"Roger," Vos, Qazvini, and Tatev replied in unison.

#

0939 hours

Both Wattana and Horikawa returned to the dinner table. However, they found Dirks and the other Iron Dutchman Services members looking at them. The former two saw that the latter four looked at them.

"I apologize for this, but could please leave us?" Dirks asked.

"Hai," Horikawa replied. "I must prepare the baths if you'll use them later." She then left the dining room. Wattana then sat down.

"So, what is it that needed Miss Horikawa's absence?" Wattana asked.

"We need to plan how to get Kravchenko's men to our trap," Dirks explained. "At this point, he must have been able to infiltrate his men here in Japan?"

"Like with Serdar Muhadow?" Vos asked.

"That's right. We need to make it look like let our guard down but what we intend to do is make them overconfident."

"I have an idea," Wattana replied.

"What is it?" Dirks asked.

"We buy clothes for Maral. We get her new clothes and get the attention we need."

"Where will you buy your clothes?"

"Hold on." Wattana began to use her smartphone's Maps application. Examining the map of Kansai Prefecture, Wattana narrowed it to Yao. Finding where Horikawa Bathhouse was located in the map, she examined the surrounding shops carefully. She then found a shop called "Artisan Store" located in the Yamamotochokita neighborhood.

"Found it," Wattana announced as she opened the link to Artisan Store's website that is provided by Maps. "It's called 'Artisan Store'. They sell clothes. However, it's located in a separate neighborhood."

"Mind if I see what that store has to offer?" Dirks asked. "We need to know if the clothes found in that shop can fit Guliyeva."

"Here." Wattana then gave her phone to Dirks. Dirks began to look over the products offered in the store's online website. He then looked at Guliyeva after accessing the link to one particular dress.

"I can see the value in this trip," Dirks said. "However, before we move out, we need Guliyeva's measurements in order to figure out what kind of dress we can buy for her."

"I'll inspect her," Tatev replied while raising her hand.

"Hold on." Dirks then gave the phone he's holding back to Wattana. He then brought out his phone and gave it to Tatev. "In this phone is an app called 'MeasureScan'. Use it on Guliyeva but… "

"Maral can't have her clothes on, can she?"

"Tragically, yes."

"I said I'll do it."

"Good. Let me and Wattana know when you're done."

Outside Horikawa Bathhouse. 1039 hours

Wattana, Tatev, and Guliyeva began to leave the bathhouse. A white Stepwagn was secretly beside the three women, but it was invisible. One of the van's occupants was Shireen Baloch.

Unbeknownst to them, Wattana, Tatev, and Guliyeva briefly walked in front of the van until they turned to their left. Now, Shireen and the van's driver watched the three women walk in front of them. Once the former three were far from the van, Shireen turned to her driver.

"Jeo saramdeuleul ttalaga," Shireen instructed.

"Algessseubnida," the driver replied.

The driver moved the van but did so slowly. This was to make sure Wattana, Tatev, and Guliyeva realized that they were being followed. Unbeknownst to Shireen and the driver, someone was behind the van and heard the van's engines despite it being invisible. That person was none other than Frederick Dirks.

That was clearly a car, Dirks thought. *But how is it that I can't see it? Regardless, I best follow it.*

#

Outside Artisan House. 1110 hours

Shireen and her subordinate arrived at Artisan House; the Stepwagn now visible. Finding a parking lot close by, the driver took the van there and once the van was parked, Shireen pressed a certain button that made the van invisible.

However, Shireen did this in front of Dirks, who had just arrived at Artisan House. He then looked at the parking lot, unaware that he was looking right at the Stepwagn used by Shireen.

Funny, thought I would see that white van here, Dirks said in his mind. *Best join Wattana and the others, because I doubt they have money to pay for that dress.*

Dirks then went inside. As a result, Shireen made the van visible again.

"I'll go into that shop," Shireen said to the driver. "Please remain here."

"Algessseubnida," the driver replied.

#

Artisan House. 1113 hours

Shireen was now inside Artisan House. After being welcomed inside, she then saw Dirks whispering to Wattana as they stood outside a changing room. She then looked toward a rack to avoid catching their attention.

I didn't see Guliyeva with that FIS agent, Shireen anxiously thought. *Are they here... to get her a dress?*

Shireen then watched the mercenary and the FIS agent standing by the changing room. Dirks in turn noticed but made she Shireen didn't notice him.

I'd like to believe that she's with Kravchenko, but she doesn't look Korean, Dirks thought. *And I just made a racist thought. But still, she's as old as Tatev and if she's looking at us, she must have a reason to do so.*

Suddenly, Dirks and Wattana heard the changing door open. Shireen also noticed. To everyone's surprise, Maral Eminovna Guliyeva came out wearing an indigo blue dress. Tatev Mirzoyan then joined Dirks and Wattana.

"How does she look?" Tatev asked happily.

"She looks great!" Wattana answered.

This reminds me of when I bought a dress for Mon's prom, Dirks thought as he looked at Guliyeva wearing the dress. He then faced Wattana. "I'll start paying for the dress," he said. "Please tell Guliyeva that she has to remove that dress."

As Dirks neared the cashier, he then caught a glance of Shireen. Shireen caught Dirks' glance in kind. Unbeknownst to Wattana, Tatev, and Guliyeva, this made Dirks and Shireen aware of each other. When Dirks reached the cashier and began paying for Guliyeva's dress, Shireen left Artisan House.

#

Abandoned Shipwreck, Crater Shore North. 1359 hours

Shireen then returned to the shipwreck in Crater Shore North that was used as the hideout for her and the Koreans she brought with her. The leader of the Koreans, Song Dong-joo, approached her as she entered the shipwreck.

"What did you find?" Song asked.

"That FIS agent and his pet mercenaries think we'll fall for his trap," Shireen replied. "Gather the men. It's time to attack that bathhouse, but we need to plan the attack first."

"Algessseubnida."

#

Horikawa Bathhouse, Yao. 1410 hours

Dirks, Wattana, Wouter Vos, and Jawed Qazvini were gathered in the dining room in Horikawa Batthouse. Tatev then joined them.

"How's Guliyeva?" Dirks asked as everyone turned to Tatev while she sat down.

"I had her review everything I taught her," Tatev answered. "What now?"

"While we were at Artisan House, I encountered a girl as old as Tatev. She could be with Kravchenko's men."

"So we'll use her to lead us to Kravchenko?" Vos asked.

"Yes. If she is following us, she could know about this bathhouse."

"So what's the plan?" Wattana asked.

"If she is working for Kravchenko, we need to get her," Dirks answered.

"How?"

"I need to talk to Horikawa first. I think it's time to open *that part* of the changing room."

"What part?"

#

1422 hours

Dirks and the Iron Dutchman Services members were now in the changing room. Finding two lockers that each had a sign with the kanji for "Koshō-chū" on it, Dirks removed the signs and simply opened the lockers. The mercenaries were surprised at what the lockers contained.

One locker contained a large bag with STANAG magazines below with 5.56x45mm bullets inside. The other locker contained cleaning kits for the rifles. Dirks then brought out the bag and opened it. Inside the bag were three Adaptive Rifles.

"Is that all?" Vos asked.

"It is," Dirks answered. "I'd say it's adequate for what will come next."

"You think Kravchenko's men will come in here, guns blazing?" Wattana asked.

"We must be prepared for that," Dirks answered. "It's why there are cleaning kits in here. We have to start cleaning up the rifles."

"I only see three," Vos asked as he looked at the locker with the rifles.

"That's where the rest of the plan comes in," Dirks answered. "For now, we clean up these rifles because it's only been a year since I installed them here and they haven't been used."

#

1505 hours

"Now that we've finished with the cleaning, allow me to explain the rest of the plan," Dirks announced, prompting the mercenaries to clean up the dining room table of the material used from the cleaning kits and putting aside the ADRs.

Dirks then laid out a paper map of Yao. A red circle was already drawn around the portion of the Takasagocho neighborhood where Horikawa Bathhouse was located at. "I encircled the bathhouse," Dirks continued. "Now, if that girl is working for Kravchenko, most likely he'll send some men to attack the bathhouse. We're to ambush them and grab at least one alive to use to get us to Kravchenko."

Dirks then brought out a red marker pen; the same one he used to mark out the bathhouse on the map. He then wrote Xs on two locations closest to the bathhouse. The first X written on the Takasagocho Sanchome Park and the second one at the apartment complex to the right of the bathhouse.

"I need someone to attack from the park behind the bathhouse and another to attack from the apartment. Volunteers?"

"I'll launch from park," Qazvini replied.

"I'll go for the apartment," Wattana added.

"Good." Dirks replied before he turned to Vos. "Vos, if in the event something does go wrong, I need you to flee with Tatev and Guliyeva. Run as fast as you can to the parking lot and escape with the Townace. Don't stop."

"Why me?" Vos asked.

"Because I'll remain in the bathhouse and attack from the veranda, but only when the firing starts."

"But where will we flee to?" Tatev asked.

"The *Iron Dutchman*," Dirks answered. "Wattana, Qazvini, and I will use the ADRs."

\#

Abandoned Shipwreck, Crater Shore North. 1514 hours

"And here, one fireteam will wait if in the event those mercenaries rush to their Townace and escape with Guliyeva," Shireen Baloch explained as she pointed at the street near the parking lot in Takasagocho using the same paper map. "That will be all."

"Clean up your weapons," Song Dong-joo ordered to all of his subordinates. "Bang Sanggŭp-pyŏngsa, once you and your men finish cleaning up your rifles, launch immediately."

"Algessseubnida," the subordinate named Bang replied.

\#

Horikawa Bathhouse, Yao. 0200 hours

"I'm sorry if my story made you… jealous," Tatev Mirzoyan said to Maral Eminovna Guliyeva; both were laying on their futon in the room Tatev shared with Sunan Wattana.

"I'm not jealous," Guliyeva said. "I'm glad you were saved. I hope to meet everyone else in Iron Dutchman Services."

"Maral, depending on how this will end, I promise you, I will protect you."

\#

1545 hours

At the same room, Tatev filled her sports bag with books. Maral assisted her.

"Are you sure this will work?" Maral asked.

"We can't give up," Tatev answered defiantly. "I said I will protect you."

"The boy you mentioned in your story, Tarou Ganji, where is he now?"

"He has his studies to finish. Most importantly, he has to keep an eye on Maria Hoshikawa."

"Maria Hoshikawa?"

"The daughter of the President of Hoshikawa Group. Think the conglomerates of the Eurasian Tsardom, but Japanese."

"Why does he have to protect her?"

"That's why Iron Dutchman Services is here in Japan. We're to keep an eye on Miss Hoshikawa while Mr. 'Smith's' employers figure out who would want to kidnap her. Months ago, the mercenary Serdar Muhadow managed to do so and Tarou was able to save her. But we were left with more questions than answers."

A knock was heard from the other end of the door. "It's 'Smith'," the FIS agent said. "Are you ladies done packing up?"

"Almost," Tatev answered.

"Wattana just bribed an owner of a nearby apartment. She's positioning herself right now. I suggest you hurry up."

"Roger." Tatev and Maral resumed filling the bag of the former.

#

1555 hours

Tatev and Maral appeared near the veranda. They found Dirks prone on the floor. Tatev signaled Maral to remain with her bag while she crawled to join Dirks.

"Tatev, is that you?" Dirks asked as he heard Tatev approach him.

"Yes," Tatev answered as she appeared beside Dirks. "Maral and I finished packing up."

"Good. Join Vos downstairs."

"Roger." Tatev then crawled back to Maral. After kneeling, she whispered to Maral what to do next. After that, both left the second floor of the bathhouse.

Apartment near Horikawa Bathhouse/Outside Horikawa Bathhouse/Horikawa Bathhouse. 1610 hours

A white Stepwagn appeared in the apartment beside Horikawa Bathhouse. Four men in black, armed with AK-05s burst out of the van, hiding their faces with balaclavas.

The men stopped at the entrance of the bathhouse. Two men each hugged the vending machines in front of the bathhouse. Unbeknownst to them, Sunan Wattana saw them from the apartment she occupied. One man at the vending machine on the left turned to the man behind.

"Niga meonjeoga," the man ordered to the one behind.

"Ye, Bang In-Young Sanggŭp-pyŏngsa-nim," the man replied.

The man in black, proceeded to the bathhouse by himself. More men in black appeared in front of the bathhouse.

The Korean gunman found Miyako Horikawa operating the counter for customers. She would then bring out a gun of her own, a P9 semi-automatic pistol, only to be shot by Bang as he joined hius subordinate and used his AK-05.

Suddenly, another gunshot was heard, starting a firefight. Bang rushed out of the bathhouse and found Sunan Wattana attacking his subordinates. Jawed Qazvini appeared from Takasagocho Sanchome Park and also attacked the Koreans. Frederick Dirks then joined the mercenaries in attacking the Koreans.

Unbeknownst to the Koreans, Wouter Vos, Tatev Mirzoyan, and Maral Eminovna Guliyeva were at the dining room, to the right of the counter. While Vos was armed with his SP2 semi-automatic pistol, Tatev wielded her P9.

"I'll jump out first and laying surpressing fire on those blokes out there," Vos silently explained to Tatev. "As soon as I fire, you and Guliyeva run like hell."

"Roger," Tatev replied.

"Watch carefully." Vos then stood up and rushed outside. He found the Koreans retreating. He then turned to Tatev and Guliyeva, using his left hand to signal to them that they can come out and follow him.

Both Tatev and Guliyeva did so, but despite glancing at Horikawa's corpse, they pressed on. Once they joined Vos, they rushed out of the bathhouse.

Outside Horikawa Bathhouse. 1619 hours

Bang and his subordinates were now trapped behind their van. Wattana and Qazvini were able to pin them there. However, Bang saw Vos, Tatev, and Guliyeva rush out of the bathhouse and turned to his subordinates.

"Ko, Hyun, jeo saramdeuleul ttalaga," Bang ordered to two of his subordinates.

"Ye, Bang In-young Sanggŭp-pyŏngsa-nim," the two Koreans replied in unison.

Both Koreans began to divert away from the van. Wattana, however, spotted them only for Bang and those still with him to fire at her. This allowed Ko and Hyun to catch up to Guliyeva only for Tatev to turn her back and fire her P9 at the two Koreans, killing them. Once she depleted her magazine, she removed it and resumed escaping with Vos and Guliyeva. It was then that Dirks appeared from the bathhouse to help Wattana and Qazvini, allowing them to kill Bang and those with him.

Nishigori Parking. 1640 hours

Vos, Tatev, and Guliyeva then reached the parking lot where their Townace was parked at. Because they used all the energy they needed to run, they were panting.

"Five... seconds, then... we climb... " Vos said, despite having spent two seconds saying that. As a result, they spent more than five seconds panting. Thankfully, it wasn't long as they were able to stand normally.

"I'll stay here. Mirzoyan, you climb first. Guliyeva, you're next, then I'm last."

"Got it," Tatev and Guliyeva replied in unison.

Vos knelt and opened his right palm while placing his left one below it. Tatev then stepped on Vos' right palm after holstering her P9 and after grasping the top rail of the fence, she jumped, followed by turning, allowing her inside the parking lot. Guliyeva was next to do so and was able to replicate what Tatev did. After that, Vos got up and grabbed the top rail, then jumped and turned. Once he joined Tatev and Guliyeva, they rushed to the Townace. After Vos unlocked it, Tatev and Guliyeva rushed inside, with Vos rushing to the driver's seat. Once he started up the van, he moved as soon as he could, but was unaware that two of

Bang's men were watching them. As soon as Vos left, the Koreans followed using another white Stepwagn.

However, there was someone else watching both Vos and the Koreans leave. That person was Pyotr Stepanovich Chadov. He had to wait, lest he was willing to be caught. Once he saw the Koreans in front of the cemetery beside the parking lot, he moved to follow.

#

Horikawa Bathhouse. 1642 hours

Dirks alone returned to Horikawa Bathhouse. He then approached the corpse of Miyako Horikawa and touched her head. He then lowered his head and closed his eyes. It was then that Sunan Wattana rushed inside and found him.

"Is that you, Wattana?" Dirks asked without moving his head.

"Y… Yes," Wattana answered. "I'm sorry if I-"

"What is it?"

"We found keys for that van. We can use it to get out of here."

"Then start it up. I'll go upstairs and pack up." Dirks then raised his head, let go of Horikawa's corpse, and began to move without even looking at Wattana.

Wattana then turned to Horikawa's corpse. She, too, lowered her head and closed her eyes. After standing there for one second, she rushed out of the bathhouse.

#

Higashiosaka Ward, Kansai City. 1649 hours

Vos, Tatev, and Guliyeva were now in Kansai City. Vos, driving the Townace, saw a stoplight and appropriately stopped as he saw the red light. The two Koreans following them also stopped.

"Mr. Vos, the van behind us stopped," Tatev said. "I was able to see who's driving it and they're also in black."

"I know," Vos replied. "As soon as I see green, it's full speed ahead."

Turning Point Part 1

Higashiosaka Ward, Kansai City, Kansai Prefecture; State of Japan. August 13, 2030; 1700 hours (Japan Standard Time)

Across Kansai City's Higashiosaka Ward, Wouter Vos drove Iron Dutchman Services' Townace van as fast as he could. Both Tatev Mirzoyan and Maral Eminovna Guliyeva struggled to remain still due to how fast the van was, but that was the least of their concerns. The two Koreans pursuing them gave chase with their Stepwagn van as fast as they could. One of them leaned from the front left seat and fired his AK-05 assault rifle at the Townace.

"What do we do!?" Tatev screamed. "They'll keep pursuing us no matter which direction we go!"

"I know!" Vos screamed in response. "I have an idea, but bear with me!"

Tatev and Guliyeva continued to hide while Vos turned right upon seeing the next stoplight. The Koreans continued their pursuit, regardless. Unbeknownst to both parties, Pyotr Stepanovich Chadov continued his pursuit of the white Stepwagn but opted to turn back.

#

1709 hours

"Are we still being pursued?" Vos asked as he continued driving. Tatev slowly rose and reared her head. She saw the Stepwagn used by the Koreans but didn't see the man that was firing at them. She then ducked again and faced Vos.

"We are, but they're not shooting at us," Tatev answered.

"Good. Listen to me. We're near Nishi High School. Once we see the next stoplight, I'll stop if we see a red light. You and Guliyeva must get off and hide at Ganji's apartment."

"Why?"

"I have an idea, but you will not like it. Just do it because if there's a slim chance this plan will keep Guliyeva safe, take it! Ganji can definitely help with that."

I promised Maral I will protect her, Tatev thought. *This seems to be the only plan that can stop those Koreans from pursuing us.*

"Roger."

It was then that the mercenaries and Guliyeva came across another stoplight. Despite the red light, Vos turned left. Unbeknownst to the mercenaries and Guliyeva, the Korean gunman had loaded another magazine into his AK-05 as he had wasted all of his magazines when he fired at the mercenaries' Townace earlier. Once he loaded his rifle, he leaned out again, aimed at the Townace, and fired once both vans crossed underneath the rail bridge used by Kintetsu Railway's Nara Line.

"They're firing again!" Tatev shouted.

"We're almost there!" Vos replied.

Vos continued dodging as much as he could, with Tatev and Guliyeva continuing to hide. Like before, the Korean gunman wasted his entire magazine and stopped leaning in order to reload. By this time, however, they neared the Takadonocho neighborhood, where Nishi High School was located at.

"Mirzoyan, it's time!" Vos announced. "There should be a car dealer to our right. Once we see it, open the right door and jump out. Take Guliyeva with you."

"But what about you!?" Tatev asked.

"I'll be fine!"

The two mercenaries then saw the car dealer. Tatev immediately open the right rear door then turned to Guliyeva.

"Maral, I'm going to jump off the van," Tatev warned. "You'll have to grab my hand!"

Guliyeva simply nodded. Tatev walked backward, then stopped. She then grabbed Guliyeva's left hand. After that, Tatev propelled herself out of the Townace with Guliyeva, holding her, also propelled out. It was then that Vos turned back while Tatev and Guliyeva got up.

"Maral, we need to run!" Tatev warned. "Now!"

Guliyeva nodded again. She and Tatev began to run while Vos charged toward the pursuing Stepwagn. Once he saw the Korean gunman firing his AK-05, Vos made another turn, making the Koreans bump into his Townace. As fast as he could, Vos used what little strength he had in bringing out his SP2 semi-automatic pistol and, seeing the Koreans, he fired until both were dead. Vos then passed out as soon as the airbag launched from the steering wheel. It was then that Chadov appeared and, after stopping his Stepwagn, rushed to the damaged Townace, opened the right front door, removed Vos' seatbelt, grabbed his SP2, and dragged him out of the van. Chadov made haste as he heard police sirens.

#

Hamilton-Ganji Condominium, Hoshikawa Condominiums. 1800 hours

While studying, Tarou Ganji heard a knock on his door. He stopped and rushed to the door. Once he reached the door, he saw through the door's peephole that it was Tatev Mirzoyan and Maral Eminovna Guliyeva. Guliyeva pressed her right hand against her heart without Tatev noticing.

Why is Tatev here? Tarou pondered. *Since there's another girl with her, it looks urgent.*

"Tarou, are you-" Tatev asked.

"Hold on," Tarou instantly replied before he opened the door. "Please remove your shoes first."

"Hai," Tatev replied. Tarou then stepped further into the condominium, allowing Tatev and Guliyeva to proceed further, but they stopped by removing their shoes. Once that was done, they joined Tarou at the condominium's dining table.

"What's going on here?" Tarou asked.

"Tarou, this is Maral Eminovna Guliyeva," Tatev explained, with Guliyeva bowing. "I apologize for bothering you, but we need your help."

"I can help. I finished my summer homework. Now, please start from the beginning."

"What about Dr. Hamilton?"

"Hold on." Tarou stood up and rushed back to his bedroom. He then grabbed his smartphone and after returning to the dining table, he used his phone's IntMail and finding "Dr. AH", he typed the following:

Doc, I apologize for this, but I might be late in picking you up tonight. Something highly urgent came up.

Tarou then pressed "Send". After that, he put down the phone and faced Tarou and Guliyeva.

"Now you can begin from the start."

Tatev began her tale. Tarou listened while closing his eyes as he realized that was why he hadn't heard from Vos or anyone else from Iron Dutchman Services, as he had his summer homework to finish.

"So that explains the firefight across Yao," Tarou said after listening to Tatev. "Nothing from Mr. 'Smith', nor Miss Wattana?"

"Nothing," Tatev answered.

"What now?"

"We still need to go to the *Iron Dutchman*."

"I'm not sure if-" Another knock was heard. *Great, what now?* Tarou anxiously pondered.

"Tarou, are you home?" a female voice asked. Tarou knew that voice as Maria Hoshikawa's. Tarou then rushed to Tatev's right ear.

"Hide and take Guliyeva with you to my room," Tarou whispered as an order to Tatev.

Tatev nodded. She grabbed Guliyeva and as she stood, so did she. Both rushed to Tarou's room. Tarou then rushed to the door and rearing his head, he found Tatev and Guliyeva gone. He then picked up their respective shoes and hid them in the bathroom. After that, he returned to the door and opened it.

"Sorry about that," Tarou said as he saw Maria Hoshikawa outside. She didn't wear her Nishi High School uniform but a cyan sundress underneath a white cardigan. "Please come in."

Tarou then stepped out of Maria's way. Once she removed the same shoes she wore at school, she and Tarou sat at the dining table.

"So, what can I do for you?" Tarou asked.

"Just came to ask about your summer homework," Maria answered.

"I'm done with all of it."

"What took you so long to let me in?"

Damn it, Tarou cursed in his mind. *I may have told her about Tatev, but she doesn't know that she's in here right now. Not only that, there's Guliyeva...*

"Sorry about that. I was incredibly busy that I didn't hear you."

"Where's Dr. Hamilton? Shouldn't you have picked her up by now?"

Great... if I tell her that I told her that I will pick her up late, she will suspect that I've been given a mission... I guess I have no choice...

"Maria, forgive me, but I've been lying to you. I told Dr. Hamilton that I'll be picking her up late because a mission did come to me, but it was someone else's mission."

"What do you mean?"

Tarou then turned to his room. "Tatev, Guliyeva, you can come out. I can't lie to Maria any longer."

Tarou's room opened. Coming out were Tatev and Guliyeva.

"I'll have Tatev explain from the beginning." Tatev and Guliyeva then sat down.

#

Outside Hoshikawa Condominiums. 1900 hours

Not only have two girls entered the condominium, but another did, Vladimir Nikolayevich Mirov thought as he hid in a nearby street while looking at the limousine used by Maria Hoshikawa. *And this girl has her own driver.*

Suddenly, he heard the safety of a pistol being released. Mirov then turned to find Jason Luke Crawley aiming his P5 semi-automatic pistol at him.

"No sudden moves," Crawley warned, forcing Mirov to surrender.

#

Hamilton-Ganji Condominium, Hoshikawa Condominiums. 0729 hours

"I… honestly don't what to say… " Maria replied after listening to Tatev and Guliyeva's story. "I guess that explains the sirens I heard when Mr. Ugaki and I neared this complex."

"Wait, did you say sirens?" Tatev asked.

"I don't know the details, but there seems to have been a car chase along Sotokanjo-sen."

"Maral and I came from that car chase. We got out of the Townace Mr. Vos was driving before he charged at our pursuers."

"We need to leave for the *Iron Dutchman* at once," Tarou warned.

"Like I said after we left Sakhalin Island, I'll help in any way in can," Maria replied.

"Then can you please get Mr. Ugaki to take Tatev and Guliyeva to Hoshikawa Shipyards? I don't think I can take two passengers with my scooter."

"I'll tell Mr. Ugaki."

"Then I'll prepare what I need." Tarou then faced Tatev and Guliyeva. "That goes for the both of you. I hid your shoes in the bathroom, so I'll get them."

Tatev and Guliyeva simply nodded. Everyone then stood up with Maria racing to the entrance and putting on her shoes. Tatev and Guliyeva rushed back to Tarou's room while Tarou returned to the bathroom.

Once Tarou retrieved the shoes, Maria had left the condominium. Tatev and Guliyeva then returned to the dining table with their bag. After leaving their respective shoes at the entrance, Tarou rejoined Tatev and Guliyeva.

"Wait here," Tarou ordered. "I need to get my pistol and ammunition. Then we join Maria outside."

"Roger," Tatev replied.

Tarou then ran to his room. Tatev and Guliyeva then sat down at the dining table again.

"What does 'Roger' mean?" Guliyeva asked.

"It's actually a name for men," Tatev answered. "In military matters, it's to positively acknowledge an order."

"What will happen now?"

"We'll be safe once we go to the *Iron Dutchman*. Hopefully, Mr. 'Smith', Miss Wattana, and Mr. Qazvini made it there."

Tarou then left his room, carrying his school bag with him. After he closed his room's door, he faced Tatev and Guliyeva. "You ladies ready?" Tarou asked.

"We are," Tatev answered as she and Guliyeva faced Tarou.

"Then it's time to go."

#

Outside Hoshikawa Condominiums. 1955 hours

Tarou, Tatev, and Guliyeva exited the condominiums. However, they found Maria atr the front gate, watching something.

"Maria, what's going on here?" Tarou asked as he, Tatev, and Guliyeva joined Maria.

"Mr. Crawley's outside," Maria answered. "He's holding a gun at someone while Mr. Ugaki and the guard of the condominium complex are apprehending the man."

"Stay here." Maria nodded just as Tarou left the complex.

Tarou then arrived just as Ugaki used plastic handcuffs on Vladimir Nikolayevich Mirov. "Why are you here, Mr. Crawley?" Tarou asked as he faced Crawley. "And who's this?"

"He's been spying on you for a good while," Crawley answered.

"If you intend to take him to the *Iron Dutchman*, I'll need your help." Tarou turned his upper body back to the condominium complex and used his right hand to make Maria, Tatev, and Guliyeva join them.

"Since you've been keeping an eye on me, I assume you know who this is?" Tatev asked as he gestured to Guliyeva, making Crawley face her.

"Yes," Crawley answered. "She's why I was ordered to keep an eye on you. Though why is she here?"

"She shouldn't be," Tarou answered. "Tatev took her here to hide. Now we need to get her to the *Iron Dutchman*. If you intend to take the man you caught to the ship, use the limo."

Ugaki tried to say something about Tarou's suggestion, only for Maria to whisper to him. Reluctantly, Ugaki nodded once Maria finished. Suddenly, engines were heard. Tarou and Tatev brought out their respective pistols and aimed at the Stepwagn van that appeared.

"Wait, it's us!" Frederick Dirks shouted as he and Jawed Qazvini appeared out of the van with Sunan Wattana remained at the driver's seat.

"Mr. 'Smith'?" Tatev exclaimed before holstering her P9. "Thank God you're alive!"

"Glad you made it, Tatev. What's going on here?"

"We were just about to leave for the *Iron Dutchman*," Tarou answered while hiding his P226. "I got Mr. Ugaki to help take Guliyeva to the *Iron Dutchman* but Mr. Crawley caught someone spying on me."

"Then let's get moving. The man Crawley arrested can come with me and Qazvini."

"I have a name!" Mirov shouted.

"You know English, but with your Russian accent, you must be an OVR infiltrator," Crawley claimed. This shocked everyone, as they all had in mind what happened in Sakhalin Island.

"Give him to me!" Dirks ordered. "We have to move now!"

Tarou, Ugaki, and the guard moved out of Crawley's way as he made Mirov move. He then pushed Mirov to Qazvini, who then dragged Mirov to the Stepwagn with Dirks following.

"Let's move out!" Tarou ordered, then he turned to the guard. "Momose-san, chūrinjō o akete kudasai."

"Wakarimasu," the guard named Momose replied before rushing to where Tarou kept his PCX scooter at.

Tarou then dragged the PCX out of the bicycle parking lot with Momose locking it again after he was thanked by Tarou. The former then positioned himself in front of the limousine after Maria returned to it. Tarou then started up the scooter and was the first to move, with the limousine following, and the Stepwagn following last.

Hoshikawa Shipyards, Taisho Ward. 2030 hours

The convoy that comprised Tarou in his PCX, the Hoshikawa limousine, and the Stepwagn used Dirks, Wattana, and Qazvini stopped in front of the *Iron Dutchman*. To everyone's surprise, they found Anita Hamilton waiting for them. As a result, Tarou parked his scooter and rushed to her.

"Doc, I apologize for-" Tarou attempted to say only for Hamilton to use her right palm to do so.

"It's alright," Hamilton replied. "Since you hadn't picked me up in an hour, Mr. Hoshikawa got me a taxi. What's going on?"

Both Tarou and Hamilton saw Tatev and Guliyeva leave the limousine and Wattana parking the Stepwagn. Tarou then turned to Hamilton.

"Please get inside," Tarou requested. "I need to tell Maria to go home."

"Her father's still waiting at Hoshikawa Group Headquarters," Hamilton replied.

"I'll tell Mr. Ugaki to pick him up, then I'll tell him to take a different route to the Hoshikawa Mansion. You'll know why soon."

#

Iron Dutchman. 2055 hours

Dirks and all members of Iron Dutchman Services, save for Wouter Vos, gathered at the briefing room. Vos and Sunan Wattana climbed to the stage and faced the rest of the mercenary group.

"I will begin this briefing by iterating what happened in the last eight hours," Dirks explained. "Horikawa Bathhouse, a front for an FIS safehouse, was attacked. Its proprietor, Miyako Horikawa, was killed. While Wattana, Qazvini, and I held off the attackers, Vos escaped with Tatev and Guliyeva on my order.

"However, they were pursued. Vos sacrificed himself to end the pursuit and on his order, Tatev and Guliyeva sought shelter with Ganji. Wattana, Qazvini, and I were able to steal one of two Stepwagn vans used by our attackers and we were able to acquire the help of Maria Hoshikawa and Tadashi Ugaki in bringing Miss Guliyeva to this ship."

"What do we do now?" Vikas Mistry asked. "Not only that, what about Mr. Vos?"

"Wattana and I will talk it over with the police later," Dirks answered. "More importantly, we know that the attackers were Koreans and that they must be working for Anton Oleksandrovich Kravchenko, a human trafficker intent on reclaiming his *merchandise*. For those who don't know, the objective is to capture one of Kravchenko's Koreans and use him to lead us to Kravchenko. Once we capture Kravchenko, the FIS will use him as a bargaining chip for negotiations with the Eurasian Tsardom. Guliyeva was bait to draw out Kravchenko into sending his Koreans to Japan."

"What about the man Mr. Crawley caught?" Tarou asked.

"We'll interrogate him soon," Dirks answered. "From what Crawley has told me, he was more focused on you so we can rule out the possibility he was there for Maria Hoshikawa."

"Any further questions?" Wattana asked.

"None," the other mercenaries answered in unison.

"For now, we're dismissed." Wattana then turned to Bartolomeu Moura. "Barto, please prepare something fast for dinner."

"I have air-fried chicken with Umami seasoning in mind," Moura replied. "It's a good opportunity to test that new air fryer."

After Moura's explanation as to what will be their dinner, the mercenaries leave the briefing room. Tarou, however, walked up to Dirks.

"Mr. 'Smith', there's something I need to ask you," Tarou said to Dirks.

"What is it?" Dirks asked in response. "Just so you know, I'm not joining you for dinner. I need to have Horikawa's corpse brought in here and store until we contact a funeral home."

"I wish to speak with our Eurasian prisoner."

OVR Safehouse, Nishinari Ward. 2055 hours

Wouter Vos began to come about. As his vision became clear, he found Pytor Stepanovich Chadov, Tatiana Ioannovna Tsulukidze, and Karim Olegovich Zhakiyanov looking at him with their dining table separating them from him.

"Glad you're awake," Tatiana said.

"Although accented, that's good English," Vos replied.

"I find that hilarious coming from a Boer. No offence."

"None taken. Who are you?"

"We'll ask the questions h-" Chadov angrily replied, only for Tatiana to stop him by blocking his mouth with her right palm.

"Calm yourself, 'Stepan'," Tatiana ordered before facing Vos again. "My apologies. Enough about my English skills. Call me 'Elizaveta'. The man beside me, who saved your life hours ago, is to be called 'Stepan' while the man to my left is to be called 'Oleg'."

"So, why 'save' me?" Vos asked while shaking his body to remind his OVR captors that they tied him to a chair.

"We intend to barter you for one of my men, who has yet to return after six hours," Tatiana answered. "He's most likely been captured by one of your men for following another subordinate."

She must have Ganji followed, Vos thought. *And Jake must have captured her spy. If they intend to use me as barter, this could be a good way for me to ask them why they're here.*

"If you intend to trade me for one of your men, why are you here in the first place?" Vos asked.

"I assumed you would ask such a question. As you can guess, we're with the OVR, the Eurasian Tsardom's intelligence agency, and we were sent here to monitor New United Nations Defense Forces activity."

"Isn't telling me stuff like this a violation of your orders?"

"You're being… it's as you English speakers put it, 'cheeky', aren't you? You're right. But the Director gave me orders to do what's needed and as long as I get my subordinate back, telling this to you will help. Now, allow me to continue."

"Fine, fine. Please, tell me more."

"Recently, my men and I have been making strange deliveries to an abandoned shipwreck in Crater Shore North. I've assumed your mercenary group is connected because you took your van to Yao. Now, why were you at Yao?"

"It's a simple protection job. My men and I were to guard a girl our… 'benefactor', for lack of a better term, retrieved from Mexico."

"And what's the girl's name?"

"Maral Eminovna Guliyeva. I assume you know her."

We have a file on her, Tatiana thought. *She was one of the girls abducted by Anton Oleksandrovich Kravchenko and yet... That's what the FIS is doing! They intend to capture or kill Kravchenko while using Guliyeva.*

"Thank you, you've been very helpful," Tatiana ultimately replied. She then turned to Chadov. "Make sure he's fed but do not untie him."

Tatiana and Zhakiyanov left the table, leaving Chadov to guard Vos. While Zhakiyanov retrieved one of the many sandwiches they've bought from the pharmacy beside Nishi High School, Tatiana returned to her room.

Tatiana then connected her phone to the satellite receiver and turned on her phone's SatCom. She opted for an audio call with "Nizhny"— Vyacheslav Leonidovich Puzanov.

"I assume you have something new to tell me?" Puzanov asked on the other end of Tatiana's phone.

"Da," Tatiana answered. "Chadov captured one of the mercenaries in the FIS's employ."

"Otlichno! What has he told you?"

"The FIS seem to be going after Anton Oleksandrovich Kravchenko because one FIS agent rescued a girl Kravchenko sold from Mexico."

"Did I hear that right? Anton Oleksandrovich Kravchenko?"

"Da."

"... Anything else?"

"Unfortunately, Leytenánt Mirov may have been captured by my captive's subordinates. I intend to exchange him for Leytenánt Mirov. If you approve."

"We need him back at Sevastopol. Do what you have to do."

"I need your help with that. Since our calls are being recorded, might I suggest giving a copy of the transcript to Deputy Director Askarova?"

"What for?"

"You know *why*. That way, we can tell the FIS indirectly about our hostage so that we can exchange our hostage for Leytenánt Mirov."

"I'll do all I can. After this, let me know when you wish to conduct this hostage exchange."

"Zametano."

#

Iron Dutchman, Taisho Ward. 2121 hours

Tarou Ganji appeared at the brig of the *Iron Dutchman* by himself, carrying a tray with food, utensils, and a glass of water. He approached the cell where Vladimir Nikolayevich Mirov was detained in.

"I'm here to give you dinner," Tarou announced to Mirov. "I also have the keys, but don't think about stealing the keys from me."

"I won't," Mirov replied.

"Then please stay back."

Mirov did as Tarou demanded. The latter put down the tray and began unlocking the cell door. After that, he immediately stood up, grabbed the tray, crouched again as he moved his upper body toward Mirov's cell, slowly slid the tray toward Mirov himself, and locked the cell door before Mirov got the chance to steal the key.

"I assume you were ordered to give me food?" Mirov asked.

"No," Tarou answered, but paused until he knew how to continue the conversation. "Actually, I was but that's not what I'm here to do."

"What is it?"

"I wish to ask about you. Why were you spying on me?"

"It's simple, I wish to know who defeated me thrice in combat: the first two times in Sakhalin Governorate and the last time in the Iran Governorate."

"Wait a second, you're-"

"I'm Vladimir Nikolayevich Mirov. Imperial Eurasian Naval Infantry, Western Regiment."

"And I assume you were able to infiltrate Japan with the assistance of the OVR?"

"Da. That means 'Yes' in Russian."

"Are you here for Maria Hoshikawa?"

"The girl who owned that limousine? No. I came here to learn about you, if in the event we were to fight again."

"And why did you take this mission?"

"Twice I've lost subordinates because of the fact we fought. If we are to meet again in battle, I hope only one of us lives."

"I see… " Tarou then turned his back on Mirov. "That will be all. Enjoy your dinner."

Tarou then left the brig. Although he took the short interrogation as an insult, Mirov began to eat his dinner.

#

OVR Headquarters, Nizhegorodsky District, Imperial Capital of Nizhny Novgorod; Eurasian Tsardom. 1859 hours (Novgorod Time)

Aigul Askarova, the Deputy Director of the OVR, appeared at the office of her Director. "You called for me, Director?" Askarova asked.

"Da," Puzanov answered. "I've received a report from 'Elizaveta'. I wish to give you a copy of the report. Please come forward."

"Spasibo". Askarova then came close to Puzanov's desk and received the three-page report.

"Since I'm here, I wish to request something," Askarova added after receiving the report.

"What is it?" Puzanov asked.

"I wish to have dinner with my wife tonight. I promised her to have dinner with her early in the evening once a month. I promise to return after dinner."

"Fine. Please give Pati my regards."

"Spasibo."

Unknown Location; Enlightenment Point. 2200 hours (EP Time Zone)

"I assume you have an update?" Sergei Akulov asked Reinhard Frühling.

"I do, Grand Gatekeeper," Frühling answered. "Shall I give it to you?"

"Yes, you may." Frühling climbed up to the throne where the Grand Gatekeeper of Knowledge sat on. The former then gave an envelope to the latter, then returned to his original place.

Akulov then opened the envelope. He retrieved a folded piece of paper that read:

Grand Duchess Tatiana has captured Wouter Vos and intends on exchanging him for Vladimir Nikolayevich Mirov. I recommend that we inform Devotee-Infiltrator McAllister, who will notify his subordinates of this.

Devotee-Infiltrator Askarova.

"What do you think of this?" Akulov asked as he resumed facing Frühling.

"I agree with Devotee-Infiltrator Askarova's suggestion," Frühling answered. "We can inform 'SB' of this, allowing her and Song Dong-joo's unit to ambush Dirks and the mercenaries while they give Mirov to Grand Duchess Tatiana and her men."

"Then inform Devotee-Infiltrator McAllister at once."

"By your will, Grand Gatekeeper."

#

FIS Headquarters, McLean, Fairfax County, Commonwealth of Virginia; United States of America. 1530 hours (Eastern Standard Time)

At a men's bathroom in FIS Headquarters, Stanley McAllister washed not only his hands but the same pager used by Oleh Bohdanovich Kovalchuk. The message read as:

Devotee-Infiltrator McAllister, we need you to tell Director Alberto Perez that Wouter Vos, the mercenary leader under your employ, has been captured by an OVR cell operating in the State of Japan. Have "Fred Smith" make contact with the OVR cell to plan a hostage exchange. Offer them Leytenánt Vladimir Nikolayevich Mirov of the Imperial Eurasian Naval Infantry, currently in the custody of Iron Dutchman

Services, in exchange for Vos. If your Director asks where you got this information, tell them you acquired it from an OVR official and that he must be given the codename "Penkovskaya". In five seconds, this message will be deleted and a new one will be sent for you to show Director Perez with this pager.

Gatekeeper United States.

Just great, McAllister thought as he saw the message be deleted and the new one appearing. *Now I have to tell Al about an asset that doesn't exist.*

#

1600 hours

"I'm impressed you acquired a high-ranking officer from the OVR as an asset," Alberto Pérez said while he read the new message the Gatekeepers of Knowledge provided for McAllister to use. "This 'Penkovskaya' simply wants an extraction team needed if he or she is compromised. What do you think?"

"I say we heed this warning," McAllister answered. "The sooner we get Vos back, we can resume going after Kravchenko."

"Then inform Caguiat."

#

Iron Dutchman, Taisho Ward, Kansai City, Kansai Prefecture; State of Japan. August 14, 2030; 0740 hours (Japan Standard Time)

Tatev Mirzoyan woke up in her room in the *Iron Dutchman* due to the alarm coming from her smartphone. Sleeping beside her was Maral Eminovna Guliyeva, who also woke up because of the alarm.

"W… What's that?" Guliyeva asked.

"It's an alarm I prepared with my phone," Tatev answered while grabbing her phone and turning it off. She then turned back to Guliyeva. "Sorry about that."

Suddenly, a message from IntMail appeared. "Maral, please wait. There's something I need to see, but I need to wash my eyes."

"I'll wait."

Tatev then got out of her bed and left the room while taking her phone.

Turning Point Part 2

Iron Dutchman, Taisho Ward, Kansai City, Kansai Prefecture; State of Japan. August 14, 2030; 0801 hours (Japan Standard Time)

After washing her face in the washroom of the *Iron Dutchman*, Tatev Mirzoyan accessed her smartphone's IntMail. She found a message from one 'MC' that read:

Miss Mirzoyan, we received a message from an OVR officer calling himself or herself 'Penkovskaya'. However, this message must be heard by all members of Iron Dutchman Services.

#

0842 hours

All members of Iron Dutchman Services, save for Wouter Vos, Tarou Ganji, and Anita Hamilton, were gathered at the briefing room. Frederick Dirks then appeared on the stage with Wattana joining him as it was the previous night. Tatev was at the projector room in her usual job. "Just this morning, 'Maria Clara' contacted Tatev," Dirks explained to the mercenaries. "She has something to tell us and it will answer what happened to Vos."

"Mirzoyan, is AudComm ready?" Wattana loudly asked as she faced the projector room.

"Almost there," Tatev replied while opening her laptop computer's AudComm. It didn't take long for it to be projected onto the screen of the briefing room.

"Contacting 'Maria Clara' now." Caguiat then pressed a button that used a telephone as an icon once she pressed "Maria Clara" from the list of contacts in AudComm. Like a telephone, Caguiat was being called.

"I assume everyone on board the *Iron Dutchman* is gathered in the briefing room?" Alicia Caguiat asked as the ringing ended.

"Everyone in the ship's gathered," Dirks answered.

"Good. Allow me to read to you the message we received from an OVR officer calling himself or herself 'Penkovskaya', who contacted us with a message explicitly for you."

"What does the message say?" Wattana asked. "Is it even in English?"

"It is in English, which makes this easier for all of us. Now, I shall read it: I wish to tell you that an OVR cell in Japan, commanded by an agent that uses the codename 'Elizaveta', is holding Wouter Vos, your leader, as a hostage. We also know that you have Leytenánt Vladimir Nikolayevich Mirov of the Imperial Eurasian Navy as your prisoner. If you wish for your leader back, you must exchange him with Leytenánt Mirov. Contact 'Elizaveta' before making any exchange attempts.

"That's all. For the sake of Mr. Vos, I suggest you move quickly." The call ended.

Should have known it was the OVR, Dirks thought before he turned to Jason Luke Crawley. "Crawley, you remember where the safehouse is, right?" the former asked.

"I do," Crawley answered.

"Get the van ready. I'll join you soon."

"What is it you have in mind?" Wattana asked as she looked at Dirks.

"We need to give this 'Elizaveta' proof that their precious Leytenánt Mirov is alive."

#

Outside the OVR Safehouse, Nishinari Ward. 1010 hours

Dirks and Crawley reached the OVR safehouse. Finding the front entrance, Dirks pressed the doorbell. After that, the two men waited until they found "Elizaveta"—Tatiana Ioannovna Tsulukidze—approaching them.

"How may I help you?" Tatiana asked.

"I'm here to show you proof Mirov is alive," Dirks announced, making Tatiana briefly step back as if she saw a corpse.

"… Come in. Quickly!"

Tatiana opened the door with Dirks and Crawley coming inside. After closing the door, the latter two saw Vos hooded.

"He's alive, right?" Crawley asked.

"He is," Tatiana answered. "And I assure you he will be if you show me proof that Leytenánt Mirov is alive."

Dirks brought out his smartphone. Accessing an application named "Videos", Dirks found a video with the name "Proof" and pressed it with his right thumb. He immediately showed it to Tatiana, and the video was simply Vladimir Nikolayevich Mirov looking at the phone's camera for five seconds.

"Now that you have confirmation Mirov is alive while my contractor and I know that our fellow contractor is alive, when and where should we have our exchange?"

"2000 hours, at Crater Shore South. One last thing, I need you to bring Maral Eminovna Guliyeva."

"Why?"

"I'd like to know if something will happen tonight at the exchange. I can imagine the people who attacked you are related to the deliveries my men and I have conducted as part of our cover."

"We need Mr. Vos alive, so we have a deal. My contractor and I will be going." Dirks and Crawley began to leave the safehouse.

#

Nishi High School, Higashiosaka Ward. 1228 hours

Maria Hoshikawa appeared on the rooftop of Nishi High School. She found Tarou Ganji eating his lunch by himself.

"Is that you, Hoshikawa-senpai?" Tarou asked without even looking at Maria.

"How could you tell it was me?" Maria asked.

"Only you would follow me here at this point. I did everything I could to make sure no one noticed me going here."

Maria then sat beside Tarou. "You shouldn't be here."

"I know. Wanted somewhere to concentrate on my thoughts."

"Thinking about Mirzoyan-san and Guliyeva-san?"

"Hai." Tarou then resumed eating.

"I didn't think girls from the Eurasian Tsardom would be captured and sold in sexual slavery. I thought the Tsardom made sure such crimes didn't happen?" It was then that Tarou finished chewing. "It's also sobbering to know that Guliyeva-san was sold by her own parents."

"From what Tatev told me about her homeland, her village was impoverished. Same with Guliyeva's. Tatev's parents must have borrowed a lot of money to make sure she went to school."

"Since you're done with your summer homework, I suppose you'll be ordered to move out?"

"I have to. There's the matter with Vos-san."

"Where's he from?"

"South Africa. You already know where Hamilton-sensei and I came from, and you learned where Tatev came from last night. Wattana-san is from Thailand, Crawley-san from Australia, Mistry-san from the Indian Combine, Moura-san from Angola, Díaz-san from Uruguay, and Bosić-san from Bosnia."

"How did you all understand each other if you all came from different countries?"

"From what I was told, everyone who joined Iron Dutchman Services before I did already knew English. Díaz-san, however, was still learning when I first ran into the mercenary group in Egypt. By the time we met Tatev, Díaz-san, and I already picked up enough English."

"And since you're mercenaries, I suppose all of knew had to have been soldiers?"

"Only Hamilton-sensei and Tatev weren't at first. While Crawley-san and Wattana-san were formerly with the NUN Ground Force, Vos-san was formerly with the South African Marine Corps. Díaz-san was formerly with the SAU Ground Force as a Walgear technician, Moura-san was formerly with the Angolan Army, Mistry-san served in the Ground Force of the South Asian Confederation, and Bosić-san from the EA Ground Force."

"What made them create Iron Dutchman Services?"

"It was Vos-san, Crawley-san, and Wattana-san who first crated Iron Dutchman Services. I can't specify much of what happened, but what I can tell you is that they were involved with the border clash between the Democratic Republic of the Congo and the Congo Federation three years ago. They left their respective militaries because of that incident and created Iron Dutchman Services. Their first contract was with the Nigerian government and that's where they recruited Moura-san, Hamilton-sensei, Mistry-san, and Bosić-san. After that contract, they needed a ship for traveling, so they went to South Africa and got the ship after Vos-san won a card game. He named the ship *Iron Dutchman*, hence the name of the mercenary group. A year later, they acquired another contract with the South American Union, where they assisted in saving what remained of a reconnaissance unit—Díaz-san—from an ambush in Bolivia launched by one of the drug cartels that hold the real power there. Then there was the contract in Libya, which was how they found me and took me in."

"Then why did you take in Mirzoyan-san?"

"Like when we first met, Hamilton-sensei appealed to everyone's humanity. Tatev earned her keep by helping us find contracts that earned a lot of money. We may not have earned much from the contract where we encountered her, but we got the books and the laptop computer those scientists made her use as compensation."

"Do you intend to be mercenaries forever?"

Tarou, who was chewing when Maria asked her question, stopped for a moment. This gave Maria pause, but that ended when Tarou swallowed.

"We… I don't want to argue about what we do, but not everyone does see it that way. Moura-san hasn't given up on establishing that restautrant. Mistry-san and Bosić-san want to set up a garage to repair vehicles."

"But what about Mirzoyan-san?"

"Ever since we met her, she never acted as if she wanted to do anything else. Of course, with this mission, she's changed."

"And you never tried to get her to school or have friends other than you?"

"She didn't seem to want any of that. While Hamilton-sensei addressed the same concerns as you did, Tatev cared little. She didn't want to volunteer to infiltrate this school when the FIS gave that contract to keep an eye on you. While Mr. 'Smith' recommended that I infiltrate the school, I didn't argue. I already told you why."

"If you do know about why you were born, will you remain a mercenary?"

Maria's new question gave Tarou pause. He had yet to insert the last of his food into his mouth. *Maria's right,* Tarou thought. *It's one thing to want to know everything about how you were born and why, but it's another to figure out what to do after that?*

Despite that, Tarou brought his food into his mouth and chewed. Maria looked on until she stopped looking at Tarou. She lowered her head and closed her eyes. *Why did I even ask such a question?* Maria pondered. *Even I don't know what to do with myself once I graduate?*

"I apologize for asking such a question," Maria said as Tarou swallowed the last of his meal. "I still find it saddening that a boy as old as I am doesn't seem to have a problem fighting and killing people. You don't know about your biological parents and you're only guarding me to answer such questions… "

"I should be apologizing," Tarou replied without looking at Maria. "I never was exposed to anything else other than weapons and war. I never asked for anything else because as long as I had something to protect me from the rain, food to eat, and clothes to wear, I believed in earning those. When you asked me such questions, I never felt this way before."

Maria rose her head. Although she continued to close her eyes, she giggled. Tarou now looked at her, confused by what she was doing.

"You know, you sound like a normal teenage boy when you said you never felt that way before," Maria said before facing Tarou.

"I'm even surprised you can ask me such questions for your age," Tarou replied.

"Again, we may be the same age, but we're senpai and kouhai, remember?"

"Hai, hai. Speaking of which, I must get going. The bell might ring soon."

"You're right. I'll help you clean up."

Tarou and Maria cleaned up as fast as they anticipated. Tarou was the first to leave but as soon as he entered the staircase, he stopped only to find Misa Todoh.

"How long were you standing there?" Tarou asked.

"I... I... " Misa said in a vain attempt to answer.

"I'd stop prying about my relationship with Hoshikawa-senpai if I were you. You'll regret what you find." Tarou continued climbing down the stairs.

Misa, as she began to leave the roof, briefly looked back at Maria but stopped before she was spotted and followed Tarou down the stairs. Maria then followed, exiting the roof.

#

OVR Safehouse, Nishinari Ward. 1400 hours

"Do you approve of the hostage exchange?" Tatiana Ioannovna Tsulukidze asked while she used her smartphone's SatCom after connecting it to her satellite receiver.

"Da," Vyacheslav Leonidovich Puzanov replied on the other end. "I had to go to the Tsar first as soon as I woke up. He saw the value in getting Leytenánt Mirov back. When do you wish to conduct the exchange?"

"2000 hours, Japan Standard Time."

"Good. I leave the rest to you."

#

OVR Headquarters, Nizhegorodsky District, Imperial Capital of Nizhny Novgorod; Eurasian Tsardom. 0933 hours (Novgorod Time)

That pervert, why did he have to infiltrate my home to give me this?! Aigul Askarova pondered anxiously while washing both her hands and the pager used by Oleh Bohdanovich Kovalchuk and Stanley McAllister. *And I have to wear it every day to be able to instantly tell Gatekeeper Int about what's happening in here. Only Pati can make me wear such a thing!*

Despite her complaints, Askarova began using the pager after opening it. She typed "Hostage exchange approved. Iron Dutchman Services will bring Maral Eminovna Guliyeva with them as 'Elizaveta' requested" and pressed the small button used to send the message.

And now I have to wear it again! Askarova then sighed.

Abandoned Shipwreck, Crater Shore North, Kansai Prefecture; State of Japan. 1545 hours (Japan Standard Time)

Song Dong-joo appeared at Shireen Baloch's room in the abandoned shipwreck they're using as their safehouse. "Saeloun geos-i issseubnikka?" Song asked.

"Eung," Shireen answered. "I heard from Gatekeeper Int. The OVR and the FIS intend to have their hostage exchange tonight. They'll bring Maral Eminovna Guliyeva with them. Give me one fireteam to use for tonight."

"I'll get Ban Chungŭp-pyŏngsa to assist you."

"Also, is my SH-6 here?"

"Junbi doetssubnida."

"Gomaweo."

Outside Hoshikawa Condominiums, Higashiosaka Ward, Kansai City. 1704 hours

Tarou then returned to Hoshikawa Condominiums. However, he stopped because he found Frederick Dirks outside. Tarou then stepped out of his PCX scooter.

"Mr. 'Smith', what are you doing here?" Tarou asked.

"To inform you about our next move, but we need to continue the discussion in your condominium."

"Just let me park my PCX and then we'll proceed."

#

Hamilton-Ganji Condominium, Hoshikawa Condominiums. 1720 hours

"The hostage exchange will be tonight, at 1900 hours," Dirks explained to Tarou at the condominium with the latter resided at. "I came here to instruct you to prepare to take your belongings."

"What for?" Tarou asked.

"We need everyone prepared for this exchange. If you have homework, do it in your room in the *Iron Dutchman*."

"What about Dr. Hamilton?"

"You can pick her up tonight but she isn't done until 1900 hours."

"Got it."

Suddenly, engines were heard outside the condominium. "Who could that be now?" Dirks asked.

"Let's find out," Tarou suggested, followed by both him and Dirks standing up.

#

Outside Hoshikawa Condominiums. 1733 hours

Once they exited the condominiums, Tarou and Dirks found Maria Hoshikawa outside the gate. "Maria, what are you doing here?" Tarou asked.

"I wanted to check up on you?" Maria asked.

Tarou briefly glanced at Dirks before answering. "I'll be sleeping in the *Iron Dutchman* tonight. All I can say is that we'll get Mr. Vos back."

"Then I wish you luck."

"Thanks," Dirks replied while Tarou dragged his PCX scooter.

#

Iron Dutchman, Taisho Ward. 1916 hours

Everyone on board the Iron Dutchman appeared at its briefing room. Maral Eminovna Guliyeva joined them but sat on a chair provided to her in the projector room so that she can be with Tatev Mirzoyan, who had just connected her laptop computer to the projector. It was then that Tarou Ganji returned with Anita Hamilton. Dirks, who stood at the stage with Wattana beside him, saw the two come inside and sitting down.

"Now that we're all here, we can begin," Wattana announced.

"Tatev, show that map of Kansai City," Dirks ordered to Tatev.

Tatev complied without responding. She opened her computer's internet browser and using the Maps of the search engine, Tatev typed in "Kansai City" on the "Search Location" bar. A map of the Japanese city then appeared on the browser, and by extension, the screen. Finding Crater Shore South, Tatev scrolled down and stopped.

"This is where we will exchange Vladimir Nikolayevich Mirov for Wouter Vos tonight," Dirks explained to the mercenaries. "We must be there at 2000 hours. In addition to Mirov, we must bring Maral Eminovna Guliyeva with us as requested by the OVR agent calling herself 'Elizaveta'." This shocked everyone, most especially Tatev and Guliyeva.

"And why do have to bring Maral with us?" Hamilton asked.

"We don't know. There's a good possibility the OVR now know we've been using Guliyeva to get to Anton Oleksandrovich Kravchenko. All we know is that they want Mirov back and we want Vos back. That is why we need to be ready for anything."

"What do you mean by that?" Crawley asked.

"Other than me, Wattana, and Crawley, I need three volunteers to come with us for this exchange," Dirks answered.

"Those who wish to go, please raise your hands," Wattana commanded.

Tarou and Hamilton raised their hands. "Doctor, why you?" Dirks asked as he turned to Hamilton.

"I want to assure Maral that everything will be alright," Hamilton answered.

"Anyone else?" Wattana asked for one more volunteer.

"I'll go." Everyone turned their heads to see Tatev leaving the projector room with Guliyeva behind her.

"You too, Tatev?" Dirks answered. "Why?"

"I promised Maral that I will protect her, so I'm coming to make good on that promise," Tatev answered defiantly.

"Then what are we waiting for?" Crawley asked. "I say we launch already."

"Before we do that, we need to load up on weapons," Dirks warned. "Since Ganji and Dr. Hamilton will be joining us, they'll need rifles. We took all the AK-05s used by our Korean attackers, so we'll each give one to Ganji and Dr. Hamilton. Wattana, Crawley, and I will continue to use the ADRs we took from the safehouse in Yao."

"Anything else?" Wattana asked to the other mercenaries.

"Shouldn't we be concerned about the Koreans?" Tarou asked.

"That's why we need to be prepared for anything at the hostage exchange," Dirks answered. "The Gatekeepers of Knowledge might be involved, hence 'Elizaveta's' interest with Guliyeva."

"I was wondering about that," Tatev said. "If those Koreans knew where the safehouse in Yao was, our movements could be watched by someone within the FIS who is providing information."

"The only way such information could be relayed to someone else is through the- No!"

"We can discuss such things later." Wattana warned. "Right now, we need to start preparations."

"You're right," Dirks answered as he turned to Wattana. "We need to make preparations now."

#

1940 hours

At her room, Tatev was able to install her ballistic vest, as well as a holster harness for her P9. Guliyeva watched as Tatev inserted her pistol into the holster.

"Why do you have that pistol?" Guliyeva asked as Tatev began to insert her pistol into the holster. Tatev stopped as a result but smiled. She then walked up to Guliyeva.

"I learned how to use a gun a month ago," Tatev answered. "I learned how to shoot so that I can be more useful than just getting contracts."

"Why do I have to come with you?" Tatev then stopped smiling. She briefly looked down and closed her eyes, but stopped and faced Guliyeva again.

"Don't worry. I'm sure those OVR agents will simply get Cənab Mirov back. I don't think they want to hurt you. Even if it might turn into an argument about Kravchenko. Now come on, we have to get you into that vest."

Both Tatev and Guliyeva turned to another ballistic vest on the bed of the former. Both girls walked up to the bed while the former hid her pistol.

1944 hours

At the same time, Tarou and Dirks appeared at the *Iron Dutchman*'s brig. Once they approached the cell where they kept Vladimir Nikolayevich Mirov, Tarou unlocked the cell door and opened it, making Mirov look at him and Dirks.

"Tonight's the hostage exchange?" Mirov asked.

"Da," Dirks answered. "Now get up or we'll be late."

#

Wonsan International Airport, Wonsan, Gangwon Province; Republic of Korea. 1944 hours (Korea Standard Time)

Two individuals stepped out of a C-141 Starlifter transport plane. One was "LS", the man who was in Mexico and in the United States. The other was an older man with short white hair, very light skin, and blue eyes. Like it was when Shireen arrived, two men appeared.

"Ulileul delileo wa jusyeoseo gamsahabnida," "LS" said. "Modeun geos-i junbidoeeeossdago bwado doebnika?"

"Ye," one of the two men answered.

#

Crater Shore South, Kansai Prefecture; State of Japan. 2019 hours (Japan Standard Time)

Tatiana Ioannovna Tsulukidze and her two subordinates, Pyotr Stepanovich Chadov and Karim Olegovich Zhakiyanov, waited in the southern part of Crater Shore. Inside their Stepwagn van was Wouter Vos, whose head was hooded.

"Oni opazdyvayut," Chadov remarked. "Oni voobshche poyavyatsya?"

Tatiana shushed her subordinate. "Ya chto-to slyshu," she said. "Oni zdes'."

The three OVR agents then saw the white Stepwagn, now used by Iron Dutchman Services, appear. Once it stopped, Dirks, Crawley, Wattana, Tarou, Hamilton, and Tatev got off and faced the OVR agents. Guliyeva and Mirov remained in the white van; the latter forcibly wearing a hood.

"As it is said in the English world, 'Better late than never'," Tatiana said. "I assume Leytenánt Mirov is in your van?"

"Da," Dirks answered. "But first, get Vos out of your van."

Tatiana simply used her head's movements to command her subordinates. Chadov and Zhakiyanov returned to their Stepwagn and forced Vos out of the van. Dirks then instructed Tarou and Wattana to do the same with the captive in their Stepwagn.

"Now give us Leytenánt Mirov!" Tatiana demanded.

"Hold on," Dirks requested just before he removed Mirov's hood. "Now go!"

"Spasibo," Mirov replied while walking to Tatiana.

"Now it's your turn," Dirks demanded aftere resumed facing Tatiana and Vos.

Tatiana removed Vos' hood. "Dankie," Vos sarcastically said before walking to Dirks and his subordinates. Tatiana then looked at the AK-05s used by Tarou and Hamilton, then saw Guliyeva inside the white Stepwagn.

"Where did you get those AK-05s?" Tatiana asked.

"Does it matter to you now?" Dirks asked. "You got your asset back. Now get out of here."

"I don't think so. If I got it right, you intend to draw out Anton Oleksandrovich Kravchenko."

"I can neither confirm nor deny that."

"Don't play dumb. Give me that girl and you can keep the AK-05s and the ammunition you took from the Koreans that attacked you in Yao."

"Don't do that!" Everyone but Dirks aimed their weapons at Tatiana and her men after her warning. Chadov and Zhakiyanov aimed their respective PM-01 pistols at the mercenaries as a result.

"What? Trying to be a humanitarian now? I don't think-"

Suddenly, metallic footsteps were heard. The mercenaries stopped aiming their weapons as a result. Everyone turned to where the footsteps were coming from and found an SH-6 Walgear approaching them, along with three armed men wearing the same black clothes and using the same AK-05s as the men who attacked the FIS safehouse in Yao.

"Impossible!" Dirks shouted. "How did they get a Donian in here?" He then turned to Tatiana. "I assume they're with you!?"

"Net," Tatiana answered. "They use AK-05s."

The Korean interlopers then stopped. The three men in black then aimed their AK-05s at the two parties. Because they had an SH-6 with them, the Koreans continued aiming their rifles.

"Give us Maral Eminovna Guliyeva at once!" a distorted voice shouted through the speakers found in the SH-6. "If you value your lives, give her to us at once!"

"This is bad!" Vos shouted before he turned to Dirks. "You didn't bring Solbein with you?"

"I didn't think we would need it until these jerkoffs showed up," Dirks replied.

"Stop it!" Everyone turned to see Maral Eminovna Guliyeva leaving the white Stepwagn and removing her ballistic vest.

"Maral, what are you doing?" Tatev incredulously asked.

"Please let me do this, Tatev. None of you must die here."

"But-" Tatev said only for Guliyeva's insistence to stop her from saying anything else.

"Please live. I'm begging you." Guliyeva continued walking toward the interlopers. Tatev attempted to pursue Guliyeva only for Tarou and Hamilton to stop.

"Let go of me!" Tatev shouted before resuming her focus on Guliyeva. "Maral!"

Guliyeva continued to ignore Tatev's pleas. She stopped as soon as the three Koreans surrounded her.

"Since Guliyeva handed herself to us, we will be going now," the distorted voice in the SH-6's cockpit said. "Farewell."

The SH-6 then grabbed Maral with its right hand. After that, it turned away, as did the three armed men, and left.

Despite what happened, Dirks and the mercenaries aimed their weapons at the OVR agents and Mirov. "W- What are you doing?" Tatiana asked.

"You four are now under the custody in the Covert Action Center," Dirks answered. "Drop your pistols and raise your hands. Now!"

"You're making a big mistake!" Tatiana complained while grabbing her PM-01 pistol and tossing into the ground and raising her hands.

"You made the mistake of taking my asset hostage. Now get in the van."

"Wait!" Wattana argued. "They have a black Stepwagn. What do we do with it?"

"Take it with us," Dirks answered. "Check the three OVR agents if any of them have the keys."

"Roger." Vos, Wattana, and Crawley respectively inspected Tatiana, Chadov, and Zhakiyanov's pockets. Only Wattana found the black Stepwagn's keys in Chadov's left pocket.

"We're pulling back," Dirks ordered before he looked at the OVR agents and Mirov. "And they're coming with us."

Except for Wattana, the mercenaries began herding the OVR agents and Mirov into the white Stepwagn. Tatev, however, kneeled on the ground. Tarou and Hamilton approached.

"Tatev, we need to get out of here," Tarou warned. "We'll save Guliyeva. I promise you that."

Without responding, Tatev stood up. Tarou and Hamilton turned to the white Stepwagn. "We'll ride with Sunan," Hamilton shouted.

"Just hurry it up!" Dirks replied.

While Crawley started the engines of the white Stepwagn, Tarou, Hamilton, and Tatev boarded the black Stepwagn just before Wattana started its engines.

#

Crater Shore East. 2231 hours

Elsewhere in Crater Shore, the Koreans reached another Stepwagn they owned. The SH-6's pilot lowered the right arm while it still held Guliyeva. The hand was opened, forcing Guliyeva to land.

"Now get in the van!" the distorted voice commanded.

Defiantly, Guliyeva got into the Stepwagn. The three Koreans followed. Once everyone was inside, the driver of the Stepwagn was the first to move. The SH-6 followed.

Cooperation

Iron Dutchman, Taisho Ward, Kansai City, Kansai Prefecture; State of Japan. August 14, 2030; 2201 hours (Japan Standard Time)

"You can't keep us here!" Tatiana Ioannovna Tsulukidze shouted while she was imprisoned in one cell of the *Iron Dutchman*'s brig. Pyotr Stepanovich Chadov, Karim Olegovich Zhakiyanov, and Vlaidmir Nikolayevich Mirov were respectively imprisoned in separate cells. Outside the cells was Frederick Dirks. Also outside the cells were Vikas Mistry and Wouter Vos.

"I can," Dirks warned. "Because the attack in Yao and the abduction of Maria Hoshikawa were committed by foreigners who shouldn't have entered Japan easily, we suspect you aided those infiltrators. Since you're spies who entered this country by pretending to be refugees from the Soviet Remnant, the police will not take kindly to that. Until my superiors decide what to do with you lot since it's pointless to ask anything out of you, we're keeping you here. I will ensure that you are fed. Now good night."

Dirks then turned away from the OVR agents and Mirov. Mistry was the first to leave. Dirks followed, with Vos as the last one to leave as he needed to turn off the brig's lights.

2219 hours

Dirks and Vos arrived at the projector room of the *Iron Dutchman*'s briefing room. They found Tatev Mirzoyan using her laptop computer's AudComm. The recipient of the call was "Maria Clara"—Alicia Caguiat. Tatev was also unlike herself as a contrast to that morning. She faintly narrowed her eyes as she used her computer.

She really wants to save Guliyeva that badly, Dirks thought.

"Miss 'Clara', Langley 3, you're online with Mr. 'Smith'," Tatev announced.

"Please shorten what you're about to say," Stanley McAllister ordered. "I only got here so I can't stay awake for too long."

Dirks summarized the hostage exchange that occurred two hours before. Tatev lowered her head and closed her eyes as she felt it was painful to be reminded of her failure to keep Maral Eminovna Guliyeva safe.

"Keep them there until I've talked with the OVR Director," McAllister ordered after listening to what Dirks had to say. "I need to think of a way to meet the OVR Director without compromising 'Penkovskaya'."

"With all due respect, Stan, but can we even rely on this 'Penkovskaya'? I was only told of this 'asset' today."

"I know, but he or she is high up that the intel cannot be ignored. I'll think of something. Good night."

#

FIS Headquarters, McLean, Fairfax County, Commonwealth of Virginia; United States of America. 1130 hours (Eastern Standard Time)

"You just had to pick a time where neither of us has eaten to disappoint me, didn't you?" Alberto Pérez sarcastically asked after listening to McAllister's report on what happened after the hostage exchange in Japan. "And now, you want to contact the OVR Director?"

"Al, it's a long shot, I know," McAllister replied. "We need the OVR's help because I doubt Blavatsky had enough intel to work with at this point and that the sooner we can sort this out, we can find where those Korean interlopers are hiding and rescue Guliyeva."

"Can I at least contact Parnell after lunch on this? She needs to know this and to approve of the idea."

"At least get her to understand that Guliyeva's life is in an hourglass."

"Yes, yes. Now go. I suggest you devise an idea on how to contact the Director of the OVR once we've had our lunches."

IC Headquarters, Lambeth, Greater London, England; United Kingdom of Great Britain and Northern Ireland. 1915 hours (British Summer Time)

At her office in the headquarters of the Intelligence Collective, Cecilia Parnell intercepted another message from Pérez through her computer's IntMail. The message read:

We have a situation. Armed interlopers abducted Maral Eminovna Guliyeva while exchanging Vladimir Nikolayevich Mirov for Wouter Vos and they have the same weapons as those who attacked the safehouse in Yao. The OVR cell responsible for Vos' kidnapping has been captured and its members are currently imprisoned in the Iron Dutchman, Mirov among them. Deputy Director McAllister suggested that we find the means of communication in the safehouse used by the OVR agent calling herself "Elizaveta". Permission to approve?

Parnell wrote "Permission granted" and pressed "Send".

#

Iron Dutchman, Taisho Ward, Kansai City, Kansai Prefecture; State of Japan. August 15, 2030; 0845 hours (Japan Standard Time)

"You've been given permission to raid the safehouse used by the OVR cell you arrested," Caguiat announced through AudComm as the screen was projected onto the screen of the *Iron Dutchman*'s briefing room. Dirks and every member of Iron Dutchman Services listened to what Caguiat had to say. "Langley 3 believes 'Elizaveta' must have been able to talk to the Director of the OVR. We need to get 'Elizaveta' to contact her superior."

"Consider it done," Dirks replied before he turned to Vos. "I need you and someone who wishes to volunteer to go with me to that safehouse."

"I'll go!" Jason Luke Crawley excitedly said as he raised his right hand.

"Then let's move out."

#

OVR Safehouse, Nishinari Ward. 0910 hours

Dirks, Vos, and Crawley examined every room in the OVR safehouse. Crawley extracted every food and drink on the dining table.

"We're not here for the food," Vos warned Crawley.

"We're going to need to feed them, right?" Crawley answered.

"Found it!" Dirks announced as he popped out of Tatiana's office, carrying the satellite receiver, making Vos and Crawley turn to him.

"What's that?" Crawley asked.

"Don't know." Dirks then looked at the satellite receiver again. "We'll make 'Elizaveta' answer, that's for sure." Dirks then saw the food Crawley took. "We're not taking all of that with us!"

"We need to feed those guys, don't we?" Crawley paraphrased his previous defense.

"You and Vos are carrying all of that. Let's go."

#

Iron Dutchman, Taisho Ward. 1020 hours

"Why do you have that?" Tatiana asked as Dirks showed her the satellite receiver.

"We need you to use it to contact your Director," Dirks answered. "I assume you use it to talk to your Director."

If I don't answer, my men and I will remain here, Tatiana thought. *And none of us can afford to die. This is also an opportunity to finally get rid of Kravchenko.*

"Da," Tatiana ultimately answered, much to the shock of her subordinates and Mirov. "I connect it to my phone and use an application called 'SatCom'. That's how I talk to Director Puzanov."

"Now talk to him. Tell him everything that happened and that if he wishes for the safety of you and your men, he must agree to a meeting with my superior."

"Fine." Dirks then unlocked Tatiana's cell. Once she stepped out, Dirks got out of her way and aimed his MCP semi-automatic pistol and forced her to leave the brig.

#

1043 hours

Outside the firing range that used to be the *Iron Dutchman*'s disco, Tatiana connected her smartphone to the satellite receiver. Vos had to hold it and stand up while it was connected to the phone. Once connected, Tatiana turned on SatCom. At the same time, Dirks began to use his smartphone's AudComm and began to contact Caguat.

"Why do I have to do this?" Vos complained while holding the satellite receiver.

"I can only get a good signal if the receiver is facing the sky," Tatiana answered.

Dirks shushed both Vos and Tatiana. "I'm hearing 'Clara' responding to me," he argued.

"Is that you, 'Elizaveta'?" Vyacheslav Leonidovich Puzanov asked on the other end of Tatiana's smartphone.

"What is it, Mr. 'Smith'?" Caguiat asked over Dirks' smartphone.

"Her first," Dirks silently told Vos and Tatiana before facing his phone. "I got 'Elizaveta' to contact her Director. Please notify Langley 3."

"Will do," Caguiat replied. "Please wait."

"Now your turn," Dirks told Tatiana.

"Sorry about that, 'Nizhny'," Tatiana replied. "I got myself into a precarious situation."

"Let me guess, you and your men, along with Leytenánt Mirov, got captured?" Puzanov asked.

"Da," Tatiana answered.

"This better be good," Stanley McAllister said over Dirks' phone.

"Yes, it is, sir," Dirks answered. "Just listen."

Tatiana began to explain what had happened the previous night. Dirks then directed his phone toward Tatiana and Vos to make sure he heard what Tatiana was saying.

"Mind if I speak to the FIS agent's superior, please?" Puzanov asked.

"Here he is, 'Nizhny'," Vos announced. He and Tatiana then made their respective phones face each other.

"Where do you propose we meet?" McAllister asked.

"Republic of Tartus. I'll have 'Elizaveta' explain the details because she knows it. I'll see you there tomorrow."

"How will I know what you look like? Not only that, how old are you?"

"I'm sixty-seven years old. I have very light skin, graying brown hair in a crew cut, and blue eyes."

"I have the same physical features as you except that I'm eight years younger than you and that I have green eyes."

"Then I will see you at the Arwad Hotel." The call ended for Tatiana's phone.

"You better start talking, 'Elizaveta'," McAllister reminded Tatiana, who sighed before she began explaining.

#

Abandoned Shipwreck, Crater Shore North. 1043 hours

"So, how are you?" Shireen Baloch asked as she found Maral Eminovna Guliyeva eating in the room used by the former.

"I'm fine," Guliyeva defiantly answered. "Don't expect me to beg for mercy."

"You have been physically defiant so no use doing that. You should be thankful I kept you away from Song's men."

"Why are you even doing this? Does Kravchenko offer you that much money?"

Shireen was unable to answer Guliyeva's question. It was as if her own heart was stabbed, causing her to grit her teeth before opting to respond. "Just finish your meal." Shireen then left her own room.

Those mercenaries must have thought her enough freedom to bark at me like that! Shireen angrily thought. *Once we take her back to Kravchenko, he and Henderson will put her in her place.*

#

FIS Headquarters, McLean, Fairfax County, Commonwealth of Virginia; United States of America. 2130 hours (Eastern Standard Time)

McAllister then arrived inside Pérez's office. The latter then stopped his phone call and faced the former.

"I assume you have good news and bad news?" Pérez asked.

"Good news is that I get to meet the Director of the OVR in the flesh," McAllister answered. "Bad news is that it's in the Republic of Tartus."

"Should have known this would involve Tartus. Hopefully, I can get Yanin to call Jacob Wong. After that, I'll contact Suliman to know you're coming."

"I promise you this will work."

"For that, I'm allowing you to leave early. You need to sleep already so that you can be early when I do hear from Wong."

"I'll take my leave then." McAllister began to leave as soon as Pérez began making his calls.

#

Outside Tadakano Drugstore, Higashiosaka Ward, Kansai City, Kansai Prefecture; State of Japan. 1710 hours (Japan Standard Time)

Tarou Ganji stepped out of Tadakano Drugstore, the pharmacy beside Nishi High School. He found Maria Hoshikawa outside the drugstore.

"Hoshikawa-senpai, why are you here?" Tarou asked.

"Why do you have that with you?" Maria asked as he pointed at the paper bag filled with groceries Tarou was carrying with Tarou, looking at it in response before facing Maria again.

"It's an order, but I can't explain what I can tell you here."

"I'll ask Ugaki-san to take me to your condominium. You can explain there."

"Arigatou."

Unbeknownst to both Tarou and Maria, Misa Todoh watched. She then left and followed her schoolmates to avoid being seen. Her younger brother Riku caught her going in a separate direction but followed her.

Hamilton-Hoshikawa Condominium, Hoshikawa Condominiums. 1749 hours

Tarou and Maria were seated at the dining table of the condominium populated by the former. The paper bag filled with what Tarou bought at Tadakono Drugstore was in the kitchen.

"What order requires you to buy from Tadakono Drugstore?" Maria asked.

"All you need to know is that Mr. Vos was captured by an OVR cell and that we captured the OVR agents because they're unwittingly responsible for Guliyeva getting abducted by armed interlopers," Tarou answered.

"Like how I was abducted months ago?"

"Yes. That is all I can tell you."

"Then thank you." Maria stood up and bowed. "I'll see you at school tomorrow."

Maria then resumed wearing her shoes and left the condominium.

#

McAllister Residence, McLean, Fairfax County, Commonwealth of Virginia; United States of America. August 16, 2030; 0430 hours (Eastern Standard Time)

While he slept with his wife Cynthia, the alarm of McAllister's smartphone rang. McAllister was able to wake up and turn off the alarm. He found what time it was and rushed to his bathroom.

While he bathed, the phone rang again. Cynthia woke up this time and answered. She found it was Alberto Pérez calling.

"Good morning Al," Cynthia said. "My husband is currently taking a bath. I assume you put him up to this?"

"It was mostly his idea," Pérez answered. "When he's done, please tell him that the plane is already at Andrews. I assume he packed up?"

"He did as soon as he returned home last night."

"Then please remind Stan." The call ended just as McAllister finished his bath.

"Was that Al?" McAllister asked his wife.

"That was him. He told me to tell you your plane is at Andrews."

"Thanks." McAllister rushed to his closet next.

#

Tartus International Airport, North Tartus, Tartus Capital Region; Republic of Tartus. 1540 hours (Tartus Time)

McAllister stepped out of Jacob Wong's Citation Longitude business jet. He found three men approaching as soon as he stepped on the soil of the Republic of Tartus. During the Third World War, the State of Israel feared another war with her geopolitical rivals. They launched Operation Sling, where they preemptively launched most of their nuclear weapons against her geopolitical opponents. One notable victim of this preemptive nuclear bombing was the Syrian Arab Republic. As a result, Syria split into fiefdoms of officers in the Syrian military, intent on recreating Syria in their image. The Republic of Tartus, by contrast, opted to be a neutral state where all parties across the world were allowed to maintain businesses. Tartus International Airport, built after the artificial island was created to accommodate it, was one such example of cooperation between the Tartus government and businesses based in the New United Nations.

Two of the three men wore the uniform of Tartus' police service, the National Police (NP), and carried *Millî Piyade Tüfeği* (MPT) rifles. By contrast, the man who stood between them wore a suit and tie. He was Ali Suliman, the Commissioner of the NP.

"Glad you made it, Mr. McAllister," the man in the suit and tie said. "How was your flight?"

"I had to sleep," McAllister answered. "Is 'Nizhny' here yet?"

"Not yet. We'll take you to the Arwad Hotel."

"By all means." Suliman and his guards directed McAllister to an Omega B Caravan. Once all three boarded the Omega B, the policemen began to leave Tartus International Airport.

"I must ask: why do you need to see 'Nizhny'?" Suliman asked while he sat in the right front seat.

"It's a hostage situation," McAllister answered. "I'm here to negotiate with 'Nizhny' about the release of an OVR cell in Japan one of my agents discovered. That is all you need to know."

#

1729 hours

Suliman returned to the airport. However, he was alone, and he entered a room with that was marked "Immigration". The original word in Arabic was found above its Arabic translation. Once he entered the room, he looked around as to find the person he returned to the airport for. That came to an end when he easily found Vyacehslav Leonidovich Puzanov and walked up to him.

"You're late," Puzanov said.

"My apologies," Suliman replied. "I had to get some sleep after taking 'Langley 3' to your room in the Arwad Hotel."

"What do you make of him?"

"Despite his age, he has proven time and again he can keep secrets. Enough of that, it's time for you to meet him."

#

Arwad Hotel. 1834 hours

Puzanov arrived at the topmost floor of the Arwad Hotel. As he neared his room, he saw a man approach it. The man then also saw Puzanov. As a result, both men slowly approached the room and, by extension, each other. They stopped as soon as they the minimum distance needed for a handshake.

"I presume that you're 'Nizhny'?" McAllister asked.

"Da," Puzanov answered. "And you must be 'Langley' 3." He then saw the paper bag McAllister carried. "Dinner?"

"Da. I left to buy at a separate restaurant because it had cheaper prices. Thankfully, they accepted UN dollars."

"You should have waited. I would have paid for the both of us if we were at the restaurant I frequent."

"But business first. Here's the card." McAllister then gave Puzanov a key card. Once he received it, Puzanov unlocked the hotel room and proceeded inside with McAllister following him inside.

Once Puzanov sat down, McAllister put down his bag and joined him in the opposite chair. "If we're to talk 'business', I'll start with this question: why are interested in Anton Oleksandrovich Kravchenko?"

"We intend to give him to you once we caught him."

"I can understand, but what do you wish in exchange for him?"

"To prove we can succeed where you failed. He was able to flee to the Republic of Korea and we're very interested in how he was able to rebuild his sex trafficking business there."

"And I assume Blavatsky told you about Kravchenko?"

"I can neither confirm nor deny that."

Puzanov sighed. *Considering what happened with Maria Hoshikawa, I might make a mistake if I continue this discussion,* Puzanov thought. "Very well, I want Kravchenko. Dead or alive."

"And you will get him. We just need *your* cooperation."

"I can imagine you know how 'Elizaveta' travels to and from Japan, so I'm going to ask that you don't capture the submarine."

While the Phantom sub is a good prize, NUN acquiring it would threaten the balance of power the Grand Gatekeeper needs, McAllister thought before he opened his mouth. "Consider it done. But we ask that Miss Guliyeva and perhaps other women Kravchenko captured aren't returned to their respective families lest any of them wish to do so."

"I wish not to talk this way about fellow human beings but you may have those that don't wish to return to the Tsardom. Now, this is my last demand: free my subordinates and Leytenánt Mirov."

"Then allow Iron Dutchman Services to use the delivery service your agents used as a front."

"Then we're done here." Puzanov offered his hand with McAllister grabbing it.

"Agreed. It's time to eat dinner."

FIS Headquarters, McLean, Fairfax County, Commonwealth of Virginia; United States of America. 0309 hours (Eastern Standard Time)

McAllister hurriedly appeared in the Communication Room of FIS Headquarters. He ultimately stopped as he appeared at the cubicle used by Alicia Caguiat as her work station.

"Contact Mirzoyan," McAllister ordered. "Now."

"Roger," Caguiat replied before using AudComm.

#

Iron Dutchman, Taisho Ward, Kansai City, Kansai Prefecture; State of Japan. 1820 hours (Japan Standard Time)

Both Tarou Ganji and Jake Crawley rushed inside the briefing room of the *Iron Dutchman* after everyone else, with the exception of Anita Hamilton, sat down. Once the former sat on their usual chairs, Frederick Dirks coughed to remind everyone that they can begin.

"Because this news came in only recently, Langley 3 will be telling us what to do next," Dirks announced.

"Thank you for that, 'Smith'," McAllister replied. "Now then, I was able to negotiate with the Director of the OVR. We are to release the OVR agents and Leytenánt Mirov after their cooperation in going after the men who abducted Miss Guliyeva."

"Why do we have to work with them?" Wouter Vos complained as he stood beside Dirks.

"Once we tell them their Director agreed to cooperate with us, they'll treat it like an order. We can't keep them there for long. Though we are to hand over Kravchenko, whether dead or alive, in exchange for the OVR's cooperation."

"Good enough with me!" Tatev Mirzoyan replied; her voice being loud enough for everyone else in the briefing room to hear. "Kravchenko needs to pay for his crimes. It won't matter if he's dead or not."

"That's good. Now, as to how having 'Elizaveta', her men, and Leytenánt Mirov cooperating with you is a problem, you will be compensated."

"With what?" Vos asked.

"Their delivery service front in exchange for their release. Some of you did mention you were looking for part-time jobs, so I felt this was adequate."

"At least we don't have to wait any longer for Mr. Hoshikawa's ultimate decision on helping us find part-time jobs," Crawley added.

"Anything else I should know about?" Dirks asked; his tone showing suspicion as to what else was negotiated between McAllister and Vyacheslav Leonidovich Puzanov.

"We opted not to capture the Phantom sub in exchange for keeping Guliyeva," McAllister answered.

"Good enough with me." Vos then faced his subordinates. "Anyone oppose?"

"None," every other member answered.

"Good. Free 'Elizaveta' and her men, remind her of much it cost to free her, and ask for everything she knows. Good night."

#

1859 hours

"Why are you freeing us?" Tatiana Ioannovna Tsulukidze asked as her cell door in the *Iron Dutchman*'s brig was opened by Dirks. The latter then gave the keys to Mistry, who then opened Pyotr Stepanovich Chadov's cell.

"Because my superior was able to contact yours. The price for your release is your delivery service that you used as a front. Also, for the cooperation of the OVR, which extends to you, your subordinates, and Leytenánt Mirov, we will give Kravchenko, dead or alive, to the OVR."

"I suppose those were fair exchanges. Since we'll be working together, what do you wish to know?"

Dirks then saw that Chadov, Karim Olegovich Zhakiyanov, and Vladimir Nikolayevich Mirov were freed. "Why don't we discuss the rest in the library? But that can wait after dinner. Since we're working together, you get to be eating what Moura made for dinner tonight."

1921 hours

Tarou returned to the *Iron Dutchman*. This time, he brought Anita Hamilton with him. Remembering it was dinner time, they immediately traveled to the mess hall but to their surprise, they found Tatiana, her men, and Mirov eating at the mess hall as if they were actual members of Iron Dutchman Services. Tarou and Hamilton then walked up to the table where Vos, Crawley, and Sunan Wattana ate.

"Why are 'Elizaveta' and her men eating here?" Tarou asked.

"We got the cooperation of the Eurasians in going after Kravchenko," Vos answered. "Just go with it."

"Then we'll sit with 'Elizaveta' and Leytenánt Mirov," Hamilton added.

She and Tarou got their respective trays and walked to the table used by Tatiana and Mirov. "Mind if we sit here?" Hamilton asked.

"You may," Tatiana answered as if it were normal. Although they found it strange, Tarou and Hamilton sat down and began eating.

"Where were you when 'Elizaveta' and I were freed?" Mirov asked.

"I needed to pick up Dr. Hamilton," Tarou answered before putting food in his mouth.

"Do you always do this?"

"In general, yes. Hamilton works at a clinic nearby. Most of the time, however, we go back to our condominium because I have studies, so we eat dinner there."

"And this is more important than your studies right now?"

"I somehow don't get failing grades because of time. We may have to work together, but we are watching you."

"Fair enough." Both Tarou and Mirov resumed eating, but the way they looked at each other embarrassed both Hamilton and Tatiana. The latter two looked at each other as if they planned on talking, but they also found it embarrassing and ate without saying anything to each other.

2030 hours

Tatiana, Chadov, Zhakiyanov, and Mirov were brought to the Iron Dutchman's library. Finding a long table and four chairs, the Eurasians sat on those chairs. Dirks then joined them with Tarou, who then closed the library door. Once he sat down, Dirks placed his smartphone on the portion of the table near his chair and pressed the application named "Recorder".

"I'm surprised a mercenary group can afford to use this cruise ship as their headquarters," Tatiana said.

"They won it over a card game," Dirks replied. "That's all you need to know. Now then, let's begin." The FIS agent then pressed the button needed for his Recorder application to do what it was named to do. "Since you and your men run a delivery service as a front, how long have you been running it and had you fulfilled any recent deliveries?"

"We began our delivery service three years ago. As for recent deliveries, we received a call on August 6 from Minagawa Group for a delivery," Chadov answered. "When 'Oleg' and I went to-"

"Wait, did you say 'Minagawa Group'?" Dirks asked, interrupting Chadov's story.

"Da," Tatiana answered. "They're a frequent client of ours."

We might have to investigate Minagawa Group for this, Dirks thought before he resumed the interrogation. "I apologize for disrupting. Go on."

"When 'Oleg' and I went to the Minagawa Electronics service center in Hirabayashikita a day later," Chadov resumed. "we were then shown what was to be delivered: nineteen cardboard boxes. We weren't allowed to know what were in the boxes, who wanted those boxes, and why. Not only that, we weren't even allowed to know where they were to be taken as we were to leave them one kilometer near a shipwreck in Crater Shore North."

"Were you given a map as to where you were to leave the boxes?"

"Da, but we weren't allowed to keep it."

"We'll sort that out later. Now then, do you remember the physical features of the boxes? How tall and how long they were?"

"How can we forget? They were long and heavy. It was as we were… carrying… people… "

That must have been how the Korean interlopers got into Japan in the first place. That shipwreck must be their safehouse.

"Since we now know what, or rather *who*, you were carrying, what about *their* weapons?"

"We were told of that shipment on August 9," Tatiana answered. "I volunteered to partake in that delivery with 'Oleg' because I ordered 'Stepan' to spy on you. A day later, 'Oleg' and I found that the shipment mostly used smaller boxes. Most likely, those were the weapons and ammunition used by the men who attacked you in Yao."

"And how did you even know about the attack in Yao?"

"I had a tracking device planted on your Townace. It was destroyed when Vos fled Yao."

"And since Mirov already told me why you were interested in Ganji, I assume you placed a tracking device somewhere close to him, too?"

"As you say in English-speaking countries, 'guilty as charged'."

"Now then, how did you know about the safehouse that it was one of your men who captured Vos?"

"After we planted the tracking device on your Townace, we visited Yao to figure out what you were up to. When the attack happened, 'Stepan' followed Vos when he escaped to Kansai City. By the time he found him, the Townace was damaged, as was the van used by the pursuers."

They clearly didn't know about Guliyeva. Vos must have told them. Punishing him for squealing won't do much at this point. Dirks then grabbed his phone and stopped the usage of its Recorder. He then opened an application called "Tracker" and once it opened, it showed a map of Kansai City with a blue dot that constantly blinked. He then showed the map to the OVR agents and Mirov.

"I assume this is where you've been making those deliveries?" Dirks asked. Tarou looked on with surprise, yet he kept his emotions in check.

"Da," Chadov answered. "How did you know?"

Shipwreck Assault

Abandoned Shipwreck, Crater Shore North, Kansai Prefecture; State of
Japan. August 16, 2030; 2030 hours (Japan Standard Time)

O n her smartphone's GOKMail, Shireen Baloch read a message
from Reinhard Frühling, calling himself "GIRH". The message
read as:

To "SB",

*A C-130 plane is being prepared to travel to Japan. Among the supplies we provided
to you is a STAR harness. We will let you know when it has left, then update you
again if it's near Kansai City. The FIS have formed an alliance with the OVR and
are planning an attack on your location. Thankfully, they won't attack until tomorrow
night at the latest but be prepared. The plane ought to be above the shipwreck should
the attack happen so by the time the attack happens, place the harness on Maral
Eminovna Guliyeva and have one of Song Dong-joo's men use it. It's guaranteed that
the FIS will use Iron Dutchman Services so keep those mercenaries away from the
shipwreck until you use the STAR harness with Guliyeva wearing it.*

Gatekeeper of Intelligence.

So it's time, Shireen thought. *Now I just have to find that STAR harness.*

\#

Iron Dutchman, Taisho Ward, Kansai City. August 17, 2030; 0900 hours

All members of Iron Dutchman Services gathered at their briefing room.
Tarou Ganji, Anita Hamilton, and Tatev Mirzoyan were the exceptions;
the former two were respectively at Nishi High School and her clinic while
the latter was already at the projector room. This time, the OVR cell that
consisted of Tatiana Ioannovna Tsulukidze, Pyotr Stepanovich Chadov,
and Karim Olegovich Zhakiyanov, as well as Vladimir Nikolayevich
Mirov, joined the mercenaries.

With her laptop computer already turned on, Tatev connected it to the
projector. Already open was the same Tracker application Frederick Dirks

had in his smartphone. Once the computer was connected to the projector, the main screen of the briefing room now showed the map of Kansai City used by Tracker and the blinking blue dot that represented the tracking device Frederick Dirks implanted onto Maral Eminovna Guliyeva.

"Secretly, I was able to place a tracking device on Maral Eminovna Guliyeva when the both of us escaped Mexico," Dirks announced to his mercenaries and their erstwhile Eurasian allies as he stood on the stage of the briefing room with Wouter Vos standing beside him. "Now, I know what you are all thinking but there's no time for ethics. Now that we know where Guliyeva was taken to, we can already plan for tonight."

"If you had a tracking device on her, why didn't you say so earlier?" Sunan Wattana asked as she raised her hand.

"I can't do anything unless given an order," Dirks answered while looking at Wattana. He then resumed looking at the projected map. "However, we can't plan just yet. I need to secure a helicopter from Camp Yao and use it to go to travel to National Police headquarters in Nagoya where I tell Commissioner Nagare everything that's happened and secure her assurance the police will not interfere when we attack the shipwreck. I'll have Vos with me and we'll use the recording of the interrogation I made with 'Elizaveta' to shorten our explanation."

"Why do you have to do that?" Tatiana asked.

"If we're to resolve everything, we need something the police can use to tell the press. We might have her men handcuff you, your men, and Lieutenant Mirov but it's only to get them to work with us for this attack. After the discussion there, we can go to Colonel Armstrong in Itami and acquire the weapons and equipment needed for the assault. Including our Walgear Solbein."

"Wait, did you say Solbein?" Mirov asked.

"Da," Dirks answered as he turned to Mirov, showing through his tone how tired he was of being interrupted. "We've kept it with the 1st Light Mechanized Assault Regiment until we need it. Now is a good time to get it.

"Once we get what we need from Armstrong, we get Ganji and Hamilton here. We inform them of the plan, equip everyone needed for the mission and what Solbein needs, and launch." Dirks then turned to the projector room. "Tatev, zoom in closely."

Without a reply, Tatev zoomed in on the map in Tracker. The portion of the map now showed the area surrounding the blue dot. Dirks then pointed at the map.

"While Vos and I will be at Nagoya, we need someone to actually go to the shipwreck and see what are the most likely areas that will be manned once we attack," Vos requested.

"Allow me and men to go with you," Tatiana requested. "We now know who made those orders and why. We wish to help put an end to their insanity."

"Good," Dirks replied as he resumed looking at Tatiana. "You can reuse your Stepwagn. I'll have Crawley take me and Vos to Camp Yao with the white one we took from the attack in Yao."

"When do we launch the attack?" Jawed Qazvini asked.

"First of all, good English," Dirks answered as he faced Qazvini. "Second, preferably at 1930 hours tonight, because we need darkness to make harder for the Koreans to find us when we attack them. We launch thirty minutes before that. We need Ganji to pilot Solbein so I'll tell him and once he comes here, we plan with the photograph 'Elizaveta' and her provide us. By the time Ganji comes, we should get the equipment from Armstrong by then and at 1800 hours, we get everything loaded and everyone in their respective vehicles before 1900."

"I have a request!" Tatev announced as she approached the stage from the projector room, making everyone look at her.

"Tatev, what is it?" Dirks asked.

"I wish to participate in this attack."

"Fine. But depending on the plans we make later this afternoon, you stick with me."

"Yes, sir," Tatev replied as she stopped and faced Dirks.

"About the attack, I have a suggestion," Tatiana argued.

"What is it?" Dirks asked as he turned to Tatiana.

"Park your truck where we dropped off those crates. We can have your...
Walgear leave the truck you intend for it to use and have it attack the
shipwreck first as a distraction."

"Good idea."

National Police Agency Headquarters, Nishi Ward, Nagoya City, Nagoya
Prefecture. 1131 hours

"Why did you show me this recording?" Miyako Nagare, the
Commissioner of the National Police Agency, asked after hearing the
recording Dirks made of his interrogation with Tatiana the previous
night. A decade older than Dirks, Nagare's black hair had long turned gray,
and she hid her dark brown eyes with glasses.

"I needed you to know that an OVR cell was in Japan. We can't hand them
over to you, and you and I both know why."

"If you came here to ask for my help with your spy games, then I can't
help you if you can't give me those responsible for the shootout in Yao,
the car chase in Kansai City, and the kidnapping of your mercenary
commander!"

"Alright, I have a proposition. You can tell the press that it was your men
who have been investigating the OVR cell since last year and that
everything was a sting operation that went wrong. In exchange, I need you
to delay the deployment of your men for one hour at most because I
found the safehouse used by the culprits behind the shootout in Yao and
the ones who pursued Vos."

"And where is this safehouse used by those Korean terrorists?"

"Crater Shore North. Specifically, what used to be Amagasaki. It's an
abandoned shipwreck."

"If you leave anyone alive, please hand them over to my men."

"Sadly, I can't do that. I'll need one of them alive as bait to get me Anton
Oleksandrovich Kravchenko, the human trafficker who sold Maral
Eminovna Guliyeva to Segismundo Alba."

"Wait, what does the leader of the Mexican drug cartel in Tijuana have to
do with this?"

"He bought Guliyeva from Kravchenko. We intend to use one of Kravchenko's Korean mercenaries to get us to Kravchenko. Sadly, we can't give him to you, but I offer you another proposition."

"And what's that?"

"In exchange for us keeping a Korean gunman, your men can hand over the OVR agents to their superiors when we release them."

"Fair trade. Just give me a picture of the shipwreck and you'll get your one hour. Also, tell me the time you'll launch your attack."

"Kansha shimasu." Dirks and Vos bowed after the former's thanks. Both then left Nagare's office.

#

Near the Abandoned Shipwreck, Crater Shore North, Kansai Prefecture. 1131 hours

The OVR agents and Mirov ultimately returned to Crater Shore North. This time, they went further than they were told in the two times they delivered to Crater Shore North. Once they saw the shipwreck, Zhakiyanov, who drove the black Stepwagn van, stopped.

Tatiana, seated beside Zhakiyanov, brought out her smartphone. She aimed the phone's lenses at the shipwreck and pressed the flash button of her phone's camera.

After that, she inspected her picture. Once she saw it was a good photograph, she signaled to Zhakiyanov it was time to leave. Everyone but Mirov agreed that this was the last time they would have to go to Crater Shore North.

#

Abandoned Shipwreck. 1135 hours

Unbeknownst to the OVR agents and Mirov, Shireen Baloch had watched their brief intrusion and while they exited Crater Shore North. She then looked at her phone's GOKMail as she received another message from Frühling hours before that read:

To "SB",

The C-130 has left Enlightenment Point at 0300 hours, EP Time Zone. It should arrive above your position at 1930 hours, Japan Standard Time. Have Song's men make preparations, prepare the STAR harness for Guliyeva's retrieval, and prepare your SH-6. Make sure the FIS and the OVR do not hinder your progress.

Gatekeeper of Intelligence.

The message had the date "08.17.2030" on the upper right with "0730 hours". Shireen then went back inside the shipwreck to obey Frühling's orders.

#

1ˢᵗ Light Mechanized Assault Regiment Headquarters/Itami Field, Itami, Hyogo Prefecture. 1340 hours

"That's quite the list for what you need to clean up your mess!" Henry Armstrong exclaimed as he looked at a list generated on the Notes application of Dirks' phone when he and Vos visited the former. "On my dime!"

"Look at it this way: we can give Kravchenko to the OVR to show them that we had to clean up their mess," Dirks reasoned.

"That sounds cathartic. I'm in. When do we need everything in that list?"

Hoshikawa Shipyards, Taisho Ward, Kansai City. 1600 hours

Jason Luke Crawley and Sunan Wattana stood dumbfounded as they saw a convoy of NUNGF trucks appear in front of the *Iron Dutchman*. Getting out of the Logistic Vehicle System Replacement (LVSR) tactical truck were Dirks and Vos. An object was hidden underneath a large sheet on the flatbed.

"This is a big step up," Crawley said. "Are you sure those trucks have all we need for tonight?"

"Yes," Dirks answered before turning to Wattana. "I even got you an ADR Sniper chambered at .338 Lapua Magnum."

"Thanks," Wattana happily replied. "You sure know what to get to a girl."

"Now can one of you please get Qazvini, Fed, Sem, and Mistry?" Vos asked. "We need to unload everything now. Also, please get those Eurasians to help. They still have to earn their keep."

#

Nishi High School, Higashiosaka Ward. 1710 hours

Tarou Ganji began to exit Nishi High School with his PCX motor scooter. However, he stopped because he felt his smartphone. After stopping, he got his phone and found that Dirks sent a message to him using IntMail. The message read:

We found where those Koreans took Guliyeva. A shipwreck in Crater Shore North. We got the equipment needed for the mission, but we need you with us as we brought something only you can use. Just tell Dr. Hamilton that she'll have to find her own ride home.

"Ganji-kun, what is it?" Tarou turned to find Maria Hoshikawa approaching him from behind.

"Can't say much," Tarou answered. "All I know is that there will be trouble at Crater Shore North."

"What about Hamilton-sensei?"

"I'll have to tell her to find her own way of going home."

"I'll pick her up tonight. The clinic is simply in front of Hoshikawa Group headquarters."

"Are you sure?"

"Guliyeva-san comes first. Hamilton-sensei would understand."

"Arigatou." Tarou then made the PCX face the direction of the Sanroku Bridge. It was then that Maria's limousine had arrived. Unwittingly, Tarou's mention of Crater Shore North was heard by Misa Todoh. She looked away just in time for her brother Riku to find her.

#

Iron Dutchman, Taisho Ward. 1744 hours

Tarou appeared at the Iron Dutchman's briefing room once every other Iron Dutchman Services member, save for Anita Hamilton, and the Eurasians, were gathered. Once he sat down, Dirks coughed to begin the briefing with both Dirks and Tatiana Ioannovna Tsulukidze standing with him. The main screen then showed the photograph Tatiana took hours before.

"Thanks to this photo 'Elizaveta' took, we can plan out how to launch our attack against this position used by those who took Maral Eminovna Guliyeva." Dirks then turned to the projector room where Tatev was. "Next slides, please!"

The main screen now showed a screenshot of the portion of a map of Crater Shore North from Tracker that showed the area surrounding the blue dot, which represented Guliyeva. Two red lines with arrow heads then appeared; one directly pointing at the blue dot and another largely traveling to the right of the first red line but also pointing at the same area already pointed at.

"From what my men and I discovered, there is only one way to enter that shipwreck," Tatiana added. "However, those Koreans most likely know we're coming, so we will be welcomed by overwhelming fire. When we made those deliveries to those Koreans, 'Oleg' and I felt that we might have carried rocket-propelled grenades. We don't know if your Walgear can survive an RPG round, but it is imperative that if we will encounter RPGs, they must be eliminated."

"Ganji, we had Solbein brought in, if in case you didn't notice that when you arrived, because we need you to use it to distract those Koreans," Dirks said to Tarou. "Other than Solbein, we have an LSAW and an ADR Sniper with us. Qazvini and Wattana will respectively use those. Qazvini will lay out suppressive fire while Wattana will eliminate any RPG users."

"I'll need a spotter, though," Wattana voiced.

"I can assist," Pyotr Stepanovich Chadov declared. "I was a spotter back in the *Spetsnaz* Demi-Brigade of the Imperial Airborne Division."

"Now who can drive the LVSR?"

"I'll do it," Vladimir Nikolayevich Mirov answered. "I wish to see how Tarou Ganji uses the silver Walger you call 'Solbein'."

"You may," Dirks replied as he faced Mirov. He then turned away from Mirov to the rest of those facing him, Vos, and Tatiana. "While Wattana, Crawley, and I still have the ADRs we took from the safehouse in Yao, we acquired additional ammunition and two more rifles for Vos and Ganji to use. Two of the AKs we took from the-"

"I'd like to point out that I was told by my Director that the Soviet Remnant suffered an attack that involved the theft of their rifles and RPGs," Tatiana interjected. "Most likely, we're dealing with those stolen weapons."

"This just keeps getting better and better," Vos sarcastically remarked. Thankfully for him, his voice was low enough no one heard him.

"My men will use the Soviet AKs in our custody for this operation."

"I'd like one for Tatev," Dirks added before turning to the projector room. Tatev, managing to hear what Dirks said, stood, faced the stage, and nodded.

Dirks then resumed facing the other mercenaries and the Eurasians. "Other than Ganji, Wattana, Qazvini, Mirov, and 'Stepan', everyone else is to storm the shipwreck once the RPG users have been eliminated."

"What about that Donian that appeared two nights before?" Tarou asked.

"If it appears, you'll have to deal with it," Dirks answered as he faced Tarou.

"It's 1800," Tatiana announced while looking at her watch.

"Then we make our preparations now," Dirks added.

"Then I must heat up all the sandwiches we bought," Bartolomeu Moura proclaimed. "We need something in our stomachs while we prepare."

"Now we finalize our objectives: we load up and we launch but once we reach Crater Shore North, we'll stop where 'Elizaveta' and her men have been leaving those crates because we need Solbein to get off the LVSR it's riding on and launch toward the shipwreck. Crawley, Vos, Qazvini, Wattana, and 'Stepan' will assist Ganji in attacking the shipwreck directly. The second team to charge into the shipwreck will take a separate route after Solbein launches and it will be composed of me, Tatev, 'Elizaveta', and 'Oleg'."

#

Hoshikawa Shipyards. 1855 hours

The vehicles used for the attack have been prepared. The white Stepwagn was in front of the LVSR truck carrying Solbein and the black Stepwagn behind the LVSR.

First to leave the shipyards was the white Stepwagn, driven by Crawley, with Vos, Wattana, Qazvini, and Chadov on board. Next was the LVSR, with Mirov driving it. Last was the black Stepwagn, driven by Karim Olegovich Zhakiyanov with Tatiana, Dirks, and Tatev on board.

I will save you, Maral, Tatev thought. *Please wait.*

#

Crater Shore North. 1916 hours

The convoy then stopped, with the black Stepwagn diverting itself as the occupants were to take a different route. With it out of its way, Solbein, hidden in the sheet, can be launched. Mirov then rushed out of the driver's seat of the LVSR's tractor and, once he reached the flatbed, he removed the sheet. He then used a radio, one of the many items Dirks asked from the 1st Light Mechanized Assault Regiment.

"I've removed the sheet," Mirov said. "Are you ready?"

"I am," Tarou answered over the radio.

"Then I'll remain in the driver's seat until this mission is over. You better survive this because I'm the only one who is to kill you in battle."

"Thanks." Mirov then returned to the driver's seat of the trailer. Tarou Ganji then made Solbein move to its left. Once Solbein's legs floated above the ground, he made the Walgear touch the ground, making it stand up. Tarou briefly walked away from the LVSR, then made Solbein turn to its left again. He then used the communicator of Solbein's control panel.

"Ready to move," Tarou announced.

"Acknowledged," Dirks replied over the communicator. "Vos, you and your group wait until I allow Ganji to move ahead. You'll have to follow after that."

"Roger that," Vos interjected.

"Ganji, you're clear to move."

"Roger." Tarou then flipped the switch that determined how Solbein should move. As a result, he now used Solbein's wheels to move on.

"Vos, you're clear to follow," Dirks said over the radio used by Vos.

"Got it," Vos replied before he turned to Crawley. "Jake, you heard him."

"Roger," Crawley replied before starting up the white Stepwagn again to follow Tarou.

#

Abandoned Shipwreck. 1931 hours

Shireen Baloch barged out of her room in the shipwreck, carrying an unconscious Maral Eminovna Guliyeva. The latter wore a harness over the dress Dirks bought for her. The shots that shook the shipwreck were the reason Shireen left her room with Guliyeva. She found Song Dong-joo in his room grabbing his AK-05.

"Is the STAR balloon ready?" Shireen asked.

"Ye," Song answered.

"What about my SH-6?"

"Also ready."

"Get me to the STAR balloon. Get one of your men to attach Guliyeva's harness to the balloon because the C-130 is almost here. I need to get to the SH-6."

#

Outside the Abandoned Shipwreck. 1940 hours

Tarou used Solbein's machine guns to fire at the shipwreck. However, two of Song's men began to aim their Type 69 rocket-propelled grenade (RPG) launchers at the Walgear.

"Rocket-propelled grenades detected," a sign said throughout the monitor of Solbein's control panel. Tarou promptly stopped firing and moved back as quickly as he could. By this time, Vos, Wattana, Crawley, Qazvini, and Chadov arrived in the white Stepwagn.

Seeing the RPG explosion after Solbein dodged it, Crawley turned to his right. As a result, Chadov and Wattana were the first to rush out of the Stepwagn because this was what they were supposed to do: save Tarou from the Koreans using the Type 69 RPGs.

Placing her ADR sniper rifle on top of the Stepwagn's engine with Chadov crouching to her right with night vision binoculars, Wattana then used the night vision scope of the ADR Sniper to take aim. At the same time, Qazvini aimed his LSAW (Light Squad Automatic Weapon) light machine gun after positioning himself far from the Stepwagn. Although he didn't aim, he kept one RPG user distracted.

Wattana then detected the other RPG wielder and aimed for her ADR Sniper. Since it was summer, both Chadov and Wattana had to worry about nighttime winds. Despite that, Wattana's shot was able to hit the other RPG user. With Chadov's assistance, she then aimed at the one whom Qazvini distracted and managing to adjust, she pulled the trigger again, killing him.

Tarou then stopped moving around. He then used his Walgear's communication.

"Mr. 'Smith', Miss Wattana's eliminated the RPG team," Tarou said. "I say again, RPG team eliminated."

"On our way there now," Dirks replied over the radio.

"Hold on, I'm seeing eight guys with who appears to be Guliyeva," Wattana interjected over the radio.

Tarou then used Solbein's camera eyes and zoomed in on the deck of the shipwreck. He found eight Koreans appearing on the roof. One of them laid the unconscious Maral Eminovna Guliyeva on the deck and another brought out a balloon whose design was that of a small airship. There was a wire tied to the balloon and below the wire was a hook.

"They have a balloon with them that's a small blimp," Tarou added. "There's a hook at the end of the wire attached to the balloon, and I think Guliyeva is wearing a vest."

"Did you say a vest?"

"Yes."

"Make sure they don't leave with Gu-"

An "Incoming" warning appeared on Solbein's monitor. "I detected something coming. I think I know who it is so I'll deal with him. Get to those Koreans."

"Will do."

Tarou then moved to his left. He then saw that it was the SH-6 that appeared two nights before.

Meanwhile, Dirks, Tatiana, Zhakiyanov, and Tatev arrived with the black Stepwagn. Once they got out of the van, they rushed to the hull of the shipwreck. Each carried a Plummet Gun. Seeing Tatev aim her Plummet Gun, Dirks ran up to her side.

"Are you sure you got this?" Dirks asked.

"I'm fine," Tatev answered.

Dirks then aimed his Plummet Gun as well. Tatiana was the first to fire hers, followed by Zhakiyanov. Tatev, then Dirks, followed. After that, they attached ascenders on the ropes that were propelled and connected to the shipwrecks but were detected by the Koreans. Only Qazvini appeared and used his LSAW to distract them.

This allowed Dirks, Tatev, and the Eurasians to continue propelling themselves upward. They used their left hands to use the ascenders while using their right hands to ready their respective rifles. Just before reaching the railing, they stopped. Then they leaned and fired against the Koreans.

Seeing this, Wattana began firing at some of the Koreans. Three of them hastily repositioned themselves while taking the STAR equipment and Guliyeva.

#

Abandoned Shipwreck. 1954 hours

Dirks, Tatev, Tatiana, and Zhakiyanov climbed into the ship. Finding some Koreans still alive from Wattana's attack, they eliminated them.

Seeing the last three using the STAR equipment while making Guliyeva stand, the former four aimed their weapons at the latter three.

"Stop what you're doing and surrender!" Dirks shouted.

The Koreans, however, laughed, and in a split second, Guliyeva was lifted into the air. The former were shot as a result. One, however, shot in the legs and Dirks, who shot him, got close and kneeled beside him to remove his mask. The man Dirks shot was Song Dong-joo.

"Where did you take her!?" Dirks asked.

"Somewhere far," Song replied before laughing again. As a result, Dirks stood up and shot him in the head, making him join the ones who were shot to death. He saw a C-130 Hercules transport plane, as did Tatiana and Zhakiyanov.

That insignia, Dirks thought as he was able to see a book with wings as a fin flash. However, he and the Eurasians would be interrupted by Tatev screaming and kicking. She stopped once she found the enemy SH-6 missing an arm but intact and sitting down. Dirks, Tatiana, and Zhakiyanov then joined her as the cockpit opened and its pilot, a girl as old as Tatev, surrendering to Wattana and Qazvini.

#

Outside the Abandoned Shipwreck. 1949 hours

Tarou, while using Solbein, charged at the SH-6 charging at them. Neither had hand weapons, so both prepared the Strike Knuckles of their respective right hands. Once they got close, their respective Strike Knuckles met and the sparks from the knuckles provided light.

Tarou then fired Solbein's machine guns, causing the SH-6 to move backward. Tarou attempted to use the Strike Knuckle of Solbein's left arm, but the SH-6 evaded the blow this time. As a result, it used its right Strike Knuckle again, but Tarou was able to realize what was happening and evaded by moving back.

As soon as the metal fist was in front of him, Tarou made Solbein grab it with both of its arms. Tarou pressed the front buttons of the arm controls as hard as he could with the intention of tearing off the SH-6's right arm. However, the pilot of the SH-6 struggled by using the SH-6's wheels.

Suddenly, Tarou felt his beating heart again. This caused Solbein's eyes to glow moreso than it did, and as a result, it was able to rip the SH-6's tight arm off. After tossing the arm aside, Tarou then used Solbein's right Strike Knuckle again and was able to stike at the torso of the SH-6, causing it to stumble into the ground.

"I… yield… " a female voice said over Solbein's communicator. Tarou widened his eyes upon hearing the voice.

That voice, it's can't be, Tarou thought. "If you yield, then power down your Walgear and get out of your cockpit!"

"I'm surprised to see that you're the prototype's pilot, Tarou."

It must be her! Tarou then watched as the cockpit of the SH-6 opened. It was then that Vos, Wattana, Chadov and Qazvini appeared with Vos using his mic.

"What do we do with the pilot?" Vos asked over Solbein's communicator.

"Arrest her," Tarou answered.

"Got it." Vos then turned to Qazvini. "You and I will go right." While the latter nodded, the former turned to Wattana and Chadov. "You two, go left."

"Got it," Wattana and Chadov replied in unison before they rushed to the left side of the SH-6 while Vos and Qazvini went to the right side.

Once both pairs got to their respective positions, the SH-6's pilot, Shireen Baloch, chose to leave her cockpit by going to her right. She surrendered to Vos and Qazvini.

In his cockpit, Tarou saw the enemy pilot he fought dragged away by Wattana once Qazvini joined her. He zoomed in on the pilot and he gulped upon seeing his childhood friend, now sixteen years old, dragged away.

Why were you my enemy, Shireen? Tarou anxiously pondered.

"Ganji, do you read me?" Dirks asked over the communicator.

"Sir?" Tarou asked in response.

"What's the matter with you? Contact Armstrong and get his men to clean up this shipwreck. We're leaving."

"Shall we take the enemy Walgear pilot back to the *Iron Dutchman*?"

"Of course. Now contact Armstrong, then return to Mirov."

"Yes, sir." Tarou leaned back and sighed. *How are you still alive and how were you able to use that Walgear?* Tarou pondered as if he were asking Shireen. He then began to switch frequencies on Solbein's communicator

The New Prisoner

Iron Dutchman, Taisho Ward, Kansai City, Kansai Prefecture; State of Japan. August 17, 2030; 2045 hours (Japan Standard Time)

"Who on Earth is that girl?" Wouter Vos asked on the stage of the *Iron Dutchman*'s briefing room. Frederick Dirks and Tatiana Ioannovna Tsulukidze stood with Vos after he asked that question and listened, as did most of the members of Iron Dutchman Services.

"That's why we need to interrogate her," Dirks suggested. "When Wattana and I caught a glimpse of her when we bought Guliyeva her dress, we suspected she was with the Koreans if she was going to Artisan House by herself without a uniform. Didn't think she was a Walgear pilot."

"She's Shireen Baloch." Everyone turned to Tarou Ganji after he named the girl that was captured in the shipwreck raid.

"Please continue," Dirks demanded.

"My childhood friend, Shireen Baloch. Thought she died three years ago. I'm as surprised as everyone that she's still alive and a Walgear pilot."

"Could explain the book with wings on the C-130 that showed up," Dirks added

"What 'book with wings'?" Tatiana asked.

"A C-130 showed up to fetch Guliyeva. On the fin was a book with wings. Only the Gatekeepers of Knowledge operate those C-130s since they use a book with wings as their insignia."

"Do you think this Shireen Baloch works for them?"

"I want to ask her that."

"You'll need me," Tarou added. "Shireen would most likely speak in Farsi out of spite. I can help interpret."

"Fine. But do not lose your cool. You talk only if there's interpretation needed and don't deliberately misinterpret."

2100 hours

Dirks and Tarou returned to the *Iron Dutchman*'s brig, where Shireen Baloch sat in front of the corner far from the door of the cell where Tatiana was imprisoned at.

"So, you want to interrogate me?" Shireen asked in English.

This makes it easier if she knows English, Dirks thought before he replied. "That's right. Answer well and I'll let you go."

"Watch your questions, though."

"We'll start with something simple: where did you take Maral Eminovna Guliyeva?"

"Back to Kravchenko."

"Why would a human trafficker want his 'merchandise' back?"

"Because Kravchenko had no intention of selling Guliyeva to Segismundo Alba."

"You're awfully cooperative with this. Now then, was that a Gatekeepers-owned C-130 that scooped up Guliyeva?"

"I can neither confirm nor deny that."

"Don't be a smartass with me. Where is that plane going and why did Kravchenko want Guliyeva back?"

"You're going to have to kill me for it."

"Sir, don't!" Tarou warned. "We still need her alive."

"She's not your friend anymore!" Dirks argued."

"Believe me, sir, having her answer for what happened to Guliyeva is understandable, but we do need to know where Kravchenko is. Based on how Shireen is answering your questions, there's a high chance Kravchenko has no intention of selling off Guliyeva."

"And what's your basis for that!?" Unbeknownst to Dirks, Shireen gave a satisfied grin with how Tarou guessed her intentions.

"Calm down. We won't be able to get Guliyeva back if we argue. We just need to shatter her confidence."

Dirks sighed. "You're right," he replied before he resumed facing Shireen. "Don't think for a second we're done with you. We'll be back."

Both Dirks and Tarou then left the brig.

#

2118 hours

"Come up with anything?" Vos asked Dirks and Tarou after they returned to the briefing room from the brig.

"Nothing," Dirks answered.

"I have an idea," Tarou added.

"What is it?" Dirks asked upon turning to Tarou.

"We use Shireen."

"Are you nuts? Not only she gave the wrong answers to my questions, what makes you think we can use her as bait to get us to Kravchenko?"

"It can work," Tatiana argued.

"How?" Dirks asked after turning to Tatiana.

"Kravchenko must use a legal front for his business. What we need to do is find it and contact them to do business."

"Good idea."

"As for me, I'll get Shireen to lose her patience. She'll most likely devise something that will benefit us." Tarou then left the briefing room again.

He really is taking this personally, Dirks thought as he looked at Tarou leaving the briefing room.

#

2128 hours

Tarou returned to the brig alone. Shireen noticed because of the footsteps of the former and once they were facing each other, the latter wasn't surprised.

"I've said it once and I'll say it again: I won't answer any of your questions," Shireen warned.

"Doesn't matter," Tarou replied. "The way I see it, only the Gatekeepers of Knowledge could have provided all those resources. You and I both know going after them at this point is pointless, so what I want to know is why you joined."

"Now you show interest in what I've been up to? You probably assumed me dead. I assumed you were dead too."

"You're right. For five years, I wandered across the desert because, by some miracle, I'm alive. That was, until I wandered into Egypt and found a mercenary group under attack. I don't know, but I felt that I must help, so I stole a Walgear."

"Thank you for the story. Still doesn't change anything."

"We could sell you off to Kravchenko. If you are working for him, he will not tolerate failure. It's only a matter of time until my client finds where Kravchenko's hiding and how to contact him."

They could, Shireen cautiously thought. *Though by now, the C-130 that picked up Guliyeva should be in Wonsan. Maybe humoring Tarou wouldn't be a bad idea if it will lead to the elimination of these mercenaries. They'll be excellent opponents for the prototype.*

"Very well, I'll talk," Shireen announced.

"Then start with why you joined the Gatekeepers of Knowledge," Tarou demanded.

"After that futile battle to defend Tehran, Commander Muhadow was able to save me. Only me. We fled to Enlightenment Point, and we both joined the Gatekeepers of Knowledge with the intent of preparing the world for a better future. I was taught everything from multiple languages to piloting many vehicles. I became a Monitor, the Gatekeepers' equivalent of a spy, as a result. If you don't believe me, I'm the one who started that fire in that hotel owned by Daisuke Hoshikawa months before in Hokkaido, allowing him to not hear about his daughter's kidnapping by Commander

Muhadow until it was too late. I even engineered the destruction of the facility before you infiltrated it, and just before its destruction, I had it cleaned up."

"That nuclear explosion... you're responsible!?"

"That's right. I'm also the reason why the Brotherhood of Freedom's offensive failed and why it was easily destroyed, save for Vahid Farahani's cell."

"Since you're telling me all of this, how did the FIS get that information about Guliyeva?"

"Another Monitor infiltrated the United States and left that file. *He's* also responsible for the events that led to Segismundo Alba's suicide."

"And you're the one who brought the Koreans here? As well as their weapons?"

"That's right."

"I can't say that I sympathize with what you're doing or why, that is, if it's true. Just be ready to face what comes next. Good night."

Tarou then left the brig. Once he finished climbing the stairs leading in and out of the brig, he found Dirks waiting for him.

"How was your interrogation?" Dirks asked.

"She talked," Tarou answered. "Wish to know what she told me?"

#

Wings of the Defenders C-130/Wonsan International Airport, Wonsan, Gangwon Province; Republic of Korea. 2138 hours (Korea Standard Time)

Two armed men in cloaks came out of the C-130 used by the Gatekeepers of Knowledge's air force, the Wings of the Defenders. They brought with them Maral Eminovna Guliyeva out of the plane toward Anton Oleksandrovich Kravchenko, also guarded by two masked men.

"Glad to see you again, Maral," Kravchenko said.

Maral, however, said nothing. "Thinking you can be smart by not talking back to me? How about after this!?"

Kravchenko furiously slapped Guliyeva. The slap was powerful enough for her to land on the tarmac. Guliyeva, however, stood up in defiance.

"Think you can be defiant with me!?" Kravchenko screamed. "Drag her to the van now!"

Kravchenko's two guards attempted to pick up Guliyeva. However, the latter was able to stand up on her own. Despite that, the former two used their AK-05 assault rifles to force her to the nearby van.

#

Abandoned Mosque, Semnan, Semnan Province, Region 1; Islamic Republic of Iran. July 21, 2023; 0835 hours (Iran Standard Time)

"Commander, I brought this crate-" Tarou Ganji, aged ten, said as he arrived at the abandoned mosque while carrying crates, having stopped his sentence as he two armed men unknowingly blocking him.

"Is that you, Ganji? Come in."

Tarou proceeded inside. He still carried the crate, which made him focus on walking to the man who called him inside, Serdar Muhadow. He didn't know that Shireen Baloch was also inside.

"Put aside that crate," Muhadow ordered. "There's something I need you to do."

Tarou did as Muhadow ordered. However, once he put the crate down, he then caught the glance of Shireen on his way to Muhadow and once he turned to her fully, he rushed to her.

"Shireen, what are you doing here?" Tarou asked.

"She's here because of you," Muhadow answered to remind Tarou where he should he have walked to. "Since you're here, bring out your pistol."

Tarou brings out a PP semi-automatic pistol. Muhadow then grabbed the pistol and turned off its safety. He then offered it to Shireen.

"Here," Muhadow said. "Take it."

Shireen wasted no time in grabbing the PP. "Now then," Muhadow continued. "aim it a him." To the horror of everyone but Muhadow, the latter pointed at Tarou.

"W... Why Tarou?" Shireen asked.

"You must not show hesitation here," Muhadow explained. "If you want to join my army, show me I can trust you. Now aim!"

Shireen began to cower as she aimed the PP with both of her hands. She closed her eyes and shook her legs as she continued to aim at Tarou. Tarou, however, opted not to resist or run, but stood and put his arms behind him.

Shireen's right index finger shook. Yet it neared the trigger. Her hesitation didn't last as the trigger was pulled, but only the hammer was heard. As a result, Shireen opened her eyes, only to find Tarou still alive and surprised. Muhadow then began to chuckle and made no effort to hide it from the children or his adult subordinates.

"You still pulled the trigger," Muhadow commented. "I made it a rule for all my soldiers to have their pistols empty when there isn't any combat. Despite that, you did what I told you to do. Perhaps I could recruit you, but you must always obey orders. Is that understood?"

"Yes… " Shireen replied, but wasn't aware of how Muhadow still acted like a soldier.

"Sir. Call me that at all times."

"Yes, sir!" Muhadow then turned to Tarou.

"Ganji, teach her how to be a soldier."

"Yes, sir!" Tarou replied with a salute.

#

Hamilton-Ganji Condominium, Hoshikawa Condominiums, Higashiosaka Ward, Kansai City, Kansai Prefecture; State of Japan. August 18, 2030; 0600 hours (Japan Standard Time)

Tarou now opened his eyes to the present. As he began to elevate his upper body, still hidden underneath his bedsheet, he found Anita Hamilton to his right.

"Dr. Hamilton?" Tarou asked. "W… Why are you in my room?"

"You hadn't woken up for your exercise," Hamilton answered. "That means something is wrong and it's related to why Maria herself had to offer me a ride back to this condo last night."

"I… I'm sorry about that."

"I can tell what happened is going to make me have to pack today's breakfast for you to eat at school. We have plenty of time. Care to explain a good amount of what happened last night?"

Tarou sighed. Despite that, he explained what happened in the raid against the shipwreck and what happened after that in the *Iron Dutchman*. Hamilton had her phone with her and realized Tarou only spent thirty minutes explaining his story.

"Is there anything else?" Hamilton asked upon looking at Tarou again.

"I suggested… that… we offer Shireen to Kravchenko," Tarou added with his guilt evident from his tone. "I know it's wrong… but Tatev really wants to save Guliyeva. I didn't wish to hurt Shireen like this, even if she was my enemy last night. But she worked with Kravchenko, and now… I don't know what to do… "

"Calm down, Tarou. This is exactly why you need to focus on being a normal teenager. Let Mr. 'Smith' and 'Elizaveta' find Kravchenko. Now get up and take a bath. If you're fast enough, you can still eat your breakfast here."

"Thanks, Doc."

"Please get up. You'll be late."

#

Iron Dutchman, Taisho Ward. 0850 hours

Frederick Dirks walked to the entrance of the *Iron Dutchman*'s shooting range. He found Tatiana Ioannovna Tsulukidze and Pyotr Stepanovich Chadov outside; the former using her smartphone connected to the satellite receiver while the latter held the receiver while aiming it toward the sky.

"Zametano," Tatiana said before the call on her phone ended. After that, she disconnected the phone from the receiver and, as she began to leave, she saw Dirks.

"… How long have you been standing there?" Tatiana asked.

"Since 'Zametano'," Dirks answered. "I assume that was your Director?"

"Da. I have to wait for his authorization from the Tsar himself on the idea of 'buying a present' from Kravchenko."

"Unlike you, my superiors in the FIS agree to the idea. They, however, will need a reconnaissance mission, and I think I can help with your plan of tricking Kravchenko into thinking the Tsar wants a concubine."

"How?"

"We buy plane tickets for a trip to South Korea tomorrow. Good way to wait until your Director hears from the Tsar."

"Excellent. When do we get those tickets?"

"Now, if you wish."

"Excellent! Also, I want to begin emptying my safehouse. The money we own is still there, as well as other effects."

"I'll get Vos and his men to help. They need something to do while we wait for our respective superiors to say anything."

"Agreed."

#

Sinpo Box Factory, Sinpo, Hamgyong Province; Republic of Korea. 0850 hours (Korea Standard Time)

Kravchenko and two of his guards opened the container where they kept Maral Eminovna Guliyeva. "Vstavat'!" Kravchenko barked.

Guliyeva got out of the container. "Selling me off now?" she defiantly asked.

"You won't have that tone after this." Kravchenko turned to one of his guards. "Blindfold her."

The guard brought out a blindfold and put it in Guliyeva's eyes. She didn't resist while the blindfold covered her eyes. The guard then grabbed her while the other aimed his AK-05 at her.

"*He*'s waiting," Kravchenko reminded. "Get her to move!"

The two guards then forced Guliyeva to move while Kravchenko led them. They traveled to a large basement found below the factory. There, the man "LS" brought with him looked at a sitting Walgear that appeared taller than those whose height was four meters at most.

"She's here," Kravchenko said to the man. The older man then faced Kravchenko, his guards, and Guliyeva.

"Let me see her," the older man requested.

T… That voice! Guliyeva thought just as the blindfold was removed out of her eyes.

Once the blindfold was removed, she now saw the older man. Her defiant attitude vanished at that instant.

"W… Why… Why are you here?" Guliyeva asked.

"I'm here to pick up where I left off," the older man answered. He then faced Kravchenko and his guards. "Get her to the Walgear."

Kravchenko ordered his two men to drag Guliyeva to the Walgear. She screamed while being dragged. Neither Kravchenko nor the older man cared.

#

Nizhny Novgorod Kremlin, Nizhegorodsky District, Imperial Capital of Nizhny Novgorod; Eurasian Tsardom. 0715 hours (Novgorod Time)

Vyechaslav Leonidovich Puzanov was in the throne room of the Nizhny Novogrod Kremlin bowing to his Tsar, Ivan Vladimirovich Tsulukidze. Puzanov bowed alongside Elmira Maratovna Borasanova, the sergeant in charge of the infantry squad of the Imperial Eurasian Army's Lifeguard Regiment assigned to the throne room.

"You two may stand," Ivan ordered to Puzanov and the female soldier.

Both stood up, with Ivan turning to the latter. "Please return to your position, Serzhánt Borasanova."

"Da, Vashe Velichestvo," Borasanova replied before standing to the right of the Tsar.

Ivan then turned to Puzanov. "I assume you're here concerning 'Elizaveta'?"

"Da, Vashe Velichestvo," Puzanov answered.

"Then we'll discuss this in my office." Ivan then stood up and began to move to his office. Only after he started to walk did Puzanov follow. As a result, the Tsar reached his office first with Puzanov following. By the time Puzanov closed the door, Ivan was seated in his desk.

"Now, what about my daughter?" Ivan asked.

"She wishes to fool Anton Oleksandrovich Kravchenko into thinking you intend on buying a concubine," Puzanov answered. "That way, Kravchenko can make a mistake that will guarantee her cell and our temporary allies the ability to infiltrate Kravchenko's hideout."

"I'll allow it. I already permitted this temporary alliance with the New United Nations. This must end."

"Da, Vashe Velichestvo."

#

Iron Dutchman, Taisho Ward, Kansai City, Kansai Prefecture; State of Japan. 1400 hours (Japan Standard Time)

"Now, let's see if 'Nizhny' had gotten permission from the Tsar," Dirks announced while watching Tatiana turning on her smartphone and connecting it to the satellite receiver as Chadov held it and aimed it at the sky.

Tatiana then turned on SatCom. She began to call "Nizhny". The ringing began.

"Is that you, 'Elizaveta'?" Puzanov asked over the smartphone.

"Da," Tatiana answered. "Has the Tsar said anything?"

"He'll allow it."

"Otlichno! I even bought plane tickets for me and Chadov. They're for a flight to South Korea tomorrow. After that, I'll work with the FIS to find where Kravchenko hides."

"Please keep me updated." The call ended. Tatiana then faced Dirks.

"Now, what do your superiors say?" Tatiana asked.

"Why don't we discuss that in the library?" Dirks rhetorically asked. "We'll need Tatev and 'Maria Clara'."

1431 hours

Dirks, Tatiana, and Chadov were now in the *Iron Dutchman*'s library. They were now joined by Tatev Mirzoyan, who brought her laptop computer with her and turning on AudComm. The ringing now pertained to "Maria Clara"—Alicia Caguiat.

"Miss Mirzoyan, you needed anything?" Caguiat asked over AudComm.

"Yes," Tatev answered. "We need documents pertaining to old North Korean factories from before World War III. Mr. 'Smith' and 'Elizaveta' have reason to believe one of them could be used by Kravchenko as a front for his sex trafficking business. Also, those documents on all legitimate businesses Kravchenko uses as a front."

"I'll send them to your IntMail address. Please wait."

"Thank you." Tatev then turned on her IntMail. She began to wait for "Maria Clara" to send her a message. Thankfully, the wait wasn't long as a message from Caguiat came. The message contained a file of a map of the divided Korean Peninsula before the Third World War. It didn't take long for another message with a file to appear, also from Caguiat. This time, the file was a map of the present-day Korean Peninsula, where the territory controlled by the Republic of Korea was now larger than the Democratic People's Republic of Korea. This was the result of the war where the ROK launched a campaign to reunify the peninsula but a portion remained controlled by the DPRK because of their alliance with the People's Republic of China, who stopped being an ally of the ROK and the United States of America as the war was coming to an end.

"Please forward this to me," Dirks instructed.

"Mind if I connect my phone?" Tatiana requested. "I also need these files for my phone."

"Before I do any of that, there's something the both of you need to know," Tatev argued.

"What is it?" Dirks asked.

1911 hours

Everyone except Bartolomeu Moura gathered in the briefing room. "Now that we're all here," Dirks announced, with Vos and Tatiana standing with him on the stage, before he turned to the projector room. "Tatev, show them."

"Got it," Tatev shouted in response before turning on her computer's Tracker. The map in the application was then projected onto the screen, showing the blue dot that represented Guliyeva at Sinpo.

"We now know where the Gatekeepers took Guliyeva," Dirks continued. "However, we can't just launch an assault to save her and to arrest or kill Kravchenko. Since our prisoner will not outright tell us why Kravchenko needed to retrieve Guliyeva from Alba, we will sneak this into Kravchenko's hideout."

Dirks then showed the mercenaries and the Eurasians a metal fly. "This is a drone we can use to infiltrate Kravchenko's hideout," Dirks explained. "As to how we'll sneak it inside, I'll let 'Elizaveta' explain."

Dirks then stepped aside to allow Tatiana to resume the briefing. "Earlier, 'Stepan' and I bought plane tickets for South Korea, made reservations, and a call to Kravchenko's box factory, which is the front he uses for his sex trafficking business," Tatiana announced. "While 'Stepan' and I pose as a recently wedded couple, we will first settle in the cheapest hotel in Incheon we could find, then travel to Sinpo, where we will then act out as Tsardom government officials tasked by the Tsar to buy him a concubine. While we deal with Kravchenko, we will infiltrate the drone 'Smith' showed earlier."

"And I assume you intend to offer them our prisoner?" Jason Luke Crawley asked.

"That's right."

"Any other concerns?" Vos asked.

"Why do we have to sell our prisoner?" Hamilton asked.

"We don't have to," Dirks answered. "We just need to trick Kravchenko. Once we get the drone inside, we can plan out our attack."

"Anything else?" Vos asked, with everyone answering no.

"Then you're all dismissed," Dirks ordered. As everyone began to leave the briefing room, Dirks saw Tarou.

"Except you, Ganji," Dirks said, making Tarou face him. "You and I need to talk to Baloch. Moura isn't even finished with dinner yet, so it's a good time for us to kill time."

"Yes, sir."

1930 hours

Both Tarou and Dirks returned to the brig. Shireen Baloch, however, wasn't surprised Tarou would be joined by his FIS handler.

"I assume you'll be selling me off to Kravchenko?" Shireen answered.

"Not really," Dirks answered. "We intend to use that as a distraction to get Kravchenko to let down his guard. We just need to tie you up and slap you into a crate, and we'll sneak in a knife for you to use after the box is opened."

"You're not going to get Kravchenko nor rescue Guliyeva that easily. Consider that a warning."

"There's something I want to know," Tarou said as it was his turn to ask Shireen. "Why take Maria Hoshikawa to that facility on Sakhalin Island? You must have helped Muhadow."

"That I can't tell you. You'll have to figure that one out yourselves, but you must be ready for the consequences of that."

"We'll work our way around it," Dirks replied. "You're going to have to wait for your dinner like everyone else. I'll have Ganji send it to you later. We're done here for now." Both Dirks and Tarou left the brig.

#

2019 hours

Tarou returned to the brig by himself. This time, he carried a tray. Once he reached Shireen's cell, he crouched to place the tray aside and once he stood up again, he brought out the key and unlocked the cell door. He crouched again to pick up the tray, only to bend half of his body when he placed it in front of Shireen. In all of this, Shireen paid no attention that it was Tarou giving her food.

"Here's your dinner," Tarou said.

"Were you ordered to do this or did you volunteer to do this?" Shireen asked.

"I guess you could say both. Just eat."

"Before I do that, mind if I ask you some questions?"

"If they're easy enough to answer, then you may."

"Why did you take that Walgear from the facility in Sakhalin Island?"

"If I answer that question, you're practically telling me that you have full knowledge of Maria Hoshikawa's kidnapping."

"Don't be smug with me. I bet you're only with these mercenaries to find out about who you really are."

She's right, Tarou thought. *Everything I've done was a step in finding out who I am. I once told Shireen I wanted to see the world when I became older. Why do I have to hide this from her?*

Tarou sighed. "Fine, I am with these mercenaries to discover who I really am," he answered. "But you should know that my mission to protect Maria Hoshikawa came first, and I only stole that Walgear as a quick method of escape."

"And you think Maria Hoshikawa will lead you to the answers about your past?"

"As long as people like you threaten her, I will use that to get the answers I seek."

"You and Hoshikawa study at the same school. Are you in love with her?"

Tarou opened his mouth as if he choked. He had never once been asked if he was in love with Maria and the question coming from Shireen didn't help. *Damn you, Shireen!* Tarou cursed in his mind. *That was uncalled for!*

"You don't have to answer immediately," Shireen mockingly added. "Though I do have to wonder how long can you continue to act that way for this mission of yours?"

"Just eat your dinner!" Tarou screamed.

"Other than that, what will *you* do if you get the answers you seek?"

Tarou, however, gritted his teeth upon hearing that question that he was asked a few times. His anger came from how Shireen asked the question. Despite that, he regained his composure and stopped looking at Shireen.

"Just eat your dinner before it's cold," Tarou warned before walking away from Shireen's cell. "I must go. I need to return to my condominium with Dr. Hamilton and resume my homework. Good night."

Shireen ultimately started her dinner, which wasn't as warm as it was when Tarou gave it to her. *Fool,* Shireen thought. *I fight to help build a world because at least the Grand Gatekeeper has a plan for the world, even if it means starting wars.*

#

Sinpo Box Factory, Sinpo, Hamgyong Province; Republic of Korea. 2019 hours (Korea Standard Time)

The screams now filled the underground complex of Sinpo Box Factory. They came from Maral Eminovna Guliyeva, now wearing a hospital gown, as she was in the cockpit of the Walgear with sticky pads on her limbs and a helmet covering her eyes. The sticky pads and helmet were connected to the control panel through wires. She no longer wore the dress Frederick Dirks bought for her, but a white hospital gown.

The older man who made Guliyeva give up in resisting the position she was in moved panels on a machine that was connected to the Walgear. As a result, electricity surged through the wires connecting the sticky pads on Guliyeva's limbs to the Walgear's control panel.

It was then that Anton Oleksandrovich Kravchenko appeared with a guard. He stopped and touched the older man by his left, making the latter turn to the former.

"Sorry if I disturbed you, but how goes the experiment?" Kravchenko asked.

"It's going great," the older man answered. "If we go at this uninterrupted, we can succeed. Thank you for providing me with this test subject."

"Thank the Gatekeepers."

The Real Reason

Marina Hotel, Jung District, Incheon; Republic of Korea. August 19, 2030; 1001 hours (Korea Standard Time)

Both Tatiana Ioannovna Tsulukidze and Pyotr Stepanovich Chadov were now at the hotel they bought a room for their mission to meet with Anton Oleksandrovich Kravchenko. Once they reached their room, they unpacked their belongings. That included the fly-based drone Frederick Dirks needed to infiltrate Kravchenko's hideout.

It was then that Tatiana's smartphone rang. Once she picked it up, she found that it was "Sinpo Box Factory" calling for her.

"Yes, this is Miss Afonin," Tatiana said.

"Glad you can hear us," a distorted voice said over the phone. "Are you in South Korea?"

"Incheon. Marina Hotel. When can we go to your factory?"

"Now."

"Excellent. Thank you and we'll see you there." Tatiana then put down the phone and faced Chadov.

"We best buy tickets for Sinpo," Tatiana instructed Chadov. "While we're on the train to Sinpo, we turn on the drone and let it go when we're in the factory. 'Smith' will handle it. We simply talk until we've made sure Kravchenko is distracted."

"Zametano," Chadov replied.

"Then let's start deciding on what to bring with us other than the drone."

#

Sinpo Station, Sinpo, Hamgyong Province. 1119 hours

Both Tatiana and Chadov left Sinpo Station. Then, they saw two men approach them.

"Are you Elizabeth Afonin and Steven Mishulovich?" one man asked in English despite his Korean accent.

"That's us," Tatiana answered.

"We'll take you to the factory now. Please follow us."

\#

Sinpo Box Factory. 1130 hours

Both Tatiana and Chadov were taken to the Sinpo Box Factory. Unbeknownst to the two men that picked them up from Sinpo Station, the former two turned on the drone. Once all four out of the Starex van, the Eurasians secretly released the drone.

Once inside the factory complex, Tatiana and Chadov now saw Anton Oleksandrovich Kravchenko approaching them. The "deal" had started.

\#

Iron Dutchman, Taisho Ward, Kansai City, Kansai Prefecture; State of Japan. 1131 hours (Japan Standard Time)

"Are you sure this will work?" Wouter Vos asked while he and Tatev Mirzoyan watched Frederick Dirks used Tatev's laptop computer to use an application called "Drone Control".

"It has to," Dirks answered defiantly. "All we need to do is hope that 'Elizaveta' and 'Stepan' distract Kravchenko long enough that he will not notice anything out of the ordinary."

\#

Sinpo Box Factory, Sinpo, Hamgyong Province; Republic of Korea. 1140 hours (Korea Standard Time)

The drone entered the main building of Sinpo Box Factory through the chimney. Once inside, the drone remained floating in the air as the drone emitted a red light. Miraculously, no one inside the factory noticed the light. After that, the drone was directed to a particular door with a sign that read "Do Not Enter" with translations in both Korean and Russian below the English writing.

Despite that, the drone began to access the lock of the door. Once that was finished, the drone entered but closed the door and locked it to make sure no one noticed that the door was open.

The drone continued toward the basement. However, most of the basement lacked light save for a certain machine. The drone flew in a certain direction despite the darkness to avoid being seen. Only through the darkness was the drone directed to the machine and got close to the man sleeping on it.

The drone was directed to elevate itself and once it was high enough, it moved to its right. It was now in front of the sleeping man, but the sound emitted from the drone's wings woke up the man, albeit briefly.

The man talked briefly, as if it was asleep. However, the drone was able to see the face and upper body of the man. After that, the drone flew back into the darkness.

Now in the darkness, the drone landed on the floor despite not seeing it. It remained there for ten seconds, then it broke into pieces.

#

Iron Dutchman, Taisho Ward, Kansai City, Kansai Prefecture; State of Japan. 1201 hours (Japan Standard Time)

"It... It can't be... " Dirks said as he looked at the man the drone made a picture of before it was destroyed.

"What's going on?" Vos asked. "Is that man the reason why you destroyed the drone?"

"Yes, and if we don't stop him, Guliyeva is done for."

"What do you mean?" Tatev asked.

"I can't tell you! Not now. Everyone needs to hear this."

"But two of our Eurasians are in South Korea right now," Vos reminded. "Wouldn't you need them to hear who this man is?"

"I can ask 'Oleg' to think of something," Dirks answered. "However, we need Ganji and Hamilton here as soon as Ganji is done with his classes. I can get to Hamilton through Daisuke. Someone will have to get Ganji later this afternoon."

"I'll get Jake to do so," Vos replied. "He can even buy us sandwiches from Tadakono DS for dinner while waiting for him."

"Good. I'll have 'Oleg' ask how 'Elizaveta' and 'Stepan's' meeting with Kravchenko went."

#

Marina Hotel, Jung District, Incheon; Republic of Korea. 1300 hours (Korea Standard Time)

"Zhakiyanov, you picked a *terrible* time to call me," Tatiana said while using her phone as she laid tired on her bed in her room in the Marina Hotel. Chadov laid beside her.

"*My* apologies for that," Dirks said over Tatiana's phone. "I discovered something that will *hopefully* shorten your stay."

"What is it?"

"Can't tell you right now. I'm going to start talking to people about what will be needed for the days ahead. You and 'Stepan' need to listen later at tonight's briefing, so I'll have 'Oleg' use his phone and make it the TV for you and 'Stepan' to listen from."

"What's so important that you need 'Stepan' and I to listen?"

"You'll know soon. Please be patient."

#

Iron Dutchman, Taisho Ward, Kansai City, Kansai Prefecture; State of Japan. 1329 hours (Japan Standard Time)

At the rock climbing section of the *Iron Dutchman*, one of the few amenities preserved, Dirks began to use his phone's AudComm to contact Alicia Caguiat. Thankfully, the wait wasn't long.

"Hello?" Caguiat asked.

"Think you could please get me to Langley 3?" Dirks requested. "I'm going to need access to resources because my operation has hit a snag."

"I'm here," Stanley McAllister said over AudComm. "Tell me what happened and what you need?"

"Long story short, all the Koreans have been eliminated, but a C-130 bearing the markings of the Gatekeepers of Knowledge interfered and made off with Guliyeva. We even captured an operative working with the Koreans most likely responsible for that. Luckily, we traced Guliyeva to the box factory owned by Kravchenko, but I discovered that Sedgwick Henderson is with him?"

"Wait, did you say Sedgwick Henderson?"

"Yes, sir. And if he's resuming the experiments we're familiar with, chances are Guliyeva will die. If I'm to take the fight to him and Kravchenko to save Guliyeva, if she's not dead already, I need all the help I can get."

"Tell me what you need, son."

#

FIS Headquarters, McLean, Fairfax County, Commonwealth of Virginia; United States of America. 0033 hours (Eastern Standard Time)

"If 'Smith' is asking for all of those, Henderson must be repeating those experiments," Alberto Pérez said after he and Yanin Saetang listened to McAllister bringing up what Dirks needed.

"I don't like all of it," Saetang argued. "There's no telling if Henderson will succeed this time. Not only that, we should be more focused on figuring out if it was a Gatekeepers C-130 that brought Guliyeva to Kravchenko and Henderson."

"We all know we can't make such an accusation against the Gatekeepers," McAllister retorted. "It's one thing to suspect them of aiding the Eurasians when they invaded Iran, tested that aircraft in the Sea of Japan, and helped create the Duchy of Finland and the Sultanate of Turkey, but outright accusing them of taking Guliyeva can harm the New United Nations."

"Stan's right," Pérez replied. "While it will be costly, I think we can make the arrangements." Perez then turned to Saetang. "Yanin, if you have dirt on the Blue House, use that to gain their help. Use Vue as your messenger."

"Will do," Saetang replied. Pérez then turned to McAllister.

"Stan, tell 'Smith' to go to Itami," Perez ordered.

"Yes, sir," McAllister.

"As for me, I'll talk to Blanchard."

#

Tsurumachi Izakaya/Outside Tsurumachi Izakaya, Taisho Ward, Kansai City, Kansai Prefecture; State of Japan. 1459 hours (Japan Standard Time)

At an *izakaya*, Frederick Dirks paid for his lunch. It was then that he felt his smartphone ring. Once he said his thanks and left, he got his phone.

The message was through IntMail and it came from "Maria Clara". The message read:

Langley 1 is currently talking to General Blanchard. For now, you are to go to Itami Airfield and talk to Colonel Armstrong about the C-5, the supplies that you asked for that come with the C-5, and the request to have the Donian II you captured be outfitted with an arm from a Minuteman.

Best get a move on, Dirk thought once he finished his message and pocketed his phone.

#

1ˢᵗ Light Mechanized Assault Regiment Headquarters/Itami Field, Itami, Hyogo Prefecture. 1530 hours

"So, what do you need now?" Henry Armstrong asked Dirks with sarcasm evident in his tone.

"Before I explain, I need to tell you that we located the girl that was smuggled out of that shipwreck and we intend to fight to get her back. However, we might be expecting heavy weaponry, so I called for additional supplies; most of which will be coming by C-5 Galaxy that should go here once my superiors succeed in arranging it with General Blanchard."

"Then why go to me?"

"You still have that Donian II taken from the battle in the shipwreck?"

"We do. You'll need it?"

"That's right. I need an arm from a Minuteman to replace the right arm Ganji tore off in that battle."

"Not a problem. I'll also give permission for the C-5 to land here."

"One last thing: I'll need to borrow two M4 Carbines: one for Solbein and the other for the Donian II with the Minuteman's arm."

"Consider it done."

"Thank you, Colonel. I must get going. I need to talk to Mr. Hoshikawa about Dr. Hamilton."

#

Hoshikawa Group Headquarters, Taisho Ward, Kansai City, Kansai Prefecture. 1641 hours

"How can I help, Fred?" Daisuke Hoshikawa asked Dirks, as the office of the former was the next destination of the latter. Unlike Armstrong, there was more sincerity in Daisuke's tone.

"I need to borrow Dr. Hamilton," Dirks bluntly answered.

"I assume this is related to what happened in Crater Shore North?"

"Can't give you the details. All you need to know is that those Korean gunmen were able to smuggle Maral Eminovna Guliyeva out of Japan and to a box factory that's a front for Anton Kravchenko's sex trafficking ring. Iron Dutchman Services, our Eurasians, and I intend to take the fight to them, so I'll need Dr. Hamilton on this. I got Crawley to tell Ganji once he finishes his classes for today."

"Sure, I can get you Dr. Hamilton's help. Please wait. I just need to give her a written message." Daisuke then wasted no time in writing with Dirks watching to wait for Daisuke to finish.

#

Iron Dutchman. 1800 hours

All members of Iron Dutchman Services now gathered in their briefing room. With Tatiana Ioannovna Tsulukidze absent, Karim Olegovich Zhakiyanov stood with Dirks and Wouter Vos on the stage.

Zhakiyanov carried his smartphone. The application he used for his smartphone was called "PT". This application allowed Tatiana and Pyotr Stepanovich Chadov, still in the Republic of Korea, to watch the briefing and participate in it.

"Now that we're all here," Dirks announced. "especially 'Elizaveta' and 'Stepan', we can begin." He then turned to Tatev Mirzoyan in the projector room. "Show them."

Tatev then projected a picture of the old man currently in South Korea with Kravchenko with information about the old man beside his picture. Dirks then faced the mercenaries and Vladimir Nikolayevich Mirov.

"This man is Sedgwick Henderson," Dirks explained. "As to why he's become a person of interest, I found that he's currently with Kravchenko." He then turned back to Tatev. "Next slide."

Now shown on the screen was the last thing the drone Dirks used in infiltrating Sinpo Box Factory as a photograph: Henderson. "I discovered that Henderson is working with Kravchenko, or the other way around, this morning. Either way, his involvement changes the fact that we need to move as soon as possible."

"Why?" Tatiana asked over Zhakiyanov's phone.

"Before I answer that," Vos replied before facing the projector room. "Next slide please".

Now shown was a video. It only played after Tatev pressed the triangle facing right. The video showed a man in a Walgear's cockpit with sticky pads on his limbs with wires connecting it to the control panel. However, as energy filled the wires, the man began to scream in pain. Tatev then stopped the video at that moment.

"This was what Henderson was known to have done: invent a way for Walgears to be used by one's mind, which we all know is needed to use our limbs," Dirks continued. "However, the experiments always ended with failure. The test subjects, volunteers from the New United Nations Ground Force, either died or became vegetables.

"Henderson didn't give up. However, he went too far by working with criminals to acquire test subjects. He was arrested, but somehow, he escaped. We tried to investigate who broke him out, but to no avail. I can imagine the Gatekeepers did it, but trying to investigate if they did help Henderson is suicide."

"And Guliyeva is Henderson's latest test subject?" Tarou asked.

"Must be," Dirks answered while facing Tarou. "That's why we need to move out as soon as we get the supplies we need."

"What supplies?" Sunan Wattana asked.

"I made a request for a C-5 transport plane to come to Itami Field. It will contain ammunition and additional weapons because if Henderson is involved, we'll need heavy firepower. I also asked Armstrong to provide us with M4 Carbines: one for Solbein and another for the Donian II we took from that fight in Crater Shore North."

"Who's piloting the Donian?" Vos asked with the intent of piloting the SH-6.

"Vladimir Mirov," Dirks answered.

"Why me?" Mirov asked.

"You came here to learn how Ganji fights," Dirks answered as he faced Mirov. "time for you to be tested by fighting alongside him."

"What about ammo for the M4s?" Tarou asked.

"It'll come with the supplies transported by the C-5," Dirks answered after facing Tarou.

"I assume we'll be using the C-5 to go to South Korea?" Jason Luke Crawley asked.

"We will," Dirks answered without facing Wattana. "However, we need the permission of the South Korean government to land at Sunchon Airport. From there, we'll use trucks from the NUN Ground Force troops in South Korea and use those to travel to Sinpo."

"What about 'Stepan' and I?" Tatiana asked. "We need to offer Kravchenko the girl we said we have in exchange for his 'merchandise'."

"Not only did I ask for a crate for Baloch, but once we're in South Korea, we can secure a truck," Dirks answered as he turned to Zhakiyanov's phone. "You'll directly approach the factory with the truck while everyone else will make their way around to avoid being spotted by Kravchenko's agents within Sinpo. He won't expect an attack of this magnitude."

"And what about Kravchenko? How will you intercept a possible escape attempt?"

"I also asked for the South Korean Army to assist in blockading Sinpo. Negotiating with them about Kravchenko will be the hard part because we've already told them about Kravchenko and they've been itching to move against him and arrest him themselves, and they'll take advantage of our plan to do so. Leave the negotiations to my superiors."

"And we'll also participate in this, yes?" Chadov asked.

"Da."

"So what now?" Vos asked.

"We wait from my superiors." Dirks then turned to the other mercenaries and Mirov. "Until then, we do not make unnecessary movements in the city until we hear from my superiors."

"I have homework tonight," Tarou warned. "I can do it here and sleep, but I need it submitted tomorrow if we hear from your superiors by then and launch."

"Do you have someone you can trust to hand over your homework?" Dirks asked Tarou.

"Riku Todoh."

"What time do you finish your homework?"

"Before one in the morning. I get up four hours later for exercise."

"Then do that and go to the Todoh house to tell Riku that you and Dr. Hamilton will be participating in a medical mission in Bolivia."

"Yes, sir."

"Anything else?" The other mercenaries and Mirov answered no.

"Then we're dismissed," Vos proclaimed.

#

Semnan, Semnan Province, Region 1; Islamic Republic of Iran. July 21, 2023; 0830 hours (Iran Standard Time)

Two men brought a child whose head was hooded to Serdar Muhadow. They forced the child to sit on the knees while the hands were tied.

"I can tell it's a child, but please remove the mask," Muhadow ordered.

One man did as Muhadow ordered. The child was a girl, which made Muhadow gulped upon seeing her. Despite that, he chuckled and stood up, walking to the girl.

"Untie her," Muhadow ordered. "Now!"

While one man raised the girl's arms, the other man prepared the "pig sticker" bayonet of his Type 56 assault rifle. The bayonet was used to untie the girl. After that, the man returned the bayonet to its original position while the girl's arms were reverted to their original position.

"What's your name?" Muhadow asked.

"S… Shireen," the girl answered. "Shireen Baloch."

"Why did my men bring you here?"

"I wish to know where a boy named Tarou Ganji is. I… was able to follow you because you took children like me and I want to know if you know anything about him."

Muhadow laughed upon listening to Shireen's reason for being brought to him. His subordinates looked at each other but didn't open their mouths. Shireen was also wise to keep silent. Thankfully, Muhadow's laughing wasn't long, as he turned to his two men once he stopped.

"Commander, I brought this crate-" Tarou Ganji appeared, having stopped his sentence as he couldn't see Muhadow.

"Is that you, Ganji?" Muhadow asked. "Come in."

Tarou proceeded inside. He still carried the crate, which made him focus on walking to Muhadow as opposed to noticing Shireen.

"Put aside that crate," Muhadow ordered. "There's something I need you to do."

Tarou did as Muhadow ordered. However, once he put the crate down, he then caught the glance of Shireen on his way to Muhadow and once he turned to her fully, he rushed toward her.

"Shireen, what are you doing here?" Tarou asked.

"She's here because of you," Muhadow answered to remind Tarou where he should he have walked to. "Since you're here, bring out your pistol."

Tarou brings out his PP semi-automatic. Muhadow then grabbed the pistol and turned off its safety. He then offered it to Shireen.

"Here," Muhadow said. "Take it."

Shireen wasted no time in grabbing the PP. "Now then," Muhadow continued. "aim it at him." To the horror of everyone but Muhadow, the latter pointed at Tarou.

"W… Why Tarou?" Shireen asked.

"You must not show hesitation here," Muhadow explained. "If you want to join my army, show me I can trust you. Now aim!"

Shireen began to cower as she aimed the PP with both of her hands. She closed her eyes and shook her legs as she continued to aim at Tarou. Tarou, however, opted not to resist or run but stood and put his arms behind him.

Shireen's right index finger shook. Yet it neared the trigger. Her hesitation didn't last as the trigger was pulled, but only the hammer was heard. As a result, Shireen opened her eyes, only to find Tarou still alive and surprised. Muhadow then began to chuckle and made no effort to hide it from the children or his adult subordinates.

"You still pulled the trigger," Muhadow commented. "I made it a rule for all my soldiers to have their pistols empty when there isn't any combat. Despite that, you did what I told you to do. Perhaps I could recruit you, but you must always obey orders. Is that understood?"

"Yes… " Shireen replied but wasn't aware of how Muhadow still acted like a soldier.

"Sir. Call me that at all times."

"Yes, sir!" Muhadow then turned to Tarou.

"Ganji, teach her how to be a soldier."

"Yes, sir!" Tarou replied with a salute.

#

Iron Dutchman, Taisho Ward, Kansai City, Kansai Prefecture; State of Japan. August 19, 2030; 1915 hours (Japan Standard Time)

Shireen, now sixteen years old, found herself in the cell of the *Iron Dutchman's* brig where she was imprisoned at in the present. She then heard footsteps and immediately went back to her defiant attitude. As she expected, it was Tarou Ganji delivering her food again.

"You're awfully slow in moving against Kravchenko," Shireen mockingly remarked while Tarou brought her dinner to her cell.

Tarou then stood up after bringing Shireen's food to her cell. "We're not reckless enough to act without authorization," Tarou retorted. "Now I must go. I have homework."

Tarou then left Shireen alone in her cell after closing and locking the cell door. Shireen then began to eat while keeping her eyes in the direction of the brig door. *You better be quick or Guliyeva will die,* Shireen thought.

\#

FIS Headquarters, McLean, Fairfax County, Commonwealth of Virginia; United States of America. August 20, 2030; 0834 hours (Eastern Standard Time)

"You called for me?" John Vue asked as he leaned his upper body into Yanin Saetang's office. "You called for me, Deputy Director?"

"Yes," Saetang answered. "Come in."

Vue proceeded further into Saetang's office. He stopped once he stood in front of Saetang. "John, I need you to buy plane tickets for Incheon now. If you leave immediately after this, you can still catch a late afternoon flight to Incheon."

"What for?"

"Long story short, armed Koreans were able to capture Maral Eminovna Guliyeva and when 'Fred Smith' and Iron Dutchman Services cornered them with reluctance from an OVR cell they uncovered, those Koreans were able to smuggle Guliyeva out of Japan."

"Wait, did you say an OVR cell?"

"Yes. While 'Smith' was in Mexico, he ordered Jason Luke Crawley to keep an eye on Tarou Ganji. The OVR infiltrated one Vladimir Nikolayevich Mirov into Japan for him to spy on Ganji to learn how he fights. 'Smith' caught Mirov, but during that debacle, Wouter Vos was captured by the OVR agents. There was an exchange of hostages but the Korean gunmen interrupted it and got Guliyeva in the process. We acquired the cooperation of the OVR cell in exchange for Kravchenko."

"What are the OVR agents and Mirov doing now?"

"Two are in South Korea, while one is still with Mirov and the mercenaries. The former two made contact with Kravchenko in order to prepare for a fake deal that will allow 'Smith' and the mercenaries to attack Kravchenko's hideout, which is why I'm ordering you to go to South Korea. I need you to get the South Korean government to allow a NUN Air and Space Force C-5 Galaxy already on its way to Itami Field. It's carrying supplies 'Smith' and those mercenaries will need for the attack and it will take them to Sunchon Airport. We need to ask the South Korean government to assist in the attack by secretly blockading Sinpo, where Kravchenko's hideout is at and we need to borrow a civilian truck for the two OVR agents to use in delivering a girl to trick Kravchenko into not suspecting that he will be attacked. We'll arrange for the NUN Ground Force in South Korea to provide trucks for 'Smith' and the mercenaries."

"Where are the two OVR agents? I wish to talk to them before I go to the Blue House."

"They're staying at the Marina Hotel, close to Incheon International Airport."

"Very well. I'll leave for the travel agency right away."

"Before you go, you'll need this." Saetang brought out a USB device. Tarou got closer to Saetang to receive the device. "All you need for your trip is in there," Saetang added once Vue received the USB.

"Thank you," Vue replied.

"Now go and buy that ticket." Vue immediately left the office after Saetang gave the order.

#

Marina Hotel, Jung District, Incheon; Republic of Korea. August 21, 2030; 1852 hours (Korea Standard Time)

Vue was now in the Republic of Korea. Having already settled in the Marina Hotel, he was knocking on the door of a particular room.

"Who is it?" Tatiana Ioannovna Tsulukidze asked from the other side of the door.

"I'm with the Company," Vue answered.

"Hold on." The wait wasn't long as Tatiana immediately unlocked and opened the door. "Now come in!"

You're bossy, Vue thought once Tatiana opened the door. He came in regardless and found Pyotr Stepanovich Chadov using his smartphone.

"Who are you and why are you here?" Tatiana asked, making Chadov stop using his phone and face Vue.

"I'm John Vue, an analyst," the FIS man said as he introduced himself. "I take it you're 'Elizaveta' and 'Stepan' from the OVR?"

"How do you know that?"

"Deputy Director Saetang told me about the both of you. Please update me about the situation because I plan on going to the US Embassy in an hour at most to get her help in talking to the South Korean President. Please tell me everything you know from the start."

#

Cheong Wa Dae, Jongno District, Seoul. August 22, 2030; 0905 hours

Vue now sat in the stateroom of Cheong Wa Dae, the executive office and official residence of the Republic of Korea, or "Blue House," as it was commonly called. Sitting with him was Mertlene Goldstein, the first United States Ambassador to South Korea. Out of every US ambassador, Goldstein was the first US ambassador to have served in the New United Nations Defense Forces, specifically the Ground Force. After leaving the NUNGF and finishing her studies did Goldstein begin her career as a liaison officer between the New United Nations and the US government. Per a recommendation by the US Ambassador to NUN, she joined the Foreign Service of the US Department of State. After appointments to various US embassies to other NUN member-states was she given her first appointment as ambassador to South Korea.

The door to the stateroom was then opened. Both Vue and Goldstein knew what that meant and stood up in response.

Iron Dutchman, Taisho Ward, Kansai City, Kansai Prefecture; State of Japan. 1130 hours (Japan Standard Time)

Karim Olegovich Zhakiyanov barged into the bridge of the *Iron Dutchman*. Occupying the bridge were Frederick Dirks, Wouter Vos, Sunan Wattana, and Jake Crawley. The FIS agent and the mercenary officers turned to the OVR agent.

"What is it?" Dirks asked.

"I got a call from 'Elizaveta'," Zhakiyanov answered. "She wishes to talk to you."

Finding a Resolution

Iron Dutchman, Taisho Ward, Kansai City, Kansai Prefecture; State of Japan. August 21, 2030; 1000 hours (Japan Standard Time)

I got a call from 'Elizaveta'," Karim Olegovich Zhakiyanov said to Frederick Dirks while holding his smartphone in the *Iron Dutchman*'s bridge with Wouter Vos, Sunan Wattana, and Jason Luke Crawley witnessing this. "She wishes to talk to you."

Dirks then took the phone from Zhakiyanov. "What do you have for me?" he asked.

"An analyst calling himself 'John Vue' wishes to speak with you," Tatiana Ioannovna Tsulukidze answered on the other end of Zhakiyanov's phone.

Vue must have been the one Saetang sent to talk to the South Korean President, Dirks thought. "Please give the phone to him."

"Is that you, 'Smith'?" John Vue asked through Tatiana's phone.

"Glad it's you I'm talking to," Dirks replied. "What does the President have to say?"

"She's willing to help, but she's asking for two small rewards."

"And what might those be?"

"She wants to claim credit for destroying Kravchenko's sex trafficking ring. Also, she wants surviving members of the sex trafficking ring to be arrested by her forces and tried under South Korean law."

"Fine." Silence followed as everyone knew they had to wait for what the President of the Republic of Korea had to say after hearing that her demands are met.

\#

1930 hours

All members of Iron Dutchman Services were gathered in their briefing room. Like it was two nights before, Zhakiyanov had to stand with Dirks and Vos so that he can use his phone's PT application to make sure Tatiana and Pyotr Stepanovich Chadov listened to the briefing.

"We've been given the green light to go to South Korea and end this once and for all," Dirks announced to the mercenaries and Vladimir Nikolayevich Mirov.

Tatev Mirzoyan then projected a map of Sinpo. There were two lines, one blue and one red, on the map. The blue map directly pointed at the Sinpo Box Factory while the red line was outside the city yet it also pointed at the same destination.

"This is how we'll launch our attack at the box factory Anton Oleksandrovich Kravchenko uses as a front for his sex trafficking operation," Dirks explained. "The blue line represents 'Elizaveta', 'Stepan', 'Oleg', and me. We'll directly approach the factory using a truck John Vue and I intend on getting to use for this operation. We'll use the truck to carry the box that is to carry Shireen Baloch. We intend on offering her to Kravchenko as a distraction. While he's distracted, the rest of you, represented by the red line, will move up to the factory while Kravchenko and his men are busy dealing with us."

"You said the South Korean military will be involved with this," Wattana reminded Dirks. "What will they do?"

"They'll secure the outskirts of the city to prevent Kravchenko or his cohorts from escaping," Dirks answered. "They'll also secure your route."

"Will NUN Ground Force troops in South Korea provide us with the trucks for later?" Tarou Ganji asked.

"They will," Dirks answered. "Vue will see to that. By the time he finishes, I'm to meet him in Seoul to secure the civilian truck."

"Will all of us be in this operation?" Vikas Mistry asked.

"No," Dirks answered. "I need Wouter Vos, Jason Luke Crawley, Sunan Wattana, Tarou Ganji, Vladimir Nikolayevich Mirov, Anita Hamilton, and Jawed Qazvini for this operation. However, if you know how to drive, I can use you and someone else who can to drive the Stepwagns on our way to Itami Field."

"I can do that."

"I'll help as well," Semir Bosić said while raising his hand.

"What about me?" Everyone turned to Tatev Mirzoyan as she had already left the projector room and neared the stage.

"I can't risk having you with us," Dirks warned. "You haven't trained at all with rifles, even if we give you an AK-05."

"I promised Maral I will keep her safe. Because she isn't, I want to help save her."

Dirks sighed while looking away from the mercenaries and Mirov. He briefly shook his head before facing them again. "Fine. But don't slow us down."

"Yes, sir." Tatev saluted after her reply.

"Then what are waiting for?" Crawley asked. "Let's go!"

"Dismissed," Vos ordered. "Now make your preparations."

"Ganji, Mistry, I need the both of you to take me to the brig," Dirks ordered to Tarou and Mistry. "It's time we took Baloch with us."

"Yes, sir," Tarou and Mistry replied in unison.

#

2001 hours

Tarou and Dirks approached Shireen Baloch's cell in the *Iron Dutchman*'s brig. The latter stood as she saw the former two approach her.

"I guess this means we're launching?" Shireen smugly asked.

"We are," Dirks answered. "And you'll help in distracting Kravchenko."

"This I must see." After he opened the cell door, Tarou dragged Shireen out of the cell. Dirks then placed handcuffs on her while Mistry joined him by putting a black bag on Shireen's head. Tarou was the first to leave the brig by dragging Shireen out. Dirks and Mistry followed, with the latter turning off the lights of the brig.

1st Light Mechanized Assault Regiment Headquarters/Itami Field, Itami, Hyogo Prefecture. 2115 hours

The convoy arrived at Itami Field. On the tarmac of Itami Field was a C-5 Galaxy transport plane as it was large enough to carry a minimum of two Walgears. Dirks and Hamilton, stepping out of the white Stepwagn van, found Henry Armstrong inspecting the supplies that were unloaded from the Galaxy.

"Colonel, we're here," Dirks announced, making Armstrong face him.

"You made it," Armstrong replied, offering his hand with Dirks shaking it. "I was just looking at the P-M02s and the MPTs you asked for, along with the ammunition."

"Thank you for doing this, Colonel," Hamilton said.

"Anita Hamilton, right?" The doctor nodded after Armstrong's question. "How long have you've used guns?"

"Just two years."

"Then good luck out there."

"Thank you, Colonel. I best get into my vest and fill it with magazines and get my weapons."

Meanwhile, Vladimir Nikolayevich Mirov saw the SH-6 Walgear he will be using. Due to Tarou tearing off its right arm four days before, the right arm now used by the SH-6 was that of an MW3 Minuteman's arm. He was then joined by Curtis Ngor, the second-in-command of the 1st Light Mechanized Assault Regiment.

"Surprised to see a Do- I mean, an SH-6 with a Minuteman's arm?" Ngor asked.

Mirov then turned to Ngor. However, he saw the insignia that indicated that Ngor was a major and as a result, he saluted by the time they faced each other.

"Major Curtis Ngor," the man said before saluting in return.

"Ley- I mean, Lieutenant Vladimir Nikolayevich Mirov," the Eurasian replied. He and Ngor then stopped saluting before looking at the SH-6 again.

"First time I got to see an SH-6," Ngor said. "I was even surprised we can slap a Minuteman's arm onto it."

"Does it function well?" Mirov asked.

"It does. Now don't get the arm wrecked."

"I promise I won't."

"Then good luck." Ngor offered his right hand and Mirov shook it with his right hand.

Mirov then proceeded to the SH-6. Since it was already sitting down, its cockpit was open. Once he climbed into the cockpit, he closed it. After that, he made the SH-6 stand up.

#

New United Nations Air and Space Force C-5. 2140 hours

Dirks, Zhakiyanov, and the mercenaries coming with them boarded the C-5 Galaxy. Two 1st Light Mechanized Assault Regiment soldiers also boarded the transport plane, but they were to put Shireen Baloch, still handcuffed and hooded, on the plane.

Once those sitting in the passenger cabin were seated, including Shireen, the two NUNGF soldiers left the Galaxy. Tarou and Mirov were next to board the Galaxy while in their respective Walgears. Tarou was the first to walk to the Galaxy and once he was close to the fin, he made the Walgear sit down. Despite that, he was able to use Solbein's wheels to board the Galaxy. Mirov also did the same to board the Galaxy.

Once the Walgears, with their respective pilots inside them, were inside, the rear ramp was closed. The pilots of the Galaxy then began to launch.

#

Sinpo Box Factory, Sinpo, Hamgyong Province; Republic of Korea. 2150 hours (Korea Standard Time)

Meanwhile, Sedgwick Henderson's experiments on Maral Eminovna Guliyeva continued. As a result, the girl was continuously electrocuted while she was connected to the control panel of the large Walgear whose cockpit she sat in. Anton Oleksandrovich Kravchenko appeared, carrying two bottles of beer. Henderson then noticed Kravchenko and turned to him.

"Is that beer?" Henderson asked.

"Da," Kravchenko answered. "I got a bottle for you."

"Thank you." Henderson took the bottle Kravchenko offered. The latter was the first to remove his bottle's cap with a bottle opener and once he finished, he gave it to Henderson to use.

"How goes the experiment?" Kravchenko asked.

"It's going well," Henderson answered before sipping from his bottle. "Because you sold her to Segismundo Alba, however, I have to re-implement the programming."

"Again, I apologize for selling her. I wasn't earning enough."

"Doesn't matter. Programming her shouldn't take too long."

"I must warn you, the police here in Sinpo are moving."

"They are?"

"That FIS agent, those mercenaries, and that OVR cell might be on their way here. Luckily, Shireen warned me they will come so I've made preparations. Though if in case… "

"I'm going to warn this to you once: I can't rush the experiment."

"I know. Just warning you."

"If you don't have anything else to tell me, please leave."

Secretly, Kravchenko grumbled. He then left the laboratory. Unbeknownst to both, "LS" listened.

#

Unknown Location; Enlightenment Point. 1800 hours (EP Time Zone)

"I assume you have an update?" Sergei Akulov asked Reinhard Frühiling.

"Those mercenaries are on their way to the Republic of Korea," Frühling answered. "They'll land at Sunchon Airport and acquired the aid of the South Korean government."

"What of Henderson's experiments?"

"He had to restart because Kravchenko sold Maral Eminovna Guliyeva to Segismundo Alba. Prior to that argument, Kravchenko warned that the National Police Agency in Sinpo has made preparations for the upcoming battle."

"Tell 'LS' to warn Henderson that if he doesn't make adequate preparations, the FIS and OVR will easily prevail."

"Henderson warned of this before. If we rush the experiment, it will fail."

"We have more test subjects, more prototypes, and replications of Henderson's notes. We can continue after the inevitable setback. Also, get 'LS' to remind Henderson that it's because of us he achieved plenty with his experiments."

"By your will, Grand Gatekeeper."

#

Sunchon Airport, Sunchon, Pyongan Province; Republic of Korea. 2259 hours (Korea Standard Time)

The NUNASF C-5 Galaxy now landed at Sunchon Airport. This airport was once an airbase for the Korean People's Army Air Force until the Third World War. Now it was used by the Republic of Korea Air Force.

A KM131 Jeep light utility vehicle approached the Galaxy when its side ramp was laid out. Frederick Dirks, Wouter Vos, and Karim Olegovich Zhakiyanov came out of the Galaxy as a result. By the time they touched South Korean soil, the KM131 stopped moving, making Dirks, Vos, and Zhakiyanov face the KM131. Coming out of the KM131 was a male officer of the Republic of Korea Army. He wore a dark green beret, the battle dress uniform of the ROK Army, and black boots. Both parties saluted upon facing each other.

"Are you Mr. 'Smith'?" the South Korean officer asked.

"That's me," Smith answered.

"Bong Do-won. Soreyong. English equivalent is "Major". I've been sent to act as your liaison for the duration of this operation. Anything you need, I will pass the request to my superiors."

"For now, my men and I need accommodations. Also, I'll be going to Seoul tomorrow."

"I'll talk to my superiors. I also have an update from the National Police Agency in Sinpo."

"What is it?"

"The box factory hasn't shown signs of activity."

"That means they know my men and I are here. Finalize the blockade. Hopefully, my men and I can start advancing to Sinpo after I finish my business in Seoul."

"About what you need in Seoul, I can accompany you because I doubt you know Korean."

"Sounds like a good idea. Now let's get my men accommodated. Tomorrow will be a long day."

#

Marina Hotel, Jung District, Incheon. August 22, 2030; 1210 hours

Dirks and Bong made it to the Marina Hotel in Incheon. The former knocked on a door.

"Who is it?" John Vue asked at the other end of the door.

"It's 'Smith'," Dirks answered.

"What are you doing here?"

"Let us in first."

"Hold on." Thankfully for Dirks and Bong, the wait wasn't long, as Vue was able to open his room's door.

"Please come in."

"Thanks." Both Dirks and Bong entered Vue's room. The latter then closed and locked the door.

"How can I help the two of you?" Vue asked.

"Located a truck for us to use?" Dirks asked. "Also, this is Major Bong Do-won of the ROK Army. He'll be assisting me and my men with the attack."

"I did. What about 'Elizaveta' and 'Stepan'?"

"We get the truck first. Then we get them."

"I was just about to get lunch. Can we please get lunch first?"

"I am hungry," Bong added.

"Fine," Dirks begrudgingly replied. "I assume you have money to pay for lunch?"

"That I do," Vue answered.

"Where do you propose we go?" Bong asked.

"What's this about lunch?" Tatiana Ioannovna Tsulukidze asked outside, surprising Bong and the FIS men.

Dirks, out of embarrassment, unlocked and opened the door. He found Tatiana and Pyotr Stepanovich Chadov outside the room.

"Sorry about that, 'Elizaveta'," Dirks sheepishly said as an apology. "We wanted to get the truck first, but Vue and Bong here wanted lunch."

"We were about to go out for lunch. You can join us, but you'll have to find your tables and pay for your own food."

"Good enough with me," Bong replied. "What are we waiting for?"

Dirks sighed and slammed his right palm on his face. *We're on a mission, not a vacation!* Dirks screamed in his head.

#

Jung-gu Repair Shop. 1345 hours

Dirks, Vue, Tatiana, Chadov, and Bong arrived at a repair shop. The proprietor of the repair shop was in the middle of talking to a man with a Porter double cab truck. Once he saw his visitors, the proprietor turned to Vue.

"Glad you made it, Mr. Vue," the proprietor said. "You wanted truck, right?"

"I did," Vue answered before seeing the man the proprietor was talking to. "Is he owner?"

"Ye."

"Who's this?" Dirks asked silently while leaning on Vue.

"Ok Ye-jun," Vue answered. "He owns this repair shop. He was once like you, but he retired to do this."

It was then that the truck owner appeared. However, he asked a question in Korean.

"He's asking 'why you need this truck'," Bong said after interpreting what the driver asked.

"Before I answer that, what's your name?" Dirks answered with Bong interpreting the question in Korean.

"Won Cheol-min," the driver answered with Bong pronouncing it in English for Dirks and Vue to understand.

"We need the truck for a delivery of our own, but we can't have you drive it. The cargo is extremely sensitive. We will compensate you after this." Bong then interpreted Dirks' reason for Won's truck into Korean. Won then gave his reply, but the way he said it gave Bong pause on how to interpret in English, which confused the FIS and OVR agents.

"What did he say?" Tatiana asked.

"He… thinks we're delivering weapons or drugs to the North… " Bong ultimately answered in English.

Dirks sighed. Everything he worked for was in jeopardy because a driver asked such a dangerous question.

"If I say yes that we're delivering weapons, what does he want in exchange for the truck?" Dirks asked with Bong interpreting the question in Korean.

Won chuckled when he listened to Bong's interpretation of Dirks' question. Now it was Vue's turn to cover his face with his right palm. That ended when he heard Won answer Dirks' question about how much he wished to be paid in Korean.

"He's asking for one million won," Bong answered. "The currency I mean."

Vue then removed his right palm from his face. "It's a deal," he said as he offered his left hand with Won shaking it with his right hand.

Unbeknownst to Bong, the FIS men, and the OVR agents, "LS" watched. He grinned once he saw the handshake and left.

Sinpo Box Factory, Sinpo, Hamgyong Province. 1558 hours

"LS" returned to the Sinpo Box Factory. As he entered the main building, he heard the standard insults used for a woman, the sound of skin being slashed, and a woman's cries.

Although he neared Anton Oleksandrovich Kravchenko's office, "LS" stopped to know what was happening. He saw two of Kravchenko's guards firmly hold the arms of a girl with long, blonde hair. Another guard, this time a woman, used a bullwhip on the girl's buttocks.

Because she used a different language, the girl's cries for mercy weren't heard. Even if it was understood, Kravchenko's minions wouldn't have stopped. "LS", however, continued on to Kravchenko's office.

Ultimately reaching the office's door, "LS" knocked. "Who is it?" Kravchenko asked.

"It's 'LS'," the Monitor answered.

"Where were you?"

"Intelligence gathering. I made sure that I wasn't followed nor spotted by the police outside."

"Hold on. Let me unlock that door." "LS" briefly stayed away from the door. Because he was close and that he stood on a wooden platform the office was a part of, he could hear Kravchenko's footsteps. Those footsteps ended when Kravchenko reached the door and unlocked it. At the same time, the whipping stopped.

"Now get in!" Kravchenko rudely ordered with "LS" complying without a complaint.

Once inside the office, "LS" closed and locked the door. After that, Kravchenko returned to his desk and sat on his chair once "LS" stood before him.

"Where did you go to conduct intelligence gathering?" Kravchenko asked.

"Seoul," "LS" answered. "The FIS and OVR have acquired a truck. Most likely, they intend to use it as some sort of distraction if they're going here."

Wait, Afonin and Mishuolovich told me they needed a truck for the girl they're offering me, Kravchenko thought. "Was there a woman with long brown hair among the people you were spying on?"

"Yes."

"I best order my men to be even more prepared. When you leave, think you could please ask for Cha to come up here? She should be done with whipping Dorokhina."

"Why were you having that girl whipped?"

"She tried to escape. You should know this."

"My apologies for asking. Very well, I will take my leave. I'll also ask Miss Cha to come here."

"Thank you."

#

Sunchon Airport, Sunchon, Pyongan Province. 1730 hours

Dirks, Bong, Tatiana, and Chadov arrived at Sunchon Airport. Once let inside, they found both Solbein and the SH-6 with a Minuteman's arm being used. Once they parked the Porter truck they bought from Won, Dirks, Bong, Tatiana, and Chadov approached Wouter Vos, who was watching Solbein and the SH-6 move.

"What's going on here?" Dirks asked, making Vos turn to him, Bong, Tatiana, and Chadov.

"You're back," Vos remarked. He then saw Tatiana and Chadov. "And I see you brought 'Elizaveta' and 'Stepan' with you."

"Did you bring Baloch with you?" Tatiana asked.

"We're keeping her in the brig until you need her. What now?"

"We need the LVSR and the Jolt-vees for transport. I'll have Bong take me to the 2nd Armored Regiment headquarters and ask for those vehicles."

"When are we going to launch? Like you said, if we don't move soon, Guliyeva will die."

"I know. If possible, we should make preparations after I get what I need from the 2nd Armored."

"Do what you have to do."

"Then I'll need Crawley and Zhakiyanov."

#

Outside Sinpo Box Factory, Sinpo, Hamgyong Province. 1730 hours

At the same time, "LS" began to leave cans outside Sinpo Box Factory. He placed them in locations no one would mind. One location was a bush.

After planting the can, "LS" moved on to the next location. What no one would suspect was that the cans had camera lenses on them.

#

Sinpo Box Factory. 1830 hours

"LS" entered the basement. He heard Maral Eminovna Guliyeva's screams while he walked toward Sedgwick Henderson. Despite the screams, Henderson felt "LS" coming to him and faced him.

"What are you doing here?" Henderson asked.

"I have a message from the Grand Gatekeeper," "LS" answered.

"And what might that be?"

"Prepare the Walgear."

"And risk the experiment?!"

"This facility will be attacked soon. I took the liberty of installing cameras outside the factory. Here."

"LS" brought out a smartphone and opened an application called "CCC". On the application was a list; each item on the list was named "Camera" with a number beside them. Pressing "Camera #1", "LS" showed one of many cameras he installed outside the factory. The camera showed a Sonata used as a police car passing by the factory.

"Why are you showing me this?" Henderson asked.

"So that you'll know when to activate the Walgear," "LS" answered. "I don't have to remind you what will happen if you disobey an order from the Grand Gatekeeper."

"Y… Yes, of course."

"Then you know what must be done when this factory comes under attack."

"Yes."

"Then I must go. I'm hungry. I also suggest you get something to eat."

#

Sunchon Airport, Sunchon, Pyongan Province. 1900 hours

Dirks, Bong, and his subordinate in the ROK Army, along with Jason Luke Crawley and Karim Olegovich Zhakiyanov, returned to Sunchon Airport. They returned in a convoy of military vehicles. While Bong remained in a KM131 Jeep driven by his subordinate, Dirks drove one JLTV while Zhakiyanov drove another. Crawley, meanwhile, drove an LVSR. Once the vehicles were parked, Dirks, Bong, Crawley, and Zhakiyanov got out. They were approached by Wouter Vos and Tatiana Ioannovna Tsulukidze.

"I guess this means we can begin?" Tatiana asked.

"Not yet," Dirks answered. "It's time for one last briefing."

"Everyone's having dinner right now," Vos retorted.

"Fine," Dirks replied. "We can start at 2000 hours. Please remind everyone."

#

2005 hours

Dirks, the Iron Dutchman Services members that accompanied him, Tatiana's OVR cell, and Vladimir Nikolayevich Mirov were gathered in a briefing room. Unlike the theater room used by the mercenaries, this room was smaller. As a result, Tatev Mirozyan occupied one corner of the room with her laptop computer connected to the room's projector. Instead of a big screen, the screen was a smaller pull-down screen. Vos and Tatiana stood with Dirks. "Now that we have everything we need for this mission," Dirks announced. "we will conduct one more briefing before we launch."

"Tatev, show the map again," Dirks ordered to Tatev.

"Yes, sir," Tatev replied before she used her computer. The map with the red and blue lines was projected.

"Again, it will be me, 'Elizaveta', 'Stepan', and 'Oleg' representing the blue line taking the shorter route to Sinpo," Dirks explained again to those he's facing. "We will pretend to offer Shireen Baloch to Anton Kravchenko as a distraction. That will be where the rest of you come in." Dirks pointed at the red line. "Vos, Wattana, Crawley, Ganji, Hamilton, Qazvini, Mirzoyan, and Mirov, you're represented by this red line. Since this is a longer route, you're to launch tomorrow at 0700 hours. When you reach Sinpo, you're to position yourselves around the favtory. The OVR agents and I will launch an hour after that. Until we reach the factory, you are to remain at your positions once you're in Sinpo. Only move when I fire from this flare gun." Dirks then showed a red-colored revolver with a large barrel.

"Any questions?" Vos asked.

"When should Leytenánt Mirov and I launch?" Tarou Ganji asked.

"You and Leytenánt Mirov can leave the LVSR when the attack begins," Dirks answered. "However, do not move until you see the flare."

"Yes, sir."

"Zametano," Mirov added.

"Any more questions?"

"How will we not be compromised by Kravchenko's men?" Sunan Wattana asked.

"Major Bong told me that he has a team of the Special Mission Group inside Sinpo to incapacitate any of Kravchenko's agents throughout the city," Dirks answered. "In addition, a flight of four Ap- I mean Guardian attack helicopters will assist should the worst come to pass. They're call sign is Subak. As for us, we'll use Dutchman. I'll be Watchman. Our Eurasian allies will be Guest."

"Anything else?"

"None," the other mercenaries, the other OVR agents, and Mirov answered collectively.

"Then we will rest in an hour," Dirks ultimately ordered. "Since you all came from dinner, it's bad to sleep immediately. By sleeping at 2130 hours, we will wake up at 0400 hours and make preparations. While we advance to Sinpo tomorrow, we'll assign the individual call signs then."

"Dismissed," Vos ordered.

#

2120 hours

"There you are," Tarou said as he found Mirov in the hangar where their respective Walgears were kept.

"Ganji, is that you?" Mirov asked without looking at Tarou.

"Da. What are you doing here? We have to return to our respective quarters in ten minutes."

"I know. Looking at our Walgears before tomorrow will help me sleep better. If I sleep well, I can concentrate on my mission better."

"Fair enough." Tarou then stood beside Mirov. The latter then moved his head to face the former. "How long have you been piloting Walgears?" Mirov asked. "You must have learned at an incredibly young age to do so."

"Actually, I just jumped into a cockpit and figured it from there," Tarou answered. "In the middle of a battle two years ago."

"Impossible! How?"

"I'd like to know that myself. I've been fighting to figure out who I really am. Being a part of Iron Dutchman Services is part of that. Even my mission of acting as a high student to monitor Maria Hoshikawa is a part of that goal."

"Before you joined Iron Dutchman Services, where did you come from?"

"Iran. The same Iran your nation invaded. My quest to know who I am stemmed from the fact that I was discovered by a community of Baloch refugees alongside a dead woman who might be my mother. I felt that I didn't belong there, and I volunteered to keep an eye on Maria because I felt that she also didn't belong in Japan."

"Is it because she has blonde hair and blue eyes?"

"You could say that, but it's mostly because she was found in the middle of the ocean as an infant. Despite her physical attributes, she saw Japan as her only home."

"Had we met seven years ago in Iran, I would have killed you."

"Same. I must wonder: why did you become a soldier?"

Mirov, however, showed hesitation in answering that question. Tarou, however, was quick to notice that hesitation. "Can't answer?" the latter rhetorically asked. "Fine."

He then walked away from Mirov. "I'm going to bed. You should as well."

Does it even matter if you know? Mirov anxiously pondered. *We'll be enemies the next time we meet. What will knowing about me will change that?*

Mirov reared his head, only to find Tarou gone. He sighed and left the hangar.

To Sinpo

Sirte District; Republic of Libya. February 2, 2028. 0900 hours (Eastern
European Time)

A boy traveled across the Libyan desert. He hid most of his body
in a white cloak. Suddenly, the boy lost the last of his strength that
he used to move and collapsed into the desert.

Is this it? the boy pondered. *Will I die here, not knowing who am I?*

However, he heard explosions. The boy somehow stood up and walked
toward the direction where the sound of the explosions came from.

Mysteriously, he was able to walk fast enough that he saw the source of
the explosions: a battle. Oil pumps appeared to be the target in the attack.
The attackers simply consisted of lightly clothed militants and pickup
trucks turned into technicals because of the DShK machine guns attached
to their flatbeds.

The boy then heard another sound. He turned to where the sound came
from and found an SH-6 Walgear approaching the oil pumps.

Everywhere I go, I find Aswārān, the boy thought. *I can't let those defenders lose
just because their enemies have Aswārān.*

After an hour of running toward the Walgears, the boy was now behind
one SH-6. "You are now outnumbered!" one militant shouted in English.
"Surrender, and you will be allowed to escape with your lives!"

The boy got closer to the SH-6. Suddenly, the SH-6 turned to its right as
one defender of the oil field fired his rifle, an MPT. The other SH-6 simply
eliminated the defiant defender with its anti-personnel machine guns. By
this time, the boy was able to climb onto the left leg of the SH-6 in front
of him. When both SH-6s continued facing the oil pumps to force the
remaining defenders to surrender, the boy had already neared the cockpit
of the SH-6 he climbed onto.

The boy then found a button on the lower left end of the cockpit. He
pressed it and as a result, the cockpit opened, much to the surprise of the

pilot. The boy seized this opportunity by climbing into the cockpit and grabbing the pilot. He then threw the pilot out of the cockpit and sat on the chair. Through the monitor of the SH-6's cockpit, he now saw the other SH-6 aiming its AKS-74U carbine at the SH-6 he hijacked.

I best hurry, the bought anxiously thought while looking around the SH-6's cockpit. Miraculously, he found the control stick for the right arm and pressed the topmost button on the front of the control stick. This caused the SH-6 he boarded to fire its AKS-74U, damaging the other SH-6 in the process. Suddenly, the boy heard and felt the SH-6 he hijacked being attacked by the militants on the ground.

Wasting no time, the boy immediately analyzed the controls. He found the switch used to make the SH-6 use its wheels and found that the words were in Russian. He flipped the switch and, finding foot pedals like those of a car, the boy pressed both, allowing him to spin and move.

I still remember how to use an Aswār, the boy thought. *Now I can really help those outnumbered defenders.*

The boy then continued moving the SH-6, making most of the militants focus their attention on the SH-6 the boy hijacked. As a result, the remaining defenders of the oil field took this opportunity to launch a counterattack despite being outnumbered.

The boy then used his SH-6's machine guns to eliminate the infantry. He then used the AKS-74U to destroy the technicals. The other SH-6, however, continued to fire at the boy's SH-6 despite the damage it took from the latter.

The boy managed to dodge the attacks from the opposing Walgear. However, the boy didn't know that he neared the oil field.

"Whoever you are, can you hear me?" a male voice said over the SH-6's communicator.

He must have taken a radio from a dead militant and tapped into the communicator's frequency, the boy thought.

"If you can hear me at least, get away from the oil field. If you get that Walgear destroyed or destroy the enemy's Walgear, the explosion will destroy the oil pumps, killing us all!"

Somehow, I can understand him. I best do as he says because Aswārān use a nuclear fusion reactor.

The boy began to move away from the oil field. The other SH-6 followed as a result and fired. The boy, however, didn't fire back.

If I fire back, I'll still hit the oil pumps. And even if we're far enough, we'll simply repeat exchanging shots and my Aswār is already taking damage. This needs to end!

The boy then stopped and faced the other SH-6. He opted not to aim and, as a result, the other SH-6 walked.

"Istaslim!" another male voice shouted over the SH-6's communicator.

Definitely not the voice I heard earlier, the boy thought. *And that language, it's Arabic… Where am-*

The other SH-6 fired its AKS-74U at the boy's SH-6. "'Iḏā astaslamt al'ān, fasawfa 'ubqī `alā ḥayātik!'"

What can I do? This Aswār can't take any more damage… That's it!

The boy then tossed his SH-6's ASK-74U aside. He then reverted the switch he pressed earlier to its original position. After that, he made the SH-6 walk toward the other Walgear, whose pilot then put down the other AKS-74U.

"Iqtarab al'ān," the other SH-6's pilot said over the communicator.

I just have to keep going close, the boy thought while he continued to make his SH-6 walk toward the other SH-6. *All I need to do is get close enough to grab that Aswār's arms.*

The boy then stopped once it was close to the other SH-6. Suddenly, the boy used the arm controls to make his SH-6's arms grab the arms of the other SH-6. The boy then pressed a series of buttons that began a self-destruction sequence.

"Māḏā tafʿal!?" the other SH-6's pilot shouted. "Da`nī aḏhab!"

The boy didn't listen. Instead, he opened the hatch that covered his SH-6's cockpit. By the time the countdown reached 5, he prepared to eject the cockpit. Once the countdown reached 2, he pressed the button needed for his cockpit to fly out of the SH-6 proper. By the time the cockpit was in the air, the SH-6 exploded. The other SH-6 was caught in the explosion, killing its pilot. As soon as the explosion ended, a parachute appeared on top of the cockpit. This was to help the boy land.

A pickup truck appeared. It stopped once the boy neared the ground. The occupants of the former, Wouter Vos, Jason Luke Crawley, Sunan

Wattana, and another man rushed out once the latter landed and the cockpit opened.

"Get out and show us your hands!" Vos shouted while aiming his MPT at the boy. Once the boy showed himself, the four mercenaries were surprised as to who saved them.

He… he's the one that saved us? Wattana incredulously pondered.

The boy, however, talked in Farsi. This confused Vos, Wattana, and Crawley, but the man with them wasn't surprised.

"What language is that, Esmail?" Vos asked.

"It's Farsi," said the man named Esmail.

"Farsi, as in Iran's language?" Crawley asked Esmail.

"Yes. The boy is saying, 'You're the one that told me to leave the oil field'."

"What's your name?" Vos asked the boy with Esmail interpreting the question in Farsi for the boy to understand.

"T… Tarou, Tarou Ganji," the boy answered.

"A Farsi speaker with a Japanese forename, that's new," Crawley remarked.

"If you have any weapons, give them to us and come with us," Vos instructed with the Esmail repeating it in Farsi.

Tarou Ganji replied. "He says that he doesn't have a weapon and is asking why he should come with us," Esmail said as he interpreted Tarou's reply.

"We won't hurt you," Wattana replied. "We just want to know why you saved us?"

Esmail interpreted the question in Farsi. Tarou then asked another question.

"What does that mean?" Vos asked.

"He's asking where we are," Esmail interpreted.

"Come with us and we'll answer every question you have," Vos answered, with Esmail interpreting.

Tarou nodded and began walking up to Vos, Wattana, Crawley, and Esmail.

Sunchon Airport Hotel, Sunchon, Pyongan Province; Republic of Korea. August 23, 2030; 0358 hours (Korea Standard Time)

In the present, Tarou Ganji woke up instantly and breathing desperately. As a result, Jake Crawley, sleeping in the bunk above him, woke up as well.

"Ganji, is that you?" Crawley asked. "What was that about?"

"I remembered… the day we first met," Tarou answered.

"Libya? What on Earth for?"

"Don't know." Tarou got off his bunk after his answer and turned on the lights of the room in the Sunchon Airport Hotel he and Crawley stayed at. He then traveled to their room's bathroom and washed his face.

"What time is it?" Crawley asked.

"Hold on," Tarou replied after he turned off their sink. Once he left their bathroom, he looked for his smartphone. Turning it on, he found that the phone was at 0400 hours.

"0400 hours," Tarou ultimately answered.

"It's time!" Crawley shouted. "We need to get ready!"

"Agreed. I'll go first." Tarou then rushed back to their bathroom.

"Be fast!" Crawley warned while he climbed out of his bunk.

#

0430 hours

Frederick Dirks then appeared in front of a room in the Sunchon Airport Hotel. He knocked on the door.

"Ganji, Crawley, are you ready?" Dirks asked.

"Almost," Crawley replied from the other side of the door.

"How 'almost'?"

"Mr. Crawley is still putting on his boots," Tarou answered. "I'm loading my pistol."

"You can finish up, Ganji. Just join me when you're done. You and I need to get Baloch into that box."

#

0438 hours

Both Tarou and Dirks entered the brig of Sunchon Airport. After the ROK Air Force guards let them inside, the former two, after being joined by one guard, approached the only cell in the brig that was occupied. Inside that cell was Shireen Baloch.

"Get up," Tarou demanded to Shireen. "It's time."

"To shove me in a box?" Shireen sarcastically asked.

"Be thankful we'll give you the means to escape," Dirks warned.

Shireen said nothing after that. Both Tarou and Dirks stepped out of the way of the guard that accompanied them as he was to unlock the cell door. After that, he placed handcuffs on Shireen. Tarou and Dirks were the first to leave the brig, with the guard following while he made Shireen move.

#

0509 hours

Tarou, Dirks, Shireen, and the ROKAF guard holding her reached the Porter double cab truck. Behind the truck was an open wooden box with holes on its four sides. The truck was guarded by two other ROKAF guards.

"You're going to put me in that?" Shireen asked as she looked at how wide the inside of the box was. She also saw a knife beside the box.

"We will," Tarou answered. "Now behave yourself!"

The ROKAF guard holding Shireen made her move closer to the box. Tarou then joined them once they reached the box.

"Now get in!" Tarou ordered while aiming his P226 semi-automatic pistol at Shireen.

Although defiant, Shireen did as Tarou told. Once stepping on the box, the ROKAF guard removed the handcuffs. "Now insert yourself into the box!" Tarou added.

Shireen did as Tarou demanded. After that, the ROKAF guard closed the box while his fellow guards brought out duct tape and sealed the box to prevent Shireen from escaping. After the box was sealed shut, two of the ROKAF men loaded the box into the Porter.

"Gomabseubnida," Dirks said to the ROKAF men. They didn't respond before they left.

"So who's driving?" Tarou asked.

"I'll leave that to 'Oleg'," Dirks answered, referring to Karim Olegovich Zhakiyanov's alias. "And now we have to eat."

"Agreed."

#

0601 hours

After their breakfast, the joint FIS-OVR task force appeared at the armory of Sunchon Airport to get their weapons. Dirks was the first to get his Adaptive Rifle assault rifle, followed by Vos. Wattana got her ADR Sniper, while Crawley got his ADR assault rifle. Tarou then got his ADR Carbine. After Tarou was Jawed Qazvini, who got his LSAW light machine gun.

After Qazvini was Anita Hamilton, who got her MPT assault rifle. Tatev Mirzoyan, who came after Hamilton and got her AK-05 assault rifle. After Tatev was Vladimir Nikolayevich Mirov, who got an ADR Carbine. After Mirov was Tatiana Ioannovna Tsulukidze, who got another MPT. Following Tatiana was Pyotr Stepanovich Chadov, then Karim Olegovich Chadov. Like Tatiana, they got MPT rifles. Unlike everyone else, who kept their usual pistols with them, Tatiana, Chadov, and Mirov had P-M02 pistols as their sidearms.

Once the FIS-OVR task force got their weapons, they began to fill their vests with rifle and pistol magazines. After the magazines, the task force members acquired grenades. When it was Tatev's turn, she hesitated, with Dirks noticing.

"Do you know how to use those?" Dirks asked.

"Read up them, but is it okay if that's enough?" Tatev asked.

"Fragmentation grenades are to kill and flashbangs to stun enemies. Get to a safe distance when using both. For flashbangs, flee far enough that the sound won't hurt your ears."

"Yes, sir." Tatev then got three fragmentation and three flashbang grenades like Dirks, Vos, Wattana, Crawley, Tarou, Qazvini, and Hamilton did. After Tatev was the OVR agents and Mirov.

The last thing the task force members got were helmets and knee pads. Tarou and Mirov got separate helmets as theirs were needed for Walgear pilots. Unlike everyone else, Qazvini placed a specific protector to cover his groin.

"Got everything we needed?" Dirks asked.

Everyone replied with either "Yes" or "Da"; both meant the same thing. "Then let's get to our respective vehicles."

#

0639 hours

While every other member of the task force rushed to the vehicles they're assigned to, Tarou and Mirov rushed to their respective Walgears, Solbein and an SH-6 using the right arm of an MW3 Minuteman. Both Walgears carried M4 Carbines built for Walgears to use and were chambered at 30x173mm.

With both Walgears sitting down, neither Tarou nor Mirov had difficulty in getting in their respective Walgears. Once inside their cockpits, they put aside their rifles and powered up the Walgears. After that, they made their respective Walgears stand up and closed their cockpits. Once the Walgears were functional, Tarou and Mirov moved them toward the LSVR truck driven by Crawley. Once close to the LSVR, Tarou was the first to approach the rear of the truck, making Solbein sit again. He then switched to using Solbein's wheels in order to get into the flatbed of the LSVR. Mirov then followed Tarou into the flatbed with his SH-6. Once both Walgears were on the LSVR, they were covered by sheets by ROKAF mechanics.

Tarou then turned on the communicator of Solbein's control panel. "Vos, are you and you and your men picking this up?" Dirks asked over the communicator.

"Vos here," Vos said over the communicator, followed by Wattana and Crawley.

"Ganji here," Tarou said. Qazvini, Hamilton, and Tatev also replied.

"Leyte- I mean, Lieutenant Mirov here," Mirov said over the communicator.

"You are to launch in ten minutes," Dirks added. "I say again, ten minutes."

"Yes, sir," Vos said, with Wattana, Crawley, Tarou, Qazvini, Hamilton, Tatev, and Mirov repeating it.

Some turned off their communicators to say prayers without being heard. Crawley, who turned off the LSVR's radio, hummed a song from 1989 that was used for the credits in a Japanese original video animation that was a part of a franchise where bipedal robots were used as combat vehicles, which helped inspire the idea of Walgears.

At the same time, in the JLTV driven by Hamilton, Tatev Mirzoyan also sang, but more quietly than Crawley, as she didn't wish for Hamilton nor Wattana to hear her. The song was called "Jujalarim"—an Azeri song composed for children. Despite her effort, both Wattana and Hamilton heard Tatev sing despite the song being in Azeri. The former two waited until Tatev finished her song.

"That's some good singing," Wattana complimented, surprising Tatev.

"Y… You heard me?" Tatev asked in embarrassment.

"What's that song about?" Hamilton asked.

"It's an Azeri children's song called 'Jujalarim'. Maral thought it to me."

"Was it wrong for us to ask?" Wattana asked as she and Hamilton heard the way Tatev answered.

"N… Not really," Tatev answered. "Sorry I kept it to myself. I only sang it to calm myself before we move out. Though truth be told, I don't know why I sang 'Jujalarim'… "

"Don't worry about Maral," Hamilton assured. "We will save her."

"R… Right."

"Vos, it's time," Dirks said over the radio. "You and your team are to move to Sinpo now. You can use GPS to remember your route."

"Starting up the Jolt-vee now," Wattana loudly announced in order for Dirks to hear.

"Starting the LSVR now," Crawley announced over the radio.

"Same with my Jolt-vee," Vos added.

"Good hunting," Dirks replied.

First to leave Sunchon Airport was the JLTV driven by Vos with Qazvini using its K-12 general-purpose machine gun. Following them was the LSVR driven by Crawley, with Tarou and Mirov inside their respective Walgears, on its flatbed. Following the LSVR was the JLTV driven by Hamilton with Wattana and Tatev riding with her.

#

0750 hours

Dirks, Tatiana, Chadov, and Zhakiyanov returned to the Porter truck they will be using for their part in the operation. The latter two loaded another crate, albeit smaller, into the rear beside the box where Shireen Baloch was kept. While Chadov and Zhakiyanov loaded the box, Tatiana used her smartphone. She dialed the number of Sinpo Box Factory. Once the number was dialed, the wait began.

"Who is this?" the same distorted voice asked over the phone.

"Elizabeth Afonin," Tatiana answered. "The package has just arrived. We're on our way to Sinpo now."

"Good. I'll be waiting". Once the call ended, Tatiana pocketed her phone.

"Now we need to remove our vests, then we move out," Dirks said.

"Zametano," the OVR agents replied in unison before removing their vests.

It's a shame this partnership has to end after this, Dirks thought. *But orders are orders.*

Once the OVR agents finished removing their vests and knee pads, they hid them in the rear cab of the Porter. Dirks began to remove his vest and knee pads and in the midst of this, Zhakiyanov rushed to the driver's seat while Tatiana and Chadov sat with the vests and knee pads in the rear cab. Once he finished removing his vest and knee pads, Dirks placed them in the rear cab, closed the rear right door, and joined Zhakiyanov in the right front seat. After Dirks closed his door, Zhakiyanov made the Porter move out of Sunchon Airport.

Watching them leave, Bong Do-won brought out a portable radio. He used it to give an order.

#

Sunchon. 0810 hours

Once they left the airport, Dirks and the OVR agents took a separate route to leave Sunchon. Dirks then turned on his smartphone and an application named "GPS tracker". He then used the application to track Vos' team and found they were using the route he designated for them.

Excellent, Dirks thought. *Now it's all going according to plan.*

#

Buchi/Outside Buchi, Sinpo, Hamgyong Province. 0830 hours

One result of the Republic of Korea annexing territory of the Democratic People's Republic of Korea was the installation of branches of businesses based in the former into cities of the latter. One business to benefit from this was Busan-based Buchi (short for "Busan Chicken"), known for their fried chicken.

As a result, Buchi restaurants can be found in former DPRK cities. Sinpo was no exception. In one Buchi restaurant, a man who didn't look Korean went to this Buchi restaurant for breakfast.

The man's breakfast consisted of a butter croissant and chocolate milk. Such was the result of the ROK being a part of the New United Nations. Once the man finished his breakfast, which he paid for before eating, he left the Buchi restaurant while unaware that a man, a local, watched him and rushed out of his sight when he left.

Once the foreign man turned to his left, he was now prone to what the local man who was watching him had planned for him. The latter turned to the dumpster behind him and repeatedly hit it. This attracted the attention of the foreign man and, once he neared the latter, the local man used a syringe and hit the foreign man at the right side of his neck. The local man then pressed the liquid inside the syringe into the foreign man, knocking him unconscious.

The local man then pushed the foreign man away where no one could see him and brought out a radio. "Target incapacitated," the local man said. "I say again, target incapacitated."

#

Sinpo Box Factory. 0945 hours

Damn it, it's been an hour! Anton Oleksandrovich Kravchenko screamed in his mind while he sat in his office.

"Sounds like you're having trouble?" "LS" asked from the other side of the door.

"Is that you, 'LS'?" Kravchenko asked as he faced his door.

"Who else is it?"

"What do you want?"

"I need permission to see Henderson."

"You may, but I need the both of you here. Bring him here at once."

"By the Grand Gatekeeper's will."

#

1004 hours

"LS" then returned to Kravchenko's office. This time, he brought Sedgwick Henderson with him. "What's this about?" Henderson asked. "I have an experiment to finish!"

"Then you better hurry it up!" Kravchenko screamed. "I've lost contact with my reconnaissance team. They should have reported to me almost two hours ago."

"Perhaps that could mean that the city was infiltrated by the ROK Army's Special Mission Group, who've been ordered to eliminate our agents across the city before the FIS and OVR arrive here," "LS" guessed.

"Then we're trapped! There's no way we can escape if the ROK military is involved."

"I've just about finished implementing the program needed for Guliyeva to properly use the Walgear," Henderson assured. "Because I had to rush it, there's no way we can test how good the weapons of the Walgear are."

"Doesn't matter," "LS" replied. "We can use the FIS, OVR, and the ROK forces as opponents to see if the weapons can work. We can even escape to the DPRK while they're distracted."

"Good idea," Kravchenko complimented. "Of course the only way for the trap to be sprung is when I hear from Afonin again."

"Then we wait."

\#

Kaechon, Pyongan Province. 1030 hours

"What's with the giant cross?" Wattana asked as he looked at a tall cross far from the road the Iron Dutchman Services members were crossing to reach Sinpo.

"I read about that one," Tatev answered. "That's just one of many built throughout the portions of North Korea that the South managed to liberate in the Third World War."

"What for?"

"To commemorate those who suffered in the prison camps operated by the North Korean government. Kaechon hosted two of those camps."

"And the government run by those animals is still functioning. All because they have powerful friends."

"They had help to prevent a refugee crisis. That didn't seem to bother the government of the South because many were killed in nuclear bombings launched by US forces during the war."

"Figures. Well, thanks for the history lesson."

\#

Sinpo Box Factory, Sinpo, Hamgyong Province. 1100 hours

Henderson then approached Maral Eminovna Guliyeva. The latter still sat on the cockpit of the Walgear her limbs were connected to.

"How are you?" Henderson asked.

"I am fine," Guliyeva answered.

"Good. The people who took away your parents are coming. What will you do?"

"Eliminate them."

"Good. I'll let you know when you're to launch. Be patient."

"Yes, my master."

#

Outskirts of Sinpo. 1700 hours

Vos' team now appeared in the outskirts of Sinpo. After the JLTVs and LSVR were parked, Vos, Wattana, Crawley, Hamilton, Qazvini, and Tatev gathered together. Then they saw a car and aimed their respective weapons at it. Once the car stopped, its two occupants shouted to the mercenaries to put down their guns.

"And you are?" Vos asked.

"Yoon Jin-young," one man said. "My rank would be 'Sergeant 1st Class' in English."

"You with the Special Mission Group?"

"We are," a woman, the second occupant of the car, answered. "I'm Kwon Ye-jin. My rank in English would be 'Sergeant'."

"How are things at that factory?" Dirks asked.

"Same as always," Yoon answered. "We already prepared a house for your men to use until you're told the attack can commence."

"Anything about the one who's supposed to give us the signal?"

"He's not here yet," Kwon answered.

"Very well. Lead us to this house."

"Some of you need to stay here and watch over your vehicles. We'll wait." Both Yoon and Kwon returned to their car. Vos then faced his subordinates.

"Some of us will have to stay here to keep an eye on Ganji and Mirov," Vos warned. "Who's it going to be?"

"I'll stay," Hamilton answered.

"I'll stay as well," Tatev answered. "Mr. 'Smith' told me not to slow us down. I feel I can help better this way until the attack begins."

"Good answers. I'll see the both of you at the factory." Vos, Crawley, Wattana, and Qazvini took one JLTV and left.

#

Sinpo. 1750 hours

Dirks, Tatiana, Chadov, and Zhakiyanov now arrived in Sinpo. Dirks used his smartphone's IntMail to contact Vos. He wrote "Are you in Sinpo" and pressed "Send".

At the same time, Tatiana used her phone to contact Kravchenko. Unlike Dirks, her wait wasn't long as she heard that he picked up her call.

"Where are you now, Afonin?" the distorted voice asked over Tatiana's phone.

"Already in Sinpo," Tatiana answered. "I apologize for being late. I had to take a route where my cargo wouldn't be seen as suspicious."

"I'll have my men waiting." Meanwhile, Dirks told Vos to standby for the signal.

Outside Sinpo Box Factory/House in Front of Sinpo Box Factory. 1800 hours

Dirks and the OVR agents now arrived in front of Sinpo Box Factory. Two guards stopped them.

"Do you have business here?" one guard asked in English, but with a heavy Korean accent.

"Talk to people in back," Dirks answered. The guard then walked to Tatiana, who sat behind Dirks.

Tatiana then opened the window. "We here to do business with Mr. Kravchenko," she explained. "Please let us in."

"He's expecting you." The guard then returned to Dirks. "You may proceed."

"Thank you." After that, Dirks used body language to make Zhakiyanov proceed further into the factory.

Unbeknownst to the guards, Sunan Wattana watched with the scope of her ADR Sniper from the roof of a nearby house. Inside the house, Wouter Vos, Jawed Qazvini, and Jake Crawley waited at the first floor of the house.

"Wouter, they're inside," Wattana told Vos on the radio.

"Roger," Vos replied. "Waiting on 'Smith'."

"Think Ganji and Mirov can get here in time should things get dicey?"

"They should. That will be up to Doc and Mirzoyan. 'Smith' and those Eurasians need to sheets removed."

Heart Attack

Sinpo Box Factory, Sinpo, Hamgyong Province; Republic of Korea. August 23, 2030; 1811 hours (Korea Standard Time)

Now in the middle of Sinpo Box Factory, Frederick Dirks, Tatiana Ioannovna Tsulukidze, Pyotr Stepanovich Chadov, and Karim Olegovich Chadov stopped their Porter double cab truck. Once they got off their truck, they found themselves surrounded by armed men once they saw Anton Oleksandrovich Kravchenko approach them.

"Glad you made it," Kravchenko said before he saw Dirks and Chadov. "Who are they?"

"Bodyguards we hired," Tatiana answered. "One's formerly with the FIS and the other's former KGB. They helped with the box."

"Well then, shall we get started?"

"Get the box," Tatiana ordered Dirks and Zhakiyanov. The latter two opened the tailgate of the Porter and dragged the box out. After sliding the box out, Dirks held it in his front while Zhakiyanov grabbed the rear end. Thankfully, the walk wasn't long, and they slowly dropped the box beside Tatiana. Chadov returned to the flatbed and grabbed the scissors needed to tear open the tape used to lock the box. Once the tape was cut, Dirks and Zhakiyanov opened the box. Shireen Baloch remained as she was even after Kravchenko saw her.

"Where did you find her?" Kravchenko asked.

"The Iran Governorate," Tatiana answered. "She was a housekeeper who argued with her master. I used my connections in the Okhrana to have her delivered her."

"And you can't give her to the Tsar?"

"He can't accept disobedient female subjects."

"And you wish to trade her for one of the girls I sell?"

"Da."

"Let me think about that." Kravchenko briefly looked away from Dirks and the OVR agents. Without voicing it, Dirks saw what might happen next and quickly placed his right hand toward the flare gun he hid. His suspicions were quickly correct when Kravchenko raised his right hand, in which Dirks subsequently drew the flare gun before Kravchenko swung his right arm downward. At the same time, Dirks fired the flare pistol. However, Kravchenko's armed guards aimed their AK-05 assault rifles at Dirks and the OVR agents. This forced Dirks to toss away the flare pistol.

"You think I would fall for your tricks?" Kravchenko said as he resumed facing Dirks and the OVR agents while the latter surrender and Shireen escaped the box. "The girl you tried to offer me works for me and she already warned me about whatever plans you had. Now tell me, are you here for Maral Eminovna Guliyeva?"

"You could say that but-" Dirks answered before a gunshot was heard.

This brief gunshot momentarily stunned everyone but Dirks and the OVR agents. This allowed them to grab their respective semi-automatic pistols while Shireen escaped as there was another gunshot.

Kravchenko and his guards saw Dirks and the OVR agents grabbing their guns and resuming aiming their respective weapons. However, more gunshots ensued, and this time, they came from automatic weapons.

With Kravchenko and his men distracted, Dirks and the OVR agents finished getting their pistols and started firing at the former. Kravchenko cowered when Tatiana aimed her P-M02 pistol only for two of the guards to block her and die protecting Kravchenko. After those two guards fell to the ground, more guards appeared. Dirks, Chadov, and Zhakiyanov joined Tatiana in aiming against them with their respective rifles: the former with his ADR and the latter two with their MPTs.

By the time they killed the last guard, they were joined by Wouter Vos. "You did this?" Vos asked.

"We sure did," Dirks boasted. He then faced Vos and noticed he came alone. "Where are Crawley and Qazvini?"

"They opted to stay and handle those outside," Vos answered. "Sunan's helping them."

"Then we best split up and look for Kravchenko," Tatiana suggested.

Suddenly, they heard wheels. That didn't last long, but then they heard machine guns.

"That must be Ganji or Mirov," Dirks said. "Now we need to-"

Suddenly, everyone heard a large door open and due to how loud it was, they instantly found where it was coming from. "I'll investigate that," Vos declared before facing Dirks and the OVR agents. "Find Kravchenko and Henderson."

"Zametano," the OVR agents replied in unison.

"Split up," Dirks added. "We can cover more ground-"

However, Dirks, Vos, and the OVR agents heard another sound in the same place where the earlier sound came from. This hastened their decisions.

Vos made it to where the sounds came from, but by the time he made it, he saw what the sound was: a large elevator carrying a large Walgear.

"N… No… way… " Vos said as he saw the Walgear.

Vos' awe and fear didn't end with the Walgear. It stood up and began to fire a laser from the top of its left arm.

#

1832 hours

Inside the Walgear was Maral Eminova Guliyeva. Still wearing her hospital gown, Guliyeva showed no emotion on her face. Her eyes, still covered by a helmet, detected a target that she didn't know was Sunan Wattana, as what she saw on the monitor of the Walgear's control panel was a man in a balaclava.

He must be one of those who killed my family, Guliyeva thought. *He must die.*

Guliyeva pressed the topmost button on the front of the control stick needed to control the left arm. As a result, the laser on top of the left arm was fired at the house where Wattana was, as witnessed by Wouter Vos.

"Sunan!" Vos shouted once the Walgear began to move.

#

Outside Sinpo Box Factory. 1839 hours

Vos reached the entrance of the factory where he came from. He found Jason Luke Crawley helping a wounded Sunan Wattana and Jawed Qazvini, who laid his LSAW light machine gun on the street, helped a man out of the rubble with assistance from two women.

"Jake, is Sunan alive!?" Vos screamed.

"I'm fine!" Wattana shouted in response. "What kind of monster are we dealing with!?"

"Most likely what Henderson was working on. We need to find a nearby hospital!"

Crawley and Qazvini nodded. Vos then joined them in helping Wattana and the civilians.

#

Sinpo Box Factory. 1839 hours

Kravchenko, guarded by two of his gunmen, reached another portion of the factory's underground complex where Starex vans were kept. Finding a Starex to use, they heard someone running to them and aimed their weapons. They stopped once they saw it was Shireen Baloch, carrying an AK-05, with Sedgwick Henderson accompanying her. Kravchenko's guards then rushed to the door.

"Good, you're here," Kravchenko said. "What took you so long?"

"I ordered Cha and her men to defend the main building," Shireen answered. "In addition, I left a bomb at your office because no doubt Frederick Dirks intends to steal from your computer there. Henderson and I even prepared the nuclear bomb underneath to blow up."

"Where's 'LS'?"

"He disappeared. It's for the best. He can escape on his own."

"Now get this van started. We need to escape to the DPRK while we still ca-"

Suddenly, everyone heard gunshots. They found Kravchenko's guards getting shot. Shireen was the first to rush to the Starex, but once she opened the front left door, Pytor Stepanovich Chadov appeared.

Kravchenko rushed to the Starex's right front door, but once he got inside, Shireen made the Starex move. Henderson rushed to make Kravchenko and Shireen wait for him, despite Chadov spotting them.

"We're leaving him!" Shireen screamed. "We have all the data, additional facilities, and test subjects to continue!"

"R… Right," Kravchenko replied with reluctance evident in his tone.

Shireen continued to escape. As a result, Henderson surrendered to Chadov.

#

1839 hours

Dirks reached the main building of Sinpo Box Factory. Encountering more of Kravchenko's guards, Dirks fought them despite being outnumbered. The former were led by Cha, Kravchenko's female subordinate. Once her subordinates were eliminated, Dirks aimed his rifle at her while Cha did the same.

"Now it's just you and me," Dirks announced.

Cha fired her AK-05 first, but Dirks dodged the shot. Dirks fired back only for Cha to hide. With somewhere to hide, Cha fired again, but Dirks now found somewhere to hide. After that, he aimed while waiting for Cha as she reloaded. Once Cha finished and aimed at Dirks again, the latter was quick to shoot her rifle, disarming her.

This made Cha flee to Kravchenko's office. Dirks gave chase, but as he got close, Cha brought out her QSZ-92. Dirks hid as soon as Cha fired.

Dirks hid at the container where the girls Kravchenko had yet to sell were kept at. The former began to hear their screams.

Thankfully, these girls aren't used as human shields, Dirks thought before he leaned toward Cha while aiming his ADR at her. However, as he fired, Cha evaded. She shot again in response, forcing Dirks to hide again.

Cha slowly moved toward the container while Dirks hid. She then placed her left palm where the OSZ-92's magazine was. Unbeknownst to her, Dirks readied his ADR. Hearing Cha come closer, Dirks flew out of the container and quickly aimed at Cha. Before landing, Dirks fired at Cha before she pulled the trigger, and as he landed on the floor, so did Cha.

As a result, Dirks was the first to get up and get close to a fatally wounded Cha. The latter, despite her wound, reached her QSZ-92. However, Dirks reached her first and after switching to semi-automatic fire for his ADR, he shot Cha in the head.

Dirks then heard knocking from the container. Seeing the padlock, Dirks simply shot the lock. It was then that Tatiana joined Dirks once the girls surrounded the latter.

"Get them out of here," Dirks ordered.

"What about you?" Tatiana asked.

"I'm going to steal some information from Kravchenko." Dirks pointed to Kravchenko's office.

"But there's not a single-"

"I found many vans to use." Tatiana and Dirks turned to see Chadov appear with Henderson.

"Is that Henderson, 'Stepan'?" Dirks asked.

"Da," Chadov answered. "Caught him failing to escape with Kravchenko and the girl we used. There are many vans below."

"Must be a large underground complex below," Tatiana commented.

"Explains how they hid that Walgear," Dirks added. "Now get Henderson and these girls out of here."

Tatiana nodded and, using both Russian and English, she was able to lead the girls to the stairs leading underground, with Chadov and Henderson following. Dirks, meanwhile, rushed to the office. Kicking the door open, Dirks found Kravchenko's desktop computer. However, he found a bomb planted beside the computer, and that it was about to detonate in two minutes.

"Not good," Dirks said. "I only have less than less than two minutes."

Once he turned on the computer, Dirks found that there was no password and easily began to find the computer's files. However, Dirks found that there were many files. Thankfully, he only found one folder that bore the name "Past Transactions." Opening the folder, Dirks saw four document files. He then brought out a USB device and plugged it into one of the computer's USB ports.

He selected all four files while making a blue square that engulfed them while he pressed the mouse's left button. He then pressed the right button, causing a small box with commands to appear. He pressed "Copy" and, finding the tab leading to his USB, Dirks pressed the right button on the tab again and pressed "Paste".

The file transfer was thankfully short. Dirks then began to explore the other folders. He found a folder called "Locations". In that folder contained documents that contained location names. One file Dirks saw was called "Libya" and he simply copied the file and pasted it toward the USB he planted. Once the file transfer was finished, Dirks quickly right-clicked on the tab of the USB and pressed the "Eject USB" command. Once Dirks saw that he was allowed to remove the USB, he wasted no time in doing so and quickly pocketed it. He now saw that the timer on the bomb was less than thirty seconds, forcing Dirks to run as fast as he could. By the time he neared the entrance of the main building, the bomb detonated, forcing Dirks to jump out of the explosion and landing on the floor outside before being engulfed by the explosion.

#

Outside Sinpo Station. 1850 hours

Guliyeva unwittingly started a rampage throughout Sinpo. She was pursued by Vladimir Nikolayevich Mirov using his SH-6. He stopped in front of Sinpo Station.

Giant or not, I must defend these people, Mirov thought while watching the Walgear piloted by Guliyeva eliminated South Korean National Police Agency officers.

Mirov then charged at the Walgear. Getting close to it, he began firing at it, but he found a field of energy blocking the 30x173mm rounds coming out of his Walgear's M4 Carbine. Although it wasn't harmed, Guliyeva turned to Mirov and fired an autocannon chambered at 20x120mm. Mirov jumped before the rounds hit his Walgear and fired in response. Like before, his shots were blocked.

What kind of monster am I fighting!? Mirov pondered.

The Walgear fired its laser, now on top of its right arm, at Mirov's SH-6. Mirov was able to dodge the laser.

If I can lure it close to the ocean, I can get it away from any more civilians. Mirov then wasted no time in making his Walgear move backward to force Guliyeva to follow her.

While pursuing it, the Walgear used its autocannon, but Mirov constantly evaded it. To keep on distracting it, Mirov continued to fire even if the shots were blocked.

#

Sinpo Box Factory. 1930 hours

Tarou Ganji, using Solbein, now appeared at the factory. He found the main building on fire and corpses of Kravchenko's guards.

"Ganji, you're here," Dirks said over Solbein's communicator.

"Mr. 'Smith', where are you?" Tarou asked.

"Behind you."

Tarou then switched to Solbein's rear camera, finding Smith on his monitor. Tarou briefly moved forward, then turned left. He opened the cockpit and faced Dirks.

"I saw a large Walgear," Tarou shouted. "Was that what Henderson was working on?"

"Yes," Dirks answered.

"Where's-"

Both Tarou and Dirks now saw the Walgear piloted by Guliyeva firing its autocannon. "I'm guessing Lieutenant Mirov must be fighting that thing," Tarou commented.

"Then help him," Dirks ordered. "I need to find another way into the underground complex in order to meet up with 'Elizaveta'."

Tarou nodded. He closed Solbein's cockpit, turned left again, and left the factory.

#

Outside Sinpo Box Factory. 1935 hours

Mirov continued fighting Guliyeva, to no avail. The former now saw that he was running out of ammunition.

I'm low on ammunition, Mirov taught. *I can't keep this up.*

However, the large Walgear was shot from behind, but unbeknownst to Mirov, it took damage. He moved away, found Solbein behind, but that caused the large Walgear to turn on Solbein and attack it. Mirov then altered his communicator's frequency.

"Ganji, you saved me," Mirov said.

"Don't think of it," Tarou replied over the communicator. "How much ammo do you have?"

"Not much. That Walgear has a shield made of pure energy. You can't shoot it easily."

"I just saved your life by shooting it and there was damage near the portion where the fusion reactor was kept."

"You may have found its weakness. Keep it distracted. I have an idea."

"I'll do what I can. Make it work."

"Ganji, Mirov, can either of you hear me?" Dirks asked over both Solbein and the SH-6's respective communicators.

"Is that you, Gospodin 'Smith'?" Mirov asked.

"Da," Dirks answered. "I found a stash of RPGs just as Hamilton and Tatev joined me. Figured we can use those."

"Good idea. Ganji is distracting that monster. We can only damage it while it's distracted."

"Why?"

"It deploys a barrier made of energy. I wasted my ammunition fighting that Walgear. Ganji was able to damage it to save me."

"Then get back to the factory. Hamilton's waiting at the entrance."

"Zametano." Mirov then altered the position of the gear lever of his Walgear, allowing him to move the SH-6 forward.

#

Outside Sinpo Box Factory/Sinpo Box Factory. 1938 hours

Mirov returned to Sinpo Box Factory. Once he made his SH-6 sit and opened its cockpit, Mirov rushed to the entrance, where he found Anita Hamilton waiting for him.

"Where are the RPGs?" Mirov asked.

"Follow me," Hamilton answered. Both she and Mirov rushed to where Dirks discovered RPGs.

Both Mirov and Hamilton reached a room at the east end of the factory. That room was an armory and inside was a stockpile of Type 69 RPGs. Dirks now carried one with a loaded warhead and two additional warheads on his back. Tatev Mirzoyan carried three additional warheads on her back.

"Glad you made it, Mirov," Dirks said. "I need you to grab one launcher. Hamilton can carry additional rockets. When I found them, I already outfitted them with night vision sights."

"Zametano." Mirov and Hamilton then rushed to the nearest launcher and warheads they can reach.

#

Near Mayang-Do Crater. 2000 hours

Both Tarou and Guliyeva were now fighting near the Mayang-Do Crater. During the Third World War, Sinpo hosted this naval base of the Korean People's Army Naval Force. As a result, the United States Armed Forces used a nuclear weapon to destroy the military installation. A crater now replaced the naval base that once stood there and it was left that way to make sure no one forgot what was done to end the war.

Tarou gave no thought as to where he was. Neither did Guliyeva. Suddenly, a flight of four AH-64E Apache Guardian attack helicopters of the Republic of Korea Army appeared. Guliyeva then stopped looking at Tarou once she was told the Apaches began firing Hydra 70mm rockets with Tarou also seeing the Apaches.

South Korean Apaches? Tarou pondered. *These are the ones whose support Major Bong guaranteed.*

"This is Subak 1-0," a male voice said over Solbein's communicator. "We're here to assist."

"This is Dutchman 9," Tarou replied. "Thank you for the assistance. Be advised, enemy Walgear is equipped with an advanced protection system, preventing your weapons from having any effect. Please provide a distraction because my men and I found a weak spot."

"Roger. We'll assist in any way we can."

As a result, Guliyeva was now distracted by their presence that the energy barrier was focused on protecting her and the Walgear from the Apaches' rockets. Tarou then wasted no time in going around the large Walgear while the latter fired its rockets at the Apaches. Guliyeva then aimed her Walgear's missiles, whose launcher was found on the Walgear's left torso, against the four Apaches. While Tarou was behind her, Guliyeva fired one missile. The Apaches then got away from the missile, but to the surprise of their respective crew, the missile split into four warheads with each warhead aimed towards the Apaches.

The ROKA pilots then launched flares to protect themselves. Miraculously, the flares succeeded in protecting the Apaches. By this time, Tarou jumped and, using the boosters on Solbein's backpack, he was high enough that he aimed his Walgear's M4 Carbine at the head of the Walgear and fired at it. As a result, the head was destroyed, depriving Guliyeva of what she needed to see. She began to scream in her cockpit. This caused her to fire her lasers without aiming at anything. One Apache was destroyed as a result, with another firing an AGM-114 Hellfire anti-tank guided missile at the Walgear. The missile hit the left arm, destroying it.

"Hamınızı öldürəcəm!" Guliyeva screamed. "HAMINIZI ÖLDÜRƏCƏM!"

Guliyeva continued firing her Walgear's surviving laser and missiles despite not being able to see what was in front of her. After dodging the laser, the surviving Apaches used their M230 Chain Guns to destroy the missiles.

By this time, Dirks, Mirov, Tatev, and Hamilton arrived using the Porter truck. Once they got out of the truck, they rushed to Solbein as Tarou simply watched what was happening.

"Ganji, what's going on here?" Dirks asked over Solbein's communicator.

"Mr. 'Smith'?" Tarou asked.

"Ganji, continue attacking that thing!"

"I know. I'm trying to formulate a way to do those. Because I destroyed that Walgear's head, the pilot can't seem to be firing properly. I can't destroy that Walgear entirely because its fusion reaction will be destroyed in the process, destroying most of the city."

"All stations this net, this is Guest Leader, do you read me?" Tatiana Ioannovna Tsulukidze asked over the communicator.

"What is it?" Dirks asked.

"Chadov and I got Henderson to talk. According to him, Guliyeva is in that Shagokhod."

"You're serious, right? If this-"

"Maral's in there!?" Tatev screamed over the communicator.

"She is. If you want to save her, you'll need to disable that Shagokhod. Destroying it won't just kill her, it will destroy this city."

"Got it!" Dirks replied.

"I'll assist the South Koreans in destroying any remaining weapons," Tarou added.

"Then do it," Dirks ordered. "Those South Koreans might kill Guliyeva by mistake and telling them will make it harder on them, but wait until Hamilton, Mirov, Tatev, and I return to the truck."

"Roger." Tarou waited until Dirks, Hamilton, Mirov, and Tatev returned to the Porter. "You can launch now," Dirks ordered.

Tarou then moved toward the direction Guliyeva's Walgear was walking to. Dirks followed with the Porter.

Meanwhile, the surviving ROKA Apache pilots continue to evade the shots from the laser on the right arm of Guliyeva's Walgear. Unaware of what will happen if they succeed, the ROKA pilots fire their Apaches' remaining Hydra rockets. Far from Guliyeva's Walgear, Tarou began to aim Solbein's M4 at the right arm. He had to wait before firing because of Guliyeva's erratic movements. Thankfully for Tarou, he didn't have to wait long as Guliyeva made one spin and when he saw the right arm, Tarou fired one bullet. The 30x173mm bullet was then able to hit the laser on the right arm, disabling it.

Around this time, Dirks, Mirov, Hamilton, and Tatev arrived elsewhere and parked the Porter. Once they got out, they rushed to the giant Walgear.

"Listen, we need to hit that Walgear with all the warheads we got," Dirks explained. "Tatev and I will go for the left leg." He turned to Mirov. "Mirov, you and Hamilton go for the right leg."

"Zametano," Mirov replied.

"Hit 'em hard."

Both RPG teams rushed to their assigned legs. Mirov and Hamilton were the first to reach the giant Walgear's right leg. Mirov then pressed his right knee while making his left knee face the street. Hamilton then removed the fuze cap of the RPG warhead and after that, Mirov aimed with the Type 69 launcher's 1PN51 night vision sight toward the giant Walgear's right leg. Like Tarou, he had to wait until Guliyeva's spinning ended. Once he saw the right leg coming his direction, he pulled the trigger. Thankfully, Hamilton was far that she only covered her ears when Mirov fired the RPG warhead. By the time Guliyeva unwittingly faced the two RPG teams, her Walgear's right leg was hit. This was to be followed by the warhead from Dirks' RPG hitting the left leg. As a result, the stability of the Walgear was thrown off balance.

With the large Walgear distracted, Tarou then jumped toward the rear and was able to cling to the cockpit. He began to use Solbein's arms to pry open the cockpit. However, the large Walgear was then able to stand up again, forcing Tarou to jump off and landing into the street.

"Mr. 'Smith', I was able to pry open the cockpit," Tarou said. "I need you and the others to continue distracting it."

"Are you nuts!?" Dirks shouted over the communicator

"I want to save Guliyeva without anyone being harmed. We need to act fast because most likely the South Koreans will send in more troops and I doubt they'll be able to disable the Walgear without hurting Guliyeva."

"We'll do what we can. Stay behind that monster and if you have any rounds left in your M4, empty the rifle."

"Roger." Tarou then aimed at the rear of the right leg. This time, he switched the M4 to full auto before firing. Again, the giant Walgear's balance was threatened. Although she was slow in doing so, Guliyeva was able to spin toward Tarou's direction, allowing both RPG teams to continue aiming at both legs.

Once Guliyeva faced Tarou, she angrily fired the autocannon, forcing Tarou to jump. While in the air and loading his Walgear's M4 with its last magazine, Tarou was able to see that it was Guliyeva was using the Walgear.

What kind of monster is Henderson for forcing Guliyeva to do this!? Tarou angrily pondered before firing his M4 to continue distracting it.

With the giant Walgear unable to move because Tarou fired at it, the RPG teams continued to aim at the rear of the Walgear's legs. Once loaded, Mirov and Dirks fired their respective Type 69s. As a result, the legs were hit at the same time.

Guliyeva was barely able to prevent the Walgear from falling. As a result, the RPG teams saw that Guliyeva was using the Walgear.

"It is Maral!" Tatev shouted. "Maral, listen to my voice! You can stop this!"

Guliyeva seemingly heard Tatev's words. However, she was then electrocuted and as a result, the Walgear stood yet again despite the legs being damaged.

"It can't be!" Dirks exclaimed. "Henderson made a Walgear that can rely on a human's brain to stand!"

"What will happen to Maral!?" Tatev asked while turning to Dirks.

"Unless we kill her, that thing will keep on going."

"Why can't we just fire one more rocket onto one leg?" Hamilton suggested. "We just need Tarou to get Maral out, right?"

"It could work, but if a leg is hit, the Walgear will collapse and not only will Guliyeva get hurt, many innocents will."

"Tarou, you're hearing this?" Tatev asked while using the mic of her radio attached to her vest.

"Do it," Tarou answered. "If I can jump close enough, I can grab the cockpit and pull it out."

"Then it leave it to us." Tatev then rushed to Mirov. "Leytenánt Mirov, I need your launcher."

"What are you doing?" Dirks asked.

"Like I said, I want to save Maral. If you won't fire, then I will!"

"… Fine."

Mirov nodded. He faced Tatev and gave her his Type 69 launcher. Once Tatev tossed her AK-05 aside and took the Type 69, Hamilton loaded a warhead into the launcher and removed its fuze cap. Hamilton, Dirks, and Mirov then got out of Tatev's way and covered their ears. Tatev then aimed at the right leg and pulled the trigger. As a result, the warhead hit the leg, ultimately ending the Walgear's ability to stand. The right arm was damaged as soon as the Walgear hit the asphalt.

Tarou, far but facing the now-disabled Walgear, jumped then used Solbein's boosters. This allowed him to land his Walgear on the portion of the giant Walgear where its head once stood. He found Maral Eminovna Guliyeva, still in the cockpit breathing heavily. However, he heard "Self-Destruction Sequence Activated" and that it will detonate in five hours. Despite that, he moved toward the cockpit and found Guliyeva, now unconscious. Tarou started by removing the helmet Guliyeva wore, then by forcibly removing her from the cockpit, separating her from the sticky pads on her body in the process. After that, he jumped out of the larger Walgear and used the boosters to land safely.

Seeing Tarou land, Dirks and Tatev rushed to Solbein after removing the RPG warhards they carried on their respective backs. Seeing the latter two from his rear camera, the former made Solbein sit and opened his cockpit. He came out carrying Guliyeva and gave her to Dirks.

"Get her to the van now," Tarou demanded. "The Walgear's self-destruction sequence has been activated and while we have less than five hours, I suggest we leave now."

"Got it," Tatev replied.

"I'll contact Bong," Dirks added.

"Good."

"Anyone picking this up?" Wouter Vos asked over the mic of Dirks' radio.

"Vos, where were you at?" Dirks asked.

"Had to get Sunan and a civilian who got hurt amongst those fleeing the city. Listen, Qazvini, Jake, and I rushed back to the factory with Yoon's help. We found how Henderson must have messed with Guliyeva, but we also found that a nuclear bomb had been set to blow. Thankfully, we still have two hours to get out before it blows."

"What!?"

"Yoon's contacting Bong right now."

"Get him to tell Bong about the Walgear we just disabled. Its self-destruction sequence was also activated after we disabled it and that it will destroy a good portion of the city. Tell him we need the ROK Army's help in saving those still in the city."

"Will do. Once we get Yoon to take us back to the Jolt-vee and the LSVR, we're go to Hongwon. I suggest you do so too. I even told 'Elizaveta' and 'Stepan' to do so too. Yoon and his men will get the surviving police to help with evacuations."

"T… Tatev?" Maral Eminovna Guliyeva asked weakly, surprising everyone.

"Maral, don't speak!" Tatev commanded. "Rest. We'll-"

"Tatev… " Guliyeva said with a smile. That was all she said.

Hamilton rushed and examined her by pressing her neck. After one minute, she stopped.

"I can't say what's become of Maral," Hamilton announced. "It's best we get her to a proper clinic or hospital."

"Then let's go," Tatev ordered.

#

Near the Republic of Korea-Democratic People's Republic of Korea Border. 2200 hours

Both Anton Oleksandrovich Kravchenko and Shireen Baloch made it to a closed shaft in a forest near the border of the two Korean nation-states. While tired, Kravchenko's exhaustion was more evident than Shireen's.

"Before we open that shaft, why don't we rest first?" Kravchenko asked.

"Agreed," Shireen replied, but not before bringing out a QSZ-92 and aiming at the head of the former, horrifying him.

"W… What are you doing?!"

"Making you rest." Shireen pulled the trigger, instantly killing Kravchenko.

After holstering her pistol, Shireen began to drag Kravchenko's corpse away from the entrance to the shaft. Once far from the shaft, Shireen left Kravchenko's body and rushed back to the shaft.

Getting into the shaft, Shireen planted an explosive device on the ladder. Once she reached the bottom end of the ladder, she brought out the explosive device's detonator and pressed it. She began to run as soon as she saw a flashlight.

Epilogue: A New Discovery

Unknown Location; Enlightenment Point. August 25, 2030; 0900 hours (EP Time Zone)

"Gatekeeper Int told me you requested an audience," Sergei Akulov said with Shireen Baloch facing him. "What is it you wish to discuss?"

"I wish to be punished," Shireen answered.

"For what?"

"Letting myself get captured and for Sedgwick Henderson's arrest."

"Do not concern yourself with those."

Shireen acted as if she was pushed back. "I beg your pardon, Grand Gatekeeper?"

"The test was a success. Your capture helped make that test possible that we can continue testing with the data we received in the battle. You also escaped in the process. As for Henderson, I'll see to it he's... *taken care of.* You may go now."

Shireen then made the Gatekeepers of Knowledge's salute. "By your will, Grand Gatekeeper."

#

Near Ishiguro's Firing Range, Outskirts of Kansai City, Kansai Prefecture; State of Japan. 1335 hours (Japan Standard Time)

A funeral had ended near Ishiguro's Firing Range. The gravestone prepared bore the name "Maral Eminovna Guliyeva". The Roman Catholic clergyman, Father Afable, gave the last rites. All members of Iron Dutchman Services, Frederick Dirks, John Vue, the Hoshikawa family, Akira Ishiguro and his wife Sayuri, and Rosarita Sanchez attended the funeral.

Once Afable finished the last rites, the time came for the coffin containing Maral Eminovna Guliyeva's corpse to be buried. Dirks, Tarou Ganji, Vue, and Ishiguro served as the pole bearers needed for the coffin. Tatev Mirzoyan watched with a tear coming out of her right eye. In her mind was what happened in the Republic of Korea two days before.

#

East Hongwon Hospital, Hongwon, Hamgyong Province; Republic of Korea. August 23, 2030; 2300 hours (Korea Standard Time)

"Is she going to be alright?" Tatev asked in a hospital room in East Hongwon Hospital while a doctor examined Guliyeva's corpse. With Tatev was Anita Hamilton and Yoon Jin-young; the latter having translated Tatev's question. The doctor was able to finish seeing Guliyeva's body but then he faced Tatev; his facing showing that he now found it difficult to answer Tatev's question. After sighing, the doctor then gave his answer but answered it in Korean. Yoon also had difficulty gathering the strength to tell Tatev the answer in English.

"Miss Mirzoyan… the doctor… he said… that… Miss Guliyeva… is… " Yoon said, his tone showing difficult it was to tell Tatev about Guliyeva.

"She… She's dead, isn't… she?" Tatev asked, now realizing what she should have realized in Sinpo hours before.

The doctor began to leave, knowing what was to come next. His prediction was right as Tatev walked to Guliyeva's corpse and cried. Neither Hamilton nor Yoon said anything and lowered their heads.

#

Near Ishiguro's Firing Range, Outskirts of Kansai City, Kansai Prefecture; State of Japan. August 25, 2030; 1421 hours (Japan Standard Time)

"Tatev, wake up!" Tarou Ganji shouted to Tatev, making her realize it was now August 25. Standing with Tarou was Maria Hoshikawa.

Unbeknownst to the three teenagers, Tatiana Ioannovna Tsulukidze watched from afar. She now opted to leave. As she began to walk away, she unknowingly passed into Frederick Dirks. "You didn't join us," Dirks remarked, making Tatiana stop. "Why?"

"I'm supposed to leave today, remember?" Tatiana asked. "The Director himself came to pick me up."

"You're right about that. Thank you for everything."

"Don't thank me just yet. You need to oversee us getting those girls back and after that, we resume being enemies the next time we meet. Before I go, what will you do with the girls we rescued that don't want to return to the Tsardom?"

"We'll seek out a women's shelter to take them in but I feel as if the files I managed to get will show us more girls to save. Do svidaniya."

"Spasibo." Tatiana continued to leave. *And now I must discuss with Slava that DNA test.*

#

Iron Dutchman, Taisho Ward, Kansai City. August 31, 2030; 1915 hours

All members of Iron Dutchman Services were now in the briefing room. Dirks and Wouter Vos stood at the stage, whereas Tatev was now at the projector.

"I doubt some of you are ready to end the mourning period, but I have urgent news and I figured now was a good time to bring them up," Dirks announced before turning to Tatev. "Tatev, show them."

Tatev opened the file that was to be projected onto the main screen of the briefing room. On the left was a picture of a woman with long blonde hair and blue eyes and on the right side was a financial paper.

"This girl, along with three others, has been sold by Kravchenko," Dirks continued. "We now know where they are because I was able to steal some of Kravchenko's files before the computer was destroyed. We are to rescue these girls."

"When do we start?" Sunan Wattana asked.

"As soon as you're ready. Other than this mission, I've also discovered something crucial that I must address to you. Before I elaborate, I'm ordering all of you to keep this to yourselves."

"Yeah, yeah, yeah," Jason Luke Crawley replied. "What is it?"

"It relates to the Gatekeepers of Knowledge."

Guantanámo Bay Maximum Security Prison, Guantánamo Province; Republic of Cuba. 0524 hours (Eastern Standard Time)

Built near the Guantánamo Bay Naval Base, a former United States Navy installation now used by the New United Nations Maritime Force, a maximum security prison was built to imprison dangerous criminals. "Henderson, respond!" a guard demanded while knocking on the door of the cell that belonged to Sedgwick Henderson. "Henderson! HENDERSON!"

The guard began to unlock the cell door. He now found that Henderson was dead.

Author's Notes

- Chapter I (New Orders)
➤ *Judogi* – uniform worn for *Judo* practitioners. Original Japanese: 柔道着
➤ *Tomoe nage* – Japanese for "Circle throw". Original Japanese: 巴投
Maya – Somali for "No".

- Chapter II (Rendezvous)
➤ Pathet Lao – officially called the Lao People's Liberation Army. Originally the Lao Issarra, the Pathet Lao fought to free Laos from French rule like the Viet Minh in Vietnam and the Khmer Issarak in Cambodia in the late 1940s. The Geneva Conference of 1954 ended French rule in Cambodia, Vietnam, and Laos but by this time, most anti-colonial fighters became Communist; most notably the Pathet Lao. This, along with movements by North Vietnamese forces (portions of Vietnam that were successfully held by the now-Communist Viet Minh) into Laos, started the Laotian Civil War that ended with the Pathet Lao's victory in 1975, creating the modern-day Lao People's Democratic Republic. "Phatet Lao" (ປະເທດລາວ) means "Lao Nation" in English.
➤ *División de Inteligencia* – Spanish for "Intelligence Division".
➤ *Fantasma* – Spanish for "Phantom".
➤ *Centro Nacional de Inteligencia* – Spanish for "National Intelligence Centre".
➤ *Policía Federal* – Spanish for "Federal Police".
➤ *Centro de Investigación y Seguridad Nacional* – Spanish for "Center for Investigation and National Security".
➤ *Inspector Jefe* – a rank in the Mexican Federal Police now used in their real-life replacement, the National Guard ("Guardia Nacional" in Spanish). In English, it means "Chief Inspector".
➤ *Comisionado General* – Spanish for "Commissioner General". The highest tank of the Mexican Federal Police. In real life, the highest rank in the Federal Police's replacement, the National Guard, is *Comisario General* (Spanish for "Federal Commissary" as the National Guard

functions differently from the Federal Police despite being a replacement).

Señor – Spanish for "Mister".

- Chapter III (The Launch)
➤ *Sí* – Spanish for "Yes".
➤ *¿Es usted el Señor 'Smith'?* – Spanish for "Are you Mr. 'Smith'?"
➤ *Gracias* – Spanish for "Thank you".

Yakiniku – Japanese for "Grilled meat". Original Japanese: 焼き肉 or 焼肉

- Chapter IV (The Raid)
➤ *¿Quién eres tú?* – Spanish for "Who are you?"
➤ *Nosotros hacemos las preguntas aquí!* – Spanish for "We ask the questions here!"
➤ *¡Dejala sola!* – Spanish for "Leave her alone!"
➤ *¡Juan, para!* – Spanish for "Juan, stop!"
➤ *Ahora cuida la entrada* – Spanish for "Now guard the entrance".
➤ *Ententido* – Spanish for "Understood".
➤ *Deténgase aquí* – Spanish for "Stop here".
➤ *Estévez, espera aquí* – Spanish for "Estevez, wait here".
➤ *Yo... puedo ayudar...* – Spanish for "I… can help… "
➤ *¿Tienes cuerda?* – Spanish for "Do you have rope?"
➤ *Luego úsalo para atarlo* – Spanish for "Then use it to tie him up".
➤ *Tengo uno* – Spanish for "I have one".
➤ *¿Por qué nos ayudas?* – Spanish for "Why are you helping us?"
➤ *Porque esto no sucede todos los días* – Spanish for "Because this doesn't happen every day".
➤ *¿Cuál es tu nombre?* – Spanish for "What's your name?"
➤ *¿Dónde está tu escalera?* – Spanish for "Where's your ladder?"
➤ *En la espalda. ¿Lo necesitas ahora?* – Spanish for "In the back. Do you need it now?"
➤ *Sí, por favor* – Spanish for "Yes, please".
➤ *Aquí está la escalera* – Spanish for "Here's your ladder".
➤ *Buenos días* – Spanish for "Good morning".

➤ *El Sr. Alba vendrá de visita hoy, él no debe ser molestado por el momento* – Spanish for "Mr. Alba will visit today. He is not to be disturbed at this time".

➤ *Vaya con Dios* – Spanish for "Go with God".

➤ *¡Mátalo!* – Spanish for "Kill him!"

➤ *¡Granada!* – Spanish for "Grenade!"

➤ *Üzr istəyirəm amma başa düşmürəm* – Azeri for "I'm sorry but I can't understand".

➤ *¿Entiendes Español?* – Spanish for "Do you understand Spanish?"

➤ Soul food – food that had its origins with black slaves in the United States of America. In the 1960s, it became a part of Black American cultural identity due to how it was promoted during the Civil Rights Movement.

➤ *Moros y Cristianos* – the Cuban equivalent of rice and beans. Means "Moors and Christians" in Spanish; *Moros* refers to the black beans and *Cristianos* refers to the white rice. This dish represents how the Moors once dominated most of the Iberian Peninsula from the 700s until the 1400s.

➤ *¿No te dijeron cómo comer correctamente?* – Spanish for "Didn't they tell you how to eat correctly?"

➤ *¡Ríndete ahora, Segismundo Alba!* – Spanish for "Surrender now, Segismundo Alba!"

➤ *¡Nunca!* – Spanish for "Never".

• Chapter V (Disguise)

➤ *Balah* – Persian/Farsi for "Yes". Pronounced "Ba-leh". Original Persian: بله

➤ *Pedar* – Persian/Farsi for "Father". Original Persian: پدر

➤ *Grach* – Russian for "rook", the bird, whose scientific name is **Corvus frugilegus**. Cyrillic: Грач

• Chapter VI (The Past and the Present)

➤ *Komitet Gosudarstvenoy Bezopasnosti* – Russian for "Ministry for State Security". Cyrillic: Комитет государственной безопасности

➤ *Mâdar* – Persian/Farsi for "Mother". Original Persian: مادر

➤ *Nal delileo on geot gat-eunde?* – Korean for "I assume you're here to pick me up?" Hangul: 날 데리러 온 것 같은데

➢   *Ye* – Korean for "Yes". Hangul: 예

➢   *Poliforum Central de la Colonia Federal* - Central Poliforum of the Federal Colony

➢   *Para el Señor Yan y el Señor Herrera* – Spanish for "For Mr. Yan and Mr. Herrera".

➢   *Tu Ángel Guardián* – Spanish for "Your Guardian Angel".

➢   *Ganji Mahsa desu ka?* – Japanese for "Are you Mahsa Ganji?" Original Japanese: ガンジマサですか

➢   *Minagawa gurūpu de hataraite imasu ka?* – Japanese for "Do you work for Minagawa Group?" Original Japanese: 皆川グループで働いています か

➢   *Kansai-shi e o-dzure shimasu* – Japanese for "We're here to take you to Kansai City". Original Japanese: 関西市へお連れします

➢   *Daleun salam?* – Korean for "Anyone else?" Hangul: 다른 사람

Neo-neun? – Korean for "And you are?" Hangul: 당신은

●   Chapter VII (Visiting Home)

➢   *Pozhaluysta* – Russian for "You're welcome". Cyrillic: Пожалуйста

➢   *Dacha* – a secondary home owned by a family that can afford to do so. The idea originated in the 17th century as estates given to the Tsar's loyal vassals, who would use these estates to host parties. Cyrillic: дача

➢   *Mat'* – Russian for "Mother". Cyrillic: Мать

Shagokhod – Russian for "walker". Pronounced "sha-gah-hod". Cyrillic: Шагоход

●   Chapter VIII (Returning to Japan)

➢   *Do svidaniya* – Russian for "Goodbye". Cyrillic: До свидания

➢   *Nevozmozhno!* – Russian for "Impossible!" Cyrillic: Невозможно

➢   *Eto poryadok!* – Russian for "That's an order!" Cyrillic: Это порядок

➢   *Rassolnik* – a soup whose primary ingredients are pickled cucumbers, pearled barley, and kidneys (beef or pork). Cyrillic: рассольник

➢   *Eto khorosho* – Russian for "That's good". Cyrillic: Это хорошо

➤ *Otpravlyat'* – Russian for "Send". Cyrillic: Отправлять

➤ *Gotovo!* – Russian for "It's ready!" Cyrillic: Готово!

➤ *Zhakiyanov, vstavat'!* – Russian for "Zhakiyanov, get up!" Cyrillic: Жакиянов, Вставай!

➤ *Oladyi* – small thick pancakes or fritters. Batter is made from wheat or buckwheat flour, eggs, milk, salt, and sugar with yeast or baking soda. Alternate sources for the batter can come from kefir (fermented milk made from kefir grains), soured milk, or yogurt. Apples or raisins can be added and is normally served with smetana sour cream, jams, powidl (fruit spread made from prune plum), and honey. Caviar can also be used. Cyrillic: оладьи

- Chapter IX (Spying)

➤ *Borscht* – a sour soup of Ukrainian origin that uses red beetroots as its primary ingredient, hence why it is normally depicted red.

➤ *Prosti za eto* – Russian for "Sorry about that". Cyrillic: Прости за это

➤ *Ya goloden!* – Russian for "I'm hungry!" Cyrillic: я голоден

➤ *Otlichno* – Russian for "Excellent!" Cyrillic: Отлично!

➤ *Teper' my mozhem nachat'!* – Russian for "Now we can begin!" Cyrillic: Теперь мы можем начать!

➤ *Onigiri* – Japanese rice formations that involve making triangles out of rice and placing seeweed wrappings (*nori*).

➤ *Kat tak* – Russian for "How so?" Cyrillic: Как так

➤ *My doma!* – Russian for "We're home!" Cyrillic: Мы дома

➤ *U menya yest' mysl'* – Russian for "I have an idea". Cyrillic: У меня есть мысль

➤ *Ya vizhu Gandzhi* – Russian for "I see Ganji". Cyrillic: я вижу Ганджи

➤ *Sledi za mnoy* – Russian for "Keep an eye on me". Cyrillic: Следи за мной

➤ *Byli sdelany. Vremya ukhodit'* – Russian for "We're done. Time to leave". Cyrillic: Были сделаны. Время уходить

➤ *Treker* – Russian for "Tracker". Cyrillic: Трекер

➤ *Ya snaruzhi verfi* – Russian for "I'm outside the shipyard". Cyrillic: Я снаружи верфи

➤ *Gde seychas furgon?* – Russian for "Where's the van now?" Cyrillic: Где сейчас фургон?

➢ *Furgon nakhoditsya v Yao* – Russian for "The van's in Yao". Cyrillic: Фургон находится в Яо

➢ *Karty* – Russian for "Maps." Cyrillic: Карты

➢ *Khoroshiy* – Russian for "Good". Cyrillic: Хороший

• Chapter X (The Truth)

➢ *Nihon Kuiristo* – short for *Nihon Kirisuto Kyoudan*; Japanese for "United Church of Christ in Japan". They're the largest Protestant Christian denomination in Japan as a result of all Protestant churches in Japan ordered by the Japanese government to form one church during World War II.

➢ *Posadili apparat* – Russian for "Did you plant the device?" Cyrillic: Посадили аппарат

➢ *Pora idti* – Russian for "Time to go". Cyrillic: Пора идти

➢ *Ty opozdal* – Russian for "You're late". Cyrillic: Ты опоздал

➢ *Ya poydu* – Russian for "I'll go". Cyrillic: я пойду

➢ *My sdelali eto* – Russian for "We made it". Cyrillic: Мы сделали это

➢ *Yox!* – Azeri for "No!"

➢ *Nani ga kotodesu ka?* – Japanese for "What's this about?" Original Japanese: 何のことですか

➢ *Siz… siz… Tatev Mirzoyan?* – Guliyeva's trying to ask "Siz… Tatev Mirzoyansınız?" (Azeri for "Are you Tatev Mirzoyan?")

➢ *Bəli* – Azeri for "Yes"

➢ *Etmə!* – Azeri for "Don't!"

➢ *Yavaş-yavaş için. Biz sizi tələsdirmirik* – Azeri for "Just drink slowly. We're not rushing you".

➢ *Por favor sígame* – Spanish for "Please follow me".

➢ *Okhrana* – short for *Otdeleniye po **okhran**eniyu obshchestvennoy bezopasnosti i poryadka*; Russian for "Department for Protecting the Public Security and Order" (*Okhrana* means "the guard"). This organization was the secret police of the Russian Empire. Like with the Russian Empire itself, the *Ohkrana* was dissolved in 1917. Since it's another Russian-speaking monarchical empire, it made sense for Ivan Vladimirovich Tsulukidze to resurrect the *Okhrana* as the domestic intelligence agency and security service of the Eurasian Tsardom. Cyrillic: Отделение по охранению общественной безопасности и порядка. *Ohkrana* in Cyrillic is Охрана

➢ *Maral, yatmaq vaxtıdır* – Azeri for "Maral, it's time to sleep".

➢ *Mən... mən... yata bilmirəm...* – Azeri for "I... I... I can't sleep... "
Cənab – Azeri for "Mister".

• Chapter XI (The Attack)
➢ *Naga fogee iyaga!* – Somali for "Keep them away from us!"
➢ *Haa mudane* – Somali for "Yes, sir".
➢ *Jeo saramdeuleul ttalaga* – spoken Korean for "Follow them".
Hangul: 저 사람들을 따라가

➢ *Algessseubnida* – Korean for "Yes, sir". Hangul: 알겠습니다
➢ *Koshō-chū* – Japanese for "Out of Order". Original Japanese: 故障中

➢ *Sanggŭp-pyŏngsa* – equivalent of "Sergeant" in the Korean People's Army Ground Force, "Petty Officer Second Class" in the Korean People's Army Navcal Force, and "Staff Sergeant" in the Korean People's Army Air Force. Hangul/Chosŏn'gŭl: 상급병사

➢ *Niga meonjeoga* – Korean for "You go first". Hangul: 니가 먼저가

• Chapter XII (Turning Point Part 1)
➢ *Momose-san, chūrinjō o akete kudasai* – Japanese for "Mr. Momose, please open the bicycle parking lot". Original Japanese: 百瀬さん、駐輪場を開けてください
➢ *Boer* – Dutch for "farmer" but it's one term for Dutch settlers who came to present-day South Africa in the 17th century because a fair number of these settlers became farmers.
➢ Penkovskaya – the feminine form of the surname "Penkovsky". Women in Eastern Slavic lands have a feminine form of the surname of their fathers or husbands ("Penkovsky" becomes "Penkovskaya"). The imaginary OVR officer McAllister claims to know having the surname "Penkovskaya" is a reference to Oleg Vladimirovich Penkovsky, the GRU (*Glavnoye razvedyvatel'noye upravleniye*; Cyrillic: Главное разведывательное управление; English for "Main Intelligence Directorate"), the Soviet foreign intelligence service for its military (the modern-day Russian Armed Forces in real life inherited GRU after the collapse of the Soviet Union) officer who provided information to the United States of America's Central Intelligence Agency about Soviet missile deployments

in the Republic of Cuba in 1962, leading to the Cuban Missile Crisis that began on October 19. Penkovsky was arrested on October 22 after the KGB received information about Penkovsky from one Jack Dunlap, an NSA (National Security Agency; the US's intelligence agency responsible for signals intelligence; unlike the CIA, the NSA is under the US Department of Defense) employee-turned-KGB asset, and developed the case needed to arrest him. Penkovsky was executed a year later.

- Chapter XIII (Turning Point Part 2)
- ➢ *Saeloun geos-i issseubnikka?* – Korean for "Anything new?" Hangul: 새로운 것이 있습니까
- ➢ *Eung* – Korean for "Yes". Unlike "Ye", this is to be used by someone for his or her equal or subordinate. Hangul: 응
- ➢ *Junbi doetssubnida* – Korean for "It's ready". Used for someone to address his or her superior. Hangul: 준비 됐습니다
- ➢ *Gomaweo* – Korean for "Thank you". Used by someone to address his or her subordinate; hence why Shireen uses this instead of "Gomabseubnida" Hangul: 고맙습니다 (Hangul for "Gomabseubnida" is 고맙습니다)
- ➢ *Ulileul delileo wa jusyeoseo gamsahabnida* – Korean for "Thank you for picking us up". Hangul: 우리를 데리러 와 주셔서 감사합니다
- ➢ *Modeun geos-i junbidoeeossdago bwado doebnika?* – Korean for "I assume everything's ready?" Hangul: 모든 것이 준비되었다고 봐도 됩니까
- ➢ *Oni opazdyvayut* – Russian for "They're late". Cyrillic: они опаздывают
- ➢ *Oni voobshche poyavyatsya?* – Russian for "Will they even show up at all?" Cyrillic: Они вообще появятся?
- ➢ *Ya chto-to slyshu* – Russian for "I hear something". Cyrillic: Я что-то слышу
- ➢ *Oni zdes'* – Russian for "They're here". Cyrillic: Они здесь
- ➢ *Dankie* – Afrikaans for "Thanks".

- Chapter XIV (Cooperation): *Millî Piyade Tüfeği* – Turkish for "National Infantry Rifle".

- Chapter XV (Shipwreck Assault): .338 Lapua Magnum – the proper name for the 8.6x70mm round. "Lapua" is the name of a Finnish ammunition manufacturer that's a part of the Nammo (Nordic Ammunition Group) aerospace and defense group in real life.

- Chapter XVII (The Real Reason): Korea Standard Time and Japan Standard Time – both time zones are in UTC+08:00. Therefore, the passage where Vos asks Dirks about the fly drone occurs a minute after Tatiana and Chadov launch their fake deal with Kravchenko.

- Chapter XVIII (Finding a Resolution):
➤ The Korean surname "Ok" – "Ok" is a Korean surname. To help understand that, it would be pronounced "Oh-k" as if you were pronouncing "Ox". Not how "Ok" is short for "Okay" in both writing and pronunciation.
➤ "Flight of four Ap- I mean, Guardian attack helicopters" – "Flight" in this case is a unit in aviation branches of militaries that can consist of four aircraft.

- Chapter XIX (To Sinpo)
➤ Libya using Eastern European Time – Libya does so because it's under UTC+02:00. Most African countries under UTC+02:00 refer to it as "Central African Time" but Libya refers to it as "Eastern European Time".
➤ *Aswār* – Singular form of *Aswārān*. While the term was first used in chapter nine (First Day) of <u>The Young Knight and His Metal Steed</u>, *Aswārān* formed the backbone of the Sasanian Empire's armies.
➤ *Istaslim* – Arabic for "Surrender". Original Arabic: استسلم
➤ *'Iḏā astaslamt al'ān, fasawfa 'ubqī `alā ḥayātik!* – Arabic for "If you surrender now, I'll spare your life". Original Arabic: إذا استسلمت الآن، فسوف أبقي على حياتك
➤ *Iqtarab al'ān* – Arabic for "Now come closer". Original Arabic: اقترب الآن

➢   *Māḏā tafʿal!?* – Arabic for "What are you doing!?" Original Arabic: ماذا تفعل

➢   *Daʿnī aḏhab!* – Arabic for "Let me go!" Original Arabic: دعني اذهب

➢   Prison camps near Kaechon: Near Kaechon are two prison camps. One is a Kwalliso (commonly referred as a prison labor camp) while the other is a Kyohwaso (commonly called a reeducation camp). Despite the differing terms, inmates in both camps have been used for slave labor.

•   Chapter XX (Heart Attack): *Hamınızı öldürəcəm!* – Azeri for "I'll kill you all!"

About the Author

A.I.V. Esguerra, from the Republic of the Philippines, was born in 1996. Throughout elementary and high school, Esguerra opted to be a writer after being exposed to various works of fiction. In college, Esguerra started writing while waiting to graduate, beginning with the short story Before Death, published by Mistwood Entertainment in 2019. Two years later, Esguerra's first novel was The Young Knight of the Desert and wrote it to be uploaded it to Honeyfeed.fm as part of the MyAnimeList X Honeyfeed Writing Contest but lost the contest. Despite that, Esguerra continued writing, starting with The Young Knight and His Metal Steed.

Esguerra intends on not only writing more books but also to venture outside books. The desire to write comes from exposure to various works of fiction and Esguerra hopes to share the same interests in fiction unto others with the stories already written and what will be written.